The Hub

NICOLA MAY

Lightning Books

Published by
Lightning Books
Imprint of Eye Books Ltd
29A Barrow Street
Much Wenlock
Shropshire
TF13 6EN

www.lightning-books.com

Copyright © May Books Ltd 2022
Cover design by Ifan Bates

Typeset in Minion Pro and Phantom Shrine

British Library Cataloguing in Publication Data
A catalogue record for this book is available from the British Library

ISBN 9781785633287

For Claire and Steve

*The smallest act of kindness
is worth more
than the greatest intention*
Kahlil Gibran,
The Essential Kahlil Gibran

The Hub: a facility for remote/flexible working. Welcoming entrepreneurs, freelancers, and home-based businesses who want a choice over how and when they work

Chapter One

'Don't you think it's a bit weird having a photo of your ex stuck on the fridge?'

'I was hoping it might kickstart my stagnant brain with some new plot ideas about how to kill someone off.'

August Saunders continued filling her red Smeg kettle. Catching sight of the tired and drawn reflection of herself in the window, she sighed. A huge ginger cat wound his way around her legs in noisy anticipation of his breakfast.

'Oh, Prince Harry, give me a second,' August huffed.

Ellie wasn't letting up. 'Well, something needs to happen. You haven't written a word for weeks.'

'And the winner of the most sensitive sister award goes to…'

'It's been nearly six months now.' Ellie's voice softened. 'Surely you're beginning to feel a bit better?'

'You don't understand.' August retrieved two mugs from the cupboard above the sink, spooned a heaped teaspoon of instant coffee into each, then reached for a sachet of cat food to pacify her miaowing moggy.

'No. I don't. He cheated on you in spectacular style, then called off the wedding with weeks to spare. I think I'd be well over him by now.'

'But you're not me, are you, Ellie?'

'No, and to be fair to you, I couldn't imagine a day without my Grant. That heartbreak diet you went on was marvellous, though. Saying that, I'd probably turn to food, rather than go off it.'

'I'm putting a bit of the weight back on now, thankfully.'

'You look great, Goose. Your skin is glowing – must be the country air, when you bother to stick your face in it. And those baby blues of yours are getting their sparkle back, even if you don't see it yourself yet.'

'I guess one advantage of moving out to the sticks is that I don't have to breathe in London fumes every day.'

'See – always a silver lining.'

August pushed her long, messy auburn waves back from her face. 'Stupid bastard.' She bit her lip, her eyes filling with tears. 'There are times when I still feel so angry, but then the sadness and missing him take over.'

Ellie went over to the biscuit tin in search of her favourite chocolate digestives, grabbed the milk from the fridge and sat down at the kitchen counter next to her sister.

'It could have been worse, I suppose. At least the wedding *didn't* happen.'

'You're not helping, sis.'

'Mum said it too. Never marry a man who looks in the mirror more than he looks at you.'

August raised her eyes at her sister. 'Maybe moving in next door to you was a bad idea after all.'

'Don't be like that.'

'Well,' August tutted and took a tentative sip from her steaming mug of black coffee, sighing with pleasure as the taste flooded her mouth. 'I didn't realise there was a standard time for mending a broken heart.' The author then assumed a BBC voice. 'Dear heart and mind, please let me completely forget the age-old cliché of my insanely fit actor fiancé falling in lust with his younger and prettier co-star. If only it was that bloody easy.'

'Sorry,' Ellie said, and meant it. 'I just worry, that's all. Sitting here alone binge-watching Netflix romcoms isn't good for you.'

'Look, Ells, you've been my rock and I do appreciate that. But when I start writing again, I'll be all right. It takes my mind of all the other stuff. And as it happens, I'm off romcoms. I'm now on to anything with Jamie Dornan in it.'

'OK, I can allow that. How hot is that man! But seriously, writing or not, you being stuck in here all day, and rarely going out… It's not healthy. There is so much life out there for the taking. Which may sound odd coming from the woman with two kids under two, whose last time *out* out was to see an Elvis impersonator down The White Horse, here in sleepy Upper Gamble. But you know what I mean.'

August sighed. 'I know you're right. I never ever thought I would say this, but I do sometimes miss working in an office.'

'You always did hate the nine to five, though,' Ellie added. 'And even when we were at school, all you ever wanted was to be a full-time author.'

August screwed up her face. 'Be careful what you wish for and all that.'

'You don't mean that. You're just in a bad place at the moment. And what are you saying? That you don't want to write any more?'

'Of course, I do! When I'm in the mood, I love it. It pays the bills and more, but it's a lonely gig when there's no one coming home to you.' August got up to flick the kettle on again. 'Anyway, dear sister, why are you around here mithering me this early?'

'I'm on a health kick.'

August smiled. 'Another one?'

11

Ellie raised her eyebrows. 'Says the woman who used to run at least three miles a day before breakfast. And yes, another one. I've gotta do it. My arse has got its own postcode.'

'So, what is it this time? The biscuit diet?'

'Ha bloody ha. I can see why you write crime now, not comedy. As it happens, I *was* supposed to be taking Colin for a walk down to Bluebell Wood, but I dropped the boys off at nursery and, well, I thought of you and wondered if you fancied going shopping instead? That threadbare old thing you're wearing could do with replacing, if nothing else.'

August dramatically grasped the familiar velour garment tightly to her neck. 'I'll have you know that this is this is the writing uniform of a bestselling crime writer and wearing it is all part of the arduous process of creating a literary masterpiece for the masses.'

'You'd better go and write then,' Ellie smirked.

'Not funny.' August rinsed her mug in the sink ready to refill it.

Ellie drained hers. 'OK, I'd better get off. But come on, let's at least get you another dressing gown for special occasions, then, shall we?'

August groaned. 'You're getting on my nerves now.'

'I know.' Ellie smirked. 'Even if it's just for while you're watching your glorious Irishman in action. Or, you never know, you might find a real man you want to snuggle up with. And you can't have *them* thinking you are a complete and utter tramp now, can you?'

'Oh, Ellie. One step at a time. Maybe shopping, but I'm not ready to be shaving my armpits or legs yet. And can we go tomorrow instead?'

'Oh, you're busy, are you?' The younger sibling raised her eyebrows.

August rinsed out a dishcloth and wiped down the draining board. 'Joking aside, Ms A.R. Saunders here really does need to try and work on a new Christmas plot for her super-sleuths, or her formidable agent will be dumping her too.'

'Good, that's great news. Not about Madame Fleurot dumping you, but...yes, get writing, lady.'

'Right! Breakfast, and then, yes, I must get that laptop open. See you tomorrow – with my best knickers on, in case I do decide to venture into a changing room.'

'That, big sis, is the best date I could wish for.' Ellie clumsily got down from the kitchen stool. 'I'd better walk that Corgi of mine before he ransacks the kitchen. See you tomorrow, kiddo, around nine-thirty.'

Ellie grabbed herself another chocolate digestive from the vintage floral biscuit tin and wiggled her ample backside. 'Oops. I've had a little snaccident.'

A smiling August shook her head and made her way upstairs. Then she caught a whiff of one of her armpits and realised that even though she intended to stay in and (attempt to) write all day, she really should take a shower and adhere to her own new-year promise of self-care, which had been decidedly remiss since her wayward ex's sudden departure.

Scrabbling around in her bedside drawer for a hair bungee, her fingers brushed against a face-down photo frame. She pulled it out and turned it over. There they were, Mr and Mrs Scanlan-to-be. 'The perfect couple', posing at the top of the Eiffel Tower just minutes after he had gone down on one knee and proposed. She blew out a noisy breath. Sometimes she still missed him so much she felt a physical pain in her stomach.

Chapter Two

It was surprisingly busy in the Swinford designer-outlet centre café for a dull Wednesday morning in March.

'Oh yeah.' Ellie began to scrabble around in her packed handbag. 'Look what came through the door yesterday.' She waved a yellow flyer in front of her sister's face.

'What is it? I threw mine in the bin without reading it.'

Ellie cleared her throat and began reading aloud. '"Looking for a fantastic shared workplace? Then the Futtingbrook Farm Hub is the answer. The co-working culture is growing rapidly. People love the flexibility of working remotely, but they miss the benefits of sharing a physical space with colleagues. Whether you're an established enterprise, scaling start-up or one-man band, we have the space for you. Nowhere will you find stronger camaraderie, better connections and a more positive community than at Futtingbrook Farm Hub. Based—"'

'Remind me: that's the Ronson's farm, isn't it?' August interrupted as she tried to catch the attention of a stressed-looking waitress.

'Yes, it is, but let me finish.' A disgruntled Ellie continued to read. '"Based in beautiful countryside just off the A267 on the outskirts of the picturesque market town of Futtingbrook, we are not only accessible, but we will cater uniquely to your needs. Email: NewFFH@rockmail.com today to arrange a show round and informal chat.'" Ellie looked up at her sister. 'I think it's a sign.'

'A sign of what?' August scoffed. 'Somebody from Futtingbrook Farm choosing to market their business locally?'

'You're such a bloody pessimist.'

'I don't think I'm ready to make small talk with other people yet.'

'I disagree. We were just discussing about you getting out and about and then this happens. You have to contact them.' Ellie took a bite of her gooey flapjack.

August finally managed to summon the waitress, who hurried over to their table. 'Another black coffee please.' She pointed to her sister. 'Do you want one?'

Ellie shook her head. 'No, I'd better have a green tea, thanks.'

August laughed. 'You've already done the damage with the flapjack. A shot of caffeine and a splash of milk really wouldn't hurt, you know.'

Ellie lifted her hand in dismissal. 'Stop trying to deflect the conversation away from you, Goose. I think a shared working space is a genius way to start making your entry into the big wide world again.'

'Futtingbrook is hardly Monte Carlo, now, is it?

'No, but it's got more life in it than our sleepy little village and it's literally a twenty-minute drive from us.'

'If you don't get stuck behind a tractor, that is.'

'What a little ray of sunshine you are this morning.' Ellie continued to dab flapjack crumbs from her plate.

'I'm surprised the Upper Gamble gossip grapevine hadn't got hold of this ground-breaking news already.' August smiled as the waitress delivered their drinks. 'I mean, a whole new office set-up in our midst. Who'd have thought it?'

'My Grant's dad did moan something about more traffic going past his farm entrance, but I didn't take any notice, to be honest.'

'My agent works out of one of these hubs in Notting Hill now. It didn't cross my mind there would be one in our little neck of the woods. Hers is proper trendy with fancy booths, a café and full of beautiful people with quirky business set-ups.'

'See, if it's good enough for Madame Fleurot… Come on. Let's look at the positives, shall we?' Ellie took a sip of her drink, flinching as the boiling liquid scalded her top lip.

'All right, I hear you. It does seem like a promising idea in principle, I suppose. But in effect, I would be paying to sit at a desk when I could be lying in bed and writing.'

'That's not the bloody point, is it? You were the one harping on about routine. You rent space and come and go as you please. That's how it works, right?'

'Yes, something like that.'

'So, you can still be your own boss. If you want to write at home, you can. At least it gives you options and who knows, a Jamie D lookalike might just be on the desk next to you. Actually, if that's the case, I'm joining up too.'

A smiling August lifted her coffee cup. 'I'm over dating actors, thanks very much. In fact, I'm over men in general.'

'You say that now,' Ellie said with a maddeningly knowing air. 'The male species aside, it could open up your social circle with meeting new friends in the area, too.'

'Scott did say I had to get on with my life.'

'So kind of your ex to leave you with such a helpful parting message. What a man!' Ellie sighed.

'Don't get me wrong, it's been lovely being here with you and Mum, but I do miss the buzz of the city. And I can't believe

I'm saying it, but I do miss Placatac sometimes too. Who'd have thought marketing toothpaste would be fun? But it was. The water-cooler banter. Even the brainstorming around new packaging and deciding which advert should go up at Waterloo Station. And those cringe-inducing leaving lunches when everybody has pretended to add money to the gift envelope and the person who was lucky enough to escape never wanted to make that speech. And I miss the routine. Yes, that's it. The routine.' Her voice assumed a monotone level. 'Walk to the overground, get a coffee from the kiosk. Grab a free newspaper. Get in carriage number four. Get off. Walk to the tube. Get off the tube. Get on the train home again at six-thirty. Drink. Dinner. Shower. A quick shag if Scott wasn't at the studios and we had the energy. And among all that monotony and presumed monogamy, God, I loved that man!' August let out a noisy groan, then took a big slurp of her now cooling drink. 'I did love life then, too.'

'And you will love it again. And if you're craving routine, well, the Hub really is your answer, isn't it?'

'Ellie the saleswoman – who'd have thought it?'

'I'm not just a crazy baby-making machine, I'll have you know. And as for a social life, you haven't actually been out of the door to give it a chance. If you look hard enough, there's much more than you think going on. Even the theatre at Swinford is attracting bigger names. And – wait for it – some farmers are even posting on Instagram.' Ellie smirked.

'Is that so?' August couldn't help but smile at her enthusiastic sibling.

'London is only an hour on the train too. It's not like we're in the Outer Hebrides, is it?' Ellie's voice had adopted an almost evangelical enthusiasm. 'And let's not forget the Futtingbrook Festival. I mean, who needs Glastonbury?'

'Blimey, what did they put in that flapjack of yours – optimism oats?' August cradled her coffee cup. 'I think the main problem is I haven't been single for seven years. That's a long time. 'When you're in a couple, you don't have to worry about all that socialising bollocks.'

'You two were always doing something!'

'I mean, when we weren't, Scott Scanlan was the best person I ever met to do nothing with. It was easy. You didn't have to worry about having no plans. Because our plans were just "us".'

A woman on the next table, spoon-feeding her baby in a highchair, pricked up her ears at the mention of the handsome soap actor's name.

'It will be OK,' Ellie soothed. 'And a man doesn't define us. But I get you on the company bit. Although sometimes, what I'd give to be able to watch all my favourite programmes without a farting husband and two children clambering over me on the sofa!'

'You're happy though, aren't you, Ells?'

'I am, but being a mum is bloody harder work than I ever thought it would be. So, listen to me now, Goose. When you do find someone else, make sure he agrees to be the house husband or he's rich enough to pay for the childcare – OK?'

Thinking that she would never allow herself to be beholden to any man or his finances, whoever he may be, August lovingly squeezed the hand of her sister. The sister who had never left the village of Upper Gamble since the day she had been born, thirty-four years ago, and the height of whose ambition was to get married, have children and lead a happy life. August almost envied her.

August was suddenly thoughtful. 'OK, so maybe the dynamic of a hub will make up my mind as to if I want to stay here or go back to London. And, I guess having a look around wouldn't hurt, would it?'

'I'm so proud of you.' The grin on Ellie's round, friendly face was suddenly replaced by silent tears. She ran her hands through her thick mop of unruly blonde curls and blew her nose loudly on her napkin.

'Oh, stop it, Ellie. I'm just going to look at a bloody office, not pick up an MBE.' She paused. 'Jesus. You're not pregnant again, are you?'

'I bloody hope not. It's just, I hate seeing you sad.' She reached for a napkin and sniffed loudly. The woman on the table next to them, her toddler now screaming at the top of its lungs, gave her a pained look as she got up to leave.

Ellie gave the fellow mum an understanding smile and said loudly, 'Listen to that little fella. It's good to let it all out.'

She signalled for the bill. 'Come on, let's shop discount designers. How exciting! And you're going to need more than a new dressing gown if you're going to join the Hub.'

Chapter Three

Before she could talk herself out of viewing the Hub, August threw her coat and outlet shopping bags on to her comfy sofa and reached for her laptop. She retrieved Ellie's screwed up yellow flyer from her handbag, sat down and began to compose an email.

To: NewFFH@rockmail.com
From: arsaunders@arsaunders.com

Scanning the leaflet and not finding a name, she carried on regardless.

Hi there,

I received your flyer through the post and would be very interested in coming along to your Hub for a show around as soon as possible. I'd be grateful if you could let me know when would be the best time for you.

Warm regards
August Saunders
Author

She had just started taking the label off her new dressing gown when she heard her inbox ping.

To: arsaunders@arsaunders.com
From: NewFFH@rockmail.com

Dear August

We've been inundated with emails since our leaflet drop, but how about Wednesday at 0930? Postcode is SF68 9PJ. Entrance is concealed.

Yours
MM

To: NewFFH@rockmail.com
From: arsaunders@arsaunders.com

Dear MM

930 Wednesday is perfect.

You say the entrance is concealed – are there any landmarks I should look out for? My sense of direction is never very good, even with a satnav ☺

Warm regards
August Saunders

To: arsaunders@arsaunders.com
From: NewFFH@rockmail.com

Dear August

Try looking for a sign!

See you Wednesday.

Yours
MM

A feeling of unease washed over August at the monosyllabic rudeness of the sender. Maybe this particular hub wasn't the right place for her, after all. Rather than reply now and regret later, she closed down her laptop and went to the kitchen to make herself a cup of tea.

Chapter Four

On this especially cold March morning, as she headed out of her sleepy village to Futtingbrook Farm Hub, August experienced feelings that had been alien to her for quite some time: hope and excitement at what might be to come. She had come to the conclusion that email tone can easily be misconstrued, so she would at least go and have a look around to see what the place had to offer, before making any rash decisions.

Driving through the scenic countryside, she realised she still felt at home in the small and pretty Upper Gamble, despite her many years away from the place. With its population of just eight hundred, it consisted of a church, a pub, a primary school, a two-pump petrol garage and general store-cum-off licence-cum-newsagent. If you had been born into its close-knit community more than sixty years ago, you were likely to die there, too.

The cricket pitch with adjoining village hall (which doubled as a club house on match days), along with the adjacent playground for the kids, made it a sought-after location for those out-of-towners wanting to move away from the madness of city life to bring up their kids. So much so that a new housing development aimed at these wealthy incomers had just been built on the outskirts of the village and another was being discussed just this week at Futtingbrook Town Hall.

To the west, a glorious walk down a one-track lane leading to Bluebell Wood could be found, and to the east heading out on the main road towards Futtingbrook, there was Penfold Farm, with its farm shop and café, which, as well as fresh farm produce, sold the legendary homemade-on-the-premises Penfold Pork Pies.

Aside from Donnybrook Close – the council estate that had gone up in the seventies – most of the houses in the village were old, thatched and full of character. They ranged from rows of old farm terraces, the likes of which August and Ellie lived in, to sprawling detached houses and bungalows. Another recent development, which had caused great local uproar, followed swiftly by excitement at the brilliant bargains, was the ASDIS discount superstore off the main road between Upper Gamble and Futtingbrook.

As she indicated off the main road, August felt unusually alert and business-like. After she'd woken from a satisfyingly good sleep that morning, she had very much enjoyed the whole experience of getting dressed, made up and ready for something that resembled a proper meeting. After wallowing in joggers and baggy jumpers – her apparel of choice for the past few months – it had felt strange pulling proper clothes on and, although she had never had a problem with her weight, she had stood back and admired her newly trim figure.

Turning up the radio of her red Mini convertible, purchased when she had left London four months previously, she surprised herself by bursting into the chorus of 'Happy' by Pharrell Williams.

As she sped along the country lane to Futtingbrook, surrounded by fields and hedgerows, she wound the window down to take in the cool, fresh country air, and began to think about the past few months.

Happiness had been a rare visitor since the day Scott Scanlan had given her the devastating news that he didn't love her any more – had told her that he had made a big mistake thinking that marriage was their destiny. Seven years of her life she had given to that man. The man who had been working as a Deliveroo driver between acting jobs when she had met him online. The man whose hand she had held through every audition and rejection. The man who was now well recognised in his desired part of a love rat in a long-running soap. A role in which, now, he didn't have to play anything but himself.

With her mind wandering, she realised a moment too late that she was driving straight past the concealed entrance and a tirade of swear words came out of her mouth. Having found a place to turn around safely, she found herself stuck behind a tractor, which evoked even more expletives. Where was this bloody sign this MM had mentioned in the email?

'OK, it must be left here,' she said aloud, ducking down to see through her windscreen, now mud-splattered courtesy of the huge farm vehicle's wheels. Then: 'Woah, OK,' as she arrived at a huge wooden gate with two high posts either side, on which were mounted security cameras. These appeared to move with her even though she was inside the car. She found it odd to see all this paraphernalia, thinking that, surely, a place like this – where she assumed people could come and go as they pleased, host visitors and receive deliveries – would have a far easier and less imposing access. She was just peering around to see if there was an intercom buzzer when the gate started automatically opening inwards in slow motion.

The long drive she found herself upon was akin to one of the many fancy country hotels she had stayed in with Scott.

Drives which had always given rise to a heady anticipation as to what the place at the end would be like, along with the glorious feelings of spending some much needed down-time together in complete luxury. Tears stung her eyes as a sudden pang of missing her handsome ex went right through her. She would have loved telling him all about this but if it wasn't for him leaving her, then she wouldn't be in this position in the first place. 'Wanker,' she muttered, then sighed.

The sight of the orange breast of a sparrowhawk sweeping down in search of prey was a welcome distraction from her memories. One of the many aspects of growing up in the countryside which she had enjoyed and taken with her through life was a wide knowledge of birdlife. There were people she had met in London who would find it hard to identify anything other than a sparrow, let alone this stunning bird of prey.

Adhering to the five-mile-an-hour signs, she eventually found herself at a fork in the road. To the right stood a smart brown-and-white sign saying 'Futtingbrook Turkey Farm' and a caricatured fat turkey wearing a Christmas hat. The other fork housed a sign made out of a scruffy piece of tree bark, with 'Futtingbrook Farm Hub' hand-painted on it in black and pointing to the left. Not quite the first impression August had imagined. It only occurred to her in that moment that there hadn't been a website for her to check anything out about the place; she was just going on the word of a flyer. Her excitement about what she was driving up to suddenly began to wane.

Luckily, when she reached the end of the lane, the barn conversion looked encouragingly smart and modern from the outside, and her excitement began to build once more. It was an impressive, wooden-clad two-storey building, with huge bifold doors to the left and a roof housing skylights. In the distance to the right, she could see a large farmhouse and various outbuildings, which she assumed must be the turkey farm. A series of lush green meadows surrounded the barn and the farms. It appeared that the two areas were linked by a short track that led from the car parking area she had just pulled in to, in which she clocked an archaic Volvo, an electric people carrier of some sort and a smart BMW. A top-of-the-range black Range Rover dwarfed her Mini as she parked up next to it. Taking a deep breath, she checked herself in the rear-view mirror. She had actually made an effort with her hair that morning – was liking how long it had got. In fact, it suited her not having her usual six-weekly trim since she had moved back to the country. And even though it clearly wasn't an interview, she felt like she was going for one.

Today, because she knew she was meeting actual people, she had decided that she should look the part, so she had put on black tailored trousers and a smart silk champagne-coloured shirt. A lick of mascara, a dash of apricot blusher and her favourite matt red lipstick had finished her look. Foundation could stay in her make-up bag until her freckles started to emerge in the spring. The designer faux-fur-collared puffer jacket and medium-heeled suede boots that Ellie had insisted she had bought at the outlet centre were, in hindsight, now a little over the top, considering the mud she was about to walk through, and the fact that she was about to enter a barn in the middle of nowhere and not a smart city office block.

'Welcome to Futtingbrook Farm Hub,' August read aloud from the red scribbly font etched on the glass door in front of her. She was just thinking she'd have to be careful when relaying the name of her prospective workplace to anyone else when a ground-floor window flew open, making her jump. A man stuck his head out and proceeded to blow a huge plume of smoke into the still-frosty air.

He was handsome, August noticed, in a Jason Statham, Machiavellian kind of way. A tight navy sweatshirt showed defined, worked-out triceps. Thick black-rimmed designer glasses. Straight white teeth and an 'I'm not going bald so I'm going to crop my hair really short' hairstyle. A minute diamond stud in his right ear finished off his look.

'Oh, a real smoker? I didn't know they even existed any more,' August smirked.

Seeming amused at this rare frankness, the man let his half-smoked cigarette hang from his mouth in James Dean sexy-style and created a crucifix with his fingers. 'To hell may I go with my nicotine-stained fingers and acrid-smelling dog breath.' Taking another huge drag, then nipping the butt with his fingers, he deftly flicked it into the sand-filled bucket on the ground below. 'Talk to the Hub owner if it bothers you, love. Although, he's a right tricky bastard. So be careful how you phrase it.'

August took a deep breath. 'Sorry, and no, I don't have a problem with it. Used to smoke myself… Like a chimney, in fact. When I was younger.'

'Younger? You can't be a day over thirty, now, can you?'

'Try seven years.' Annoyingly, August found herself blushing. 'Er…and tricky, you say? I did wonder. His emails were abrupt. Verging on rude.'

'Oh, really? Interesting.' He nodded slowly, still holding court from the open window. 'Let me guess where you're from, then. The glitzy world of PR and marketing.'

'God, no. Actually. Well, yes. When I was in London, I… How did you?... Jesus. Am I that much of a stereotype?' She carried on swiftly, not wanting to hear his answer. 'Well…I was, but I write books now.'

He raised his dark eyebrows, looking reluctantly impressed. 'Wow, a real-life author in our midst. Not sure if Futtingbrook

Farm is ready for such a cultured animal.'

August laughed. 'I'm a top-twenty bestseller in the UK. Sadly, not made the Sunday Times Top Ten yet, but it pays the bills.'

'Not as rich as that Fifty Shades woman, then? Talking of arses—'

'Were we?' August muttered.

'—he's rough as a badger's one, he is. The owner of this place, I mean. A pig has better manners. That's who you've come to see, I guess?' August nodded. 'Anyway, I best shut this window before I let all the bloody heat out. What time you meeting him?'

'Nine-thirty.'

The man checked his flashy Patek Phillipe watch. 'You better get a shift on. He can't abide lateness, either.'

'Let's hope he talks of you so highly, eh?'

The man's full lips twitched in amusement. 'Go on in. Mrs G is in the kitchen by the sound of all the clattering. If you ask her nicely, I'm sure she'll show you where to go.'

'Thank you. And by the way, my name's Aug—'

The window slammed shut.

Slightly taken aback by this rudeness, August entered the Hub thinking that if everyone was as spirited as smoker-man, maybe this whole experience would furnish her with some interesting characters she could plagiarise for her Christmas mystery, at least.

The entrance door opened onto a plain reception area to the left, where there was a long white desk and an empty black swivel chair. On one side of the desk sat a pile of scruffy-looking files, on the other a plate with a half-eaten bacon roll and an empty mug. Three clocks, showing Paris, London and New York times, looked down at her from the otherwise plain white wall. The barn was much bigger inside than she had expected. Pleasantly surprised, she looked to her right to see a modern open-plan office area, housing different coloured chairs and more plain white desks, as well as a couple of more discreet, enclosed booth areas. Four glass-fronted offices ran along the back wall; three had black blinds pulled down so she couldn't see into them, but the one that was open offered a beautiful extended view over the meadows beyond. It was as if her modern Soho office had been boxed up and transported all the way to Futtingbrook – but instead of a view of concrete and brick, there was gorgeous, rolling green countryside. After a moment, she noticed that there was not one person in sight, which was strange, given the number of cars she had seen in the parking area.

'Mrs Saunders?' A thick local accent appeared in the reception area followed by a short, stout body that housed a pair of the biggest, most pendulous breasts August had ever seen. As the woman waddled from foot to foot, her breasts moved with her. Her baggy, grey wool dress was covered with a waist apron, her thick calves with American tan tights, and she was wearing trendy pink Nike trainers. To complete the look, over her tight grey curls she wore one of those hats that school dinner ladies used to wear. The genius comic writer that was Victoria Wood would have had a field day with her, August thought, before hoisting a hasty smile onto her face.

'Oh, hi, yes, that's me. But yet to tie the knot. I'm August. August Saunders.' She never usually laughed nervously, but for some reason did so now. 'Quiet here, isn't it?'

'What a pretty name. There's an April, a May and a June in Lower Gamble – that's where I come from – but August, that's a new one on me. Born in August, I take it?'

'Er, no on Valentine's Day actually.' August didn't want to get into the whole story right now: that her father had loved the name Augusta, her mother not so much, so she had lied to him

30

her whole life that the registrar had written it down wrong on the birth certificate and, on a snowy February morning, August Rose Saunders had been born.

The woman's breasts bounced as she laughed.

'A sense of humour too. We like those here in the Hub, we do.'

The woman stared at August intently. 'And as for quiet? Oh yeah. Here, well, it's the quietest place you'll ever find to work in Futtingbrook. So, so quiet. Pins drop and you don't hear them.'

'Oh, OK. That quiet.' August was now really quite amused. She was also finding it hard not to stare at the woman's grey monobrow.

'I'm Beryl, Beryl George. In charge of reception, the lunches for them "Hubbers", and for the turkey workers in and out of season. I clean for old Mrs Ronson up at the farm, too. Plus, keep this place shipshape. In fact, I do bloody everything around this place and I'm rather good at it, if I say so myself.'

Thinking that if she really was that thorough, there wouldn't have been food left on the reception desk, August checked out the row of world clocks. Ten-thirty in Paris – she'd better get a shift on. 'I know this sounds weird, but I've come to see someone with the initials, MM?'

'I know that. Now follow me, dear.'

The six-foot Jason Statham lookalike smirked and shook August's hand firmly.

'Hi. Max Ronson. I run this shit show.' He held her questioning gaze.

'So who's MM then?'

'MM?'

'Whoever sent me an email re this meeting signed off MM.'

'Oops, didn't realise I'd put that. Mad Max. It's what the Hubbers call me, on occasion.'

August gaped at him, thinking that all this was as clear as the mud she had just dirtied her new boots with.

August's chaperone stood in the door frame as if waiting to be excused to leave. 'Mrs G, could you be a diamond and bring me some more coffee capsules, please? I'm running low.'

The big-bosomed woman rolled her eyes, tutted, then winked at August as she waddled off.

'I appear to have met your rude twin brother on the way in.' August hid her initial shock with a grin. 'What was that all about?'

'You gave as good as you got. I want this place to be a fun working environment, and no dummies allowed.'

'If I'd known there was an initiation ceremony, I'd have reread my book on hub etiquette.'

'Talking of books, I wonder what your Lovelace & McGee characters would make of all this?'

August felt herself redden. 'You know who I am?'

'Wiltshire's answer to Agatha Christie, so your website tells me. I can see the new titles already; *A Cat among the Turkeys*, *The Mysterious Affair at Futtingbrook Farm Hub*.'

August laughed. 'I'd kind of hoped I might be able to keep my head down here and just get on with my job.'

He gave her a lazy smile. 'I'm all about heads being down, aren't you?'

Despite herself, August felt herself blush. 'You're incorrigible.'

'It's your mind that's the dirty one. Coffee?'

Too smart for his own good, this one, August thought. 'Yes, black, please.'

After a pause, Max said: 'So you've moved out of London?'

'Yes. Six months ago.'

'Like it in deepest darkest Wiltshire, then, do you?'

'Do *you*?' August held his gaze again. She really wasn't in the mood to elaborate on her sordid tale of relationship woe.

Pointedly ignoring her question, Max leant back in his swivel chair and put the coffee machine, which stood on the wide windowsill behind him, into action. 'So, I take it you're not just using us for research, then? I've always thought I'd make a great character in a book.'

August faked a yawn. 'If I got a pound for every person who said that to me, I could give up writing.'

'Ooh, sorry for being so bloody unoriginal.'

Despite the faint smell of cigarette smoke clinging to the air, August noticed that the Hub owner's office was OCD-tidy. A smart MacBook Pro was open in front of him. There was not a piece of paper in sight. Even his wastebin was empty. A model of a red Ferrari sat in a square glass display case in front of him. The words, 'You'd make a good mafia boss' flew out of August's mouth, without thought, bringing with them renewed blushes. 'I love the noise when they start up,' she said swiftly, pointing at the model of the car. 'Do you own one?'

'Done that, worn the t-shirt – owning the car, that is. I haven't been a mafia boss – more's the pity.' Max grinned. 'The problem is, I do have a mind with the speed of a Ferrari, but the brakes of a push bike.'

August laughed. 'Brilliant! I may have to steal that for one of my books. The expression, not the model, that is. I guess if you want to slow down, this is the area to do it.'

'It doesn't matter where you are, life is as slow as you make it.' The Hub owner handed August her coffee.

'A wise man too.' August was beginning to feel slightly high on this natural and unaffected banter. And were they flirting? It had been so long since she'd done that, she wasn't even sure.

'OK, I take it back. Maybe you *can* be a character in my next book.'

'And to think you mocked me.' He opened his drawer and pulled out a packet of cigarettes. 'It pained me to sell the car, but sadly it just wasn't practical to continue careering around these country lanes pretending I was Sebastian Vettel with a death wish.'

'Were you having a mid-life crisis, Max Ronson?' August mocked.

'If forty-one equates to my actual middle age, then I will be very happy given the amount of toxins I've thrown into my body over the years.' He took another cigarette out of the packet and spun it in his fingers. 'The last vice saloon. I keep saying I'll give up on my birthday.'

'When's that then?'

'It was two weeks ago.'

August laughed. 'You'll do it when you're ready. It took me a lot of attempts.' She looked at the wall to the side of him, which displayed an impressive array of black-and-white photographs of Formula One champions of old. 'Stunning prints, by the way. Are they originals?'

'Yes, yes, they are. Such a talented photographer...' His voice tailed off. He put the cigarette to his lips, then removed it again.

'My birthday was two weeks ago, too. What date was yours?' August asked. 'Mine was the fourteenth.'

'You can never moan that you don't get any cards on that day, then,' Max winked. 'I know what you women are like.'

August tried hard not to smile but failed.

'I'm a Valentine's baby, too, as it happens. But what a load of commercial bullshit all that is. If you love someone, tell them every day if you have to.' He paused, then said in a much quieter voice: 'Before it's too late.' He pushed open his window, lit a cigarette, took one huge drag, then aimed the half-smoked butt at the bucket full of sand.

'Good job I'm not one of those angry ex-smokers,' said August.

'Good job I'm the boss. And yes, I'm an Aquarius. But look at me; of course I am. Attractive with a sense of style. They're the main attributes, aren't they? Apart from that bit, I think that's all absolute bullshit, too.'

August shook her head. 'We clearly have so much in common.' When he gave her a wry look, she laughed. 'OK, maybe not, but we do share a birthday.'

'One out of three ain't bad, princess.'

August looked past his shoulder out to the parking area. 'I'm surprised you didn't pick a room with a better view as you are "*the boss*".'

'Nosey, that's why.'

'I guessed that from the number of cameras around here. It's like bloody Fort Knox.' August assumed a dramatic voice. 'Infiltrate the Futtingbrook Farm Hub at your peril!' Despite the joking, her mystery-writing mind really had started to wonder.

'I like to see the comings and goings of this place, and being sat this side of the barn keeps me away from the riff-raff.'

'What riff-raff? It's like a morgue in here.' August screwed her nose up.

'I assumed as an author you'd want proper quiet to concentrate.'

'Well, yes, sometimes, but I also wanted some kind of vibe around me. It's a solitary old business living and writing at home alone and I do have an innate ability to zone out once I've got my teeth into a plot.'

'I see. You'll have to speak to Cat; she runs a matchmaker service from here.'

'Did I say I was looking for someone?'

'Are you?'

'Bloody hell, what is this?' August hated herself for feeling an attraction towards this man. The words 'frying pan' and 'fire' whizzed around her brain. Scott Scanlan had already led her a merry dance and she didn't want to make any stupid mistakes again. And first impressions told her that Max was clearly a player. She'd have to be on her guard. 'Not that it's any of your business, but for the record, no, I'm not.'

'Sorry, got to keep my Hubbers happy.' He grinned his perfect, expensive smile. 'Only way to keep the rent coming in.' Max drained his espresso, and his voice became more business-like. 'Let me tell you a bit more about how it works here.'

'Halle…bloody…lujah.'

Max laughed. 'I like you.' Inwardly glowing at his comment, August took off her jacket and placed it on the back of the chair. 'So, the Hub is officially open five days a week, Monday to Friday, seven-thirty am to six pm, in line with the main gate before the forks. If you did want to stay late you'd just need to let me know so that I could manage the alarms, but I'd rather you pissed off on time. You can obviously come and go as you please, though. It's your space. I am just starting to market the place, so we are by no means full.'

'You implied you were heaving.'

'I lied.'

'I love your honesty.' They both laughed. 'You need a website.'

'I know I do.' He sighed deeply. 'Fancy doing a bit of work for me? You can be my marketing bitch.' He winked, then glanced down at the phone on the desk as three concurrent messages flashed in.

'Hmm.' August stroked her chin mockingly. 'Great offer, but I think I'll pass on that one.' The twinkle in his chocolate-brown eyes caused her to bite her lip.

'Anyway, back to the Hub. I have a hard-core trio who are here most days, and then a few others who just use the space sporadically, as fits with their business needs. We have a kitchen-cum-eating area where Mrs G, who you met earlier, offers up a hot meal daily – for the workers here and also for the turkey-farm staff, in and out of season. She also makes sandwiches. And there are snacks available. Prices it as she goes. Be warned, she likes to know the minute you walk in the door in the morning if you want one of her hot delights. Go with it. She's a loyal old bird and I can't fire her because she's on my mother's payroll.' He took a slurp of the coffee he had just made for himself. 'All drinks are free. There's a water cooler in the kitchen as well. Power points at every desk. The Wi-Fi is included in the rent, and is amazingly fast. Umm.' He ran his hand over his shaved head. 'What else? Oh yeah, there's a gym. And we gift you a free-range Futtingbrook turkey at Christmas. Plus, you get the chance to talk to me every day.' Max grinned. 'What more could an internationally bestselling crime author want?'

August found herself laughing. 'Hardly international. Like I said I'm big in the UK, but my agent is of course working on worldwide domination.'

'If one can say they are big in any area, that's a win for me.' His slightly posh twang was suddenly accentuated.

August shook her head. 'You're so wrong.'

'But oh so right, writer girl.' Max smirked.

She let this particular 'Maxism' go. 'OK, in principle, renting space here sounds great. It's such a beautiful outlook. And, well, I need this.'

'In principle?'

'Yes, how much is it?'

'How much do you want to pay?'

August laughed. 'Business degree, I take it?'

'The school of life.' Max smiled. 'I'm teasing you. It's three grand a year – two hundred and fifty pounds a month. Ideally, a six-month commitment up front, then it can roll on monthly with a month's notice.'

'That's reasonable.' August's tone lilted. Cheap rent and an undeniably witty and attractive man to be paying it to – maybe things were looking up.

'You can pay more if you like,' Max teased.

'Ha bloody ha. Can I just ask, though – is it always this quiet?'

Max assumed his faintly amused face. 'I tell you what, it's the middle of March now. How about I give you a two-week free trial, and at the end of it you can let me know if this collaborative working life is for you?'

'How could I refuse such an offer?' August smiled. 'I'll come in tomorrow morning, say ten-thirty. If that's OK, of course?'

'Sure. I'll sort the paperwork and email it over to you…just in case you do want to sign up, which I hope you will. I'll give you a proper show round then, too, but now I've got to dash.'

'I look forward to it.' August got up and reached for her coat. Max, now up from his desk, helped her on with it. 'See, you can be a gentleman.'

Holding the door open for her, he grinned cheekily. 'And for the record…Agatha…*I'm* not looking either.'

A smiling Max watched from his office window to see his potential new 'Hubber' get into her car, then went out into the primary office and shouted.

'You can come out now. After all that, she didn't want quiet. Thanks everyone – appreciate your support.'

The black blinds flipped up from the three meadow-facing offices. A radio was turned on and started sounding out from the mini Bose speakers that were dotted around the beams of the barn.

'Christ knows what she'll think when the turkeys start kicking off.' A tall woman in her mid-fifties with a sharp black bob, tight leggings, riding boots and bright pink lips stated, as she sauntered towards the kitchen area.

'I'm surprised the "alpaca assassins" weren't out there humming and spitting when she arrived this morning, too.' A tall, gangly man in his early twenties yawned and stretched his arms upwards.

Beryl appeared at his office door with the coffee capsules. 'Can we trust her, do you think, Max?'

He put his finger to his lips to shush her. 'Mrs G, I reckon she's going to be as good as gold.'

Chapter Five

August knocked for the third time, then huffed as she hunted in her messy bag for the key to her parent's bungalow. She could see her mum through the kitchen window, so why couldn't she hear her? Letting herself in, the March wind suddenly caught the front door, causing it to slam behind her.

'Ellie, is that you, darling? I thought you were at Music Minis with the boys this morning.'

Radio 4's *Woman's Hour* was on at full volume.

Without looking up, Pamela Saunders continued placing sweet pea seeds into tiny pots on her pine kitchen table, which was neatly covered with yesterday's newspaper. There was soil all over the place. An old black Labrador lay snoring in his basket next to the Aga.

August turned the radio down, finally causing her mum to look up at her and beam with delight. Rubbing her hands of soil, she jumped up to greet her first-born with a string of fast butterfly kisses on her cheek. 'My beautiful August Rose, how lovely to see you. Eleanor told me you were feeling better. Are you, love?'

'I'm getting there. What are you doing, with all this mess?'

'What I'm always doing.' Her local twang was soft; to August, it sounded like coming home. 'Gardening. Sweet peas today, my favourite. They remind me so much of your dad. Every year he would plant them, the old-fashioned ones with the beautiful scent, and every day they were flowering he would cut some for me. And, our shifts permitting – what with his at the station and my nursing ones – he would either bring them up with my waking cup of tea or leave them in my favourite vase by the kettle if I was sleeping.'

'I vaguely remember him winding them around the sticks in the garden, but I didn't know he had such a romantic streak.' August felt herself welling up.

'I still miss him terribly, you know.' Pam Saunders went to the sink, washed her hands, then began to fill the kettle.' Twenty years, it will have been this Friday. Twenty years and still bloody cancer prevails like an unstoppable juggernaut.' She let out a big sigh. 'Have you got time for a cuppa?'

'Yes, tea please. In my yellow mug.' August sighed. 'And of course you miss him. He was the best.' She then let out a little laugh. 'All that bloody home-made wine he used to make. That Marrow one… We had litres in the shed, do you remember? I used to be captivated watching him make it, like some mad professor with all those tubes and huge glass containers.'

Pam laughed. 'That I don't miss. It was potent, wasn't it?'

'Oh god, yes, I once pinched a bottle and snuck it to a party when I was sixteen.' August remembered. 'Me and Bobby were so drunk, we literally fell asleep on the sofa and missed the whole night.'

'Happy days. The station still send me a Christmas card every year, you know.'

'Because he was an amazing policeman too. Without him, I wouldn't have become a crime writer. You know that.'

'It's so sad he will never know that, though.'

'I don't believe that he won't,' August said gently.

Her mum's face lit up with a smile. 'You're right. You dressing up as teenager super-sleuth Nancy Drew on school fancy dress days was a definite clue.'

'Ha! Yes. That bloody magnifying glass you both bought me one Christmas, too. I used to sleep with it under my pillow. And I think the reason he bought me my special signing pen for my sixteenth birthday was that deep down, he kind of knew it was the path I would take.'

'Aw. I didn't realise you still had that.'

'Yes. Amazingly I can still get the same cartridges for it. I carry it with me everywhere. I feel it's a link between him and my writing. I used to love hearing all his stories – the good, the bad and the ugly.'

'Oh, August Rose, that's so lovely.' Pam turned away to swirl some boiling water around the blue-and-white stripey teapot and push back the hot tears that had snuck up on her.

August leant down to stroke Barney's ears, causing the old Labrador to let out a contented sigh, smack his mouth and carry on with his doggy daydream. She then took off her coat and sat down at the very same pine table where she had eaten thousands of meals throughout her thirty-seven years of being on the planet. She looked around at the long country kitchen, with its big grey flagstones and blue-and-white gingham curtains at its tiny windows. The place where family Saunders would laugh, talk and, on the insistence of her dad, always eat together so that they could discuss the highs and lows of their days. There had been so much laughter but also, with the passing of time and departing generations, tears too. It had been an idyllic childhood – that was, until the premature death of Ron Saunders, when August had been just seventeen and her sister fourteen.

August took in the very same pictures that had been on the walls for all those years. The now-vintage ceramic chicken-shaped egg container, still full to the brim with eggs from the local farm shop, as it had been ever since she could remember. She looked across to her mother and realised that she had been so wrapped up in her own self-pity for the last six months that she hadn't noticed that she looked different, older all of a sudden. Her once-auburn hair was now grey all over. Her sun wrinkles were that little bit deeper on her forehead. Her blue eyes had less of a sparkle. August felt a swoop of regret. This was a wake-up call. Her own wallowing had to stop. She should spend more time with her lovely mum. Not just pop in for a few minutes as she always had done, unless it was her birthday, when, for the past few years, she would get the train down from London and go to The White Horse in the village for lunch (her mum's choice), and Ellie, Grant and the grandkids would all be there. Scott's feeble excuse of staying home to learn lines last year suddenly made sense.

August had lived here at Orchard Cottage, just a ten-minute walk from the Victorian terrace cottage she was in now, for her first twenty-seven years on earth. And if it hadn't been for her being offered a promotion and relocation offer to London by Placatac, the toothpaste company she had worked for in Swinford, the very same year she'd split from her childhood sweetheart Bobby Collins, she would probably still be living in this sleepy village now.

There had been no dramatic heartbreak. She and Bobby, after eleven years together, had just grown apart. Last heard, he had his own plastering business and was living in a new-build in the Kingston Homes development on the outskirts of Swinford with his wife, three kids and an Alsatian called Jason.

When the time had come to up sticks, she had found it far

sadder leaving her friends, family and Barney the family dog than finally saying goodbye to her long-term lover.

It had been a difficult and somewhat scary decision to leave, but she had been ready for an adventure – realised that it was the right time to leave a sleepy village and see what lay beyond it. Plus, with her first book being submitted to London agents, she felt maybe it would somehow be easier to achieve her dream of turning her hobby into the reality of becoming a full-time author if she were in London.

She had found a room in a shared house in Clapham with two women of a similar age. And what an adventure it had been. There, she had not only made up for Bobby being the only man she had ever slept with, but had partied hard, enjoying what a single life in a big city had on offer. That is, until she met Scott Scanlan and, at first sight of him, suddenly realised the meaning of true love. Or so she'd thought.

'Do you not ever think about finding someone else, Mum?' With the radio now off, silence filled the kitchen, aside the soft snoring of Barney. 'Me and Ellie would welcome it, you know. We don't like to think of you being on your own forever.'

Pam groaned. 'Not again, dear, please. I loved your dad so much and anyway, I'm not on my own. I've got Barney.'

'I know you did, but—'

'August: enough. Worry about yourself, before me. My garden is my solace. Plus my friends at the WI and my book club. Not forgetting my gorgeous grandsons and you two girls, of course.' She smiled lovingly at her daughter. 'I'm more than fine with the company I keep, thank you very much.'

Pam moved the seed- and soil-filled pots to one end of the table, then placed a floral tray with the teapot, two unmatching mugs, a bowl of sugar and a packet of chocolate digestives in front of August. She was about to sit down opposite her daughter when she jumped up, leant over and grabbed the tray, nearly pulling it on to her lap. Her face looked suddenly pained.

'Mum, what are you doing?'

The older woman stuttered. 'What am I thinking of? Let me pour. So rude.'

'Mum? You're being really weird.'

Then, suddenly twigging what was going on, August walked around the table and moved the tray away. 'I thought it was odd, you buying the Sun.'

'Mrs Dye took great pleasure in pointing it out to me when I was at the checkout at the Spar yesterday. Haven't you seen it?'

'Obviously not.' Wondering what had been going on with her ex-lover now, August's pulse began to race in woeful anticipation.

Wiping a bit of soil off his expensive veneers, she sighed deeply as she began to read the offending newspaper article aloud. '"Heartbreak for Scott Scanlan fans as he announces second engagement in two years."'

August's face twitched as she looked at the ceiling to control her shock and dismay.

'I'm so sorry, love. I didn't want to call, and for you to think I was meddling.'

August's face contorted with anger as she pushed the offending page away. 'What about heartbreak for his ex-fiancée? Fuck him, I say!'

'August! Language! Actually yes, FUCK HIM!'

'Mum!' They both started laughing.

'He didn't deserve you anyway.'

'No. He didn't.' August took a deep, calming breath. 'Time for a clean slate – which is just about to happen, in fact.'

'Ooh, what's this then?'

'I'm signing up to work out of one of these collaborative hub things.'

The smile that had lit up her mother's face dimmed a little. 'Oh. I thought for a moment you were going to tell me you'd met a new fella.'

August pulled a face. 'I kind of want to get over the other one first.'

'Want and need are hugely different things, August. I say you need to get under someone new to get over the other one. Especially as the other one was such a complete and utter bastard.'

'Mum! You can't say that.'

'I'm speaking for your father; he'd have kicked his arse to Acapulco and back again.' Pam took a deep breath and started to calmly pour the tea. 'A hub? What's that all about then?'

'It's like a shared workplace where people from different companies and entrepreneurial types – like me, I guess – work together under one roof.'

'That sounds interesting.'

'Yes, and it will get me out of the house and hopefully inspire me a bit. I need to get cracking with the writing again.'

'Ah, yes! Is it over at Futtingbrook Farm? I got a flyer through. The Ronsons' place.'

August nodded. 'Yes, that's it.'

'I guess it's one of the brothers who's set it up, is it?' Pam Saunders offered.

'I met with a Max yesterday. I don't remember him from growing up. He didn't go to either of my schools, I don't think.'

'Hmm. He was the disruptive one of the two, that one. I remember when you were little, I heard that his mum and dad sent him off to a posh private school to try and sort him out. In fact, both boys went there, I think. He came back from living in London himself, I hear. According to Mrs Dye, whenever it was, it was in a hurry and nobody knows why.'

'Well, let's concentrate on the positives, shall we?' August tutted, not wanting any negativity to stain her decision to sign up at the Hub. 'I shall take as I find, as you taught me to, Mother.'

'Handsome, is he?'

August avoided her gaze. 'Why do you ask that?'

'Just be careful, darling, as I hear he has an eye for the ladies. And you need to be on the search for a nice boy now, not one who mucks you around.'

'A ridiculous assumption on no grounds whatsoever, I expect.' August huffed. 'Mrs Dye really should put her energies into working for a tabloid. She'd be perfect at that!'

Pam laughed. 'You sounded like your Lila Lovelace character then.'

August shook her head. 'And for the second time this week, I'm not looking for love.'

'And that's exactly when love starts looking for you,' her wise mother replied, reaching for the sugar bowl.

Chapter Six

It was like a different office when August pushed open the door to the Hub the next day. The local radio station blared out across the barn and there were three people sitting at desks in the open-plan office area. Spread out but close enough that they could chat if they wanted to, she noticed. She was thankful that today she was wearing jeans, a baggy cashmere jumper and flat boots, as it felt a bit chilly. Plus, it had certainly been a lot easier negotiating the muddy car parking area than in yesterday's heels.

Before she had a chance to even smile at anyone, Beryl appeared, breasts in full swing. 'Hot, not or a sandwich?' she asked, her strong local accent enquiring.

'Umm.' August didn't know what to say. She didn't want to disappoint the woman, but she had had a bowl of porridge literally just before she left the house and wasn't hungry.

'Hot, not or a sandwich, young August?'

'Err. I'm not sure.'

'I need to know if you want a hot meal, a sandwich or nothing at all. It's not brain science.'

'Err. I hadn't really thought even if I'd be here until lunchtime.'

Beryl's voice raised an octave. 'I need to know for the

numbers.'

Autumn panicked. 'OK, hot would be amazing. Thanks, Beryl.'

'It's shepherd's pie, is that OK?'

'Perfect, thank you.'

Beryl gave her an approving look, as though she had passed some sort of test.

'She got you.' August looked up to see a strikingly attractive woman approaching her. 'Six-foot-one with heels, before you ask.'

'She did. And yes, you definitely trump my five-foot-eight there. I thought I was tall. Good to meet you. I'm August.'

'Cat Bachelor, but the bastards here call me Big Cat. Max has had to pop out for a bit, said for me to meet you and show you the ropes.'

August noted a faint Scottish accent. 'If you're sure you've got time.'

'Of course, I have. It's good to see another female other than Beryl in here. Who, being honest, isn't quite on my level of converse, if you get my drift? Come on into the kitchen, we can grab a coffee.'

The kitchen area was modern and airy, made up of smart black units, small, white oblong wall tiles and a grey slate floor. A long white table and eight chairs could be found at one end and an expensive coffee machine rested on the counter next to a kettle and various boxes of different fruit teas. There were two glass-fronted fridges. One looked empty aside from a pot of humous and some salad cream, but the other housed a selection of soft drinks and juices alongside bottled sparkling water and fresh milk. A water cooler finished off the beverage offerings. A snack machine featuring every kind of chocolate bar and crisp flavour was against the wall next to the table and chairs. There was a double oven with a gas hob and a dishwasher as well as a Smeg toaster – the same as August's own, but in black.

'So, it's all here. Max is very generous; he makes sure we are all fed and watered. It's all included in the rent – what's on show – including the snack machine. Being honest, the food Beryl prepares is very touch-and-go – in fact, it's mainly go.' Cat laughed a deep throaty laugh. 'But it gets so bloody cold in here sometimes, it's worth risking just for the warmth.' It was August's turn to laugh.

'Amazing what we get for the monthly cost here, though.'

'I know. I think he feels it's so remote here, and so far removed from what he was used to in London, that if he keeps the price down, it gives him a better chance of getting some more people in. Despite that, it's only been a few of us here, for just over a year now.'

'What did he use to do in London, then?'

'None of us know. We don't even know what he does here, to be honest. He is the master of not answering direct questions.'

'Yes, I kind of got that.'

'Coffee?'

'Yes, black please. So, Max hinted you were a matchmaker?'

'Yes. I moved here from Edinburgh twenty years ago, for the love of an Englishman. As we do. We split five years ago. Me and husband number two as I used to call him. No drama, no kids with him, so it was a clean break, but at the grand old age of fifty-five, I started to internet date and found it so demoralising that I thought, if Pattie Stanger can do it on *Millionaire Matchmaker*, why can't I set up my own agency?'

August laughed. 'Bloody brilliant. I love that show.'

'Don't grass me up, but my clientele are not all millionaires, sadly, or I'd be charging them double and living in a mansion in Morningside by now. But I'm doing OK. My aim is to find love for others in a remote area, and maybe for myself eventually. Who knows?'

'Well done you for taking the initiative. Any business is hard to set up I should imagine, but when you are trading in the transient commodity of love, I guess it's especially hard to forecast.'

'You're not wrong there, but God, I've had some fun, I tell you. When I realised it wasn't a good look having sex with all my son's mates' – August's eyes widened – 'I immediately dropped the "no sex with my clients" rule. I'm not frightened to say I love a good bang. Consenting, clean, with no ties unless they are on my wrists. Luckily, so far nothing has bitten me in the arse – not even literally.'

'Right.' August suddenly felt that her own sex-life had been demoted from vanilla to a simple off-white.

'My son's thirty by the way, not thirteen, in case you were wondering. Conceived in the toilets after half a bottle of Tequila at a particularly outrageous office party. I was twenty-five, his father was an arsehole and my Catholic upbringing stopped me from doing what would have been the sensible thing at the time. But he's turned out bloody well considering the starting odds. And he's moved near here recently, which is even better.'

'Wow! I'm looking for characters for my next book. Max is a contender but maybe I should be basing one on you.' August laughed.

'God! No publicity, thanks, unless you just mention the agency of course.' She assumed a posh voice. '"The Country Matchmaker. A five-star route to rural romance."' Her voice returned to normal. 'Although at the moment, I really am considering dropping the o, the number of incongruous bastards I seem to be attracting on to my books.'

August laughed. 'I can see why you and Max get on so well.'

'Yes, I'm of the "think it and say it" kind of era too. Jonah hates it. I goad him.'

'Jonah?'

'I'll introduce you in a minute. He's bonnie too.'

'My good ear is burning already.' A clean-shaven, black-haired man, the same height as August, appeared in the kitchen wearing dark jeans, a plain brown jumper and a pair of muddy green wellies. His voice and energy were gentle, and he smelt of pine needles. August aged him in his mid-forties.

'Wore these in and forgot to bring my shoes to change into.' He pointed to his feet. Smiling warmly, he held out his hand to August, who was now sitting opposite Cat in the dining area. 'Hi, I'm Jonah Lin.'

'Nice to meet you. August Saunders.'

'Just to warn you, I won't be ignoring you, just not hearing you sometimes, as I turn these aids right down or off when I want some peace.' He fiddled with the small device in his right ear.

'That's what he tells us, but he has selective hearing even when they're on.' August could sense Cat's affection for the quiet man. 'But I learnt fuck off in sign language, so he never escapes me.'

They all laughed. The water cooler gurgled as Jonah filled his reusable bottle then sat down to join them at the table.

'So, we have a writer among us. How exciting.'

'Oh, did Max tell you?'

'No, Beryl did. You can't do a lot around here without her having knowledge of it. So, what have you written? Anything I'd know?'

'I doubt it. Agatha Christie meets Val McDermid, I like to call it. Also known as the Lovelace & McGee Mystery series.'

'Tell me more.'

'Not much to it, to be honest. Two women detectives solve

mysteries in the West Country. Lila Lovelace is glamourous and pretty useless. It's the plain, Northern Irish underling, Marie McGee, who really is the genius of the two in the crime solving, but she never gets any of the credit, nor any of the crop of usually undesirable men that seem to flow Lila's way.'

'Interesting. I'm more of a non-fiction man myself, but my wife would love that. Saying that, she doesn't have much time for reading at the moment.'

'Kids?' August guessed.

'Yes, two sets of unexpected twins, plus she runs a homeopathy clinic out of our place now.'

'Wow, busy lady. How old are they?'

'The boys have a *made-on honeymoon* sticker on their soles. Then, oops she promptly fell again a year later, with the girls. Fourteen and thirteen respectively. They are pretty self-sufficient on most fronts, but currently our world seems to be a hotbed of hormones and chauffeuring to various sports clubs and friends' houses. Poor Sukie. I come here for a rest. Do you have kids?'

'You shouldn't ask a woman that, Jonah.' Cat piped up.

'Oh, sorry August... I didn't think that—'

'Honestly, it's fine.' August's voice was full of reassurance. 'I'm not in that place yet. I have two gorgeous little nephews, though, whom I adore.' He was still looking sheepish, so August cast around for a change of subject. 'So, what do you do then, Jonah? If you don't mind me asking.'

'No, not all. I used to run a tailor's shop in Piccadilly. Had a team of ten working for me, mainly making suits, mainly for the rich and famous. Crazy hours, crazy times. Then I started learning about this even crazier planet and realised that I wanted not only to do my little bit to try and save it, but to give more to my family than just money. It took me a long time to realise that time is the most expensive but also easiest thing you can give anybody.' His kindness was palpable, and August felt increasingly drawn to his affable demeanour. 'So, we upped sticks from the big smoke and now live a mile down the road from here.'

'Good for you.'

'Luckily we've been accepted into the community and more importantly the kids and Sukie love their new surroundings.'

August grinned at him. She couldn't imagine anyone not liking Jonah. 'So, what do you do now?'

'I run a business called Touching Cloth.' A surprised laugh burst out of August. 'I know, I know, it means being near to shitting your pants. I hadn't heard of that offensive little phrase until after I named it! The website and cards were all sorted before anyone cared to challenge it. My online store is all about ethical fashion, so I was thinking about touching in the emotional sense, not the other kind. And now I'm stuck with it.'

He looked so rueful that August felt a surge of hilarity-tinged pity. 'Maybe it could work in your favour. Who knows?'

'Well, this is the funny part, August. It certainly did do that, as the press picked up on it and asked to interview me about my business and, well, it went a bit viral. The partially deaf Anglo-Chinese man with the funny-named company was quite the hit. Even my kids were impressed. And I got a lot of business out of it.'

'We need more of you in this world, clearly.' August took a sip of her coffee.

'Thanks. You'll meet Tyler tomorrow if you're here. He helped me make a brilliant TikTok reel on the backside of it. Ha! Backside. See what I did there? I've got loads more followers and clients using the website now.'

'Brilliant! So sorry to sound dumb, but how does it all work?'

Cat stood up. 'I've got to interview a new recruit on Zoom in a minute, so I'd better go and get set up. Our state-of-the-art gym is the last door down to the left on Max's office side, just in case you're interested.'

'Sure, thanks so much, Cat, and lovely to meet you. Sorry Jonah, carry on.'

'So…in short, I host sustainable clothing brands under the Touching Cloth umbrella and advise them on their customer journeys and if they need any financial advice, I can help them with that too. I will only deal with those who use renewable energy, natural materials and plastic-free packaging. Some of my clients even recycle garments when they're worn out, turning them into other clothing items. It's so inspiring. Like I said, I'm very much all about protecting our wonderful planet, and thankfully my kids are following suit, too. All vegetarians, except for my Frank, who just won't give up his chicken. But that's his choice. And life is about choices, isn't it?'

'Yes, it really is.' August's mind spooled back to her own life choice of moving back here to be near the people who really knew and loved her and she suddenly realised that, despite everything, she was beginning to feel a renewed sense of happiness and vigour.

'Come on. Let me show you the gym,' Jonah enthused.

They stood up and walked down past Max's office, the door of which was closed. Looking around, August noticed a lift. 'Talk about hi tech, this really is an amazing barn conversion. What is upstairs, anyway?'

'All we know is that it is off-limits. We see Max going up there sometimes, but when we ask him, he always smiles and says the same: 'Can't a man have a cave?''

'Oh, really?'

August's mystery-writer mind began to work overtime.

Maybe Max had a secret woman hidden up there and that was why he had made it clear that he wasn't looking for anybody. Or worse still, a body that needed to be buried! Or maybe he was a drug dealer and was growing weed, hence all the skylights to let out the pungent smell, and the cameras for security. Her vivid imagination was interrupted by Jonah pushing open a door labelled simply: THE GYM.

'OK, it's not quite your David Lloyd.' August started laughing and then couldn't stop, for the Futtingbrook Farm Hub gym consisted of one upright exercise bike and a running machine. Jonah shrugged. 'Better than nothing. None of us use it, to be fair, but it's there if we do want to. Some lunchtimes, I take a walk up and around the whole farmland area. If you've got time on your hands, there's a public footpath that takes you all along the fields and into Futtingbrook itself. It's so pretty around here.'

'Are you daring to laugh at the luxury fitness area that I am providing completely free of charge?' The slightly posh twang of Max Ronson reached them, annoyingly causing August to feel herself redden immediately. 'Bloody expensive equipment, that was, and I'm the only bugger who uses it. Thanks, Jonah, and sorry I wasn't here when you arrived, Agatha. Had to see a man about a pig – you know what it's like. But good to see you've met Jonah.'

'Yeah, and I caught up with Cat too.'

'Our very own Big Cat. Signed you up yet, has she?'

'No! But if there are some millionaires in her midst then maybe I should.' She made a doubtful face.

'So, are you going to grace us with your presence at the happy Hub and do some work today, then?'

'Laptop is in my bag, so that's the plan. I've ordered hot food, too.'

She saw Jonah and Max grimace at the same time, and her

trepidation at the thought of the impending meal doubled.

'Have you got time to pop into my office for a second?' Max asked her.

'Sure.' August duly followed him.

'Shut the door behind you.' She did as she was told. 'I just wanted to check you're all right?'

She frowned at him. 'Why wouldn't I be?'

'Being honest, I only did a really quick Google search minutes before you arrived yesterday. The author bit in your email had intrigued me. But I had no idea who you were until then. I may have been flippant with you. Sorry.'

'Oh. Well, don't worry, it's fine. You were fine. I just want to be August here. Not A.R. Saunders, the bestselling author. If you know what I mean. I'm not exactly a rocket scientist now, am I?'

'I totally get it. When I lived in London, I used to have friends in showbiz, and they were just that: friends whose jobs happened to be in the public eye.'

'Thank you. And look at me, saying I'm not a diva, then spouting like one.'

Max kept his voice level. 'I wanted to say sorry you've been through such a shit time, personally. It was out of order me going on about you being single yesterday. I wouldn't have if—'

August felt a dart of alarm at the idea of discussing her recent romantic failure with this man she barely knew. 'It's OK, but I don't want to talk about it now.'

'And I don't need or want to know about it now. I'm not trying to pry; I just wanted to apologise.'

August suddenly felt overcome at this unexpected thoughtfulness. She looked up at the ceiling to try and stop tears from falling.

Max bit his lip. 'Fuck me, don't start blubbing on me. See.

This is why I'm rarely nice.'

August managed a smile. 'It's the bloody stench of fag smoke making my eyes water.' Her voice softened, and Max, who clearly didn't have the tools to deal with an emotional woman, looked relieved. 'But I appreciate you saying it, Max.'

A loud noise from the kitchen made August visibly jump. 'What the hell?'

'Your hot food is here.' Max's face remained deadpan.

August checked her watch. 'It's only eleven-thirty.'

'Yes, I know, and yes, Mrs G has a gong. She also bangs it for another reason, but I'll let you find that one out for yourself.'

August put her hand to her forehead. 'At least being here is going to liven up the dullest days, that's for sure.'

'Good. Now, go and get your lunch before you get in trouble. Shepherd's pie today, isn't it? Made from a real shepherd's scrotum, I believe. And don't worry, there's a microwave in the kitchen if you're not hungry right this minute.'

'Oh, God. I hope there is a wastebin too.'

'Yes, and plenty of sick bags under the sink.'

'Too funny.' August got up and opened the door.

'Talking of fun, it's Friday fun day tomorrow. I usually get pizzas delivered. One day less to get food poisoning.'

'Free pizza and a state of the art running machine – what more could a girl wish for?' August picked up her bag. 'OK. Onwards. Is there a Wi-Fi code?'

'Yes, it's "gobblers", all lower case, followed by exclamation mark.'

'Of course, it is.' August caught his smiling brown eyes.

'Have a good day, Agatha. And could you shut my door behind you, please?'

Chapter Seven

That evening, August sat on her small two-seater sofa, stroking a purring Prince Harry and watching television. *Celebs go Dating* had just started. 'Don't bother, girlfriend,' she said aloud as the first woman sat there nervously awaiting an ex-boy band member. 'Whoever they are, or think they are, they will still act like a bloody Neanderthal.'

Switching the TV off, she made a mental note to go and see her mum before she headed for the Hub in the morning. She had popped into one of the gift shops in Futtingbrook on her way home earlier and found some silk sweet peas for her. August didn't usually like fake flora, but these were particularly good, set in what looked like water in a plain glass vase.

In one way, the years had flown since her dad had passed, but also it seemed a complete age since she'd seen that open, friendly face of his, and felt the warmth of his huge bear hug. She sometimes got frightened she would completely forget that feeling or, worse still, his face. Photos never quite did him justice.

'Ow! Stop it, you naughty boy.' Prince Harry was kneading her thighs with his paws, sticking his claws in as he did so. She gently pushed him off her lap and headed for the kitchen to make herself a hot chocolate. It had been six months since she had moved back to The Terrace to live in the rented cottage owned by her sister and husband, who resided next door with their sons, Wilf and James, almost two years and six months old respectively. And not forgetting Colin the Corgi, of course.

It had been pure serendipity that they had started advertising for a new tenant just days after Scott had struck his cheating blow. Luckily there had not been a London house to split or a divorce to settle. Their fancy serviced apartment had been fully furnished, so when her brother-in-law had pulled up in his mobile fish-and-chip van to move her out, all she'd had to do was throw in two large suitcases and a wailing Prince Harry.

As well as kicking off the whole way back to Wiltshire, the agitated moggy did a stinking protest pee in his basket. This caused Grant to swear the entire length of the M4, certain that health and safety would shut him down if there was so much of a drop of cat urine left in there. With August caterwauling in unison with Grant's rant, it had not been the most peaceful journey.

When she had eventually arrived at her new country abode, she realised that all she physically had to show for her nineteen years of working was a box full of shoes, a wardrobe of clothes – half of which didn't fit her now, due to the heartbreak diet – and a fat ginger tomcat gifted to her by the cheater a week before he had told her that he was leaving her.

A large hungry miaow from Prince Harry jolted her out of her thoughts and reactivated her potty mouth. 'Bastard!' she said aloud, a mixture of grief for her father and bad memories of her ex manifesting. 'Manipulating bastard!' Then, to her now startled moggy, 'Not you, darling. I'm happy you came to me.' She reached for some cat treats and threw a few on to the kitchen floor, and the ginger tom gobbled them up as if he hadn't been fed for months.

August bashed about getting a mug, slammed the fridge door shut, then set the microwave to heat her milk. She ran upstairs, got the framed photo from her drawer, tore back down the stairs and threw it with force into the bin.

The engagement news had been the last straw. Realising the speed with which his relationship had developed had made her wonder just how long the affair with bitch-faced actress Delila the Dog – a.k.a. Bella from the Café in the UK's longest-running soap – had been going on before the coward had actually had the balls to tell her it was over.

But if she were honest with herself, the finality of Scott's approaching wedding to someone else was probably a blessing in disguise. Throughout her heartbreak, she realised now that she had still been holding onto the forlorn hope that he may realise the error of his ways and come back to her. Because, despite all the rules about self-respect and a leopard never changing his spots, fundamentally she had loved him dearly. And if she were honest, still did, a little bit.

She was just about to go upstairs with her hot chocolate and get ready for bed when her mobile rang. August closed her eyes. 'Bugger.' It was Brigitte again.

Brigitte Fleurot was a force to be reckoned with. A literary agent who fought for her clients and got deals like no other. She was both respected and despised within the industry – the perfect combination for any kind of agent – and for all her faults, August got on well with her. But it was late on a Thursday night, and she really wasn't in the mood for a serious talking to. She would let her go to voicemail, then listen. Sitting down on the sofa with her chocolatey drink, August found the message on her mobile, then pressed speaker.

'Augooste! C'est Brigitte. Remember moi!' There was a wine

slur to her loud voice. 'Fine, avoid me, but do you want a bloody writing career or not?' August wished she'd left it until the morning, now. 'I fear I may murder you at this rate, and I would get away with it as there'll be no Lovelace & McGee to solve it!' August couldn't help but smile at the feisty Parisian. 'The good news is that I have details of the new deal, and it's not just a Christmas book. They want to sign you for three more. *Trois!* You hear me? And it's a good offer. Makes sense, as that will make ten books in the series. *Magnifique!* So just bloody ring me, will you? Or at least answer my emails. If I don't hear from you, I will come to deepest darkest Wiltshire tomorrow and drag you out of a bloody *champ de choux* if I have to.'

August googled *champ de choux* and laughed out loud. Were there even cabbage fields around there? She had no idea. But what she did know was that Brigitte Fleurot only left London for funerals or holidays, so her threat was obviously an idle one.

Blowing out a big puff of air, August thought for a second. Another three books was great, but with that came intense pressure, as three more would of course need to be written. How long had they given her, she wondered? Maybe this was the kick up the arse she needed now. She would head to the Hub straight after seeing her mum the next day, then ring her agent, find out what the exact offer was on the table, what the deadlines were, and finally get things moving.'

She lovingly stroked the ginger tom as he walked across her legs. 'At last, we have a plan, my little man.' Then, suddenly overcome by a combined sense of relief and excitement, she felt herself welling up. Three more books, whatever the deadlines – that was amazing! Not only that her publisher wanted to make the offer and give her renewed financial confidence, but also because it made her realise just how much she had needed such a boost and appreciation.

Walking back through to the kitchen, she retrieved the framed photo of Scott and herself from the bin, gave it a wipe with a dishcloth and headed upstairs, clutching it and her now-cooling bedtime drink.

Chapter Eight

August could hear strange wailing-type noises coming from a slightly ajar window as she approached Orchard Cottage. Peering through the window, she saw her mother lying on the floor face-up with all limbs spread out, her body resembling that of a crime scene from one of her novels. Unlike August's fictional victims, Pam was moving her limbs very slowly, as if swimming on the floor.

Intrigued, August knocked loudly on the door, and through the window saw her mother jump up with a start.

'August Rose, what on earth are you doing here at this hour?' Looking embarrassed, she brushed down her jogging bottoms and fussed with her hair. The noises continued their eerie lament from her mother's phone.

'It's not that early. I thought I'd catch you before you took Barney out.' She looked at her mother quizzically. 'What are you doing, anyway? And what on earth is that noise?'

'Oh, it's nothing.' Under her daughter's stern gaze, she relented. 'Well, OK, it's my *Chant des Baleines* tape. Me and Margaret – you know, my friend from the WI? – well, we decided that we'd try a bit of this New Age stuff. All the rage, this whale music, we heard. I find it ever so relaxing.' She fiddled about with her phone until there was silence. Then, acting like she had been discovered in the shameful act of coitus, she rushed through to the kitchen and flicked on the kettle. 'Have you time for a cuppa, darling?'

August followed her. 'No, don't worry. I just wanted to drop something in for you.'

'I'm meeting Carol on the corner for our dog walk at seven forty-five, so we've got a few minutes.'

'It's fine, I need to get working anyway.' August rustled around in her handbag and pulled out a floral-patterned paper bag and handed it to her mother.

Pam Saunders tutted. 'What do I tell you girls about buying me things?' Pulling out the glass vase containing seven very realistic and delicately coloured sweet peas, the older woman let out a sigh and August could see tears forming in her mother's eyes.

'I thought they could maybe sit on your bedroom windowsill until the real ones grow.'

'As thoughtful as your father, you are.' She kissed her daughter on the forehead. 'Twenty years today, he's been gone. My darling Ron, your dear dad. Who'd have thought it? He'd have been so proud of you and Ellie, you know. As am I.' She took August's hand and squeezed it. 'Thank you. It's a beautiful gift.'

'It still hurts, even after all this time.' August sighed.

'Yes, it does. But we have to be grateful that we have each other, and just remember that your dad lives on through you and you sister. So he's always with you.'

'It's not the same.' August bit her lip to stop it from quivering.

'We knew the day he died that life would never be the same, but we've got on, just as he wanted us to. And what more can we do?' Pam washed up a couple of stray mugs and put them on the draining board. 'Shall we go to the grave on Sunday? I mentioned it to Ellie; she's around.'

'Yes, of course.'

'I'll do us all a nice roast after, like we usually do. All right?'

'Lovely.' August gave her mum a sudden, tight squeeze, and she squeezed back just as firmly.

'Right. I best take this hound out. You look nice. Are you off to the Hub today?'

'Yes. Which reminds me, I have some good news: my agent phoned last night and she's got me a new three-book deal with Big Red.'

Pam gasped, her hands flying to her mouth. 'Oh, darling, that's wonderful!'

'Gives me no excuse not to write now.'

'Well, you'd better ink that quill of yours and get on then.'

August laughed. 'Indeed. Have a good day, Mum, and see you Sunday.'

Chapter Nine

'Hot, not, sandwich or a pizza?' Mrs G accosted August on arrival.

'Do you know what, Beryl, as much as I love it, I'm going to pass on the pizza. I would like a tuna mayo sandwich, please. On brown bread with a packet of salt and vinegar crisps, if that's OK?'

'It's not one of those fancy London delicatessens here, young lady. I only do cheese. With tomato, pickle or salad cream.'

'Oh.'

'I haven't got all day, August.'

'Cheese, tomato and mayonnaise, please. Brown bread, if I have a choice.'

'I didn't say mayonnaise, did I? ASDIS own salad cream all right for you?'

August kept her face straight. 'Salad cream will be absolutely divine, then, thank you, Beryl.'

'There we go, we got there at last.' The woman puffed. 'It'll be in the left-hand fridge at eleven thirty. You get your own crisps out of the snack machine. That will be three pounds, please. Pop the money in the tin marked Beryl's Benidorm Fund on top of the microwave, there's a good girl.'

August had to admit that although bizarre, she kind of liked this antiquated system. Life down here was certainly real and it felt both refreshing and freeing to be living it without a constant Instagram filter. Yes, as an author she had to keep a certain number of posts going out to the world, but gone now were the selfies Scott had seemed to want to take of them both doing everything bar going to the toilet, in order to satisfy his fans – and his ego. After all that public intrusion, she felt now that she wanted to keep her private life as private as she could. Which, at the moment, was easy, as it was nigh on non-existent, anyway.

Making a mental note to ensure she carried some cash at all times for fear of the wrath of Beryl George and her gong, she walked into the main office area.

'Morning, Agatha. You're up with the tits today.' Max appeared from his office, his eyes framed by dark circles. He yawned loudly.

'Someone keeping you up?' The moment she said it, August cringed inwardly at her comment.

'Well, the same couldn't be said for you. You obviously couldn't wait to see me again.'

'Obviously,' she said, her face and voice deadpan. 'But no, I popped to Mum's before I came here and it appears her social life is busier than mine, so here I am.'

'Look at you, being the world's best daughter?'

The words, 'My dad died,' fell out of August's mouth without thought.

'Oh, shit. I'm sorry.' Max put his hand on her arm.

'Twenty years ago today, actually. And it's OK.'

'It's never OK, losing someone you love too soon. Time covers the mind with scar tissue, so the pain lessens, but it never goes.'

August paused, taken aback by Max's profoundness and understanding, but also shocked at her own openness with this man.

She felt vulnerable, all of a sudden, and cast around for a change of subject. 'I've got a new idea buzzing around for my Christmas book and I need to get it down. Can I use one of the private offices this morning?'

'Look at you, Miss Efficiency.' Normal Max had returned, to her relief. 'I bet you were head girl, weren't you? I can see it now, long socks and short skirt. Parading around, flicking your hair, spouting literary prose out of those rosebud lips of yours.'

August worked to keep a straight face. 'I could report you for talk like that.'

'Report away. I'm sure the owner of the Hub will be most sympathetic.'

August tutted. 'Like I said before, you're lucky I'm a good sport.' She fixed him with a stern look. 'But less of the impertinence in future please, mister.'

'You can't be throwing words around I don't understand just because you is a big-shot author,' Max joked.

'Consult Mr Google – you're good at that.'

Max shook his head. 'And Agatha.' August bit back a stinging comment. 'You don't have to ask. The run of this place is yours.'

'Except upstairs, clearly.' August gave him a sour look and made her way into to the kitchen.

'Can't a man have a cave?' Max shouted after her, and she heard him pressing the button for the lift.

August, now completely intrigued to find out what was going on up there, but feeling like it would be completely unacceptable to follow him, waited restlessly for the coffee machine to do its thing. A man's voice spoke behind her.

'Hey, you must be August.' She turned around to face a gangly, six-foot lad in his early twenties, with blonde hair that was in better condition and as long as hers, and an eyebrow piercing.

'Welcome to the mad house. Tyler Trinder, or TikTokT as I'm known in the world wide web of online fakery. Creator of all things digital and freelance designer at your service. Check me out.'

August smiled at his self-assurance. 'Well, it's very good to meet you…TikTokT.' He had a distinct eau de weed about him, and she had to make an effort not to wrinkle her nose.

'You too. I've never met a real-life author before.'

'Well, here I am – and you're soon to be disappointed, I'm sure. I'm no different to anyone else, I just happen to put words on paper in an order that people like to read.'

'Man! Don't do yourself down like that, but I do blame you for ruining my sex life, actually.'

'Err, OK. Dare I ask why?'

Tyler laughed. 'Reece – that's my partner – let's just say he's a bit of a fan boy of yours. Totally obsessed with your bloody mystery books. It's because you base them around here. Told me to tell you, he loves your "Queen of a lead" – his words, not mine.'

'That's all very lovely, thank you, but I'm still not quite getting the bedroom connection here?' August picked her mug of coffee off the machine and took a hesitant sip, then a bigger one, pleasantly surprised by the quality.

'Oh, as soon as a new book of yours comes out, the sex ban commences.'

'Err, I'm not sure I want to hear any more.' August smiled.

'He turns into Agatha bloody Christie himself, boring me with his theories about who he thinks has done it and why. No disrespect at your craft there, obviously.'

'None taken.' August laughed. 'And I'm sorry to hear that, but it's also nice to know I have such a super fan.'

'Anyway, don't worry, I won't mention it again.' At her

enquiring look, he explained: 'Max said we're to treat you like anyone else.'

'Did he, now?' August laughed again. 'I was kind of hoping everyone would curtsey on my arrival. But if you'd like a signed copy of my recent one to give to your man, I can sort that.'

'Amazing!' Tyler suddenly held his stomach. 'Oof, sorry, I need to go. Reece and his experimental cooking. Goat curry last night.' The young lad looked suddenly pale as he exclaimed, 'My guts are doing a dance of a thousand flounces.'

A slow trickle of dark blood seeped under the two-part stable door, creating a red-and-black muddy swirl in the puddle outside. Lila Lovelace's current logic was that if she stood still as a statue, the whole enormity of the situation would disappear. It wasn't until a huge gust of wind took hold of the lower panel and swung it open, that Lila's scream amplified the horrific sight in front of her.

Composing herself, she checked her hair in her compact mirror, then reached for her phone and proceeded to ring for an ambulance.

August was just rereading the prologue to her last novel to try and glean some inspiration for this year's Christmas mystery when she heard an all-out commotion in the reception area. 'Shit!' There was only one dog in this world that she had heard howling like that before. Peeking through the black blinds that had created such a peaceful writing environment up until this second, August leapt up, then flew to reception to be faced with a red-faced Mrs George, a disgruntled basset hound and a perfectly made-up French woman, wearing a black velvet fedora.

'Oh, August, you didn't say you had a visitor coming, and this woman is insistent she sees you.' Beryl's face was getting redder and redder. She was puffing like a blowfish. 'You are supposed to put names in the visitors' book. You are lucky I opened the gate for her.'

'Sorry, Beryl, it's OK. I know this lady. It's fine. Thank you very much for all your help, I can take things from here.' With a harrumph, Mrs George waddled off to the kitchen. And August realised that her agent must mean business to have left the confines of her office and London town.

Brigitte Fleurot tugged gently at the pink sparkly collar belonging to her soulful-faced dog. 'Jean-Claude, if you don't shut up, I will set you free outside and you will never see me again.'

August intervened. 'Brigitte. How did you know I was here?'

'I knocked on the door of your *maison* and your sister came out and she told me. It is *très petite, non*?'

'It's fine for just me, and I don't even know if dogs are allowed in here.'

As Max appeared from the lift, Jean-Claude threw back his head to let out another long, loud and distressing yodel. Completely unfazed, the Hub owner took the liberty of taking Brigitte's free hand and kissing it.

'*Enchanté, madame.*'

August expected an outburst from her agent at this intrusion of her personal space, but as she looked at Brigitte's face, she was astounded to find it softening. Not even a photo of twenty puppies made her do that normally. It was clear that, despite looking like he had just jumped out of either prison or an action movie, this man possessed what so many men didn't: pure Max appeal.

Max put a treat in front of Jean-Claude, who immediately scoffed it down then plonked himself down in front of the reception desk with a huge huffing sound.

'Of course dogs are allowed here. We have a cocker spaniel up on the farm.' He squatted down and stroked the hound's soft ears. 'And look at this fine fella. A Grand Bleu de Gascogne, I believe. Haven't seen one of these in a while.'

August could tell Brigitte was as impressed as she was at his obscure knowledge of dog breeds. '*Oui, oui.* A *grand* pain in the *derrière* at the moment. He's bored. He hates trains and one of your local taxi drivers made him sit in the boot, which, even though he could see out, he couldn't bear it.'

'I didn't realise that basset hounds were French?' August said.

Max glanced up at her. 'Yes, *bas* means "low" and the attenuating suffix of et makes it mean "rather low". My mate's mum used to have one. Such loyal dogs too. I'm Max, by the way.'

'A pleasure, Max. Brigitte Fleurot, Augoost's agent, for my sins.'

'In all the commotion I didn't introduce you, I'm sorry.' August was slightly flustered herself now and would never admit it, but also feeling a tad jealous at Max's obvious flirtation with the older, married woman.

'So, Brigitte, how about I take Jean-Claude here for a walk and you do whatever an agent needs to do with her *protégée.*' He looked to August for approval, who winked and nodded.

'*Merci*, thank you Max, that would be *formidable.*'

The loud and haunting sound of Mrs George's gong suddenly echoed around the barn, causing Jean-Claude to start to howl again and the big-breasted woman to come waddling out of the kitchen rubbing her hands on her lap apron, shouting, 'Who was it?'

Tyler, who was sitting at one of the general desks in the open-plan office, raised his eyes, grimaced, then carried on scrolling through his phone. Max ushered the two women to the office where August had been working earlier. A now remarkably quiet Jean-Claude, followed slowly, his droopy and mournful eyes giving him a look of devil-may-care nonchalance amid the dramatics that were unfolding.

The perplexed author turned to Max and mouthed, 'What's going on?

Managing to contain his laughter, he turned and headed towards the door, singing tunefully into the air the words: 'skid marks.'

It was six pm when Max knocked on the door of the office where August was working. He poked his head in to find her manically typing. 'Eight am start and still here. Maybe the life of an author is not as easy as I had presumed it to be. Have you not got a home to go to?'

'The wrath of Brigitte Fleurot is enough to make anyone work hard.' August looked down and quickly finished the sentence she was writing. 'It's such a good feeling when the words start flying.'

'I bet. And I can tell she's a feisty French fox, that one.'

'Another one for your lair, perchance?'

Max's brow furrowed. 'And what's that supposed to mean?'

Taken aback by his sudden abruptness, August flushed. 'It doesn't matter.'

'It does to me.'

'Err. I heard you had to move out of London for undisclosed reasons. And rumour has it you are a bit of a womaniser, too.'

'I didn't "have to" do anything. I was offered a chance to take this barn over and that's what I did.' He shook his head, his expression stony. It changed his whole face, and August experienced a dart of alarm. 'I had forgotten about small-town mentality, and I don't have to explain myself to anyone.'

'You don't – of course not. Shit, I'm sorry Max, I'm already turning into the people around here that I myself wanted to escape from.'

After a moment, a smile cracked onto his face, and she felt a wave of relief. 'Never apologise, never explain, Agatha. And I rather like the fact that you care.'

August tried to lighten the mood. 'Beryl puts the fear of God in me. I'll be keeping a bottle of bleach in my bag at this rate. I bet you don't get that kind of treatment in one of those fancy London hubs.'

'Well, nobody's forcing you to sign up.' August searched his face for a sign of a return of his bad mood, but he was smiling as he perched himself on the desk.

'Thanks for walking Jean-Claude. That really helped. Brigitte did warn me she was coming, but I didn't believe her.'

'It was no bother. I should walk at least once a day to keep my head clear, so it was a good excuse to do that.'

August shut her laptop down. 'I feel better now. Contract for another three books signed and I'm about done on a draft synopsis for the Christmas one. Will finalise it next week – which means a happy Brigitte and a happy publisher.'

'Just need to make sure you're a happy author, too.' Max stood up. 'Up to anything good this weekend?'

'To be honest, I've only just emerged from the nightmare that you read about. So, I don't plan much of late – just take each day as it comes. Maybe a walk, and I've promised Mum I'll go to Dad's grave with her on Sunday.'

'Tough stuff, this adulting business, isn't it?'

'Yes.' August sighed. 'It really can be.'

'So, Mrs G aside, how are you finding it here? Do you think you might stay?'

'I have to admit it's perfect. The view across the meadows is so inspiring.' August was then shocked to find the words *you're perfect* popping up on the tip of her tongue, and she had to fight hard to stop them spilling out. Yes, he had the Max appeal, but he clearly wasn't her type, with his bald head, un-PC attitude, secretiveness and smoking habit. She pushed the thought from her mind, hoping it wasn't showing itself in the blush of her cheeks. 'How about you?'

'Nothing much.'

'Max Ronson, you are harder to read than Shakespeare.' He smiled his amused smile. August shut down her laptop and stuffed it into her messy bag. 'Blimey, it's dark out there. I was so engrossed in Lila Lovelace's festive felonies that I didn't even notice you turning the lights on. Can't wait for the lighter evenings, to be honest.'

'Not long now. The spots should come on automatically when you go outside, but I'm happy to walk you.'

'OK. I'm going.' August laughed. 'And, nah, you're fine, I'm a big girl now. Have a good weekend, Max. And by the way, I have decided that I will be joining you and your happy Hubbers. I'll get the signed contract back to you Monday.'

A grin transformed his face. 'Agatha, that really is the best news I've had all week.'

August arrived at the main gate and typed in the exit code that Max had scribbled down on a Post-it note. As she was pulling out, a big lorry passed her at the entrance and the huge security lights lit up the cabin, illuminating the driver. She did a double take when she saw who it was. The gates had already shut behind her, but checking her rear-view mirror, she noticed them opening automatically to let it through. Nothing odd about a lorry delivering stuff to a farm, maybe. But what was odd, was the fact that she was sure it had been TikTokT who was driving it.

Chapter Ten

Holy Trinity Church in Upper Gamble – also labelled 'the family church' by Pam Saunders – was where August's mother had been christened and married, had buried her husband and where both sets of her girls' grandparents lay. A magnificent sixteenth-century stone building with its imposing clock tower and storytelling stained-glass windows, it had a magic about it that only old churches hold. The cemetery was separate – a huge expanse of stoneware, grass and memories, fenced off with views of fields and woodland outside its spiritual perimeter.

It was a bright April morning and Ellie and August drove into the familiar church car park in convoy. Mid-morning Sunday service was due to start in half an hour and it was starting to fill up already. Familiar to the women, not because they were regular churchgoers, but because they had been visiting their dad's grave for the past twenty years religiously around his birthday, death date, Father's Day and Christmas.

They got the boys out of Ellie's car and made their way to the graveyard, shutting the gate behind them.

August ruffled Wilf's hair as he sat upright in the double buggy, bashing a toy elephant against the side of it. 'Goooose! Goooose!' He held his arms out to her.

'Leave him in there for a sec. How was your run, anyway?'

'More of a fast walk to get me back into it, but I had forgotten how beautiful it is through Bluebell Wood. Some are already coming up, too. So pretty.'

'Yes, it's been so mild, that's why. Give it a couple of weeks and it will be a carpet of colour. Good for you, though.'

'Yes, I needed that. I think I've got a cold coming though. My throat is a bit sore, and I'm really bloody snotty.' August pulled a tissue from her sleeve and gave her nose a big blow.

'Get home, have a nice bath and rest up. It's probably because you're beginning to relax, at last. Come on then, big man.' Ellie gently lifted the toddler out of his chariot.

'Nice flowers. Well done with those.'

'I popped into the farm shop on the main road. They're gorgeous, aren't they?' Her tone changed abruptly. 'Wilf, no!' Ellie just managed to stop her two-year-old pulling a handful of daffodils off a grave. He sat down in protest and started screaming, which in turn woke his little brother, who had been sleeping soundly in the bottom of the double buggy. They immediately started to howl in unison.

'Blimey, they'll both be waking the dead, at this rate.' Ellie took Wilf in her arms and started bouncing him up and down while singing his favourite nursery rhyme. 'There's a Sippy cup in the bag under the pushchair for his lordship here and a teething ring will sort James out. I knew I should have waited until he'd had his morning nap before I left the house.'

'I should film this and advertise it as the best form of contraception ever.' August's laugh covered Ellie's whispered, 'Too late.'

'Where's Grant this morning? I thought he might come along.'

'Old Mrs Trinder the other side of us has got a water leak.

He's gone in there to help fix it.'

'I mean to tell you, that's Tyler's nan. The young lad I work with at the Hub told me she lived on The Terrace, just the other day.

'Ah, right. But that doesn't surprise me. You know the degrees of separation in these villages are far less than six.'

August smiled. 'He's a good egg, that husband of yours, isn't he?'

'I lucked out there. Never off duty, my Grant.'

Dear, kind and funny Grant Jenkins. Ellie's lifelong sweetheart – or Mr Cod, as the locals lovingly called him – owned a mobile fish-and-chip van in which, five evenings out of seven, he would go from village to village – and in the summer, campsite to campsite – selling his fried wares. When not doing that, he was the local odd-job man. 'Rich' to Mr and Mrs Cod was a take-away once a week, their annual two-week holiday to the same caravan park in Devon and, most importantly, a huge family Christmas with all the trimmings. There was a lot of love in that Jenkins household. Love with arms that had stretched around August in her time of need, housed her, fed her and eased her through the last few difficult months, unconditionally and without her ever having to ask.

Teething ring administered successfully, and with Wilf now settled back in the top tier of the pushchair, bashing his cup on the side, the sisters carried on walking down the central path of the graveyard.

'I thought Mum would have been here by now.' August placed the cut flowers in the bottom of the buggy and started to fill a watering can from one of the graveyard taps that poked up through the grass to the edge of the pathway.

'It's her turn for church flowers, I think. She'll be here soon. Thank God it's sunny today.'

'Yes, it's gorgeous and it doesn't seem quite so bad doing this with a bit of warmth on our faces.'

'I agree, and they do say the sun only shines on the righteous,' August laughed. 'Hence me being shrouded in such a bright light.'

'Ha, bloody, ha!' Ellie gave her a playful push. 'Sorry again about Madame Fleurot, I had no choice but to tell her where you were. She pulled up in a taxi with that howling bloody hound of hers, so I knew it must be urgent. She's so abrupt. God knows how her husband puts up with her.'

'He's a family lawyer so she never upsets him, or the divorce settlement would be distinctly not in her favour.'

Ellie laughed. 'I don't have that problem. Poor old Grant would be getting half of nothing if we split up.'

'It's all good. It's given me the kick up the arse I needed. I actually really enjoyed writing, the last few days. When I get into my groove, it's the best job in the world, in my humble opinion.'

'Aw, that makes me so happy. And how is the lovely…Max, isn't it? Mum assures me that you fancy him.'

August tutted. 'Of course she does. I barely mentioned the bloke. And in mum's case, as always, it's assumption not fact. I don't fancy him. Well…'

'Goose?'

'OK. He is hot, but I'm also assuming he's a player, and I left London myself to escape men like him.'

'No, you left London because you wanted to be near the people who genuinely love you.'

August shook her head at her sister. 'You're so bloody smug. What I do know for sure is that I could do with some sex. It's been months! And for someone who's rarely been without it, that's tough. I went from eleven years being in a relationship with Bobby, to then being a Tinder trollop, where I slept with a different bloke most weekends, then seven years with the arse. And for all his faults, Scott Scanlan was bloody good in bed.'

'Do you think that's wise, though, contemplating sex with Max?'

August's jaw dropped open. 'I didn't mean sex with Max! Not sure how you just came to that conclusion, Ellie. How awkward would that be? Especially now I've agreed to sign up to the Hub. I know I'm going to like it there.'

'Then, I'm really pleased about that, too. Good. And as for the other, get yourself a vibrator, or swipe right on Tinder if you really can't go without the real thing. If you set up your profile and state you are looking for nothing more than a one-night stand – which I assume you are, at the moment, anyway – then there will be a stampede across the green.'

August laughed. 'I don't even want to talk to them. Just pure filthy sex in a hotel or at their place, then leave immediately.'

Ellie shook her head. 'Well, don't take any risks. Meet them first in a busy place before getting jiggy. Or you could just abstain, August.' Ellie let out a huge sigh. 'Like I wish I had on Valentine's Day.'

'Shit, I knew it. You are, aren't you?'

'Yep, my period is late. Tits are already swelling. Without doubt or even doing a test, another baby Jenkins is on its way.' She gave August a rueful glance. 'And the only positive I can see at the moment for having three kids under three is that I don't have to go on a bloody diet for another nine months.'

August put her arms around her sister and squeezed tightly. 'Well, I, for one, am excited, and I know you are too, really. Congratulations, sis.'

August felt Ellie relax into her embrace. 'I blame you. That birthday bottle of bubbly at yours set me off.'

'You need to start watching some contraception videos yourself.'

'I know, I know, but James is only six months, and I kind of wanted to give my body a rest from the pill, and my Grant hates condoms. I thought we had been careful, but six months' abstinence, a glass of bubbly, two bottles of Shiraz and playing naked Twister on the kitchen floor obviously doesn't count as careful.'

Trying hard not to imagine her sister and brother-in-law in this particular throw of coitus, August couldn't help but burst out laughing. 'Well, I'm absolutely delighted. Every new bubba you pop out takes the pressure off me having one any time soon. Mum will be bloody ecstatic.'

'Yes, she will, bless her. And Goose,' Ellie inhaled sharply, 'I might as well tell you this, too…while I'm at it.'

August felt a rush of foreboding. 'Oh God, this sounds ominous.'

'It's just, well, me and my Grant have talked about this before but, well, we said if we did have another one, rather than move we would convert the two terraced houses into one, which means you'd have to move out, probably end of summer latest, for us to sort everything in time for the new bubba. I'm so sorry.'

Despite the initial dismay she felt on hearing this unwelcome news, August knew how hard it must have been for her sister to relay this information, so she put on a determined smile. She had only just started to feel comfy in her space, and the idea of moving again so soon unsettled her. But she had got through worse. 'It's fine. I understood it was never a long-term thing. Maybe that's when I'll move back to London. I can already tell now, after working at the Hub for just a day, that my evenings will need filling with something other than staying in. I can't just sit and talk to Prince Harry and watch back-to-back dating and quiz shows, both of which are my new television addiction.'

'London isn't the only place you can have a bloody social life. You just said yourself the Hub is great, too. Sit and settle for a bit, Goose. Let life happen rather than look for it.'

'Max said that he had a mind the speed of a Ferrari but with the brakes of a push bike. I'm beginning to feel the same at the moment. There are so many things going around my head.'

'See, you already have something in common with him.' Ellie smiled. 'Give it a chance, living here. You've only just come out of your shell. See what's about, evening classes maybe, or volunteer somewhere to meet new people. I dunno. Is there not anyone at the Hub you could do stuff with?'

'Maybe, but it's early days and joining stuff just to meet people…it all feels like such an effort.'

'You say it yourself about your writing: if you don't put the effort in, you don't get results. And I hate to say it, sister, but that is true in most areas of life.'

'It all happened so naturally before, and there's so much to do in London.'

'But that doesn't make it less lonely, if you're empty inside,' Ellie said gently.

'When did you become so wise, little sis?'

Ellie smiled at her fondly, then looked into the pushchair and stuck out her bottom lip. 'When they're sleeping like babies, they're so adorable.'

'Yes, they're so cute. I love them dearly. Aw.' August stuck out her bottom lip, too. 'Maybe it will be a little girl this time. That would be cool.'

'I hope so. Here comes Mum. She's got a spring in her step.'

'She'll have even more of one when you tell her your news.'

Pam Saunders waved wildly as she appeared at the gate at the top of the cemetery path holding a bunch of white roses, and started to walk down to join them.

Ellie glanced at her sister once more. 'Sorry again about the cottage, and I obviously want the best for you, but on a purely selfish front it would be lovely if you stayed around for a bit longer, at least.'

'Don't get me wrong, I do love being near you and Mum and these two munchkins – soon to be three.'

'See? And you never know, you could meet the love of your life in deepest darkest Wiltshire, and it'll be you telling me that you're the one who's up the duff next.'

'I thought it was me who was good at making up the far-fetched stories.'

They both laughed.

'And what's amusing my girls so much on this sunny Sunday?'

'Sorry Mum, we shouldn't be laughing.'

'Quite the contrary. Never ever apologise for that. When did a Sunday lunch go by without your father telling one of his dreadful jokes? He would want us all to be happy. Now come on, let's go and say hello to him.'

Chapter Eleven

August awoke with a streaming nose and a head full of cold, but also with a wondrous realisation that the thing that she always told other people would happen to them when they were going through heartbreak or grief, had just happened to her.

She had learnt it from losing her dad at such an early age. She would tell people that for a while they would wake up every day and that the first thing that they would think about was the person they had lost. Then one day, without even realising they would wake up and something totally different would be on their mind. And it wasn't that they had forgotten the other person, it was just that the acuteness of the pain was dwindling, and it was time for them to move on.

That morning, her first thought hadn't been of Scott Scanlan but of Max Ronson, and whether or not she should join him at the Futtingbrook Farm Hub.

The thought of getting up and dressed and driving to the Hub was all a bit much when she felt so rough, so she pulled on her new dressing gown and went downstairs to make herself a mug of honey, lemon and fresh ginger, all of which she had purchased the day before when she had started to feel unwell. Then, retrieving a box of tissues and her laptop from her writing desk in the spare room, she blew her nose loudly and snuggled back into her warm bed and flicked her television on to *This Morning*. A contented Prince Harry snuggled his way into the gap between her legs. She hated being unwell, but she also felt it deliciously decadent having a legitimate excuse to watch daytime TV and just drop off to sleep when she felt like it.

Opening her laptop, she found a copy of the signed publishing contract Brigitte had sent to her over the weekend, then reached for her diary to make sure that, as well as alerts on her phone, all her deadline dates were written in bold. Despite supposedly being on August's side as an agent, Brigitte could abide a missed deadline about as well as an ageing actress could bear missing a Botox injection.

She was just about to close her email when a new one popped into her inbox. Subject: *Wherefore art thou, Agatha?*

Knowing it could only possibly be from one person, she smiled broadly as she read on.

Agatha, are you OK? I know this is a come-and-go-as-you-please place, but you did say you would sign the contract to join this happy hub of hope and hilarity so I thought you may be in today.
MM

She settled back against her pillows and wrote:

MM, Look at you, missing me already ☺ I've got a stinker of a cold so I'm in bed watching daytime TV and eating chocolate digestives.
ARS

Only a minute later, her computer pinged with another email.

Oh, Agatha, trust me, my feelings don't run that deep. Just thinking of the annual three grand on my top line. Remind me to organise a show round of the farm for you when you're back. Get well soon, writer girl ☺

MM
You must give me the address of that charm school you went to. I will see you soon, holding aloft a contract signed with the blood of one of my victims. It may just be for a few months though, so don't get too excited. I have to move out of my rented place at the end of the summer, and I may be heading back to London.
ARS

Agatha, did you realise your initials when spoken sound like ARSE ☺?

Shaking her head, a smiling August shut down her laptop and promptly let out a huge sneeze, which caused Prince Harry to jump up and fly off the bed. Then, snuggling under the covers, and feeling suddenly peaceful, she closed her eyes and slid into a dreamy doze.

Meanwhile back at the Hub, Max Ronson hung out of his office window, lit a cigarette and sighed deeply. There had been too many goodbyes in his life and he sure as hell didn't want there to be another one. Not quite this soon, anyway.

Chapter Twelve

Ade Ronson really was a mountain of a man. His features were strong. His hands huge. His light eyes kind. He was just finishing off a call on his mobile as he emerged from the entrance of the Futtingbrook Turkey Farm office reception and almost bumped into August. He grinned at her and stuck his hand out.

'You must be August. I'm Ade, Ade Ronson.'

'You won the height and hair competition over your brother, then?' August checked out his stocky six-foot-three frame and full head of shiny almost black hair as she shook his hand. His matching dark beard was trimmed neatly.

'He won on the gift of the gab front though, I'm afraid. The only birds I'm charming now are my turkeys – not even my wife or three daughters can be reeled in.' August smiled. 'I even think they love their Uncle Max more than me. The children, that is. Not my good wife, I hope.' He grinned an imperfect smile. 'That would be awkward.'

'Three children! Wow, how lovely.'

'It's wonderful, and enough for me, but Beth – that's my wife – is desperate for a little boy.'

'Sounds like my sister. She's pregnant with her third, got two boys and wanting a girl.'

'Hmm. Maybe her people could talk to my people, and we could somehow arrange a swap.' Ade put his hand gently on her shoulder. 'So, you're after a show round.'

'Yes, please. Max said I need to know what to expect, and any forms of defence I may need to adopt as the months go on, as we'll soon be surrounded by marauding death row inmates.'

Ade couldn't help but laugh. 'That brother of mine. Well, I promise they won't peck you to death, but I can't promise they won't be noisy as they get older. They're such social creatures. It is quite funny. I have videos on our website of me saying hello to them and they literally reply, in spectacular style.'

August tutted. 'Now you're joking with me.'

'You wait and see. You don't believe me now, but I guarantee you'll fall in love with my turkeys.' They both laughed. 'So, a tour won't take long as there are no turkeys here yet to distract us. But the one-day-old chicks will be arriving soon, and that's when this place comes alive. I have a skeleton staff of workers on the farm in the winter, but a turkey army for the months leading up to the big day.'

'I have no idea what a turkey chick looks like. In fact, I've never even imagined what's involved in rearing them.'

'They are ridiculously cute, but I have to keep it real. The kids like to give the characters among them names, but ultimately, they're our livelihood, and the Christmas dinners of around thirty thousand households. It a serious business.'

'Wow, thirty thousand of them!'

'Yep. Bird flu and foxes permitting.'

'Foxes?'

'Yes, our biggest nightmare. That's why we have the alpacas: to kick the shit of them.'

'"Curiouser and curiouser, cried August."' She laughed. 'Honestly, this place is a hotbed of future plot ideas.'

'I didn't you know you wrote. Anything I would have heard of?'

'Probably not.' August wasn't in the mood to promote her wares and Ade seemed to know not to push it, for which she was grateful.

'OK, let's go. You OK on one of these?' Ade pointed to a red quad bike. 'I'd rather you wore a helmet, if that's OK?' Thankful that Max had suggested she wear jeans and wellies, August nodded. Suddenly feeling the cold, she pulled her thick puffer jacket around her, hopped on and placed the old-fashioned-looking, open-faced helmet over her thick auburn locks.

It felt alien but also rather nice to have her arms around the thick-set body of a stranger, who smelled of a mixture of soap and coffee.

They set off out of the farm gates and down the lane, where there seemed to be miles of meadows either side. Ade stopped at various points to play the proper tour guide. And each time they set off again, August let out a little scream, as the thrill of being on a quad bike and the wind hitting her face and causing her hair to flow behind her was both exhilarating and exciting.

'So, here's the turkeys' sunflower field.' Rows and rows of dead sunflowers, their heads bowing, faced August. 'Love the seeds, the birds do. We'll be planting again soon.' They carried on to the next meadow. 'And here is their very own cherry orchard.'

'They really are spoilt, aren't they? What are those?' August pointed to a row of what looked like tambourines hanging down on string from a metal frame.

'Oh, that's their play area. Instruments, they love playing those.'

'You're obviously joking?'

'Not at all. See how the red one is more bashed. Turkeys love red, if any of them cut themselves we have to be on full alert to pull them out quickly before there is a feathery blood-sucking stampede.'

August gaped at him. 'That's so mad. And that huge, long barn?'

Ade rode on and pulled up next to it. It was full of hay bales, food containers and water feeders.

'They bring themselves in here to rest and sleep. That's the old stuff in there. When the new staff start, it will be spotless and dry. We also pipe some classical music in to keep them calm, especially after fireworks night.'

'That's so cool. So, if you have them from one day old, how do they arrive?'

'In boxes. You'll have to come up and see them. It's very sweet, and a big day for us. Jarvis – that's the farm's cocker and official turkey dog – he rounds them up like sheep. They spend a few months under cover, growing, and then we let them loose when they're big enough, so that they can have the full run of these meadows.'

'Oh my God! A turkey dog? That's crazy. I never would have imagined such a thing. But what a life they have. Well, for seven months, at least…'

'Yes, we really emphasise the free-range side of things. We have to, as the average bird sells for around seventy to one hundred pounds. Their meat is the best in the area. Our repeat business is proof of that.'

It seemed quite strange to August that these birds were treated like royalty and then summarily executed. Although, unless she herself became a vegetarian, who was she to even so much as comment on the ethics of it all?

Ade started the quad bike up again. 'Let's go and meet the bad boys of the farm, shall we?'

They arrived at the field furthest from the farm to see seven similar-sized, brown-and-beige alpacas. Among them, one random white one stood out, making a total of eight. 'Here they are.' They both hopped off and approached the animals. 'Meet Snow White, Sneezy, Bashful, Dopey, Sleepy, Happy, Grumpy and Doc, cleverly named by my beautiful daughters. However, one thing you must know is that despite the Snow-White moniker, they are all male and all, in fact, very grumpy.'

August laughed. 'Really?'

'Yes. I told you the turkeys wouldn't peck you, but I can't guarantee these won't bite.' Ade smiled. 'My dad informed me that the feistier the alpacas are, the better. We buy them off owners who can't cope with them. We need them to be aggressive so that they act as a deterrent and attack any foxes who dare to tread their path. We do have electric fences, but it's true, foxes are the wiliest of creatures, so we need these boys to kick arse.'

'This is like a whole new world to me.'

'If you do ever walk up here, be careful, as they spit. It's usually reserved for each other but occasionally they'll aim it at us. The girls find it hilarious.'

August laughed out loud. 'As will I. How old are they? Your girls, I mean.'

'Five, seven and nine.'

'Aw, sweet. And you mentioned your dad. Did he run the farm before you?'

'Yes, this place was Dad's life – until he had a stroke and passed away three months afterwards.' The man's face dropped. 'He was a good man – the font of all turkey knowledge – and I am still his biggest fan.'

As she watched him remember his beloved father, it suddenly struck August how different Ade was to Max. His air was softer, not so edgy. He had a feel of earthy reliability about him. Where it was more exciting spending time with Max, it was easy to be in Ade's company.

'I'm so sorry, Ade.'

The big man sighed. 'He was eighty. He worked up until the day he fell ill. I miss him, but we hold so many happy family memories in this place.'

'Is your mum still around?'

Ade nodded. 'Very much so. Soon after Dad had his stroke, I moved here with the family to help Mum and keep the farm running. I had a smallholding up the road and, luckily, I'd always helped him with the turkeys, so had some knowledge. But it's still been a steep learning curve. After Mum's accident, she was insistent that they stay living at the farmhouse, so they moved their bedroom to the ground floor. But after Dad's stroke we kitted out the annexe for the pair of them. It was a happy release for Dad when he passed. He couldn't bear to feel useless. We used to let their place out to turkey workers, but it made sense to make it completely wheelchair-friendly. It looks over one of the many meadows, and that's where Mum decided to stay.'

'That's nice that you can look out for each other.'

'She doesn't need any looking after herself yet, that's for sure. She's seventy-five going on fifty-seven. Painting rather than farming was always her passion. She does have a soft spot for the alpacas, though. I reckon it's because she feels an affinity with their feisty characters.'

August laughed. 'She sounds like my kind of woman.'

'Good. Don't be surprised if you come across a forthright grey-haired lady in a wheelchair with an easel on her lap when the weather gets better. If you think my brother says it how it is…' As he spoke, it started to rain.

'Is that why Max came back? Because of your dad, I mean.'

She noticed Ade's face fall. He paused. 'Partly.'

'And your poor mum. Was it a car accident?'

94

'Er. No. She…umm… She came off one of her horses. She doesn't like to talk about it. So, it's probably best if you don't mention it to anyone – not even Max.'

August felt a bit wrong-footed at yet another secret this family seemed to hold. Ade had seemed so open at first, too. 'Oh, OK. Bless her. I didn't realise you had horses.'

'We don't – now.' For the first time, Ade sounded abrupt. 'Now, come on, August, let's get back, shall we? We can scoot the scenic way to the Hub.'

Realising she had pushed too much, August silently cursed her lack of tact, but all was forgotten when the quad bike roared to life once more. She screamed again in exhilaration and held Ade tighter as they accelerated along a main lane and then shot off down a muddy one. As they reached a crossroads, he slowed to turn left. Looking to her right as she slowed along with him, August glimpsed a closed wooden gate, and through its slats a short driveway, at the end of which was another barn. The building was almost identical to the Hub in size and shape, but this one did not seem to have been renovated, by the look of it. As they pulled up close to the side of the gate, she could make out what looked like the same lorry she had seen the other night, from which a man was offloading boxes with a small forklift. A black Range Rover sat to the side of it. At that moment Ade picked up speed, so she didn't have time to check out the number plate, but unless she was very much mistaken, it had looked a lot like Max's. Her mind went into overdrive again. If it was Max's car, what was he doing in the barn? And if it was the same lorry, had it been Tyler driving it? And just what was in all those boxes? There was something going on here and she wanted – no, needed – to work it out.

Thankfully, the rain had stopped by the time they reached the Hub. August hopped off and gave her helmet back to Ade.

She could see Max pulling into the parking area.

'That was so fun, and gave me such a brilliant insight into the world of turkeys – thank you. And I already love the alpacas. What's in that other barn, by the way?'

Ade frowned. 'Which barn? There are a few.'

'At the crossroads.'

Max headed over to join them.

'I think Max has another grand plan for it, don't you, bro?' The tall man looked at his brother.

'If it isn't my two favourite people?' Max grinned. 'And what are you on about?'

'The Cross Barn.'

'I thought I just saw your car there,' August explained.

He screwed up his face in apparent puzzlement. 'No, I don't think so. I've just been to the dentist.'

August wasn't convinced that a trip on the main roads would have caused quite so much wet mud to be caked on the wheels, but thought it would be rude to question him further.

'You and your pearly whites.' Ade grinned his slightly off-white, crooked smile.

'So, you know all about the Futtingbrook fowl now, then? They have a better life than me.'

August laughed. 'They have a better life than any of us, by the sound of it. Bit too short an innings for my liking though, bless them. I didn't realise how many acres were here either. The grounds are so beautiful.'

'Yes. Beats London. That's for sure.'

'I've started running again, so if you're happy for me to make use of all that lovely land, that would be amazing.' August ran her hands through her long hair, which had been pressed down into the helmet.

'Of course, that's fine. Just keep a wide birth from the seven spitting dwarves and their snowy leader.' August laughed again as Ade went on, 'Actually, Max, talking of running, I meant to let you know. The Sebastian Line – you know, the charity that moved into the building that was the old post office? Well, they approached me and asked if they could use the footpath that goes up through here then circles back to town for their annual sponsored run, and also if we minded them setting up a refreshments station somewhere en route.'

Max nodded. 'That sounds fine to me.'

'Ooh, I'm looking for a challenge. Maybe I'll have a look to see if I can join in,' August piped up.

'I think the woman said that all details and sponsorship forms would be online from today,' Ade said encouragingly. 'I think directly outside the Hub would be the perfect place for a station, as we can use the concrete area where you park the cars. It's just before the chicks arrive and the weather should be better by then, and hopefully not too muddy, so I said yes.'

'Exciting,' August said. 'OK, I must get on, I've got a book to write. Thanks again, Ade.' She made her way inside.

'The Sebastian Line? That's the suicide charity, isn't it?' Max licked his cracked lips.

Ade's voice was soft. 'I wouldn't have said yes to anyone else. You're OK with it, then?'

Max gave a weak smile. 'Of course, I am, bro…and thank you.'

Ade put his hand on his brother's shoulder. 'I donated a hundred pounds, too.'

'You'll be organising your own bloody Live Aid, next.'

'Very bloody funny.' Ade nodded towards the Hub. 'She seems lovely.'

'She is. Smoking, too. Look at her.'

'So?'

'You know I don't play with fire on my own doorstep.'

'Not now you don't, matey.'

'OK, OK. You don't have to keep reminding me that I'm indebted to you. I'm sorting it – you know that.'

'Sorry, bro. I didn't say it for that. So, August is a writer. What does she write?'

'Crime novels. Pretty successful, by all accounts.'

Ade laughed. 'You really do need to behave yourself now, then.'

'Always.'

'And what *are* you doing with the back barn anyway?'

'Nothing much.'

'Max?'

'It's fine. You've given me a second chance with these two barns, and I will never forget that. I'm determined to pay back every single penny that I owe you, and I will.'

'OK. As agreed, some rents need to be coming back to me by the end of June at the latest. How's the sign-up going for the Hub? August is the only new one in a long time, isn't she?'

'I know, I know but you don't need to worry about it, bro. I won't let you down, I promise.' Max's face took on a pained expression.

'Beth asked if you fancied dinner with us tonight. Around six, so we can eat with the girls – on their insistence that Uncle Max joined us, of course.'

'Perfect. And Ade, the Sebastian Line... Tell them we'll provide the refreshments here on the day too. Free of charge.'

Ade watched Max walk back into the Hub with a look of love for his kind and troubled brother. His sibling had a heart of gold; he just wished he could direct it in the right places and find some of the peace and happiness he deserved.

Chapter Thirteen

August headed into the kitchen to get herself a coffee. Cat was pushing a creamy pasta dish around a plate, a slight grimace on her face. Jonah was eating a vegan snack bar while perusing his phone.

'Nice t-shirt, Jonah.'

'Recycled by one of my website companies from two old ones of mine.'

'I love the fact you're a walking advert for your business. I keep thinking I must have a look at your website.' August joined them at the table.

'I've just recruited a new company on board this week. They make funky handkerchief dresses, which I think would be right up your street.'

'Fab, I'll definitely look, then.' She turned to Cat. 'You went hot; you're brave.' She took a sip from her coffee.

'I mean, macaroni cheese. I thought, how could she possibly go wrong with that? And she's put bloody stilton in it instead of cheddar.'

Jonah laughed. 'I don't even trust her sandwiches. She professes to buy vegan cheese, and to be fair it does taste like it, but she's so scathing of plant-based diets that I wouldn't be surprised if she snuck a minute piece of ham in somewhere, just to make a point.'

'After hearing about the poor turkeys' fate, I'm surprised you actually work here, as a vegan,' August said boldly. 'It's like those poor birds are welcomed with open arms by the hotel concierge, have a magnificent five-star stay and just as they are all fat and happy, they are murdered at the check-out desk.'

'August, really! But it's OK. Thankfully they're far enough away for me not to hear their dying screams, even with my aids in.'

'Jesus, Jonah.' Cat got up and forked her lunch into the bin. 'How do they kill them, anyway? Did you ask, August? I didn't really want to know when I went up there for my show round.'

Jonah immediately turned his hearing aids down and resumed perusing his phone.

'Ade told me it's an electric wand thing. They just tap the birds on the head, and they die instantly. It's all very humane. What I can't believe is what a life they have before they meet their festive fate! They're treated like kings and queens.'

'The female meat tastes better, so I'm told,' Cat said, perusing the snack machine for a suitable lunch alternative.

Max walked in just as she said that, and said: 'Of course, it does.'

August shook her head at him in mock-disapproval. 'We're talking about turkeys.'

'So was I. Much rather have young female meat than a tough old bird.'

'Max Ronson. I don't know how you get away with it.' Cat opened a packet of salt and vinegar crisps and sat munching them at the table.

'What?' he replied innocently. 'And anyway, it kind of turns me on – the thought of a gang of marauding feminists whipping me into shape with their acute disdain.' Cat couldn't help but laugh. 'Anyway, how are you and your five-star rural romances doing?' Max enquired genuinely.

'It would be so much better if you signed up, Max, you know that.' Cat smiled. 'The women far outweigh the men at the moment and I could do with a diamond among the rough.'

'Surely that should be the other way around?' August interjected to an eye-roll from Max.

'Like I've said before, I'm not looking, and when I am, I sure as hell don't intend to pay for it.'

'Well, that suits me perfectly. After all, I do want to keep my reputation,' Cat smirked.

'That ship sailed long ago, didn't it?' Max pretended to correct himself. 'Oh, you mean the company's.'

'Ha bloody ha. It's a good job I like you.'

Max grinned at her mischievously, grabbed a chocolate bar from the snack machine, and headed back towards his office.

August sat down at the table. 'I know what I meant to ask. I saw a lorry pull in here that night I was here late, Max.' Max stopped in the doorway. She watched his face intently for a reaction. 'Anyway, I had to double-take, as the driver looked just like Tyler.'

Max laughed a little too loudly. 'He can just about ride the bloody scooter he tears about on, so him driving a lorry? Really? It would have been sacks of food being delivered ready for the chicks' arrival, I expect.' Max spoke heartily. 'It's a busy time for Ade now.'

'Maybe I shall add a trucker doppelganger in my next book, anyway.' August laughed it off but her intuition was telling her that whatever it was, there was definitely something not quite right around here and she was determined to get to the bottom of it.

'The vivid imagination of an author, Agatha. I think I may need to get you to sign a non-disclosure agreement at this rate.'

'I only put people I don't like in my books, so you'll be all right.' She felt herself reddening.

'Is that so, Agatha?' Max smirked.

August took a sip of her coffee, breaking their eye contact. 'So, any of you up for doing a charity fun run with me? I've started exercising again and there's one happening in a few weeks' time and it's going right past the Hub. Isn't it, Max?' He nodded. 'It's only 10K.'

'Only 10K! August Saunders, you've got nearly twenty years on me and, for the record, I've never even run for a bus.' Cat carried on eating her crisps. 'But I do need to get fitter and I guess it is for charity. Let me think on it.'

'I'm going to pass as I'll be in charge of the drinks station, but I will need a hand with that,' Max added.

Tyler came in and pressed the button for a Diet Coke from the machine. 'What am I missing, then?'

'The Sebastian Line, charity race, the runners are coming through here. We're talking about taking part, or giving Max a hand with the drinks bit.'

'It's the suicide and crisis line charity, isn't it? So yeah, defo.' Tyler took a deep breath. 'I didn't know him that well, but I went to school with that Sebastian, poor fucker. When is it?'

'Saturday before Easter weekend,' August said. 'And that's so sad, if I'm right in thinking what you mean?'

'Yeah. Proper tragic. I'll defo run. That's cool.'

'Good man,' Max said fervently.

'Brilliant.' August beamed. 'So that's me and T running, and maybe Cat. Max is on drinks duty…and Jonah? Jonah?'

Cat went right in front of his face and signed *fuck off* to him. A laughing Jonah turned up his aids. 'I can lipread when I want to, you know. My knee's a big dodgy at the moment, so I'll pass on the run, but if I can do anything to help on the day, that's fine. And I'll happily make a donation for such a worthwhile charity.'

'Well, now we clearly have a social secretary in the Hub, I shall leave it to her to organise. Agatha, OK?'

Taken aback, August felt she had no choice but to go along with it. 'Umm…sure. OK.'

'See. I knew you'd end up as my marketing bitch,' Max smirked.

August reddened. 'Hardly.'

'Sorry, am I being impertinent?' Max winked, and August felt more drawn than ever to the handsome Hub owner. 'And I'm not that mean, really. Of course I'll support you, every step of the way. It's important to me.'

'Very good.' She was beginning to learn that Max Ronson's steel-like demeanour was just a veneer that covered a much deeper and more sincere man below it.

'Right. I've got a couple of spare trestle tables in the barn; my mum will have some cloths and jugs. So actually, we just need water and squash and energy bars and drinks. Oh, and maybe some shots of brandy.'

Jonah's face screwed up. 'What for?'

'I read it in one of the Sunday papers. I think alcohol – namely champagne, brandy and even strychnine cocktails – used to be used as performance enhancers. It can't hurt and it is supposed to be a fun run.'

'Strychnine is rat poison, isn't it?' Cat quizzed.

'Yep.' Max shrugged. 'We'll leave that out, eh, Cat? But yeah, that is so mental. Apparently, in the 1908 marathon at the London Olympics, Canadian gold medal favourite Tom Longboat drank so much alcohol along the route he collapsed at mile nineteen and failed to cross the finishing line. A bit like what may happen to our very own elite athlete, Mrs G here.'

They all laughed as Beryl waddled in with some clean tea towels in her hand. 'What you up to, you lot? How was the mac n cheese, Cat?'

'Delicious as always, Mrs G, thank you.' Cat winked at August, then got up and hastily threw her empty snack wrappers in the bin.

'You up for the charity fun run then, Beryl?' Tyler kept his face straight. 'It's only ten kilometres.'

'What's that in real money? All this bloody metric lark. Give me pounds and ounces and yards and miles, please. And anyway, I do enough exercise running around after you buggers.' She huffed. 'As for more bloody do-gooders around here, charity begins at home, I say.'

'August, can you give me a hand quickly?' Cat called over her shoulder as she made her way across the Hub.

'Sure.' She followed the tall woman into one of the private offices.

'Hold this end.' Cat handed her a white cloth featuring the most beautiful scene of swans swimming on an ornamental lake. 'We just need to pin it up on the wall behind my desk.'

'It's so pretty, but why exactly are we doing this?'

'Darling, my punters are paying seven grand for seven dates. I can't have them thinking I'm based out of a barn in a shitty turkey farm in Futtingbrook, now, can I? First week here, it was turkey season. Not only did a couple of the bloody alpacas start fighting behind me, but somebody also tooted a horn, and when the birds get startled by loud noises, well, you will never hear anything else quite like it. Dreadful. The woman was a complete raving snob anyway and I would have found it hard to place her, but seven grand is seven grand, and I could have given her a good run for her money.'

'Do they fall for this then?'

'Of course. It looks far more realistic on the screen.'

'Cat Bachelor. You are bloody hilarious.'

'Use me as a character and I'll be setting an assassin alpaca on you – and there will be no sparing the spitting.'

'Good luck with the potential new dater.' August giggled and headed for the office next door.

'And I must let you have a look at *my* newly signed men and see if there is anyone you fancy,' Cat called after her.

'She's not looking for any,' Max shouted across the office.

'Who says *she's* not!' August shouted back. Max walked towards her.

'I'll have you know, Agatha, that this is a very calm and zen workplace, and I won't accept that kind of attitude in my Hub.'

'Oh, fuck off, Max.'

They both burst out laughing. 'Now go and finish that bestseller and then you really can be my marketing bitch.'

'I'd rather be the cook.'

Dong! The familiar sound of Mrs G's gong reverberated around the barn.

'We'd all rather you were the cook,' Tyler offered, speeding his way to the toilets with a bottle of bleach in his hand.

Chapter Fourteen

'Goose, will you slow down?' Ellie huffed and puffed as her sister marched ahead of her in the aptly named Bluebell Wood. 'I'm a pregnant woman, don't you know.'

'It'll do you good. Come on, you love it here as much I do. And, it's not often you don't have the kids or Colin causing havoc. Just make the most of Grant looking after the whole menagerie for a while.'

They came to a little bridge with a tinkling brook running under it, and a blanket of colour on either side.

'See, that was worth the stomp, wasn't it?'

The sisters gazed over the carpet of deep violet-blue flowers moving slightly in the soft breeze of the sunny spring Sunday morning, taking in both their sweet smell and calming aura.

'If it's a little girl, I'll call her Bluebell,' Ellie announced suddenly, retrieving her water bottle from her rucksack.

'Aw, sis, that's so sweet.'

'I might even add Rose as a nod to her auntie. You never know.'

'And that is even sweeter. Are you going to find out the sex?'

'Definitely – for admin reasons, more than anything else. If it is a little girl, she'll need a separate bedroom eventually. It'll help with planning the refurb of the cottages.'

August sighed. 'I wish I could think as far ahead as you.'

'No, you don't. It's much easier to just live in the moment sometimes. How are you doing, anyway? You seem a lot brighter.'

'Yes, good, thank you. The Hub lot are fun. Max is fine eye candy too, and it's good to brush up on my flirting, at least.'

'I can't believe you're not all over him.'

'At first impression, he's too similar to Scott: a bit arrogant, and definitely a player.'

'And you're the one always ready to tell *me* not to judge a book by its cover.'

'Anyway, there's a 10K run for the suicide and crisis line charity that's based in Futtingbrook. As some of the route is through the Hub's grounds, I've been tasked with helping organise the refreshments, which we'll be providing. Not loads to do, but it's giving me a purpose other than sitting at home and watching TV. You don't fancy joining me running it, do you?'

'As in running the refreshments, or physically running it? When is it, anyway?'

'Saturday before the Easter weekend. And no, I mean moving that fat arse of yours.'

Ellie laughed. 'Bitch! Only you could get away with that. And from my side, that'll be the negative then. I will happily join in your training out here, though. You can run back and forwards to me, like you used to, while I walk.'

'That's a deal. It will be good for both of us.'

'Yes, I agree. Joking aside, I know I do need to keep this pregnancy weight in check, or I'll never get over the stiles when we go walking, let alone through a kissing gate.' A peaceful silence descended between them and after a minute, Ellie said,

'I'm pleased you're feeling better, Goose.'

August turned to smile at her sister. 'Yes, it's all about filling my time and mind with stuff. I only Google Scott's name every other day, rather than every other minute, now. And I've at last found a bit of a routine around here, so thanks for pushing me to check out the Hub.'

'That's great to hear, but it does make me feel even more guilty about you having to move out.'

'Please don't feel like that. Guilt is such a wasted emotion.'

Ellie put her hand over her sister's and squeezed. 'You're so brave, sis. What's the love rat up to, anyway?'

'Dearest Delila was last seen trying on a pair of Jimmy Choo glittered courts in Selfridges. It hurts, but it is what it is.' She sighed, thinking back to the night when she had found this particular article and had cried herself to sleep. 'It's not about being brave. I'm kind of more intrigued now than anything else. And as for me moving again, it's another new adventure, which can only be a good thing.'

'So, is going back to London still on your mind, then?'

'I don't know for sure what I'm going to do. But what I do know, is that not one of our so-called joint friends has asked how I'm doing – not one. I'm sure as hell not going to reach out to them, not now.'

'People are busy, August, and when you haven't got so much going on yourself, then you tend to notice it more. That's all.'

'You've got two kids and you find time for me.'

'That's family, innit?' Ellie put her hand on her sister's shoulder.

'I hear you, but there's busy and there's sending a quick text, which takes two seconds. They don't even have to mean it, but it would at least show they were thinking of me. When we were together, it was Scott this, Scott that. I wonder if they'd have been the same when he was a bloody take-out delivery driver.'

'Maybe you're better off without them all.'

'Yes, all those shallow bloody Hals.'

The girls started their walk back to the village. 'How's the internet dating going – or luring, in your case?'

'Can't believe I'm saying this, but I've not had time.'

'That must mean you're busy, so that's a positive.'

'Maybe the running is taking the edge off my carnal urges. And the fact that Ann Summers is the best friend any girl could ask for helps.'

Ellie burst out laughing. 'And that is why you are such a good bloody writer.'

They arrived back at their row of terraces to see Grant waiting to greet them at the gate, one babe asleep in his arms, the other asleep in his pushchair in the doorway, and Colin the Corgi flat out in the spring sunshine on the pathway.

'What have you done wrong, Grant Jenkins?'

'We missed you.' He kissed the red and sweaty cheek of his wife.

'Have you emptied the Calpol bottle?'

Grant laughed. 'No. But there is a six nations match on later, and Grumpy Mick asked if I could join him at The White Horse.'

August put her hand up. 'I'm not getting involved. See you tomorrow after work.'

'After work – hark at you,' Grant grinned. 'Good to see you looking so well, Goose.' The nickname, created by Ellie when, as a child, she was not able to say August, sounded even more endearing coming from her brother-in-law.

'In!' Ellie demanded, gently negotiating the pushchair with its precious cargo over the front step. 'While we can still have a modicum of peace together.' At the word peace, Wilf woke up and started screaming.

'Maybe it will be easier with three,' Grant said gloomily.

'Only a man would ever dare make that comment,' Ellie laughed. 'Come on, my stallion, let's get this little lad some lunch.'

'See you soon, sis.' August opened her front door to be greeted by an affectionate Prince Harry, who continued to butt against her legs until she filled his bowl with crunchies.

She made a little noise of contentment. Real life may be basic back here in Upper Gamble, but real life was good. The deep love of her family filled her with a warmth and safety she had almost forgotten existed while she had been living in the world of show business with Scott. The Hub was proving to be more fun than she had ever expected, and she had already written the first three chapters of her new book; working title: *A Christmas Mystery in Futtingbrook Fallow*.

Chapter Fifteen

Max was already at the concrete parking area at the front of the Hub, setting up trestle tables for the fun run, when August appeared, rucksack in hand.

'Morning, Agatha. Thanks for getting up so early on a Saturday.' He handed her some clean white linen cloths.

'I'm sure you'll put them on neater than me. Thank God it's not raining, for everyone's sake.' He looked around. 'Where's your car?'

'I left it at the farm and walked across. Guessed we'd need as much space as possible, over here.'

'You're so thoughtful.' Max smiled warmly, lit a cigarette and looked out over the meadows.

'You actually are the only person I know who smokes.'

'That sounds like judgement to me.' Max carried on puffing.

'I didn't say you should give up.' She paused. 'But you *should* give up.'

He laughed. 'Not only thoughtful, but funny, too. The whole package. And like I said, I will on my – our – birthday, next year.' He took another big drag and blew out the smoke noisily. 'The only important question of the day is: are you dressing up?'

'What, for a playroom dungeon or the race?' Needing sex

was obviously affecting her more than she realised.

He stared at her. 'Blimey, Agatha, where did that come from?'

She felt her cheeks redden. 'The day I met you, you said something about fifty shades. That's all.'

'The day I met you I was just showing off.'

'And every day ever since.' She smirked. 'Anyway, today, Mad Max, I will be Wonder Woman.'

'Oh god, that outfit she wears!' Max let out a loud wolf whistle. 'You can come at me with your lasso of truth anytime.'

She tutted. 'You're relentless.'

'I'm winding you up.'

'Good job I like you.'

Max raised his eyebrows. 'You still do?'

'Somebody has to, you miserable bastard.' A smirking Max took another exaggerated drag of his cigarette, then, with a deft throw, headed the still-smoking butt on its way to the sand bucket. 'Ah, yes,' August said, 'while I remember, you need to turn on the hot water urn for tea.'

'It looks as prehistoric as half the women who attend the WI.'

'You are so bloody rude. One day you'll be old, you know. And Mum got that from her group especially.'

'Let's hope we have that luxury.' His voice dipped and August glanced at him, intrigued at the sudden change in his demeanour. She was about to ask but then he made a visible effort to return to his previous jollity, and the moment passed. 'And we must put some plastic glasses out for brandy.'

'Are you really doing that?'

'Of course. The vicar is running, isn't he? I hear he loves a tipple, and I've got a lot of making up to do if I am going to get through those pearly gates.' He peered around and frowned. 'Actually, why are we making tea? Nobody will want tea if they've been careering round country fields with a sweat on.'

'They might do, later. Darcy suggested that some of the organisers come back here at the end. That is OK, isn't it? Not everyone drinks alcohol.'

'I guess I have no choice. Jesus, I said I wanted a marketing bitch, not a managing director.'

'Are you ever serious?'

'Are you being serious?'

'Yes.' Then the question they'd been dancing around since they first met came spilling out of her mouth. 'Why *did* you come back to live here, Max?'

A prolonged silence caused August to suddenly feel awkward for pushing the subject.

'London can be a lonely place on your own,' Max muttered.

'I was just having the same conversation with my sister.' She could tell that Max was a little choked. August found this sudden vulnerability endearing, but today, quite clearly, wasn't the time or the place to explore his obvious demons further. 'Come on, let's get this set up. Wonder Woman had better not be late getting to the start.'

August was just coming out of the Hub with some plastic glasses when she heard raised voices coming from the car parking area. She stopped at the door to see Max in heated discussion with a very glamourous woman. A silver Porsche Carrera was parked to the side of them. Her poker-straight, shiny black hair and immaculate dress sense suddenly made August feel totally inadequate with her scraped-back locks, tracksuit and trainers.

'I don't bloody care if it's for charity – we had an agreement. You can't just let me down days before. It's not right.' The woman's huge dark glasses covered nearly the whole of her face.

'If you hadn't booked yet another holiday at such short notice, this wouldn't have happened. I got the dates mixed up, that's all.

Giulia, please don't be like this. I promise I'll make it up to you.'

'Well, you'd better – or you know what will happen, don't you?' August detected an accent, but try as she might, she couldn't recognise it.

Feeling a mixture of not wanting to know and really wanting to know, she boldly started walking over to the pair. On noticing her, the raven-haired beauty got into the car, slammed the door, and with the meaty roar of a high-performance engine, she sped off up the drive.

'You OK?'

'Just give me a shot of that brandy, will you?' Max's face was contorted in anger.

August's mouth acted without brain engagement as she handed over a large measure. 'She's a cutie.'

'No, Agatha, she's a cunt!' Draining the strong spirit in one go, he stormed inside.

Shocked at this reaction, August initially froze, then just as she was about to follow him in to make sure he was all right, a fresh-faced lady, all in black sports gear with a Sebastian Line-branded sash in bright blue, came jogging towards her.

'Morning!' she sang. 'I'm Darcy Webb. And I'm guessing you must be August.'

'Oh, hi Darcy, yes, that's me. I wasn't expecting you this early.'

'Yes, I thought I'd get a little warm-up in before the race and I had to drop these to you anyway. The gate was open.' All the while jogging on the spot, the woman took a compact black Nike rucksack off her back and pulled out a couple of charity collection tins.'

'Ah, right, great.' August took them from her. 'One of them is actually for Max's brother. He's happy to keep one permanently at the turkey farm office. It gets a great visitor flow up there, apparently.'

Darcy beamed. 'That's superb. I really appreciate your help, August. It's been so easy to work with you and this set-up looks great.'

'We're expecting one hundred and fifty runners – is that still about right?'

'Yes, save the odd drop-out.'

'Are you and some of the others still joining us after the race? It's such a lovely spot here, with this view over the turkey meadows.'

'Let's see how everyone's feeling, shall we?'

'So, how do you fit with the charity, then, Darcy? Do you work as well as volunteer?'

Darcy took a noisy swig from her water bottle and sniffed. She reminded August of Davina McCall. Fit and fifty-something. Calm but direct.

'I give most of my time to the Sebastian Line, to be honest. We do our best to keep the phone line open twelve hours a day, from midday through to six am the next morning. Suicidal thoughts don't work to time or season, but that's the most I can fill without burning out at the moment, I'm afraid. Early hours of Sunday and Mondays are particularly busy and, frustratingly, that's when we tend to be short of volunteers.' Her eyes looked sad all of a sudden, and August patted her on the arm.

'So, as well as taking calls, you arrange events like these. That's a lot, and so good of you to give up your time like that.'

'Sebastian was my boy,' Darcy said quietly. 'And I don't see it as giving up – just giving.'

Horrified, August gasped. 'I'm so sorry,' she whispered. She could feel herself welling up.

'Seventeen, full of life and energy, he was. A beautiful soul.'

'You don't have to tell me this.' Just the thought of anything happening to her beloved nephews gave August a knot in her stomach. But she couldn't exactly say what she really wanted to, which was, 'I don't want you to talk about it to me', could she?

'I want to. He had the biggest heart but sadly his depression was deeper. He split from his girlfriend and was feeling stressed about his upcoming exams. I didn't realise his head was troubling him in such a profound way. "If only" are two words those of us bereaved by suicide use a lot.'

'I can't even imagine the pain you are going through.'

'My pain is nothing to what his obviously was.' Tears filled the lost mother's eyes. 'It will be three years soon.' She sighed deeply. 'Setting up the Sebastian Line has helped me so much. It's the little things that upset me. Catching a glimpse of a lad who looks like him or hearing another mum call out his name in the street.' Darcy took a second to compose herself. 'And if we, as an organisation, can help people chat through their feelings in their hour of need, and hopefully get them out of a moment they feel stuck in, then that comforts me. I'm doing it for all the parents out there, as well as those with the suffering minds.'

'I think what you are doing is amazing.' August didn't think she'd ever meant something so sincerely in her life.

In that moment, a seemingly recomposed Max joined them.

'Do you know Darcy, Max?' asked August.

'Hey, how're you doing? Max Ronson.' He double-kissed the sportswear-clad woman. 'Great turnout, according to this one here.' He nodded in August's direction.

Darcy cleared her throat and gave a brittle smile. 'Yes, doing it late April, one hopes the weather will hold out. While I remember, please thank your brother for such a generous donation. Greatly appreciated. And it's so good of you letting us traipse through your grounds. Are you running, Max?'

'No. Today, I shall be administering substantial amounts of

cheerleading and copious shots of brandy to all who desire it.'

Darcy looked confused, and August patted her on the arm. 'Don't even ask,' she said indulgently. It occurred to her that Max had clearly had far more than one shot already.

'OK. I will do my best to join you later. Not sure for a shot, but let's see how painful my legs are. You never know, I might be needing a bottle.'

August noticed Max's gaze momentarily fixated on the woman's Lycra-clad bottom as she jogged back up the drive.

On turning to face her, he noticed that she had tears in her eyes.

'Oh, Agatha, I'm sorry if I was too much with my outburst. I promise I do only save the c-word for really special occasions.'

'Jesus, it's not all about you, Max. And as for the c-word, it's decidedly underused in my opinion. In fact, the correct use of it on occasion, is poetry. I try and slide it into my books at least once.'

'Bravo!'

'Yeah, the prudish reviewers hate it, but I was told not to write for anyone else but me. So, that's why I do it.'

'So, why the tears?'

'It was Darcy's story that set me off. I can't even imagine losing a child – or anyone, for that matter – to suicide. It's incomprehensible. And to be in such a dark place as to want to take your own life – that's immense.' She shook her head. Max put his hand gently on her shoulder.

'Yes, it is. The poor woman. While it might appear that someone has everything to live for, it must not feel that way to them.'

'It puts life into perspective, it really does. And well done you for being so accommodating. I wouldn't have thought of putting Max Ronson and charitable causes in the same breath when I first met you.'

'Everyone has at least one dark horse in their stable,' Max replied quietly.

'And underneath all that brash bluff and bluster, I genuinely believe there is a decent person waiting to get out, Max Ronson.' He looked slightly taken aback at her comment, but perhaps a little gratified, and this emboldened her to ask: 'Who was that woman you were talking to, anyway? Or should I say shouting at?'

They both turned at the sound of approaching footsteps. Although August loved Jonah, she was as annoyed as she noticed Max was visibly relieved to see him. As Jonah approached in full walking apparel, trekking poles included, Max placed another cigarette in his mouth, quickly lit it and waved.

'Saved by the bell,' August said under her breath.

'I didn't see the memo that we were climbing Everest.' A plume of smoke hit the air as Max greeted his fellow Hubber.

'Oh, that little hill? Just the fallows of Futtingbrook today, so just as dangerous,' Jonah smirked. 'I walked from home. It was gorgeous, all through the fields. The birds were singing their spring sonnet, the trees and plants are already a vibrant green and the bluebells are an abundance of colour.'

'All right, David Attenborough, calm down.'

Jonah laughed. 'Tried to convince the kids to come, but four-nil to the mighty iPad, I'm afraid. They might come down later with Sukie.' He eyed the refreshments area. 'This all looks very professional. Oh, shit, yeah, Tyler said he's designed up and mailed you the refreshments sign to put out here, you just need to print it off.'

'I thought he was coming here to do that.'

'No, he's badly hungover. Said he'd try and find August and Cat at the start.'

'That kid! OK. I'll go and print it now.' Max butted his cigarette and headed back inside. 'Jonah, Agatha, do you want a coffee?'

'Yes please,' They replied in unison as Jonah walked over to the table. 'Everything OK with you, August?'

She had started to unpack a box of energy drinks. 'Yes, I'm good thanks. Slightly nervous about running 10K for the first time in a while, but apart from that, all good.'

'You'll be fine, don't worry. You can always walk a bit if it gets too much.'

'Yes, I want to try and get round in one without stopping, though.'

'I feel like we haven't had a proper chat for ages. You've been head and blinds down, lately.'

'That's what happens, once a story starts flowing. I lose days and weeks sometimes. Barely stopping for a pee, let alone dinner.'

'I may have to read this one if you're naming and shaming.'

'Like I said to Max, only people I don't like get in there.'

He raised his eyebrows. 'Has he made the cut?'

August laughed. 'Despite his ways, you can't help but like him, can you?' She paused for a second before taking the plunge. 'Jonah? Have you ever seen him with a woman before?'

'As in, a girlfriend?'

'Yes. It looked like he was arguing with someone who pitched up here in a silver Porsche earlier. She looked kind of familiar.'

'Long dark hair? Italian-looking?'

'Yes!'

'I have seen her once before, but I've no idea who she is.'

'Oh.' August laughed aloud at the disproportionate disappointment she felt at not getting to the heart of this particular mystery just yet.

'August, Max has a good heart, but you must have realised by now that he's not an open book.'

'Who's not an open book?' A familiar voice greeted them.

Jonah looked up, his eyes nearly popping out of his head. 'Bloody hell, Cat!'

August's mouth dropped open. 'Oh my god, you look stunning.' August felt an instant girl crush take hold as the tall goddess strutted her stuff in front of the drink's tables adorned head to toe in a rubber-look jump suit, ears and mask.

'Fuck me sideways and call me Batman.' Max appeared with a coffee in each hand, gawking at her. 'How many of your operatives did it take to shoehorn you into that little number?'

'Well, I had to be Catwoman really, didn't I?

'I hope you've got lots of Vaseline. PVC is a bugger with chafing. And aren't you going to sweat like mad?' Jonah added seriously, taking a coffee from Max.

'Of course I am, but it never occurred to me that it might be twenty bloody degrees in April. On the plus side, I figured there will be hundreds of sweaty local men running around me. If not for me to hit on, it'll be good for the business.'

'Jesus, Cat. I thought I was mercenary. It is for charity, you know.' Max took a gulp of his drink.

'As if you are not doing this to market the Hub, too?'

'Shit, I honestly hadn't thought of that,' Max replied, and August could tell he was being truthful.

'Anyway, I've already raised a ton of money from my clients.' Cat straightened one of her ears. 'I'll have you know, my business may not have many successful matches but financially there are certainly some catches.'

'I can feel a new slogan coming on there, can't you, Agatha?' Max winked, handing Cat one of the collection tins. 'I reckon if you shake this and that delicious booty of yours on the way round, the Futtingbrook Farm Hub, The Country Matchmaker and even you will be having it off later, for sure.'

August shook her head in disbelief. 'Not quite the kind of marketing plan I've worked on in the past.' She checked her watch. 'Shit, I better get changed. It's a good twenty-minute walk up to the start.'

August noticed Max do a double-take as she appeared from the Hub ten minutes later in full fancy dress: short blue skirt, red and gold bodice and clean white trainers included. Her long auburn hair was tied up in a high ponytail.

'Wow. Agatha has legs and cheekbones, everyone. Bagsy me to stick your race number on.' Initially glad that she'd had this effect on him, she then suddenly felt a little self-conscious that she had too much flesh on show to be running around the neighbourhood. Too late to do anything about it, though.

Cat was now animatedly chatting to Ade, who had just arrived on his quad bike to check out the proceedings.

'Come on, Cat, we'd better get going,' August shouted over to the pair.

'Wonder Woman,' Ade sang loudly out of tune, and waved across at her.

'Like a virgin.' A singing Beryl suddenly appeared from the front of the Hub, a cone bra stuck on the top of her own pendulous breasts and a long hairpiece ponytail. Her signature sweater dress, tights and trainers remained the same.'

'What the—? Where did you spring from?'

'Hollywood, of course. For today, Maximillian, I am going to be Madonna Ciccone.'

He snorted, then worked to rearrange his face into a serious expression. 'Mrs G, you said yourself you're designed for comfort, not speed.'

'For goodness' sake, I'm not running! I just wanted to get

into the spirit of things and make sure you untidy buggers don't mess up my kitchen. Now, where did you put that brandy?' She waddled over to the refreshments table, where Jonah was now unboxing energy drinks.

August checked her watch. 'Cat! We'll miss the start if we don't hurry.'

Max retrieved his car keys from his pocket. 'I'll drive you. I mean, my two favourite superheroes in one go – what more of a fantasy could one man ever dream of?'

It was Ade's turn to shake his head at his brother. 'Good luck ladies! And I don't just mean with the race.'

Chapter Sixteen

'Here comes Wonder Woman,' Max grinned, as a red-faced August approached the table.

'So tell me, who picked the hottest day in April to run 10K?' She grabbed a brandy and downed it in one. 'Good idea, this.' She bent down to hold her knees and get her breath back.

'How did you do?'

'Considering I've been a couch potato for the last however many months and have done limited training, I did OK. Came thirtieth, I think, and did it in one hour ten. Which means Ellie's Grant has to give me an extra twenty quid for the Sebastian Line, as he reckoned I'd never make the top fifty.'

'A win-win then. How about Cat?'

'Last seen with the sweaty bank manager, strutting towards the office she assures me he uses for important business meetings, with a bottle of Chablis.'

'I bet she was! Although, if its Roger Weeks you are talking about, I wouldn't have put her with a short old silver fox like him. Good on her, though.'

'Not really that good. He was wearing a ring.'

Max reached for another shot of brandy and downed it. 'Well, not everyone has a happy relationship, and nobody's perfect.

Life doesn't work like that.'

'Clearly not, and thanks for reminding me of that, Max.'

'Oh shit.' He put his hand to his head. 'Sorry. Sometimes I speak before I think.'

'It's OK.' August took a deep breath and shut her eyes for a second to regain her composure. 'Weddings are so overrated, anyway.'

'No, that was heartless. Shit, I can be so tactless. Sorry, Agatha.'

Just seeing Max looking right at her for more reassurance allowed her initial fizz of offence and woe to be replaced by a genuine growing affection for the complicated man standing in front of her. 'Honestly, Max, it's fine. I've moved on and I agree: give me imperfect, any day.' She looked towards the Hub for a change of subject. 'Where are the others?'

'Jonah's wife and brood showed up to help with the drinks station. Didn't you see them when you came through?' Max asked.

'I was obviously flying, Max Ronson, so no, I didn't,' August smirked.

'Wonder Woman,' he sang, then smiled. 'Good kids they are, and Mrs G – well, she did her bit, then hit the brandy. George – that's her old man – just picked her up. I didn't see Tyler at all, did you?'

'No, but I could have just missed him among the throng, I guess.' August yawned loudly.

'Nah, he'll still be in bed, that one.'

'Hang on a minute, I need to rewind here,' August piped up. 'So Beryl's husband is called George?' Before Max could answer, she downed another shot of brandy and grimaced. 'I'd better have some water. I'll be falling over.'

'Yes, George George. Far out, ridiculous and amazing all at

the same time. You country folk are a funny lot, aren't you?' Max picked up her hand. 'Phew, just the five fingers.'

'Max! You can't say that.'

'I just did. Stop worrying about what everybody else thinks or says, Agatha. Because the bottom line is, the majority of people are so wrapped up in themselves and their lives, they don't even notice yours.'

'Well maybe you should check your own toes, then, as my mother's friend reliably informed her that the Ronsons have been around this area far longer than the Saunders clan.'

Max sighed deeply and pushed away her hand, his face suddenly darkening. 'Blah, blah, blah. Gossip, gossip, gossip. I thought better of you.'

She frowned at him. 'Max, are you drunk?'

'So what if I am?' Max lit a cigarette and checked his watch. A smart two-seater convertible Mercedes pulled up beside them. 'Shit, I better shut the gate. Shhh Agatha, don't tell anyone about the gate.'

'Tell anyone what?' August screwed up her face. What else did she need to find out? This place was becoming more like a plot from one of her books every day. Realising she couldn't beat him, so she might as well join him, August fired down another shot.

Darcy Webb smiled sweetly up at them from the driver's seat.

'If it isn't the gorgeous Mrs Webb again,' Max enthused.

'Yes. Just me though, I'm afraid. Everyone else wanted to get off.'

'No worries. I said to August I thought the tea urn was a glorious extra.' August gave him a sarcastic smile. 'Brandy for the leading lady?'

'I won't, thanks, now that I'm driving. I just wanted to come down and say thanks for all your support today.'

'Has it been successful?'

'Very. The local press covered it and it looks like the sponsorship is higher than I ever imagined. The tins seem lovely and heavy, too. Should at least cover part of the centre's fuel bills for the year.'

'Well, well done you – that's fantastic. And you can use the land here anytime. My brother is very amiable, you know that.'

'And thanks for your help with the co-ordinating, August.' Darcy beamed at her. 'It means a lot when somebody gives up their time, and like I said, please do bear in mind if you know anyone who'd like to volunteer. We are always on the lookout.'

'Sure, and if you need any raffle prizes at any time, I'm happy to donate signed copies of my books, if you'd like them.'

Darcy beamed at her. 'That's really kind. OK, I'd better get on. I just need to do a final check that the course is clear and nobody's face down in a cow pat somewhere.'

They both waved the woman off.

'You're a good girl really, aren't you Agatha?' Max hiccupped. 'All these good people, doing even more good for people they don't even know. What's that about?'

'It's called compassion, Max. Darcy's son died. He took his own life. She has made a purpose of his loss, which seems to happen a lot after tragedy. I was thinking as I was running around how hard it must be for those left behind.'

'That's the thing. Everyone thinks they are a bloody expert, but they haven't got a fucking clue. Little Miss Know-Everything, you are.'

August gasped, and anger descended like a mist. 'Max! Stop it. There is a line and you've just crossed it. I'm tired and I'm hungry and—' She noticed with a jolt that the pseudo hard man had tears in his eyes. As he turned and started marching towards the Hub, August swiftly followed and spun him around.

'Then tell me, Max. Give me a clue. From the minute I met you, I wanted to ask you what's really the matter. But it's nigh on impossible to have a straight conversation with you. You make it impossible.'

'When you realise that everyone must die and nothing lasts forever, then your pretty little head may understand. Life isn't like one of the little stories you write, Agatha – it's real. It hurts, it's dark.' He pushed past her and headed for the front door. As he marched towards the lift, his face contorted with pain.

Following him in, August rushed around to block him from going upstairs. 'Don't you think I know that, too?' Fuelled by brandy herself, August found herself shouting. 'You patronising prick. It's not all about you, Max. Everybody has their own pain. And if you don't talk about it then how will you ever feel better? Everything is a bloody joke to you. You can't even call me by my real name.'

Max took off his glasses and wiped his face roughly with the back of his hand. 'If you feel like that then go home…August… I'll see you on Monday.'

'My dad died too, as you bloody well know, so don't try to tell me I don't know the meaning of loss,' August continued to shout. 'But you have to get on with it and keep living, and not allow grief to destroy you.'

And then the lift arrived with a plonk and suddenly they were both inside – and kissing. Kissing as furiously as though their own lives depended on it.

The lift finished its short journey and, as the door opened to let light in, Max broke free and quickly pressed the button to make the door shut again, but it was too late – August had seen what she needed to see.

'No, this can't happen,' he gasped. 'You can't come up here. I can't do this. We need to go down.'

The lift started to descend. Max rubbed his hand over his shaved head. 'What am I thinking? That was a big mistake – I shouldn't have – I'm drunk. Sorry.'

The change in Max's face made August realise that he actually was really angry, and her pulse started to race with alarm. With her own eyes wide with red-headed anger too, she began to breathe even more rapidly than when their lips had been locked.

On reaching the ground floor, she hurried out of the lift and turned around. 'Well, thanks for that, Max. And for the record, I'm not anyone's mistake. I don't know who the fuck you think you are.' The doors shut.

Drunk and angry and confused and oh so horny, with a huff and a flick of her wonder-woman skirt, August stormed outside to ring a taxi.

Chapter Seventeen

Easter Sunday, and Bluebell Wood was in full bloom. Chattering birdsong filled the warm air, as well as the deep, fragrant aroma of the flora all around. The vibrant blue flowers matched the cloudless sky, making for a perfect late-April morning. Couples and families were on the main path, enjoying their long weekend and making the most of the spring sunshine.

August held Wilf's hand to steady him as he leant down to pick some of the inviting blue flowers for his mum. Ellie, happy that her morning sickness seemed to have already dwindled, was walking, face to the sun. Grant strode ahead, carrying a sleeping James in one arm and pushing the double buggy with the other. Colin the Corgi had jumped into the bottom of the buggy, and was snoring like a piglet.

Ellie caught up with her sister. 'Goose, you're being very quiet. In fact, you've been quiet all week. I was beginning to wonder if you were avoiding me on purpose. Are you all right?'

'He's had a poo, doll, and I forgot to put the nappies in,' Grant shouted back to them, strapping James into the top of the buggy. 'How about I head home, get the boys sorted and I'll meet you back at your mum's for lunch at one? I've got the dog. Come on Wilfy,' the loving dad called out.

Wilf handed his mum the one bluebell he hadn't dropped then started toddling to Grant's now outstretched arms.

'Thanks, love,' Ellie called to him.

With Colin now awake and reluctantly back on his lead, the three Jenkins boys and their four-legged friend headed back to the village ahead of them.

August smiled. 'He's such a keeper.'

'He has his moments. So come on, stop changing the subject. I heard you rattling around in the cottage all week, so I know you didn't go to the Hub, did you? And where's your car?'

'Bloody hell, I didn't realise you constituted the whole Upper Gamble neighbourhood watch in one household!'

'I just don't want you going under again, that's all. Has Scott upset you?'

'No. Of course he hasn't. In fact, I think he has actually forgotten I even exist. Which would have upset me before, but I really am over it now.'

'Then what is it?' August avoided her gaze until Ellie gasped loudly, making August jump and spin around, thinking she might have tripped over a root and fallen.'Oh my god, you've slept with Max Ronson, haven't you?'

August took a deep, calming breath, glad that her sister was fine but not pleased with the direction the conversation was taking. 'I hate the fact that you know me so well.'

'Goose!'

'No, I didn't shag him. But something did happen, and I can't even tell you how mortifying it all was.'

'Well you can, and I'm all ears.'

'We were drunk – had too much brandy after the race. I only need to sniff a drink when I've been running and – well, we ended up shouting at each other and then – well, we kissed.'

Ellie blinked at her. 'Oh. That's a good thing, isn't it?'

'We were in the lift, which literally takes two seconds to go upstairs, and when we got to top and the door started to open, he went a bit manic and told me I had to leave.'

'What, before you even got out of the lift?'

'Yep.'

'Who started the kissing?'

'I dunno, it was if as if we both wanted it badly. But maybe that's because I'm craving sex at the moment. Every port in a storm, and all that.'

'How was the kiss? Proper passionate, like?'

August blushed and looked away from her sister, suddenly intent upon studying a particularly lovely bluebell. 'God, you need to get out more, Ellie. Yes, it was amazing, but he's such an arse.' August started to gabble. 'Said it was a big mistake. I got a glimpse of what was up there and it looks like he lives in the barn as well. It was like Great Aunt Betty's hoarder bungalow used to be up there. Not millions of newspapers and carrier bags, but stacks of boxes, literally piled everywhere. He's a bloody enigma, as well as an arse.'

'Maybe he's just moved in there and hasn't unpacked yet?'

August pulled a doubtful face. 'It all seems a bit fishy.'

'Fishy? That's what Marie McGee would say. You're morphing into one of your own characters.'

August gave her a reluctant smile, which quickly turned into a frown. 'The difference is she'd sort him out with one lash of her tongue. He confuses me. My feelings are confusing me.'

'Maybe he just likes living there. I mean, from what you tell me, the grounds are beautiful.'

August stopped in her tracks. 'I've only just remembered that a woman visited him at the barn – shouting at him, too. Absolutely stunning, she was. Like a movie star, and she was driving a kick-arse Porsche.'

'He sounds complicated, Goose. Maybe she's a girlfriend or an ex – who knows? But what I do think is that I'd stay well away from him romantically. You told me yourself that Mrs Dye told Mum he was troubled. You don't need another broken heart.'

'I hear you, but the problem is that chemistry has no bloody ears!'

'Goose, listen to me. How many red flags do you need to be waved in your face with this one? Really! Come on, sis. At least with Scott he started out well, then turned into a bastard. You have a way out before you even go in to the starting stalls with this one.'

'Don't worry, he clearly doesn't want me anyway. And, I know you're right. He talked to me like dirt. That's why I haven't been back to the Hub, plus I feel completely embarrassed about it all. To top it all I left my bloody car at the farm.' August blew out a long breath.

'You should have just called me. One of us would have come and got you.'

'I wish I had. After he shouted, there was me in a Country Cab, in a bloody Wonder Woman outfit, with snot running down my face singing "I Will Survive". Quite the drama queen.'

Ellie giggled. 'Oh, Goose, sorry to laugh but that is really funny. Can you stay working there, do you think? You must remember it's about what's good for you – nothing to do with him.'

'I don't know. I need to just face him and get that bit over with first. If he apologises, then maybe.'

'Where there is anger, there is almost always pain underneath, Goose.'

August nodded. 'Yes. Something is clearly not right. His brother did tell me that their dad died around a year ago.'

'Aw, and we know how hard that can be. Don't worry, sis. You've done nothing wrong. Has he tried to message you?'

'No, nothing. Cat sent me a brief message asking if I was OK. I just said I was getting in the groove writing at home this week and left it at that. She'll probably tell him, if he asks.'

'You want him to know you're all right, then.'

'I suppose I do.' August sighed. 'Actually, of course I do.'

'Who said it was boring down here, hey, kiddo?'

August smiled. 'I know, tell me about it. A fun run and a snog in a lift all in the space of twenty-four hours – what's a girl to do? Ooh, I know what else I wanted to tell you.'

'Go on.'

'You mentioned about me volunteering to meet new people, and after you mentioned it, well, it seems too much of a coincidence not to give it a try. You know the Sebastian Line?'

'Of course, the charity you were running for.' Ellie widened her eyes in anticipation.

'Well, they are always looking out for new listening volunteers, apparently, and now I am in the enviable position of being able to write full-time and choose what hours I work, I thought I'd give it a go.'

Ellie suddenly looked doubtful. 'Wow. What, listen to suicidal people, you mean?'

'Well, yes, it's a crisis line, so there will be all sorts of people who call in who are down or lonely, too.'

'You're a better person than me, if you can do that.'

'I was so affected by Darcy Webb's story of losing her son that I kind of imagined it being a youngster I knew, like Wilf or James needing someone to talk to in their hour of need. It almost feels like I have no choice but to volunteer.'

'Well, when you put it like that… You're so sweet, Goose. How old was her son?'

'Seventeen.'

Ellie put her hand to her heart as tears filled her eyes. 'Oh my

God, I can't even imagine how you'd ever get over it. Do they train you properly?'

'Oh, yes. I read about it online. It's about time I gave back. It's just one shift a week standard, and more if you have the time. I figured a night shift would suit me, I can have a little kip after, or just do a weekend one, even.'

'Aw, bless you, Goose. And despite this little wobble with Max, you're doing so well now.' Ellie checked her watch. 'We'd better get a move on. If we are late for Mum's Easter feast, there will be hell to pay.'

August was stuffed when she got home from her mother's. Bless Pamela Saunders – she did love a special occasion with her family and that day was no exception. A huge roast chicken with all the trimmings and both August and Ellie's favourite: home-made cherry pie with thick custard. She had even planned a surprise egg hunt for her big girls as well as Wilf, who had proceeded to eat so much chocolate that he'd projectile-vomited under the kitchen table and Barney the old faithful Labrador had to be dragged away before he slurped it up.

After pouring herself a glass of wine, August put food down for a miaowing Prince Harry. In his annoyance at being left all day, he promptly turned his nose up at it then sauntered upstairs to leave even more ginger hairs on the new black velour throw she had put on her bed. *Apparently I can't please any of the men in my life*, August thought despondently.

Lying on the sofa with her jeans open, she began checking her phone for messages. Disappointed there were none, her thoughts turned to Max. Despite his dramatics, the whole lift scenario had been super sexy and could have been more so with her in her short-skirted outfit and the feeling of complete passion that had flowed between them so undeniably before he cut it short. But for whatever reason, Max had not wanted her, and for whatever reason, that rejection had affected her badly.

Thinking about the whole scenario suddenly made her feel horny, but at that moment, even if Jamie Dornan had appeared on a white charger, she really was too full to do anything, let alone jiggle about having sex. She went to the notes section in her phone and typed the words, Too Fat to Fuck. Was TFTF already an acronym, she wondered? Lila Lovelace was a sucker for an acronym; maybe she could use it in the Christmas book. Just thinking about it had made August laugh to herself.

With thoughts now moving to her Tinder days in London, and how much fun she'd had then, she decided it was time to jump back into the magnificent mire of men again. And with the encouragement of alcohol, within seconds she had downloaded the app and there, staring back at her like one big messy memoir, was her old profile.

There she was, a fresh-faced twenty-nine-year-old who, despite showing far more cleavage than she would dare to now, looked hot. Something, if she was honest, she hadn't felt since the day Scott had cheated on her.

Should she be naughty and keep these old photos of her younger self to lure a man in? Maybe she would keep the one of her and Caroline, an ex-Placatac work colleague, at Ascot races and replace the others.

'Hmm,' she said aloud, thinking she should maybe use a pseudonym for a bit. She didn't want anyone finding her Facebook, Instagram and Twitter author accounts and professing to knowing everything about her in a couple of clicks.

After much deliberation, and realising that her needs at this moment were purely sexual, *Poppy, 37, marketing consultant, looking for someone to butter my muffins,* was the chosen alias, career and desire.

She had only been swiping for a few minutes when MATCH! popped up on the screen. Heart pounding, she clicked it and staring back at her was Ian, a property developer from Swinford. Blonde, blue eyes, trendy haircut, nice clothes. Thirty – nice! – with a beautiful smile. Younger was perfect. She wanted sex, not a ceremony. She just hoped he was looking for the same thing as her. Completely forgetting that she felt TFTF, August started messaging immediately, *Lucky you, we've matched!*

She smiled at his speedy reply. *Quite! Hi Poppy! Cool name btw. I just want to be totally honest in that I'm not looking for anything serious at the moment but I am a dab hand at buttering muffins x*

That night, the sex in Ian from Swinford's bedroom, in his rented flat in the centre of town, was just what the lust doctor ordered. Experienced, pure and safe filth, which had satisfied a need they both obviously felt. The property developer was handsome, and a really cool and intelligent guy. He worked out too, so his 'mind for business, body for sin' quip on her arrival at the local pub where they had done their official introductions, really hadn't been a joke.

He told her that he had just moved into the area to concentrate on his career, and was not ready to commit to anyone, so their timing had been perfect. He had an early start in the morning so, if it was OK, she wouldn't be able to stay over. He didn't even balk when, in the aftermath of an explosive orgasm on August's part, she had burst into tears and blurted out that it was because he was the first man she had slept with after seven years of being with someone and it just felt odd. He had given her a big hug and laughed that he was more than happy to oblige, whatever the situation.

She sat in the taxi on the long journey home, fully sated and armed with the number of a decent bloke who had said she could call him anytime for some more mind-blowing, no-strings sex.

All in all it had been an enjoyable and empowering experience, and despite it bringing up the obvious feelings about Scott, and her confused feelings about Max, it had felt good to be a woman back in control of the narrative of her own sex life.

On reaching home, she saw Ellie's upstairs curtain twitch, and rolled her eyes fondly. Her younger sister had never been able to understand the appeal of casual sex, and August realised that it wasn't everybody's cup of tea. But she had always been of the opinion that as long as the sex was safe and consenting, independent single women should be able to access pleasure and have the confidence to explore and honour their true sexual selves, whenever and however they so wished.

Without even taking her coat off, she made her way up the stairs to her bedroom. Retrieving the framed photo of her and Scott from her bedside drawer, she ran her finger over his face. God, she had loved him. But tonight she had overcome another hurdle on the road to finally moving on.

There was no getting away from it. Love was forever complicated, in whichever guise it raised its indomitable head. Family love, casual sex, deep, committed love and even misunderstood feelings, like those that Max had thrown at her just a week ago. They all had their own place.

Feeling overwhelmingly tired all of a sudden, August moved the framed photo to her general box of memories under the bed, stroked a sleeping Prince Harry, then, taking off her clothes, headed for a quick shower before falling into bed.

Chapter Eighteen

The next morning, a bleary-eyed August could feel a frisson of excitement on entering the Hub.

She had felt knackered when she woke up, and also deliciously achy after her bedroom gymnastics of the night before. But her tiredness was lifted by the upbeat music coming from the beam-perched speakers and the smell of spring on the breeze, which was blowing through the many open windows and the pulled back bifold doors of the bright and airy Hub, on this fine May day.

Her plan had been to grab a coffee, stay incognito, get her head and some words down until lunchtime, get some air by walking up to the farm and retrieving her car, then driving back home for a siesta. Bless Ellie for giving her a lift that morning after dropping the boys at nursery. She was thankful that Max's car was nowhere to be seen, so that her mission of hotfooting it in, going straight to an office and pulling the blinds down was possible.

'Hot, not or a sandwich?' Beryl caught her as soon as she put her foot through the door.

'Definitely not today, thanks, Mrs G. I'm heading off early.'

'Not for August.' Beryl George said aloud as she made a note in her little pad. 'We missed you, my love. Where have you been?'

Both Cat and Jonah waved wildly from the across the office. Tyler sauntered past and gave her a cheeky wink.

'I'm here now, and everyone seems in a good mood. What's going on?' She silently congratulated herself on side-stepping the question so neatly.

'The one-day-old chicks are arriving today!' Beryl was beaming. 'Means I get busier with the new staff and what not, but it creates such joy to have those little darlings scooting around in the barn. And you wait until they get a bit older and are let loose in the meadows. It's hilarious.'

'Aw, bless. I can't wait to see them.'

'That reminds me, Ade was asking about getting your car moved. There will be a lot going on up there today and he wants it shifted, he does.'

'Of course! I didn't realise it was such a big day for the farm or I'd have got my sister to drop me there and moved it first thing.'

'Don't worry, love. Max is helping his brother today so why don't you give him a call; he can come down and fetch you.'

'Err. No, it's fine, I'll walk, thanks, Mrs G. The fresh air will do me good,' August stuttered.

At that moment, a quad bike pulled up outside the entrance. August saw a dark, stocky, strong-jawed man get off it and make his way to reception. Beryl waddled to meet him.

'Morning, Ivor. You're after the Cross Barn key, aren't you?' The man nodded. 'Actually, August, why don't you get a lift back up to the farm on the bike? OK with you, Ivor?'

'Sure. Come!' he said in what August recognised to be a Croatian accent.

'*Pozdrav,*' August said, quietly hoping she'd remembered it right.

'*Pozdrav*,' Ivor smiled to reveal a crooked smile nestled in his weathered face.

August hopped on to the back seat. 'Just one of the three words I know.' She spared him the detail that she had worked with a Croatian girl in London and had learnt the very basics from her over coffee one morning.

Ivor dropped August in the Futtingbrook Farm courtyard and sped back down the lane. She could see Max, wearing a Peaky Blinders-style cap, with his back to her, chatting animatedly to Ade at the front of one of the barns. The very same barn that her bloody car was parked alongside. She began to walk comically on tiptoe behind them, feeling extremely foolish – but it was no good, Ade spotted her.

'August, thank goodness. I was just about to put it up for sale on We Buy Every Single Car On The Planet dot com.' He laughed.

August was so discombobulated at the sight of Max, she couldn't match his mirth or his wit. 'I'm so sorry, I didn't think you'd need it moving. Selfish of me.'

'Agatha.' Max politely doffed his hat. She noticed that he looked awkward in front of her for the first time ever. The trendy headwear, along with his thick-framed glasses, made him look even more handsome than usual. She felt herself redden.

'I…err…umm…better get out of your way. I hear you have a busy day ahead.'

'Have a look in here, first.' Ade sounded like an excitable child, and August found it impossible to resist his enthusiasm. 'We're all ready for them.'

August peered into the huge barn, which had been covered in thick, clean sawdust. There were several low, round pens made of wire and several red, rubber, dome-like water feeders dotted

140

around. Jarvis Cocker, the turkey dog, was running around sniffing everything out as he went.

'He's all set to herd up any unsuspecting stragglers.'

August peered around, feeling dazed. 'It's all so new to me. It kind of blows my mind. I wouldn't have even thought of putting dogs and turkeys together.'

As they walked back outside, a Range Rover similar to Max's pulled up beside them. Max, who had been on the phone, leaning on a fence that bordered one of the meadows, now headed towards them, holding his arm up in greeting to the man in the SUV as he did so. In the rush to avoid Max, August hurriedly pulled her car keys out of her bag and promptly dropped them right at the feet of the driver now getting out of the Range Rover. They both bent down at the same time to pick them up, and bumped heads.

If August had felt herself gently redden on seeing Max, it was nothing to what she felt when she realised who exactly was in front of her. She was worried that her whole face now resembled a beef-steak tomato.

'I'm so sorry,' they said together, each rubbing their forehead. 'Ian?' August questioned quietly.

'Poppy?' He whispered back.

'Greetings! You must be Sean.' Ade came up and patted the handsome blonde man on the back. 'This is my brother, Max, and meet August. She writes books, so we try not to upset her in case she puts us in them.' August froze on the spot. 'You two, this is Sean, Cat Bachelor's son and our new poultry vet.'

August made a weird noise between a cough and a laugh and wished a sink hole would appear and swallow her up.

'Good to meet you all. August, you say?' Having clearly regained his composure, Sean directed a sneaky wink at her. 'And a writer – that's pretty damn cool. Beats a normal day job like marketing, I guess.'

'She's very big in her genre, so we hear.' Ade sounded almost proud.

'I bet she is,' Sean smirked, then pulled a professional expression onto his face. 'So, Ade, what time are these baby birds arriving, then?'

If the human body could physically sick up embarrassment, August Saunders' would have done so right at that moment, all over the Ronson and Bachelor boys' wellies. It was not a big deal that 'Ian the property developer' was in fact Sean the vet; she could deal with that. After all, in the whirlwind world of dating, she was Poppy, marketing manager. She got it. But the fact that she had not only recently kissed the owner of the Hub but had now slept with her Hub mate's son, who was probably going to be on her work doorstep for the next few months, was a little bit more difficult to get her head around.

August parked back up at the Hub and lay her head on the car headrest, shutting her eyes for a moment. Her instinct had been to drive straight out of the farm and Futtingbrook and head to the peace of Upper Gamble, but she had a book to write, and Beryl had told her that Max was helping Ade with the influx of their fluffy new arrivals, so hopefully she wouldn't have to face him again – today, at least.

She headed to the kitchen to be greeted by a smiley-faced Cat, who was getting herself a coffee. 'Where have you been, then?' August could immediately see that she had the same eyes as Sean, an indigo blue, dark and soulful. Almond-shaped, a bit like a dolphin. He must have got his blonde hair from his father, she thought, although Cat's jet-black locks were clearly dyed.

'I left my car up at the farm.'

'Jonah has had a conspiracy theory running, imagining you'd been killed in your own bed by one of the suspects you are writing about.'

'Jesus, Jonah needs to get out more! That level of imagination beats anything of mine. Nothing half as exciting, I'm afraid. I just couldn't be bothered to make the effort – sometimes I do that. I wake up, put my laptop on at some ridiculous hour and get so engrossed in what I'm doing I just stay in bed and write.'

'For a whole week? Beryl thought you'd had a fall out with Max.' Trust Cat not to hold back, August thought, her heart leaping as she worked to keep her voice level. 'Did she now?'

'He's had a face like a smacked arse all week, to be fair,' Cat added, sitting down with her drink. 'Has barely left his man-cave upstairs, and when he has come down, he's been monosyllabic. He's upset people before with his rudeness, you know.'

'I can believe it.'

'But Max is Max – no filter; take him or leave him. You know that.' Cat stood up to go to the snack machine.

'Oh, I'd take him every time,' Max interjected, striding into the kitchen and making them both jump. Getting himself a glass from a cupboard and filling it from the water cooler, he ignored Cat and turned to August. 'Agatha, have you got a minute?'

'Good luck,' Cat whispered.

Holding her coffee in her slightly shaking hand, August apprehensively followed him into his office. He nodded for her to shut the door and sit down.

'I thought you were busy with Ade,' she stated tentatively.

'I wanted to talk to you.' He held her gaze. So what was all that about up at the farm, then?'

Her heart skipped a beat. 'What do you mean?'

'You seemed a bit flustered to see Cat's son, that's all.'

'I don't know what you're on about.' Frightened of a confession from her eyes, she glanced down.

He gave her a disbelieving look. 'I've been around the block enough to know *that* look.'

She visibly cringed, then felt a wave of angry defiance crash over her. How dare he ask about her personal life, when he'd refused to tell her anything about his? 'What I think we really need to be discussing here is the elephant in the lift from last Saturday, don't you? I'd kind of hoped an apology might have left your lips, rather than some sort of accusatory bullshit.'

Max sighed. 'I was drunk.'

'The universal "get out of all arsehole behaviour" card,' August sighed.

'OK, and I'm sorry. I'm sorry that I kissed you. Is that what you want me to say?' He folded his arms tightly.

She scowled. 'You don't have to be so bloody defensive.'

'It was a difficult day for me, all right?'

She rolled her eyes. 'I get it, you had a row with your fancy woman.'

He looked away. 'You wouldn't understand.'

'We've been here before, Max. And I might if you tell me.'

Max looked at the black-and-white Formula One photos on his wall. 'Actually, you'd better, go.'

She stared at him. 'As in, leave the Hub, you mean?'

'No. I just don't want to talk to you right now.'

'You're like a bloody spoilt child, Max Ronson. You're the one who called me in here and seemed to think you had a right to pry into my private life. I'm not going anywhere until we've had this out. It wasn't the kiss; it was what followed. I was drunk too, but not so much that it was a mistake. Not at the time, anyway…' August's voice tailed off. 'But as it was so much of a disaster for you, thinking about it, it's good I left before something happened that you so obviously would have regretted.'

He looked at her with a pained expression. 'Don't be like that. It's not you…it's…'

'Give me credit and spare me the bullshit, Max. We are both grown-ups. Well, I think I am anyway.'

'Ouch, that hurt.' He fiddled with the diamond in his ear. 'It's complicated.'

'It always is,' August sighed. 'And I told you, I'm not looking for anyone, seriously.' She put her head in her hands. 'God! Bloody drink has so much to answer for.'

He nodded. 'It does. And I couldn't even see anyone if I wanted to. Not at the moment, anyway.'

She looked up at him sharply. 'Why? It's the Porsche woman, isn't it?'

Max nodded. 'But it's not what you think. I promise.'

'It never is.' August made a noise between a laugh and a huff. 'Open the window and let's get this this swarm of clichés out of here, shall we?'

'A red-headed temper *and* a sense of humour. Hot!' Max lay back confidently on his office chair. August huffed. He leant forward. 'The things I do to try and become a character in one of your books. Surely you dislike me enough for me to get in there now.' Max held her gaze with his, and suddenly she couldn't look away.

'Anyway, please tell me you are going to stay. Working here, I mean. It wouldn't be the same without you.'

She tore her eyes away. 'Max Ronson, you're unbelievable!'

'I know you want to.'

'I'll have to think about it.'

Max grimaced and bent down, exaggeratedly rubbing his foot.

'What are you doing?' August asked, completely baffled.

'Rubbing away all the bullet marks from the number of times I shot myself in the foot.'

August just about managed to keep a straight face. 'Don't be thinking you're the funny one, now. OK. Yes, I will stay, but because it suits *me* to do so – not to satisfy your pathetic plea.'

Max bit his lip, held out his hand across the table, and wordlessly she gave him hers. He held it softly. 'Good. I'm glad. Really glad.'

He had the most beautiful hands, August noticed. Long, strong fingers with beautifully manicured nails. A spark of lust went through her and he gave her one of his amused smirks, almost as though he could sense it. 'Friends?'

Feeling suddenly flat, she let go of his hand, stood up and headed for the door. 'I dunno. Friends respect each other, Max. Tell each other the truth.'

'Fair point.' He picked his Ferrari model up and began to study it. 'So, *did* you sleep with him then, or not? The vet, I mean.'

Without turning around, a flustered August Saunders scurried out of his office, headed to a private one and pulled down the blind.

Chapter Nineteen

The Sebastian Line centre was located in the main high street of Futtingbrook, a small market town consisting of one wide, straight road with car parking bays either side. It was home to an eclectic mix of cafés, boutiques, craft shops, charity shops, a butcher, a baker, and now taking centre stage, a small Waitrose supermarket. The actual market took place on a Saturday, as it had been doing for hundreds of years, eight until three, mainly selling food from nearby farms and occasionally the odd artist or crafter would come and flaunt their wares. At Christmas it was the place to come and get that special something for the dinner table or a bespoke stocking filler.

The Sebastian Line centre itself was housed in a little, low-ceilinged Victorian building, which had previously been home to the old post office. A low black door opened from the street into three small rooms downstairs: two call workstations separated by the original counter, plainly decorated and each housing a desk, office lamp, swivel chair and phone; a kitchen to the rear of the building, which led to parking space enough for two cars, and a toilet with a tiny handbasin.

On each workstation wall was a white poster with the Sebastian Line logo in the top right corner and simple black text, stating: LISTEN with LOVE. SPEAK without JUDGEMENT. A round white clock with simple black digits completed the wall space.

A rickety old wooden staircase led up to a shower room on one side and on the other, a small bedroom, housing a single bed and a bedside table.

'So, this is us,' Darcy Webb announced to August, on completion of her speedy show-around. 'Small but cosy. I make sure it's warm all the time as there's nothing worse than coming out on a winter's evening to sit for hours in the freezing cold.'

August pointed to one of the posters. 'I love your mission statement.'

Darcy smiled. 'That makes us sound very corporate, August. We're dealing with feelings, not fancy goods here. Would you like a cup of something?'

'Sorry, that's too many years of working in marketing in my old office job. Black coffee, please.' August followed Darcy into the kitchen, which, despite its nod to the eighties, was almost as well equipped as the Hub's, with decaf coffee and herbal teas among the jars of hot chocolate and chai tea.

'The milkman comes twice a week, but we bring in what we fancy drink-wise and share. There's a biscuit tin, too. Which, if you do choose to join, you will soon begin to view as an essential requirement. Cakes are widely accepted as well, obviously.' Darcy Webb smiled, her thin top lip disappearing into her face.

'Once trained up, we ideally like you to take at least one shift a week. At the moment, we're open for twelve hours a day. Shifts are six pm until midnight, and midnight to six am. That later shift is tough – I won't lie. From a personal perspective, I mean; you will feel very tired anyway, even without the emotional toll of taking some of the calls you'll get. The bed is up there for if you need to rest and clear your mind. In the bedside drawer there is a donated CD player with some meditation discs. Just put the Do not Disturb sign on the door and you'll be left alone. There are three of us in the main volunteer team: me, Melanie and Emma. We try to do at least three shifts a week each. My husband David does the odd shift to fill in, too. I'm hoping to get some more men on board now that I'm putting the word out for volunteers, as I would ideally love for us to be available for twenty-four hours. We see it as more of a vocation than a simple volunteer role.' The efficient woman handed August her coffee, then peered off into space. 'Hmm, now what have I missed? Oh yes, I try to have two volunteers on the night shift, firstly because it is usually the busiest and secondly, it's good to have the support at that time of night, I think.' Darcy took a sip from her steaming green tea, then checked her watch. 'If you've got time, I'm on this six pm shift on my own today, so you can listen in to any calls that may come in, if you are interested? You don't have to stay for the whole shift, if you don't want to.'

'I'm having dinner at my mum's at seven thirty, so I'll stay for an hour if that's OK, but will do longer next time.'

'That's perfect. Is she local?'

'Upper Gamble, down the road from me.' August suddenly felt a rush of appreciation for the relationship she had with her mother. It was truly tragic to think that Sebastian would never be having this conversation about his mum, and that Darcy Webb would never again have dinner with her son.

'That's nice,' Darcy, oblivious to August's thought pattern, replied breezily.

August was relieved to change the subject. 'So, what does the training involve?'

'I've found that working on the job with someone has proved the most beneficial. There is a manual with suggested questions you can use, especially if the caller is suicidal, and organisations that you can signpost callers to. For example, we have a bereavement charity we work with in Swinford. And a national drug and gambling addiction helpline we can share with callers. I will mentor you for as long as it takes for you to feel comfortable taking calls on your own. If you do agree to volunteer, I also need to get a DBS Certificate sorted for you, but that doesn't take long.'

'Considering what the calls entail, you make it all sound so straightforward.' August felt a sudden mixture of nerves and fear. 'I'm not going to lie – it does frighten me that I could be talking to someone who may be in the process of taking their own life.'

'If it didn't make you feel that way, you wouldn't be human,' Darcy replied gently. 'Not everyone can do it. I've trained a few who, when they were no longer being mentored, fell apart, but being honest, a good dose of empathy is the main ingredient for this working out for both you and the caller. And if you didn't have the required level of empathy, you wouldn't be here considering volunteering your time and energy in the first place.' She gave August an appraising look. 'Why did you decide to give it a go, August? I should imagine you are remarkably busy.'

August hesitated, wanting to sort her thoughts before answering. 'A mixture of things, but mainly hearing your story made me think about my own nephews and how I'd want them to be able to call someone in their hour of need. Suicide has never crossed my mind, but I have been in a dark place before.'

'I'm sorry to hear that.'

August shrugged. 'Just life, really. My dad died when I was seventeen and I recently went through a horrid break-up.'

'Aw, that's tough stuff.'

August shook her head. 'It is, but it is a work in progress and

I've found that the old adage that time is a healer is really true – for me, at least.'

Darcy patted her arm. 'Sometimes we all need an ear, August.'

'Yes, we do – which is why I'm here. And I'm also in the enviable position where I can write at any time, so I don't have to restrict myself to a nine-to-five.'

'That's great, and thanks so much again. How I like to advertise this line is that it's not all about suicide; the crisis line bit shows that we are also here for folks who are in despair and just need to feel held. Sometimes the voice of a non-judgemental stranger is all somebody needs to pull them through a difficult moment.'

The phone rang and Darcy pointed for August to put on the headphones next to the handset. 'We aim to pick up in no more than four rings,' Darcy instructed.

'The Sebastian Line, Victoria speaking. Is there a name I can call you by?'

Victoria? August thought, and then felt her heart beginning to race as she heard a man's voice at the end of the phone. She really hadn't expected to be thrown in at the deep end quite so soon. With her mouth going dry, she forced herself to focus on what the caller was saying.

'You can call me anything you like sweetheart, but it's Doug,' the man continued.

'Hello Doug, thank you for calling us. What's going on for you today, then?' Darcy's a.k.a. Victoria's voice was soft and caring.

'What's your name then?' The gruff voice questioned.

'As I've said, it's Victoria. But we are not here to talk about me.'

'I'm finding it really hard; really, really hard.' Darcy then raised her eyes knowingly and met August's scandalised expression as the male voice at the end of the line continued.

'What's so difficult for you, then? Do tell me.'

'I didn't say difficult, I said it's hard, didn't I? Stupid bitch.' The caller laughed manically, then hung up.

Darcy looked at August with a pained expression. 'I should have warned you first about that type of call. Some men – and occasionally women – unfortunately find it a turn-on to speak to one of us. I didn't expect one at six pm on a Thursday, but that's the nature of this sometimes, I'm afraid. You don't know what you are going to get and when you are going to get it. See how I didn't entertain his use of the word hard?'

'I'm dumbfounded.' August took another gulp of coffee. 'People waste your time like that with sexual calls? I actually can't believe it.'

'Yes, we get a few like that, and worse, I'm afraid,' Darcy said conversationally. 'We don't tend to talk about those sorts of calls outside of here. In fact, all calls are confidential. It's also up to you if you even tell anyone you volunteer with us. The fewer people who know the better, actually. I think maybe if we're anonymous, we're more likely to get calls from the local area. Yes, I am the face of the Sebastian Line, obviously, but hardly anyone knows I take the actual calls. And as you heard, when I'm in the centre, I am Victoria.'

August put down her mug. 'Yes, why do you do that?'

'All volunteers are assigned a pseudonym. I find it helps to separate yourself from the more difficult calls. I walk in here as Victoria but leave as Darcy. Feel free to hang up on someone like Doug there. He's obviously got issues, but not the kind I'm prepared to clog up my phone lines with.'

'Good old Doug, having a tug.' August cringed at her thoughtless statement as soon as she'd said it, but luckily Darcy laughed.

'Has that put you off? I hope not because I'd love you to join me for some training, August.'

'I'm certainly up for giving it a go. I've no idea how I'll be, but thank you.'

'And that's the kind of volunteers I want, not someone who says, "I've got this, sounds easy." Because it's not – it's bloody hard. Learning how to listen properly is a difficult skill, but it does become much easier with practice.'

'What happens if you do recognise a voice?'

'We aren't just restricted to calls from the local area. We go as far as out as my advertising reaches, so it would be unlikely. But if it does happen, you can ask if they still wish to talk to you. If not, put them on to your fellow volunteer, or if you're alone, you could highlight our sister organisation in Swinford, or if it is a specific concern or addiction, then some of the others I mentioned already, which are on a list in the desk drawer.'

'Is it a free call?'

'Sadly no, not yet, but I would love it to be eventually. So, when can you do your first shift? How about next Monday six pm?'

August reached for her diary. 'Yep, I can do that.'

The phone rang again. 'You head off if you like,' Darcy smiled.

August checked the clock above the desk. 'I'll listen to one more, I've time.'

Darcy nodded as she picked up the handset. 'The Sebastian Line, Victoria speaking, is there a name I can call you by?'

The woman at the end of the line was sobbing, her breath hitching as she relayed her sadness.

'I'm Maggie. Hello. I'm so sorry to bother you but my husband died three weeks ago. I'm so very sad. I just need somebody to talk to.'

August stuck her lip out and put her hand to her heart. Darcy scribbled a note and passed it over to her new volunteer.

This is why we are here x

Chapter Twenty

'Hot, not or a sandwich?' Beryl was scrubbing the draining board in the Hub kitchen with gusto when August arrived. Cat was sat at the table, scrolling through her phone, a steaming coffee in front of her.

'Morning all,' August breezed. 'No pizzas today then? I thought Max always ordered pizzas on a Friday?'

'Not today. He's gone away for a few days.' Beryl carried on buffing the glass fridge door with an orange duster.

'Oh. But his car is out there?' August was surprised at how disappointed she felt. 'Where's he gone, then?'

'He didn't say,' Cat said. 'I just saw him being picked up earlier by a woman in dark glasses.'

'That was his architect,' Beryl suddenly piped up.

'Ah, right.' August didn't dare ask if it was the same 'architect' that he had been fighting with on the day of the 10K run.

The words, 'Does he have girlfriends?' fell out of August's mouth before she could stop them.

'Well, sadly he's not batting for my side, that's for sure.' Tyler poured some milk into his coffee and sashayed out of the kitchen.

'Who knows? He refuses point blank to join The Country

Matchmaker.' Cat sighed for dramatic effect. 'But that says nothing. Seven grand is a lot of dosh and I rarely push people together, as then they don't sign up again.'

August gasped in mock horror. 'Cat Bachelor! That's awful.'

'What is?' she smiled. 'It's a business.'

'Don't you want success stories to show on your website?'

'I have those. Lots of my friends agreed to do some fake ones before I started out. More chance on Tinder, I reckon – at least there's a bigger selection pool of men and women in search of that elusive chemistry we all seek.'

'Right.' August gulped, trying not to think about the last time she went on Tinder, and now unable to look Cat in the eyes.

Beryl was puffing and panting now. 'Ladies, do you want any lunch or not?'

'I'll have a cheese and tomato sandwich on brown then, please. With salad cream and brown pepper.'

'Heavens alive, August Saunders, you'll be asking me to cut them into triangles next!'

Cat laughed. 'I don't know what we'd do without you, Beryl. And not for me, thanks. I brought some soup in with me.'

Cat took a mirror out of her handbag and started studying her face. 'I'm thinking of having a little bit of work done. I hit fifty-five and literally felt my facial muscles drop. And this bit of saggy neck skin' – she put her hand to her jaw – 'where did that come from? I'm turning into a bloody turkey, myself.'

'If I look like you when I'm in my fifties, I'll be incredibly happy.' August joined her at the table.

'Thanks, August, but just you wait 'til you get here. It's true, youth and beauty are wasted on the young. I was so hot in my thirties, and did I realise it? Of course, I didn't.'

Beryl sniffed. 'You young women today. I don't know why you don't just enjoy life and stop worrying about what you look

155

like. Bottom line: if you are lucky enough to get older, you either go jowly like that basset hound of your fancy French agent, or your cheeks go so hollow you could rest your drinks in 'em. And what's the alternative? You go under the knife and look like a blinking cloned alien or Frankenstein's daughter with slugs for eyebrows. And what's with all those kids with those puffer-fish lips? It must be like kissing a rubber ring.'

'Welcome to Beryl George's Beauty School.' Cat put her mirror away, smirking.

'Well, grow old disgracefully, I say. If it's not your wrinkles, it's worrying that you're too fat or too thin. One of my tits weighs more than young August here, and do you hear me moaning? Health is what's important – without that, you're buggered.' She took off her pink rubber gloves and threw them under the sink. 'I'm off up the farm to sort the food orders. You must come up and see the chicks, August, before they get too big.'

'Yes, I think my boy is up there again today, making sure everything is in order.' Cat drained her cup. 'Have you met Sean yet?'

Amid her mortification, August felt distinctly relieved that Cat's handsome son obviously hadn't mentioned their night of debauchery to his mother.

'Er, yes – in passing. The day the chicks were arriving.'

'It's just so lovely having him nearby. He was living down in Somerset with his girlfriend, but she got far too clingy so when a placement came up at the Swinford Veterinary Centre, he jumped at it. He likes the fact he's nearer London – and his mumma, of course. I'm hoping he will find a nice woman and settle down, now. And as much as it will gall me to be called a grandmother, or to share him with someone else, it would be lovely at the same time to have a little baby or two to cuddle and spoil.' August found it weird to imagine Cat changing the nappy of the man she had had hot sex with just weeks previously, let alone her being a grandmother.

'Why don't we go for a walk up to the farm at lunchtime?' Cat continued. 'I can introduce you two properly, then. I actually think you'd really get on.'

August had a sudden flashback to her and sexy Sean doing just that, and her face seared red. 'Er, another day, perhaps. I have to get this Christmas book written or I'll be in real trouble.'

Cat finished off her coffee. 'You're allowed a lunch break, surely?'

August looked out and over one of the turkey meadows and smiled stiffly, her palms pricking with sweat. 'Well, it is a beautiful day so, umm, let me see.'

'Good girl.' Cat stood up. 'I don't want to pry, but how are you doing now? I love the soap your ex is in and I'm always looking at the gossip pages. And then all of a sudden, there was a photo of you and him, and him and her. What a twat, doing what he did.'

'She was younger and prettier; how could he resist?' August's sarcasm was palpable, and she gave a quick smile to soften it.

'She's got high-maintenance written all over her,' Cat scoffed. 'And look at you – you're stunning, August, and a bloody bestselling author to boot. These men! He'll be back for you, mark my words – they always are.'

Despite herself, August felt her heart leap. 'Don't say that, Cat. I'm just beginning to get over him.'

But Cat was on a roll. 'You wait. The grass won't be greener – more like Astroturf. Fake and easy to replace. He'll be back.'

'He's engaged to her.'

'Sorry to be blunt, but he was engaged to you and that didn't stop him.' August winced, but couldn't deny the truth in her words. 'Anyway, more fool him. From the little of you I know

157

already, I think you are a diamond of a woman.'

'Aw, thanks Cat. I have to say, it's so much easier being away from London and everything that living there brought with it. And I love being here and chatting to you lot.' August smiled, feeling suddenly warm inside. 'It brightens my day. Talking of men, I forgot to ask what happened to you after the fun run?'

Cat eyed her mischievously. 'I needed a new business account.'

August's mouth dropped open in shock. 'What are you like?'

'Five-foot seven, with the smallest cock, and nigh on white pubes. Ew! But I've got the biggest limit on my new gold card now.'

August shook her head, laughing. 'Cat Bachelor, you're a bad woman.'

'Bad? I much prefer bold. And the added benefit of them being married and ugly is, well, apart from them making more of an effort in the bedroom department, it's so much easier for me to play the "I don't feel good about myself doing it again" card, too.'

'I love the month of May.' August lifted her face to the sun as she and Cat set off from the Hub. 'The weather gets better and it means summer is just around the corner.'

'Agreed. I'm glad you could find the time for a walk with me. It's too nice to just sit inside all day.' Cat became animated. 'And I can't wait for you to see the chicks.'

'Aw, I'll take some photos and share them with my nephews.'

'You know, I'm sure Ade wouldn't mind you bringing them up to the farm. We'll ask him when we get there. Shall we make it a long one and walk up to the crossroads and over the back meadow?'

'Yeah, let's do it.'

'Shame my Sean had to get off.'

'I'll get to meet him properly again, I'm sure.' August's relief on finding out about his early departure had been monumental.

Cat looked pensive. 'He's thirty… You're thirty-seven, aren't you?'

August shot her friend a warning look. 'Cat, don't even go there.'

'Why not? Bit of an age gap, but with my true matchmaker head on, I know you'd be good together. Same sense of humour. He loves a redhead, too. Maybe I should set you two up on a date?'

Oh God, thought August. 'Cat, the only date I'm interested in at the moment is with me, you and these baby turkeys.'

They walked in companionable silence for a while, their conversation giving way to the buzz of insects and chatter of birds. The pure blue sky was dotted with fluffy white clouds that drifted lazily in the gentle breeze, causing them both to relax and get lost in the moment.

A couple of men, Ivor included, were working in the sunflower meadow, removing the old plants and replacing with new. The big man waved at the pair of them, and they waved back.

'I need to get him on my dating books,' Cat muttered, taking in the big man's tight t-shirt with its obvious sweat marks.

'Not sure a farm hand's wage will quite cover your seven-grand price tag. Unless you're offering a discount, of course.'

'God, I am so not talking business. There's something about a working man with broken English and huge hands. I bet he'd be filthy, too.'

'You make me look like Snow White.'

Cat laughed. 'Even I'd draw the line at an alpaca.' The furry llama lookalikes had just come into view in the next field.

August gave a bark of laughter. 'I can't believe you just said that.'

'Nor can I. Anyway, I know what I meant to ask: what did Max want with you in his office the other day? You looked serious when you came out.'

August hesitated, but couldn't think of a story quickly enough. 'We had a bit of a…for want of a better word, an indiscretion. The day of the fun run.'

Cat whooped, and August couldn't help but smile. 'He tried it on with you, didn't he? I'm not blind, August. It's obvious there's a frisson between the pair of you. Deep down he's a good bloke, but I'd stay away on the relationship front, if I were you.'

'It was a mistake. We both had too much of that bloody brandy he insisted upon.' August sighed. 'I do fancy him, though. It's not like me to try to force my head to rule my heart, but I am trying.'

'I like the bloke, but I've been around the block enough to tell there's a lot going on for that man upstairs – literally, as well as metaphysically.' She tapped the side of her head.

'I hear you. Yes, what the fuck is going on in that flat of his? Have you been up there? And there's something a bit odd about the Cross Barn up here, too.'

'I've no idea. I keep my head down. It's his business and I think it's probably best not to ask. Being honest, I also thought I saw Tyler driving a lorry one night when I was staying late. I'm all about letting people get on with their own shit, though, August. If we were meant to know, then we would.'

'The crime writer in me is intrigued, that's all.'

'All I can say is, if you get too busy in the snooping sense, then you'll be writing at home alone again.'

August frowned. 'What do you mean?'

'Somebody else started asking too many questions, and Max said their contract was no longer tenable.'

'Oh, really?'

Cat nodded.

They reached the crossroads and went over to the padlocked wooden gate, where a short drive led to the Cross Barn. There were a couple of cars parked alongside it.

'Isn't that Mrs G's ancient Volvo?' asked August.

'It looks like it.'

'Listen.' August stood up on the bottom rung and craned her neck towards it. 'It sounds like some kind of machinery whirring away in there.'

All of a sudden, they were startled by the roar of a quad bike approaching at speed. It screeched to a halt by their side.

It was Ivor. 'You ladies go to the farm? Squeeze on with me, I take you both now.'

The women looked at each other. 'Bagsy I go in the middle,' Cat smirked.

Chapter Twenty One

August pulled up on the little concrete drive area in front of her terraced cottage and gathered together her ASDIS bags from the footwell. The road in front of the house was quiet aside from the noise of pigeons cooing and a couple of kids playing on the swings in the park across the road. The sun was going down, leaving a slight chill in the air. Ellie appeared at the front door, a smudge of flour on her cheek. 'I've just made a chicken pie. I'll cut you a slice for your dinner when it's ready, if you fancy it?'

'Lovely. Thanks, sis.'

'All OK with lover boy today?'

August put her carrier bags down on the front step. 'He's gone away, evidently. And I think it's best I don't pry into his private life and just use the Hub for work, not play.'

'That's probably a good idea. So, what you up to this weekend then?'

'Eating chicken pie and watching Gogglebox tonight, by the look of it.'

August's phone beeped with a message.

'You're welcome to have dinner with us, if you want to?'

August scrabbled in her bag for her phone, then grinned as she quickly checked the message. *Pop Pops, Fancy some Friday night fun? You bring the baps; I've got plenty of sausage. Ian* ☺ *x*

'Unless you've just had a better offer, of course?'

'This is all very civilised.' August sipped on her white wine as Sean flicked a beer mat in the air and caught it. The trendy Swinford bar was beginning to fill up with Friday night revellers in anticipation of the live band that was due to come on at eight.

'Well, now I know you're a famous author and not a mere marketing manager, you have my full attention.'

'Mercenary as well as a fantastic fuck – two qualities one must admire in a man.'

Sean laughed. 'I literally couldn't believe it when I saw you at the farm. Thank God I like you, or it could have been just a tad awkward.'

'It was awkward enough for me. What sort of name is Ian, too?' August laughed.

'I was watching football when I filled out my profile. Ian Wright was on as a pundit.'

'Brilliant! That's how I get my character names sometimes, randomly like that.'

'So, how's it been going on Tinder since we met, then?' Sean took a swig from his bottle of San Miguel.

'It hasn't. I've been busy.' August removed a stray hair that had stuck to her lip. She had made an effort tonight. Bodycon dress, with suspenders and stockings underneath, as Sean had said how much he loved a woman in full underwear regalia last time they had slept together. Heels, too, to accentuate her long legs, and a deep red gloss to highlight her rosebud lips.

'Nah, I don't think you've been busy. If you've had the best, why try out the rest, I reckon.' He looked deep into her eyes as he took another swig.

'God, vets and surgeons. Is it because you've studied for so long that you're generally such cocky bastards?'

He grinned. 'You've got to admit there's something quite sexy about a man who changes animals' and people's lives.'

She considered that a moment. 'Maybe I do that with my writing. Change lives, I mean.'

'Which one would you recommend I read, then?'

August smiled inwardly. She much preferred that level of interest to the egotistical character requests. 'Let's see how you perform tonight, and I'll see if you deserve a signed copy or not.'

'I take it you have the full works of Ms A. R. Saunders to hand then.'

'You're incorrigible, Sean Bachelor.'

He flipped the beer mat again. 'I'm not a Bachelor – well, in name, anyway. My surname is Ross. Mum reverted back to her maiden name, thought it more appropriate for the business.'

'I still can't believe that Cat is your mum.'

'Yeah, she looks great for her age, doesn't she?'

'I didn't mean that; I meant the embarrassment of it all.'

'Cheers for that! She thinks we'd get on famously, by the way. Once a matchmaker, and all that. And we can't deny, we did have a laugh the other night.'

August fixed him with a serious look. 'I'm looking for a fuck buddy, Sean. I'm on a deadline. Nothing more, nothing less.'

'Yes, yes, I know that, and quite clearly on the rebound too, after the waterworks last time.'

'Oh, yeah, sorry about that.' She looked away, feeling uncomfortable for the first time that evening. 'You really helped. Can't believe my own mother said this to me, but getting under someone to get over someone seems to have worked.'

'Well, a big thumbs up to both our mums, and I'm glad I

could be of service. I'm all up for the friends with benefits treatment – or FWB, as stated on many a Tinder profile.'

'I didn't even realise what that stood for. Thought it was some strange kink.'

He chuckled. 'You're sweet. Great film that, too, *Friends with Benefits*. But don't be going all Mila Kunis and start falling in love with me.'

The word 'friends' suddenly led her thoughts to Max. But Max clearly didn't want the benefits, had rejected her, and she would be foolish not to enjoy the moment, especially after all the heartache she'd been through. 'Maybe if you looked even remotely like Justin Timberlake,' August smirked. 'But I do have to say it really is a great feeling to realise you're not sad any more about something you thought you would never get over.'

Sean dropped the beer mat he had been playing with, then slowly ran his hand up her leg as he retrieved it. She gasped slightly at his touch. 'Stockings, too? What a good girl you are.'

'So, Sean Ross, do you really want to wait for this band to come on? Because I know what I'd rather be looking at.'

'What's that then, my little bestseller?'

'Your bedroom ceiling, of course.'

'Dirty bitch.'

'You love it. Now drink up and let's get naked.'

Chapter Twenty Two

Monday night, and it was pouring with rain. August shielded her hair with her bag and rang the buzzer to the Sebastian Line centre. She was not expecting the door to be opened by a man whose wrinkle-free face didn't quite match his bright white hair.

'Sorry, was just finishing up a call. I didn't realise the weather. What a gloomy old Monday, especially after such a glorious weekend. Remind me to give you the door code, too.' They made their way into one of the call rooms and she was relieved to be out of the cold.

'So, you must be Geri.'

She stared at him. 'No, August. August Saunders.'

'Not here, you're not. I'm David, Victoria's husband, when I'm taking calls. Mike when I'm not. I didn't realise she hadn't told you your Sebastian Line name yet.'

August grinned. 'Your wife clearly has a sense of humour.'

'Yes, and every single album the Spice Girls ever made. As for humour, you wouldn't think it was appropriate here, but it absolutely is. It's sometimes required in the darkest of times to get us through.'

'Yes, look at all the good comedians – it's the same principle.' August thought for a second then decided to address the elephant in the room. 'I'm so sorry about Sebastian, David.'

He gave her a sad smile. 'Thank you. Thank you so much. The grief still rips through us like a tornado. It's not like we have any other kids to concentrate on. We always wanted just the one. He was such a good kid.'

'I'm sure he was.'

'Right!' David then said with a sudden, deliberate exuberance. 'Let's get us a cup of something before we take a call. And, sorry, meant to say, you're with me today as Darc...I mean, Victoria, isn't feeling great. Bloody menopause. I don't cover often but if the boss summons me, I do as I'm told.'

'Ah, poor her.'

'She's all right, she's on that UHT stuff now. Feels much better for it, evidently. Just not this evening.'

August didn't feel it was the time or place to correct him; just tried her hardest to keep a straight face.

Ring, ring, ring, ring...

'Shit.' David bolted back through from the kitchen. 'Finish making my coffee can you, Geri, please. Lots of milk, two sugars, then pick up the headphones when you're ready.' He threw the headphones on. 'The Sebastian Line, David speaking. Is there a name I can call you by?'

'Hello Barbara.' David listened intently for a bit. 'Yes, yes, they are like family, aren't they? And fifteen, what a great old age for a Chihuahua.'

August put the two cups of coffee down on the desk and sat to her fellow volunteer's side, pulling the headphones on as she did so, so she could hear both voices. Barbara was sobbing. 'He was my baby. It was six years ago today. He just fell asleep on my bed, peaceful as anything.' The sobbing continued.

'Yes, that's so sad.' His voice sounded strange, and August glanced over at him. 'But he wasn't your baby, was he really,

Barbara? He was a dog, and he lived a long and happy life by the sound of it.'

August cringed at the man's distinct lack of empathy. Barbara's voice took on a more aggressive tone. 'I thought you would care about my little Fluffy, but clearly you don't. You're supposed to help.' The phone went down with a clunk. David reached for his coffee, then retrieved a hip flask from his trouser pocket and poured what smelt like whisky into it with a shaking hand.

'Oops, it's a good job Victoria isn't here – that wasn't my finest moment. Don't mention you saw that, either.' He patted the pocket where the hip flask had come from, and took a deep, measured breath. 'OK, this is a good lesson, Geri. I haven't done that for a while. We don't bring our past in here with us. We all have triggers, but we can't act on them. That person on the end of the phone, whoever they are, needs us. However trivial their problem may seem, they've rung us for a kind voice, whatever they need to get them through. Not everyone in life has had any kind of terrible thing happen to them, so if their internet goes down the same time as a bulb blows, it can throw people into some kind of panic. I even had a bloke the other week ranting that he couldn't get through to the tax office and it was affecting his nerves.'

'If I ever feel triggered, I'll just keep looking at the poster above the phone. "Listen with Love, Speak without Judgement",' August stated.

'Exactly. You'll be fine. Just remember, it's not about you, ever. It's all about them. We can't fix people, but we can hopefully help untangle their moment, whatever it may be.'

'It must be so hard for you sometimes,' August said, feeling an almost painful level of sympathy for the man.

'It's hard for all of us. I do struggle though, with some of the calls, as it's kids like Sebastian I want to be here for and God, I really have helped a couple, I know that.' She saw tears well up in his eyes. 'I'm not a monster, honest. Well, unless I get a bloke pleasuring himself – then you should hear me.'

August smiled nervously.

Ring, ring, ring...

'Another one! It's only six-thirty, it's going to be a busy shift, I can feel it.' David took a slurp directly from his hip flask this time.

August took a short intake of breath when she heard a young girl's voice at the end of the phone. David's face turned serious.

'How old are you, Claire?'

'Eighteen. You don't tell anyone, do you...about talking to you, I mean?'

'No, this is a confidential, non-judgemental space and I'm here to listen.' David's voice was soft and comforting.

'I feel like I don't want to be here any more.'

David's voice was surprisingly calm. 'I'm by your side and I'm not going anywhere. What do you mean exactly, when you say that?' August felt tears stinging her eyes. 'Make some notes,' the white-haired man mouthed to her.

When David needed to be good, he was brilliant – and who was she to judge him for being a bit short with the woman who'd lost her dog years ago and needing a sneaky shot to get him through? He had lost a child far too soon, so in her humble opinion, he was allowed to be as grumpy as he liked.

Chapter Twenty Three

'Hot, not, sandwich or pizza?'

'If the lovely Mr Ronson is paying, I'd like pizza today, please, Beryl. Something hot and spicy, just like me.' August had broken her own friends-with-benefits rule and stayed the whole night with Sean for the first time the previous night, and was feeling particularly sprightly, if slightly hungover.

'That's nice – a full house for pizza today, then.'

'You're in a jaunty little mood today, August.' Jonah was in the kitchen doing his daily word puzzle. 'That's not even in the dictionary, is it?' He threw his phone on to the table, then huffed loudly. 'Bloody hell. Right. That's it. I'm not doing it tomorrow.'

'You so know you will.' August looked over his shoulder. 'I've purposely not got involved, for fear of addiction. A daily word quiz – wish I'd thought of that. Such a clever concept in this new world of bingeing everything we can get our hands on.'

Tyler walked in, smiling. 'Puts a new spin on playing hard to get, doesn't it? Although not sure anyone does that any more with internet dating being so throw-away.' He acknowledged August with one of his legendary winks. 'How's the new bestseller coming along, then?'

'Tyler Trinder, there are two things you must never ask an

author. One: how's the writing going? And two: can I be in your book?'

'It came from Reece, not me. Take your time. Believe me, I'm not ready for another sex ban any time soon.' The lad laughed, grabbed a coffee then headed back out to the main office.

'I must get on, too.' Jonah got up, stretched and went to fill his water bottle.

'All right, boss,' August heard him say, and her head whipped around.

'Jonah,' said Max. 'Good to see you mate.'

'Agatha.'

'Max.' She was annoyed at feeling herself redden and her heartbeat rising. Why did her feelings have to show themselves when her mind was doing its very best not to play ball? She looked out of the kitchen window to catch a smart white Audi SUV with the personal number plate CORA13 heading back up to the security gate.

'Have you missed me, writer girl?' He dumped his wheelie case in the middle of the doorway.

She turned back to him and smiled. 'Like the deserts miss the rains.'

He smiled back. 'That much, eh?'

'You're always away.' Damn! Why had her mouth let that escape too?

'Busy man.'

'Where did you go?'

'Not far.'

'Not far enough, clearly.' August shook her head at him. 'I don't know why I bothered asking – you'd never tell me in a million years. And I don't actually care.' She got herself a coffee, then flounced off to a private office and pulled the black blind down. She opened and switched on her laptop, found the word

171

document for *A Christmas Mystery in Futtingbrook Fallow* and began typing:

Lila Lovelace stared into the molten brown eyes of the farmer's son. 'You were the only one who could have been in the stables the night of the murder.'

Even as she said it, she thought to herself that she must stop this fetish of fancying every suspected felon.

'I was in Majorca, Detective Lovelace. You need to get your facts right, love.'

'What were you doing in Majorca?'

'That's none of your effing business.'

Lila found the handsome, balding man's swearing a real turn-on. 'Did you love her? Elise, I mean. And do you have proof?'

Marie McGee shook her head in dismay at her haphazard partner's line of questioning.

'Satisfaction guaranteed or take your love back.' The suspect sang in fine tune. 'Proving love ain't a science, last time I looked, is it?' The man threw back his head and guffawed.

Lila's lips twitched. 'If only it was. I mean, don't be silly – not that kind of proof.'

'I've got a duty-free receipt if that 'elps. Much cheaper getting her Christmas present that way.'

'You went all the way to Spain to get Elise McGill a gift and then killed her?'

'Give over, blondie. She was my bird. Of course, I got her a present.'

'So, who were you with on holiday?'

'I was on my own. I told ya.'

'You're confusing me now, Mr Jaggard.'

'It doesn't take fecking much.' Marie McGee whispered *under her breath.*

August was so engrossed in her writing that she didn't even notice Max sneak in and close the door behind him.

'You look really cute when you're concentrating.' August nearly jumped out of her skin and accidentally deleted a chunk of what she'd written.

'Fucking hell, Max, you scared me. What do you want? I'm mid-flow.'

'I could tell.' August took in the handsome face of the man on whom she had quite clearly based Isiah Jaggard, the baddy of her Christmas mystery.

'Have I made the grade yet?'

She didn't want to offer him any kind of flattery. 'How many times, Max? I only put people in I don't like.'

'I'll take that as a compliment. You won't mind me asking if you fancy coming out with me one night, then? I know you said you were struggling finding stuff to do around here and…well, seeing as we are now friends.'

August regarded him uncertainly. 'I'm not sure.'

'Not sure you can resist me again, you mean.'

August cocked her head to the side. Her immediate mental response that that was exactly what she was scared of was swiftly overtaken by the one that came out of her mouth: 'Get over yourself, Max.'

'Agatha. Come on. A mate of mine has invested in a new little wine bar opening in the high street next Friday. I said I'd support him. We can pretend we're in Soho for the night without the commute or commotion.'

'Relentless.' August shook her head.

'I told you: mind quick as a Ferrari, brakes of a bike.'

She congratulated herself on having such a good go at resisting, but knew she'd reached her limit. 'OK,' she relented. 'But I'm driving.'

'Deal. And totally understandable you not trusting yourself to drink with me again.'

She felt her cheeks flame red. 'I didn't say—'

Max laughed and stood up from the desk. 'I've started reading your *Love, Lies and Lupins*, by the way. More sex required, if you ask me.'

Not wanting to show how flattered she was that he had bothered to pick up one of books, she replied brightly, 'I don't recall that I did. Now, go! I need to get on.'

'Pizzas at one sharp.'

'Lovely. Now please kindly bugger off and shut the door behind you.'

He shut it then opened it again and stuck his head back around. 'I love it when you're bossy.'

She gently threw her pen at him, just missing his grinning face.

Chapter Twenty Four

'Are you not going into the Hub today, then? I thought you always went in on a Monday.' Ellie puffed and panted as she tried to keep up with August, who was marching ahead in the Bluebell Wood.

'I can't hear you properly.'

Ellie was now not only red with breathlessness but also annoyance. 'Well bloody slow down, then. I was already carrying an extra stone before bloody Grant added the baby.'

'Sorry.' August eased off and kept pace with her sister, who repeated herself. 'I'm going in later. I need to concentrate on house hunting this morning.'

'Oh god, I feel so guilty about taking your place over. But honestly, there is no rush.'

'Guilt is such a wasted emotion, Ells. It's fine. And looking at your tummy, the timescale is obvious.'

'She is a big baby, I reckon.'

'Bless. I'm quite excited now, for a change of home. And Madame Fleurot may have her faults, but she got me a bloody brilliant advance for the next three books, so I figured, put it into property, rather than it just sitting in the bank.' August grinned. 'I can't believe I'm getting sensible in my old age.'

Ellie made a screeching noise. 'Wow, you're buying somewhere? That's amazing! Please say you're staying around here. I'll be so happy if you do, Goose.'

'Yes. Well, I'm looking as far out as Lower Gamble. The peace around here is really helping with my writing. Not to mention the benefits of being in the area where my books are set.'

'Us mere mortals don't think of things like that,' Ellie laughed. 'Oh, for some peace. Maybe I'll come and live with you at weekends and Grant can have the kids.'

'We can do that.' August was thoughtful for a second. Or you can look after it for me if I do decide to go back to London, maybe? I always had the dream of a chocolate-box cottage with a stream running past the end of my garden, and roses growing up the side, if I'm honest.'

'You and half the country, I expect.' Ellie smiled. 'So does this mean you're definitely not moving back to London? Yay!' Ellie did a little jig on the spot, causing both her boobs and baby bump to jiggle at the same time.

August looked at her sister fondly. 'You're crazy. Never say never. Whatever happens, this gives me options. If I do decide to go back London, then I'll have somewhere I can rent out, or even Airbnb, which would cover my rent, so it's a win-win.'

'Well, me and bump and the boys and Colin are all willing you to stay here. Mum will be too – she was just asking this morning what you were up to.'

August tutted. 'I must go and see her this week. I've had so much going on.'

'Look at you, Miss Busy Pants. It was only a few weeks ago you were crying you had nothing to do.'

'I know. Be careful what you wish for, and all that.'

'How's the vet?'

'Hot.'

Ellie gave her a sideways glance. 'You've been seeing a lot of him, haven't you?'

'Too much, really, for someone who's supposed to be purely for mutual sexual gratification.'

'Maybe he could be more than that?'

August shook her head emphatically. 'No. It is what it is with him. He's Mr Right Now, not Mr Right.'

'Does Cat know you're seeing him?'

'Not as far as I know. Give her her dues, if she does, she hasn't mentioned a thing since she said we'd be good together. I do feel a bit bad not telling her but sometimes I think it's OK to keep things back. My philosophy is that we don't have to tell everyone all of our business, especially if it doesn't affect them directly.'

'I agree. I don't tell Mum everything if I think it will worry her unnecessarily.'

'Same,' August nodded.

'But don't stop yourself with Sean because you're scared of getting hurt, though, will you, August? Go with your feelings.'

'It's not like that. I'm keeping my options open.' She took a deep breath. 'Actually, Max has asked me out. There's a new wine bar opening in Futtingbrook High Street, apparently.'

Ellie's head whipped around, but August's gaze remained fixed on the bluebells. 'Ah, so here lies the real reason.'

'No, it's as friends. I'm not going to lie; whatever he says or does, I still feel attracted to him. But I'm going to be a grown-up and realise that not everyone we fancy is right for us to be with.'

'Bloody hell, Goose. What's happened to you?'

She shrugged. 'I feel like I wasted years with Scott. And if I do decide to go down the kids route, I need to get a move on – and with the right man.'

'So how does Sean fit with that, then?'

'He's not stopping me finding someone else – I am. You know what I'm like when I'm writing – I haven't got time to make the effort. If anything, he's acting as a useful block, stopping me from succumbing to the charms of Mr Ronson.'

'Can I just rewind a second there? Kids? Shit, that's the first time you've ever said you wanted them. What's going on?'

'Maybe I'm just growing up, eh, baby sister. I can't just drift forever in an imaginary world, living vicariously through my characters.'

'That sounds like a perfect life to me.' Ellie stopped and put her hands on her ample hips, puffing loudly. 'And give yourself a break, you haven't even been single for a year yet.'

'Yeah, you're right. I'm happy now, though. I've also started volunteering at the Sebastian Line.'

Ellie stared at her as though she'd just sprouted another head. 'Wow, you really are busy.'

'I'm not going to say much about it though, as it's confidential, you know. I've just started training and I want to make it work.'

'Aw, I'm so bloody proud of you, Goose.'

'Don't think too well of me, sis. I'm doing it for me, too.'

'And that's OK.' Ellie gave her sister a massive, sweaty kiss on the cheek. 'Awww. I think I'm going to cry.'

'Oh, stop it.' August started laughing. 'You're so funny. How're you feeling, anyway?'

'At this moment in time, bloody knackered. Can we head back home, please?' Ellie checked her watch and groaned. 'I was hoping I could fit in a cheeky nap before I pick the little terrors up from nursery and they start rampaging again.'

'Come on. We're so lucky living here and it's lovely and warm today. Smells like summer is on its way, too.'

The women wandered back towards the car park.

'When are you going out with Max, then?'

'This Friday.'

'Ah, OK. Mum mentioned that wine bar. Mrs Dye told her some bloke from London had taken it on. Evidently the locals weren't too happy that an interloper had taken the lease. It'll be interesting to see how it does.'

'Like anything, if it's a good place to go, people forget the controversy and embrace it. And it's one of Max's friends, so I'm interested to see what he's like.'

Ellie's voice became uncharacteristically serious. 'You will be careful with him, won't you?'

'Don't worry. I'm keeping Mr Red Flag tightly on his flagpole.'

'Good. He may be handsome, but he smells of trouble, that one.'

'And Tom Ford, which seems to be much more of a problem.'

Laughing, the sisters pushed open the kissing gate and headed up the single lane track towards home.

It was a blustery but warm May afternoon as August drove through the security gate and towards the Hub. She noticed a woman in a wheelchair with a large sketchpad on her lap up close to one of the meadow fences. Wearing a large white floppy sun hat, a navy jumpsuit and white designer pumps, the woman looked far younger than her seventy-five years. The alpacas were milling around nosily as the woman deftly moved her pencil around the page.

Driving past slowly, so as not to disturb her, August gave the artist a quick wave. Just then, a slight gust of wind took the woman's hat and it landed right on the Mini's bonnet. August pulled over to the side and walked back up to the woman she assumed, from her previous conversation with Ade, must be the

Ronson boys' mother.

'Oh, hello dear.' She was tiny, August noticed, with a youthful and serene beauty to her face. Her voice was quite posh, far removed from the local twang August had been expecting. Her hair was styled in an immaculate silver-grey short bob. Holding her hand out, she smiled, 'Judith Ronson. I take it you work with one of my boys?'

'I'm August. I rent space at the Hub. Here.' She shook the sun hat and handed it over. 'Thankfully, just a bit of dust, now all that mud has dried up.'

'Thank you, dear. I don't really understand what my Max is doing. I mean a hub. What is a hub?' Judith put the hat back on. 'All this fancy wording. Why can't he just call it an office, like everyone else? I don't get it, but if it's working for him, and he's happy, then we're all happy.'

'It must be lovely to have both your sons so near you, Mrs Ronson.'

'Do call me Judith, and yes, I suppose it is now, especially after losing my Tony and, well, since…since the accident that left me in this bloody chair. Ade is the spit of him, you know. My husband, I mean. I sometimes have to take a second glance.'

Deciding that now wasn't the time for her inquisitive mind to enquire about the accident, August peered at the art pad, instead. 'Wow, that's an amazing sketch.'

'Thank you. It's for my boy's birthday. Forty-one on the first of June, he is.'

'Oh, I thought his birthday was on Valentine's Day?'

'Max's is, yes. This is for Ade.'

'Ah, right.' August's mind started to whirr, she was sure Max had said he has just turned forty-one this year, too. How weird. She must have misheard him.

'OK. I need to concentrate, dear, get this done while I still have some sunlight. It was lovely to meet you, August.' She distinctly looked her up and down. 'And don't you be taken in by any claptrap from that younger son of mine. His bark is far worse than his bite and his heart is bigger than a lion's, if he ever cared to show it to anyone.'

Chapter Twenty Five

'The Sebastian Line, Geri speaking. Is there a name I can call you by?'

Darcy fiddled with her headphones then put her thumb up and nodded furiously at August. This was her second training shift this week and she was already beginning to feel more confident.

'It's Emily. I'm so sorry to call you, but I just need someone to talk to.'

'That's OK. I'm here to listen.'

'It will probably sound silly to you, but it's the first anniversary of my mum dying today and I'm struggling.'

'Do you mind me asking how old you are?'

'I'm nineteen.'

August put her hand to her heart, then blew out a big breath. This was the call she had been waiting for where she could offer so much but was also so worried that digging into the depths of her own grief might cause her not to be able to hold it together.

'How are you struggling, Emily? Tell me.'

'Just wishing she was here, really. I passed my driving test this morning and she was the first person I wanted to tell. I miss her so much.' The teenager burst into tears. August looked to the ceiling and took a deep breath. Darcy put her hand on her shoulder and mouthed, 'You OK?' August nodded.

'Your driving test, you say? Well done you, that's a great achievement.'

'Thank you,' Emily replied softly.

'Do you have people to talk to when you're feeling like this? Friends and family?'

'My dad and my brother Callum, but I don't like to upset them. I love them very much.'

'Sometimes they might surprise you, you know. Grief has no script, I'm afraid. Rears its scary head up on days like these and then, when you least expect it, trickles in like a tiny stream. It does get easier though.'

'Did somebody you know die too, then?'

'We're not here to talk about me, Emily, but I do understand. I understand very well.'

'It's so difficult.'

'Yes, it truly is, and I am so sorry you are hurting.'

'You do get it.' The girl started to cry again. 'That means a lot.'

August sniffed back her own tears and looked up at Darcy, who also had tears in her eyes but put her thumb up for her trainee to carry on. 'Don't be scared to share your feelings with others who love and understand you, and who knew your mum. And you can call us, too. We're open every night from six pm through until six am the next morning.'

'That makes me feel a lot better, thank you so much.'

'Good. So, have you got a car to whizz around in now, then?'

'Yes, I'm so excited. My mum saved five pounds a week for me and my brother since the day we were born and invested it for what she called happy days, just like these.'

August bit her lip. 'How truly lovely is that? She sounds like a real-life angel, who is still looking after you even though you can't see her.'

'I hadn't thought about it like that.'

'She will always be part of you and from what little I know of you, enormously proud of you, too.'

The girl sniffed. 'Geri, I think I'm going to go now. I feel so much better for talking to you.' She hung up.

August started to cry. Darcy went to the kitchen and came back with a glass of water and a sheet of kitchen roll.

'You were brilliant.'

August took the kitchen roll with a grateful glance. 'Look at me, crying like a baby.'

'We're all human and what you said will stick with Emily forever now. We can rarely fix people, just help them step out of a moment. And she knows she can ring again, if she needs us. You're going to make a wonderful volunteer.'

August blew her nose. 'Thank you. I really want to do it.'

'Fantastic! Being honest, I think one more session and I am happy to let you take calls on your own. How do you feel about that?'

'Slightly nervous but I know there is massive support here, so I'm not on my own really. So, yes, I very much want to do it.'

'Great. Have you received your DBS Certificate?'

'Yes, sorry I forgot to tell you last time.' August nodded.

'Good, and David said you listened in to a suicidal caller the other day, too, so you have an idea of what's to come, without any form of sugar coating. If it helps, I think you're a natural, though; you really are.'

'That's kind of you to say.' August felt a rush of warmth go through her. 'And yes, I've taken loads of notes, too.'

'Well done. Every call is of course different and if you don't have anyone shadowing you, you can text any one of us and we can be here in minutes should you need extra help, or for me to call an ambulance.'

This gave August a sudden, sobering reality check as to how important being at the end of this phone really was. Darcy checked her watch. 'I'm hungry. Waitrose is open until eight, I think, so there's just time to go and grab a sandwich. Do you fancy anything?'

'Just a packet of ready salted crisps and a smoothie of some sort, please.' August reached for her purse.

'Don't worry, I'll get it. You can get the next one.'

As the door shut, August checked her phone and saw two missed calls from Sean and a message: *Where are you my little bestseller? You're so elusive this week... I'm beginning to think you've found a new toy...*

She wasn't ready to divulge anything about her volunteering work yet as, despite liking him and having given him privy knowledge of every inch of her body, she still hardly knew him. She hovered over her reply. A little white lie wouldn't hurt: *Writing has really tired me out, so a night in with Prince Harry and reruns of* Friends *for me. You OK?*

'Now I've heard from you I am ☺ How about Friday? A night in with a horny vet and reruns of what we did last Thursday?

The centre phone ringing made her jump, and she threw her mobile back in her bag. 'The Sebastian Line, Geri speaking. Is there a name I can call you by?'

185

Chapter Twenty Six

'Thursday night always used to be Toad-in-the-Hole night when your dad was alive.'

'Did it now, Mother? I'm not sure I really need that level of information.' August raised her eyebrows in mock horror.

Pamela Saunders laughed and tutted. 'August Rose, behave yourself. You're just like your dad, you are. He used to love all that classic Carry On film-type humour.'

'Aw. He was so funny, wasn't he?' August could feel Barney creeping nearer her feet in hope of some sausage and batter titbits. The stable door out to the garden of Orchard Cottage was open, letting in the soft May breeze and the soothing noises of early evening bird song and chatter.

August noticed her mother looked more vibrant than she had seen her in a long time. 'You look nice.'

'I had my hair coloured today; it was such a treat.'

'It really suits you. We could pass as sisters now.'

'Hardly, but I'll take that. Do you want some ketchup with that?'

'Yes please. I'll get it.' August stood up and went to the fridge.

'I love having both my girls near me. I would never stand in your way – you know that. But it's great having you around. It has really lifted me.' August noticed that her mother did look younger, almost serene.

'Aw, Mum. Same.'

'We'll be able to start eating al fresco soon. I'll keep an eye on the forecast. With Flaming June on the way, I was thinking I could have you all over for a barbecue in a couple of Sundays' time, maybe? If you're not busy, that is.'

'That would be lovely.'

'Your sister tells me you've started volunteering. I'm so proud of you, darling.'

August stuck out her bottom lip, then huffed loudly. 'Oh. Did she now? I wanted to tell you myself.'

'You know what she's like. Don't you remember? She let slip to Mrs Dye that she was pregnant first time around. It carried on the Upper Gamble gossip grapevine and the vicar had the christening in his diary before even Grant, me or you had any idea.'

'You can make light of it, but she really annoys me sometimes.'

'Be kind. Eleanor doesn't have as much going on to talk about as you do.' Pam lifted her tone to try and break the tension and the subject. 'How's it all going with the volunteering, anyway?'

'Great. It's rewarding and emotional and tiring all at the same time. I really do hope that I am helping in some way.'

'Well, that's lovely dear. I'm sure you are. And well done. Oops, I forgot to offer you wine.'

'No, I'm good with just water, thanks. I'll save it for tomorrow. There's a new wine bar opening in Futtingbrook.'

'Lovely, you're getting out too. That makes me happy. Who are you going with?'

'Oh, just someone from the Hub.'

'Ooh, does that someone happen to be Max Ronson, by

chance?'

'Mum! Yes, but we are just friends.' Just saying the word 'friends' didn't feel right. They were clearly more than friends, but what she felt they had couldn't be labelled. Not at the moment, anyway.

'If you say so, dear.'

'I do.'

'OK, good – because I've always believed that whatever level of help they may get, a troubled child will always take with them a troubled soul.' Pam began to move her food around the plate, without touching it. She then sighed heavily.

'What's up, Mum?'

'Oh, August Rose, I've done something terrible and you're going to be cross with me.' Pam's face looked pained.

'It can't be that bad.' August wiped her mouth on the floral serviette her mother had just handed her.

'It was talking of reputations that's reminded me.'

'Go on.'

'Scott phoned.'

'He phoned here, you mean?' August felt alarm mixed with annoyance sweep over her.

'Yes,' Pam muttered.

'I take it you didn't tell him where I was living?' August suddenly felt a little shaky. 'And surely, he still has my mobile number, so why call you?'

'Well, you know how well we used to get on; he said he was phoning for a chat to see how I was and – well, I might have told him where you are living.'

'Oh, Mum!' August exclaimed but then, clocking the horrified look on her mother's face, softened her tone. 'It's OK, that's fine. He's engaged and looks happy so he's hardly going to just pitch up now, is he? How did he sound?'

'Like he always used to, our old chatty Scott.' August suddenly felt a pang of loss among her swirling emotions. How dare he raise his head when she was just getting herself together again? Pam looked like she might cry. 'I'm sorry, darling, but I also let slip you were volunteering and working out of the Hub too.'

'Bloody hell, Mum! I didn't want him knowing anything about my new life. Wanted to let him wonder.' August ran her hands through her hair. It annoyed her that she was feeling this way. Scott Scanlan had wrong-footed her enough already.

'Well I just felt he should know how well you are doing without him. I was civil and didn't speak long. My loyalties are with you, my darling, of course, and damn me for saying too much! Silly old woman.'

'Don't say that. It is what it is, and you've done it now.' August pushed her dinner plate away from her with a touch too much force. 'It's OK, honestly, Mum. He is a wanker though, isn't he? I'm just getting my life back together and he peeps over the parapet in true Scott Scanlan style. Just letting me know he's still there. If he thinks I'm a back-up plan if things don't work out with Delila the Dog, then he can fuck off.'

'August Rose!'

'Sorry, Mum, it's just got my back up, that's all. Wheedling in again via a back door.' She took a deep, shaky breath. 'Actually, can I have that glass of wine, please?'

It was eight-thirty when August returned home from her mum's. She threw her keys on the side, fed a miaowing Prince Harry, went to the fridge and poured herself a cold glass of Sauvignon. Two glasses of wine on a week night was a lot for her these days, but knowing that Scott had phoned had knocked her for six. Seven years was a long time to be with someone. Seven years of memories, a lot to just pack away and forget. A lot of those years had been great and, in hindsight, if she hadn't thrown herself so much into her writing, maybe he wouldn't have strayed. Maybe it had been all her fault?

She was just about to flop onto the sofa and switch on the TV when she heard a car pull up in front of her little driveway. Sneaking a peek under the blind, she saw a black Range Rover there and her heart began to pound.

How awkward that both the men showing interest in her had the same car. It was like a lucky dip as to who was going to knock on her door. Checking herself in the hall mirror she readied herself for the doorbell.

'The vet or the vagabond – who do you reckon eh, Prince Harry?' The ginger tom raised an uninterested ear at the mention of this name.

When she saw who it was, she felt a swoop of disappointment. 'Sean. What are you doing here?'

'I wanted to see you.'

August could sense that Ellie's curtains were twitching.

'I've just been to my mum's for food and was going to have an early night.'

'I won't stay long. It's just you didn't answer my message yesterday. I was worried.'

'Shit, sorry. I totally forgot. Come in. Glass of wine?'

'Have you got a beer?'

'No, wine or wine – that's it.'

'Nice gaff.' Sean began to look around. 'I was beginning to think you had a man stashed away in here.'

August handed over his drink and yawned loudly. 'I should be so lucky.'

Prince Harry was fully stretched out on the sofa. Sean leant down and stroked his head gently. 'Who's this fine fella of a feline then?'

'Prince Harry. He's loving his new country life.'

'Prince Harry! What a cool name for a ginger cat. Ouch!' Sean jumped back as the moggy, annoyed at being disturbed, scratched his hand, then leapt off the sofa and ran upstairs.

August laughed. 'Oops, sorry. He can be a moody little sod sometimes.' After a moment's slightly awkward silence, she said, 'Anyway, Sean Ross, as much as I'd love to entertain you, I'm knackered and really not up for anything other than sleep.'

'Oh. Not just the cat who's moody, I see.' The tall blonde put his wine down on the side, put his arms around August's waist and went to kiss her neck. She wriggled away from him. 'My little bestseller, what's wrong?'

'Honestly, nothing's wrong.' August reached for her wine and downed half of it. She could feel her hackles rising. 'It's...er... just a bit weird you showing up here without warning, that's all. And I've just had some news about my ex and...I kind of just want to be on my own tonight.'

'OK, OK. I get the message.' Sean, reaching for his wine, accidentally knocked it to the floor.

'For fuck's sake!' August ran to the kitchen to get a cloth.

'Give it to me. Shit, sorry, I'll clear it up.'

'Just go, Sean.'

'So, tomorrow night?'

'I'm busy.'

'Saturday, then?'

'Maybe. Look, let's keep in touch. I thought friends with benefits meant we don't have to plan ahead like this.'

'No, no, you're so right, I'm sorry.' Sean headed to the front door. 'I'll see you, soon.' He blew her a kiss, hurried to his car, then screeched off, causing her to grimace and Prince Harry to appear and start winding his way around her legs as if to console her. Picking him up and putting him over her shoulder in the weird way he loved, she sighed and snuggled into his fur. 'And there was him telling me not to go all Mila Kunis on him, hey, boy?'

Chapter Twenty Seven

'Hot, not or sandwich?'

'Beryl, what about pizza? It's Friday.' Jonah was pouring over his daily word game as August arrived and headed for the coffee machine.

'Max isn't here.'

August looked up at her.

'Oh, where is he, then?' asked Jonah. 'And I don't know why you can't just pay, and get him to pay you back.'

Beryl George harrumphed. 'He's meeting a man about a rabbit, and you know it doesn't work like that. Now, what do you both want?'

'I want pizza.' Jonah laughed. 'The vegan one they do is so tasty.'

'I heard a joke about a vegan the other day. Now, what was it?'

'Mrs G, if you're going to be mean I don't want to hear it.' Jonah fiddled with his hearing aids.

'Oh yes! This is it. Have you heard the one about the pessimistic German vegan?' She left far too long a pause, for effect. 'He always feared the Wurst.' Beryl's pendulous breast bounced as she laughed to herself.

August stifled a grin. 'Come on, Jonah, you have to admit you've heard…worst.' August then burst out laughing. He remained mute, an expression of injured dignity on his face.

'Hot, not or sandwich, young August?' Mrs G bellowed, making August jump.

'Not for me, thank you.' August took a sip of her scalding drink. 'I'm going home at lunchtime.' She didn't want to convey that she was actually going to the hairdressers for a cut and blow dry and to get her nails manicured before her night out with Max.

Cat appeared, looking slightly jaded, quickly followed by Tyler. 'Jesus, Big Cat, you've been burning that candle, haven't you girl?'

'I might have been.' August noticed that Cat was decidedly grey around the gills.

'You have to tell us who with, now.' August bent down and picked up the flapjack that had just clonked into the snack machine drawer.

Cat leant over Jonah's shoulder and, gleefully sabotaging his word game, shouted, 'TIGHT.'

He turned to glare at her. 'I can't believe you just did that.'

'I was helping you, Jonah.' Cat went to the snack machine, got herself two Diet Cokes and started to drink one down straight from the can, as fast as the bubbles would allow her.

'My one pleasure of the day.' Jonah harrumphed, turning his hearing aids off and staring back at his screen.

Tyler tapped him on the shoulder so that Jonah looked up into his face and, clearly, so that Jonah could lip-read, said, 'You need to get out more mate.'

'Fuck off!' Jonah relayed in sign language, causing Cat to guffaw.

'Children,' Cat then said in a calming voice as Jonah and

Tyler stormed off through to the main office.

'Don't tell me you were with the bank manager?' August unwrapped her breakfast.

'I was bored.'

'No way! Cat, read a book or watch TV like anyone else.'

The tall woman laughed. 'I have to say that what he lacks in endowment, he makes up for in effort. He really does makes me laugh, too. Anyway, I forgot my laptop, or I wouldn't have come in. I'm away to Edinburgh tonight to stay with old friends for the weekend.'

'That's nice.'

'Yeah. I've been down south a long time now, but I do miss the old homeland. How about you? What you up to?'

'Umm. Not much. There's a new wine bar opening in town.'

'Oh yes, Max mentioned it. He's going, I think.'

'Er, yes. I'm meeting him there.'

'Excellent. That'll be a laugh – until he hits the spirits, I expect.'

'It'll be fine. I'm driving so if he starts to kick off I can just escape without having to wait hours for an Uber.'

'Oh, yeah, the pluses and minuses of country living – one being having no decent taxi service.' Cat drained every drop from her first can of Coke, then let out an unladylike belch. 'Pardon me. That's better.'

August grimaced. 'Good job the bank manager's not here now. Right, I'd better get some words down.'

'Well, just be mindful of Max and enjoy yourself tonight. I still need to get you together with that boy of mine. He's been so busy lately; I've hardly spoken to him myself.'

Feeling her face colour, August filled her mouth with flapjack to buy herself some time. 'Have a great weekend, Cat.'

'You, too. I want a full report on the new wine bar. I could do

195

with a fresh five-star rural romance hunting ground.'

August was laughing to herself as she walked to a quiet office when a message popped in. It was Darcy Webb.

Geri, I wouldn't normally do this to you at short notice, but my midnight to six am volunteer has cancelled with a sickness bug. Me and Mike have booked a rare weekend away, so is there any chance you can step in? You'll be on your own, but I know you can more than manage.

August rolled her eyes. Sod's law that she actually had plans, but as she wasn't drinking anyway, she could do both. She doubted the wine bar would stay open until midnight and, as it was Saturday tomorrow, she could just get back into bed at six am and catch up on some sleep.

Sure. Have fun. x

You complete angel, thank you SO much. You'll be taking over from Melanie but just in case you need it the door code is 1010SEB. My phone will be on in case you need me. Toodlepip x

Chapter Twenty Eight

'Wit, woo, sister. You look bloody amazing.'

In her cooking-stained jogging bottoms and baggy Nike sweatshirt, Ellie appeared at her front door with an excitable Colin ready for the last of his daily walks around the block.

August's long hair had not only been cut perfectly but also tonged, and now hung in voluminous waves around her shoulders. Her nails looked smart and fresh with their French manicure. She had even put on false lashes and, with her newly applied matt red lips, looked like she could have stepped off a movie set. She wore tight jeans, ankle boots and a black V-neck top to show off her tiny cleavage. The look was topped by a pink faux-fur bomber jacket that matched her colouring perfectly.

'Thanks. I feel like it's the first time I've been properly out out since I moved here.' She gave a slightly nervous laugh.

'Well, have the best time, and I want to hear all about it. Me and my Grant were just saying we could do with a night out ourselves.'

'You know I'll always babysit.'

The blue-and-white Mr Cod van pulled up with a grinning Grant waving out of the window.

'Talk of the devil.' Ellie smiled with love at her doting partner, who took the opportunity to sound out the 'Simply The Best' track he used to attract customers to his fishy wares, and began to dance in his seat to his audience of two.

'Turn that off, you silly sod. You need to either walk Colin or watch the boys for ten minutes.'

'I've got to be parked up at the cricket club by seven-thirty. You know that's my busiest fish stop on a Friday night.'

'I know that. That's why I've summoned you now.'

He jumped out of the van. 'Your wish is my command, my angel. Let me take Mutley here. Have you got some poo bags?'

'On his collar.'

Grant took Colin's lead, causing the Corgi to start running around in circles, barking. 'Look at you, Goose. Dressed to kill.'

'Don't give her ideas, you know what her imagination is like.'

'Who's the lucky fella then?'

'She's meeting Max Ronson.'

'Not like that though,' August added swiftly.

'Good. He's allegedly had more women than me and your sister are going to have babies, that one.'

'Ha, bloody ha.' Ellie mock-swiped him. 'Get off or you'll be late.'

'Yes, my love.' Grant trotted off down the road with Colin at his heels.

'Ells, just so you know, and in case you are worried, I won't be coming home tonight.'

Ellie's head whipped around. 'Crikey, who else have you got lined up, then?'

August laughed. 'Nothing like that, I've got a Sebastian Line shift midnight to six am.'

'You're going to be knackered.'

She shrugged. 'It'll be fine. It's Saturday tomorrow and volunteering isn't always about choosing what's right for you.'

'You're so lovely. I'll make sure I take the kids out in the morning, so they don't disturb you through the wall.'

'Bless. You don't have to do that.'

'Right, I'd better get them ready for bed. Have the best time. Keep your legs closed, Goose, and your wits about you. And good luck with your shift.'

August put her lights on high beam and began to drive down the dark road to Futtingbrook. It was the first time in a while that she felt confident, and she liked it. It was freeing. Life was suddenly on one of its positive paths in its journey of ups, downs and roundabouts. She also had a wonderful feeling of anticipation about meeting Max away from the Hub. Whatever his faults, he did, after all, have the Max appeal.

Checking herself in her rear-view mirror, she tutted. 'Fuck!' One of her eyelashes had fallen off already. She pulled into a layby, put the light on and peered around frantically. She finally found it stuck to the accelerator pedal, now covered in dirt. She swore again, thinking furiously. If she was quick, she could get to ASDIS before it shut; she was sure they sold them there.

Screeching into the car park of the discount superstore, she was surprised by how busy it was. Not wanting to be late for Max, she drove right to the front, and was just parking in a mother-and-baby parking bay when she noticed an attractive blonde woman with a neat bob, wearing a fitted black trouser suit, heading towards the white car next to her. Giving August a filthy look, as if to say, *you ain't got no babies on board*, honey, she drove away, leaving August looking at a reserved space marked STORE MANAGER and wracking her brains as to where she had seen the familiar number plate of CORA13 before.

The wine bar, simply named Jaxon's, was at the very end of Futtingbrook High Street, where the war memorial acted as a roundabout so you could easily head back down the other side. The wide high street was typical of many English market towns, with parking bays running down the middle; unless it was market day of course, when you crammed into the two pay-and-display car parks on offer.

August parked in a bay as close to the wine bar as possible, where her heels would take her easily on the cobbled path and far enough away that Max wouldn't see her arriving. There was nothing worse than walking towards someone and not knowing where to put your face. She put on her new eyelash, reapplied her lipstick and checked her watch – she was just about on time. She took a deep breath and got out of the car.

'Here she is.' Max was having a cigarette at one of the two tables on the pavement outside, with a single ashtray and one large outdoor heater servicing both. She could tell that he had been looking out for her. Noticing that he was already slightly the worse for wear, she inwardly cringed. She had learnt that a drunk Max was not necessarily a nice Max and she had really hoped that they could have a nice evening together and get to know each other a lot better.

'You brush up all right, don't you?' Max grinned. 'I love your jacket. Like a fluffy pink rabbit.'

'You don't look too shabby yourself. New glasses?' August was taken aback at just how handsome he was looking.

'They are my going-out pair.'

'You're so flash.' If she was honest, she liked the fact that he looked after his appearance – one reason she had fancied Scott, also. A good dress sense in a man was important to her.

'I'm such a wanker, you mean,' Max laughed. 'Come on, let's get to the bar. What's your poison?' Max put out his cigarette.

The sensation of him putting his flat hand on her back to usher her inside caused her to flush slightly.

'Just sparkling mineral water and fresh lime for me. I'm driving. I told you.'

'Go on, just the one. There's a gorgeous local sparkling that Jaxon is flogging.'

'No, Max. I can't.'

He rolled his eyes. 'You're no fun.'

'Well, I might as well leave then.' Realising she could be in for a rollercoaster of a night, August half meant this.

He gave her one of his amused smirks. 'Don't you dare go anywhere.'

August looked around her at the other well-dressed clientele. On glancing at the wine list, where the cheapest price tag per glass was nine pounds, and with bottles going up to over a thousand pounds, she realised why.

Max caught the eye of one of the model-looking barmen, who was wearing a black t-shirt and smart black jeans. 'All right, mate. Perrier and fresh lime for the lady, please.'

'So how do you know Jaxon then?' August asked.

'He used to run the wine bar round the corner from where I lived in Holborn. The change in people's working habits lately buggered his lunchtime trade, which regrettably forced him to shut down. He's in the kitchen at the moment, helping his chef out with the canapés. Wants it to be all perfect on opening night.'

'Has he moved from London too, then? This isn't just an investment he's running from afar?'

'He's here to stay if it works out. Him and his missus are living in the flat above here at the moment. I admire him. He fell on his arse but is giving it another go. Now follow me, madame.'

Max led her to a table at the back of the small bar, which it seemed he had reserved. He lit the fancy-looking candle with his lighter. A bottle of the sparkling wine he had mentioned was already sat there in an ice bucket. He poured some into the glass he was holding and clinked it against August's tumbler with a 'Cheers, Agatha. Seven years bad sex if you don't look me right in the eye.' He stared right at her, causing her to laugh out loud.

'You're so pretty when you laugh.'

'I bet you say that to all the girls.'

'Nah, just to all the pretty ones.'

August felt herself blushing, then ignoring what Cat had told her about not asking questions, she turned right into her feisty, straight-talking character, Marie McGee. 'Talking of pretty, how do you know the ASDIS store manager?' Max's face contorted slightly as the unexpected interrogation began. 'That was who you were away with the other week, wasn't it? I saw her car at the Hub.'

'We do a bit of business together – that's all.' Max's face had 'why are you asking?' written all over it.

'Ah, business. I see. And Max, don't worry – you don't owe me any explanation. I just hope you're happy with your little harem.' August sighed deeply.

'What's wrong with you, tonight?' He raised his voice slightly, causing a couple on the next table to turn around, despite the music. Anyone would think you cared.' Max took a huge glug of his drink, then reached for the bottle of fizz. 'But you're right. It's none of your business, and actually it isn't what you think.'

'Jesus, here we go again. If you want to act out like Tony Soprano, carry on. I'm surprised you didn't keep your red Ferrari.' August felt a fire in her belly she had not experienced since she found out Scott had cheated on her.

At the mention of his Ferrari, Max's face suddenly fell. He took a deep breath and jumped up. 'I need a pee. Back in a sec.'

She had just taken a canapé from another ridiculously good-looking waiter when she felt a message buzz in on her phone. It was Sean. *Poppy, sorry about the other night, I don't know what came over me. Let's go back to plain old muffin buttering.* She laughed, feeling suddenly guilty for being slightly off with him since his uninvited visit. And if Max was going to have secret dalliances with other people, why shouldn't she? She replied straight away: *I'd like that*

Later? x

Tomorrow x

Send me a pic of your tits x

She was just replying *No! x* with a smile on her face when Max returned, smelling of a heady and intoxicating mixture of cigarette smoke and Tom Ford.

After one look at her face, he said, 'The vet?'

'It's none of *your* business if it is.'

'Touché.' Max clinked glasses again. 'I'm pissed already.'

'Get some canapés in you.'

'I'd rather have some chips.'

'Ask your mate. I'm sure he'd do you some.'

'He's got enough on his plate. It's fine, I'll stick to my liquid diet, thanks.'

'Well on your bad head in the morning be it.' August suddenly remembered something she'd meant to ask him. 'How old are you, Max?'

'Forty-one, last time I looked.'

'Oh. So how come Ade is the same age as you then? I saw your mum. She told me it was his forty-first birthday coming up.'

Max took another big slurp of his bubbles to stall his answer. 'She's old. She's always getting muddled.'

'She seemed very with it to me, and bless her, being in a

wheelchair. Do you mind me asking what sort of accident she had?'

Max suddenly stood up.

'What the fuck is this August? I've invited you out for a nice evening and I feel like I'm on the set of bloody *Line of Duty*.'

'I'm just trying to make conversation. You know, when two people talk about things that interest them? I'll just shut up, shall I?'

'Yes, bloody shut up.'

She stood up, suddenly furious. 'I don't have to take you talking to me like this. What's the point of going out for the evening if every topic is off-limits? I'm going.' August reached for her coat from behind her.

One of the waiters came over to clear their table and she gave him an apologetic smile. Thanking the tall, smart man behind the bar on her way out – assuming he must be Jaxon – she headed to her car, swiftly followed by a staggering Max.

'Agatha, wait.'

'No, Max. You ask me out, you're on the way to being completely smashed when I arrive, and then you're rude to me. It's not acceptable.'

'I just don't like talking about myself, that's all.'

'I was asking you simple bloody questions. Silly me for being interested in you and your life.'

She checked her watch as Max snapped again. 'Hot date, have you? Why else would you not be drinking on a Friday night?'

'Max, not everyone is the same as you, you know.'

He hiccupped. 'Agatha, Agatha, boring but hot little writer girl.'

August sighed. 'Just stop it, Max.' She checked her phone. It seemed crazy to drive home and come back to Futtingbrook again, but it was way too early to go to the Sebastian Line centre.

'Can you give me a lift back to the farm?'

'No. Get yourself a bloody taxi.'

He groaned. 'You know how hard that is around here.'

'You'll be fine. It's not that late.'

August looked at Max's handsome and now somewhat sad-looking face and remembered the words of her wise younger sister: 'Where there is anger, there is almost always pain underneath.' She softened.

'OK, but you need to get in, right now.'

As they reached the main security gate to the farm, Max pressed a button on his phone, and they opened automatically. 'Spooky down here at night, isn't it?'

'It really is.'

'Boo!' Max said loudly, right in August's ear, causing the little red Mini to go off the lane and on to the grassy area. He started to laugh uncontrollably.

'Max! Stop it!'

As they approached the barn it was as if every spotlight at Wembley was now lighting their path. August checked her watch again as her drunk companion struggled to get out of the car. As he lifted his arm to wave goodbye, he somehow fell out of the seat, ending up on the gravel outside the Hub's main door on his hands and knees.

August huffed but, not wanting to leave him in this state, she got out.

'I blame the fresh air,' Max slurred, his scuffed right palm bleeding.

'Not the copious amount of local wine, then,' August muttered. 'Where are your keys?'

He looked down at his jeans pocket. She reached for them, and he put his hand over hers. 'You just need a code. But see, I knew you wanted to touch me.'

'Max!'

He meandered over to the keypad. 'I can do it.'

'Let me just see you upstairs, then I really have to go.'

'Agatha just wants to kiss the bad boy again, don't you, Agatha?'

'Not when the bad boy's in this state, she doesn't.'

'Honey, honey, honey, must mean money in a rich man's world.' He sang out of tune.

'What are you on about?'

'I need to pay the money, honey.' Max made a noise between a laugh and groan. 'The door code is 6661XO, because I'm devilishly handsome.'

As she opened the door, the alarm started buzzing.

'Quick, Agatha, don't call the police.' He giggled childishly. 'The alarm code is 6662XO. It's in the kitchen. I like you like XO.' Max sang a line from the Beyoncé track, which August realised had been playing at Jaxon's as they left. She managed to manoeuvre him into the lift as he carried on relaying distorted lyrics. 'You better kiss me before our time runs out, Agatha?'

'What are you on about?'

'Beyoncé,' Max slurred.

'Max, my mission here is purely to get you on to your bed safely.'

'Ow, my hand.' He put his bleeding palm to his lips.

Without another word, August pressed the lift code, which she had, amazingly, memorised from before and they reached the top floor and his messy living space. She helped him to the bed.

'Sit there, I've got some wet wipes in my bag,' she ordered.

'You'd look great in a nurse's uniform, Agatha.'

August was just dabbing at his hand when Max fell back on the bed and began snoring like a warthog.

Leaving his bedside light on and making sure he was lying on his side and that a half-empty bottle of water from her handbag was right next to him, she checked the time again. She still had plenty of it to get back to the Sebastian Line centre. It was fine.

As she was pressing the button for the lift doors to open, she noticed a couple of the boxes that were piled high all around the upper floor to the side of it. The same boxes that she was sure she had seen on a forklift at the Cross Barn, too. The top one was open. With her curiosity getting the better of her, and her heart beating fast at the thought of what on earth she might find, she pressed the torch on her phone and shining it down, tentatively slipped her hand under the box lid.

She had no idea what to expect, but was surprised to feel glass. Opening the lid up wide, she could scarcely believe her eyes. Looking down into the box, she found herself staring at jar upon jar of ASDIS-branded runny honey. She quickly checked the labels of a few of the other boxes piled around and realised they were the same. A million different thoughts started to run through her head.

What on earth would Max be doing with thousands of jars of cheap honey, and why should it be such a secret that he had them in the first place? And what on earth was he doing with them in the Cross Barn? While this discovery had given rise to far more questions than answers, August was certain of one thing: she now knew how Max knew CORA13, the store manager of ASDIS.

Chapter Twenty Nine

'Hi, you must be Geri, I'm Melanie. Nice to meet you.' A woman in her early forties wearing a track suit and designer trainers greeted August at the door of the Sebastian Line centre with a yawn. Her hair was tied back in a messy ponytail. 'Good of you to step in at such short notice. For a Friday evening, it's been really quiet, actually. I can't wait to get to my bed, I tell you.'

August thought it best not to mention that she had driven around listening to Tony Parsons' new audiobook for a while as she had been far too early for her shift and couldn't be bothered to go back home and change.

'You get off, then. I'm all set.' August threw her bag down on one of the desks.

'You look gorgeous, by the way, Geri.'

August beamed. 'Thanks! I've been to Jaxon's – you know, the new wine bar up the memorial end of the high street?'

'Ah, yes, I heard about that opening. How was it?'

'It's a really cool space actually – was packed in there. I'd definitely recommend it.'

'I must try it. Not drunk on duty, then, I hope?' Melanie grinned.

'God, no, it's hard enough being sober doing this, isn't it?'

August chuckled, but Melanie said, 'We'll leave that to David, shall we?'

Not wanting to get involved with any insider politics, August busied herself by taking off her jacket and put it on the back of one of the chairs.

'So, what led you to do this then, Melanie?'

Melanie's eyes met August's. 'I was in an abusive relationship. Felt I had no place to go. And then I found the number of a crisis line. It really was a lifesaver.'

'I'm so sorry.'

'Don't be. I was young. Talking to somebody made me realise that there was help out there. To not only get away but understand why I accepted being in an abusive relationship in the first place. I sorted myself out. I'm with a kind, loving man now and have a beautiful daughter.' They smiled at each other. 'How about you?'

'I heard Darcy's story and it really affected me. Plus, it might sound selfish but I wanted to meet new people. I'm just out of a relationship, felt a bit lonely. I have time to give.'

'Aw.' Melanie put her arm gently on August's. 'How are you feeling now?'

'So much better, thank you.' August felt as if the Sebastian Line offered a sea of empathy to its volunteers too. That already it felt like a space where she could talk openly, and nobody would judge. She liked it, a lot. August checked her watch. 'You get off home to that husband and baby of yours.'

'Baby! She's nineteen going on twenty-nine.'

'Ah, you must have been a child bride.'

Melanie smiled. 'The kettle's just boiled, and I brought in some of those lovely soft cookies from Waitrose to keep you going.'

'That's kind.'

'That's kind…of our job spec really, isn't it?' They laughed again. Melanie headed to the back door. 'Have a good night, take care and don't answer the door to any strangers.'

Feeling slightly unnerved by that comment, August watched Melanie go. Then, checking the front door was locked and the blind firmly down, she went to the back door and checked all was secure that side of the centre, too.

She was just getting settled at her desk with a cup of instant hot chocolate when she nearly jumped out of her skin. For, coming from the back door, she suddenly heard a light tapping sound. With her heart beating out of her chest, she reached for her phone, then luckily before she had a chance to call Ellie's Grant to come and rescue her if required, she heard a familiar voice. 'August, it's me.'

She went to the back door and pulled up the blind.

'Sean? What the fuck are you doing here?'

'I'm staying at my mum's house while she's away. I er…I just saw your car pulling in here…was just picking up a Chinese.'

She peered at him suspiciously. 'This late?'

He answered by holding up a brown paper bag. '…And, well, I was right. Here you are.' He craned to look through the door. 'What are you doing here? What is this place?'

'You can't come in.'

'Why not? Who are you here with?' August really didn't like the accusatory tone that Sean was now adopting.

Wondering what on earth had she done to attract two very sexy but emotionally unbalanced men, August sighed heavily and pressed the exit button on the coded door. 'OK, but literally for five seconds and if the phone goes you have to leave immediately.' She pulled the blind back down securely.

Sean entered and peered around, his enquiring gaze finally catching on one of the Sebastian Line posters. He bit his lip. 'Oh, baby girl. You are a real-life angel. Shit, and there's me being an absolute arse about not seeing you. Have you been doing this all the time?' He placed the bag down on one of the desks and made a woeful face.

'Yes. You are being an arse. I've always said we just need to be honest with each other. I told you I was too busy to be seeing someone seriously. I thought what we had was OK.'

'Well, you clearly haven't been that honest, or you'd have told me about being here.'

August took a deep, steadying breath. 'Sean, let's get this straight – yet again. We are not a couple. You do you, and I do me, and this is part of my life. I don't want to share *this* and have been asked not to share *this*.'

'I get it.' Sean sighed. 'Come here. You look super-hot, tonight.' He pulled August to him and with all the stresses of dealing with Max suddenly melting with his touch, she couldn't resist the urge to kiss him. Getting turned on by the thrill of doing this where they really shouldn't be, and feeling his hardness pushing into her, she suddenly had an overwhelming urge to have sex. Pure, filthy, no-strings sex, just like they had had the first time they had met.

'Upstairs.'

He stared down at her. 'You what?'

August's breath was coming in gasps. 'We fuck and you leave. If the phone goes, I have to take it. And make sure to leave me some food.'

Chapter Thirty

'You look as rough as I feel,' Tyler greeted Cat at the coffee machine. 'I'm modelling sunglasses for a TikTok video today, so I figured I could get away with it. Good weekend?'

Cat glared at him. 'Thanks for that, youth. Edinburgh is not for the faint-hearted and yes, it was great to catch up with some old pals.'

'Yes! In two.' Jonah punched the air, peering down at his phone. 'Look at me go.'

'His word game, I take it?' August got up to fill her water bottle from the water cooler. 'Do they ever use swear words?'

Jonah gave her a martyred look. 'Will any of you ever take this seriously?'

'I love words, so yes, I will, but it would be funny if they mixed it up a bit with a few offenders. Good weekend, Jonah?'

'Yes, thanks. All six of us headed to Dorset and did some kayaking and paddle boarding. It was great fun.'

'That's an Enid Blyton book right there,' Cat added.

'Who's she?' Tyler looked perplexed. 'Nice one though, Jonah. I've convinced Reece we need to be doing that when the weather gets better. Right, I'd better get filming. I'm only doing this job because I get to keep all the shades.' Tyler drifted off to one of the offices.

'I'd better get going too,' said Jonah. 'I've just taken on a new client who wants to provide branded and personalised sustainable t-shirts and water bottles for her whole company, as well as sell them. Pretty cool, eh?'

'Can't see Max doing that for here,' Cat said.

'Bottles of Courvoisier, maybe,' August added, feeling relieved that she hadn't seen him that morning. His Range Rover wasn't in its parking spot either, so she could relax. 'How was your highland adventure?'

'Brilliant. I do miss Scotland, I'm not going to lie. The weather was amazingly warm too. Even had brunch by the beach.'

'I thought you were in Edinburgh?' August quizzed, sitting down at the table and nursing her coffee.

'I was. Portobello Beach is just a short hop from the city centre.'

'Wow, well, shows how much I know. How lovely is that?'

'So, the big question to you is: how was the wine bar, and how did Maximillian behave?'

'Hot, not or cold, ladies?' Beryl suddenly appeared. 'I need to get a wiggle on. Bloody car didn't start this morning. Had to wait for Mr George to find his jump leads and get it started.'

'I could have done with a pair of those to get me started.' Cat gave a throaty laugh. 'And I'll have cheese and pickle on brown, please, Beryl. Thick-sliced, if you have it. I'm starving.'

'Cheese and salad for me, with mayonnaise, please.'

Mrs G fixed her with a stern look. 'August, how many times? I don't do mayonnaise.'

The writer giggled. 'OK. Salad cream is fine.'

'For goodness' sake, I'm busy enough already, aside you mucking up my orders pad,' Mrs G huffed.

'No Max today, then?' August really hoped he wasn't going

to come in as, even though she had done nothing wrong, the more time to dilute the goings on from Friday night, the better.

'He's up at the farm. Those baby poults are being let loose outside today and he's giving his brother a hand. Right, now, where are those boys?' Beryl waddled off in search of Tyler and Jonah.

August stood up. 'I'd better get on, Cat. I'm already behind on my word count for this month. I need to get my head down.'

'Tell me quickly, then. Was Jaxon's full of hot potentials, or not?'

August thought back to the hot, crowded room and sultry vibe. 'I can see it becoming popular. The waiters were like models but can only have been twenty at most. The music was really good. I didn't really notice any other men to be honest.'

'Hmm, twenty – that is a little young, even for me,' Cat smirked. 'And sounds like you only had eyes for our Mad Max, eh?'

'In his dreams.' August gave a brittle smile, really not in the mood for getting into detail. 'I tell you what, Cat, how about a walk tomorrow at lunchtime? We can have a proper catch-up then. Weather looks like it's going to be gorgeous and we can go and check out those baby turkeys.'

Later that day, August was in full writing flow when a tentative knock sounded on her office door. On realising who it was, her heart started to race. Max.

'Hey.' She'd never known him so subdued. He came in, shut the door and sat in the office chair opposite her. 'On a scale of one to wanker how bad was I?'

She gave a reluctant smile. 'Let's just say you made Hannibal

Lecter look like a vegetarian.'

He snorted. 'Very good, Agatha. Particularly good, in fact. Me and Jaxon always used to say that if you don't remember, it didn't happen.'

'That only works if you aren't with somebody sober.'

He grimaced. 'Do you know how I cut my hand?'

'You fell out of my car. It was stationary, might I add. Although you were lucky I didn't throw you out of it.'

'That bad, eh? Shit, I'm so sorry. That makes sense now. I wondered how I got home. I do remember how lovely you looked in your pink fluffy jacket though. That can't have been for me. You were going off to a date afterwards, weren't you?' Max winked.

'Quite the selective memory, you have, don't you, Max Ronson? And don't push your luck. You were bloody rude. I asked you a few questions and you got the right hump with me.'

'Like what?'

'It doesn't matter now.'

She could sense that he wanted to push, but thankfully he seemed to think better of it. 'Thank you for getting me home. And I am sorry if I was a total twat. I thought if I stuck to sparkling wine, I'd be OK, but it appears that alcohol of any sort turns me into a monster.'

'If I, were you, I'd stick to water, as, yes, it really does.'

'I guess I need to make it up to you. If I promise not to pop one cork' – he gave her one of his best amused looks – 'shall we do it again?'

August was just trying to decide how to answer when she noticed Cat approaching with purpose from across the office. Her face fell. For not only did the tall woman have a predatory grin on her face, but she was carrying the pink jacket that Sean had picked up by mistake in her hurry to get him to leave the

Sebastian Line centre the previous Friday.

'It appears I'm not the only little minx on the block,' Cat bowled in uninvited. 'Oh, hi Max.' August visibly cringed, then mouthed 'No' to her lover's mother, but it was too late. 'Yours, I'm told. Oh, I love it when a plan comes together.'

'Don't tell me The Country Matchmaker has actually made a match,' Max sneered.

Cat caught the look of horror on August's face and seemed to realise, far too late, that she'd made a big mistake. 'Don't be ridiculous, but I'd better head off and get working on it.' She scurried out, shooting August a look of agonised apology.

'I told you I knew that look.' Max's voice wobbled slightly. 'Sean the vet, I take it. "Friends tell each other things," you said. "I wasn't going on a date," you said. "I didn't sleep with him," you *didn't* have to say, as you snuck off out of my office with your tail between your legs, rather than answer.'

August said nothing, but could tell that her cheeks were on fire. That would tell him all he needed to know. He sighed heavily. 'There are many things I've wanted to call you, August Saunders, but a liar was never one of them. I think you'd better leave.' Max stood up. August could see that every part of him was shaking.

August stood up to her full height. 'You were the one who said the other night was a mistake, that you couldn't be with anyone because of Porsche woman, whoever the fuck she is. And I may not have told you some things, but what makes you think you have a right to know what's going on in my life, anyway? At least I'm not withholding the truth about absolutely everything, like you seem to be.'

'I thought you were good with words. Is there even a difference?'

'So, tell me then, Max, what is with that woman? And what

are all those jars of honey doing upstairs?'

'Enough now.' Max raised his voice. 'Leave. Yes, leave. Run off to your lover boy. And stick to bloody writing about solving mysteries at home. I don't need someone else meddling in my affairs and mucking everything up.'

'What the…?' August was now red with anger. 'This has got totally out of hand. We have a contract, I've paid for six months upfront, and I have every right to—'

There was a sudden sharp knock at the door. 'August?' It was Beryl. 'I'm bloody fuming. Another unannounced visitor. What did I tell you before when your agent and her bloody smelly hound arrived here? Put names in the book!'

August felt like she was going to explode, but Max beat her to it. He opened the door with force, causing Beryl to sidestep, then hold both her palms up in confusion.

August tentatively looked out of the office door and on seeing who was in the reception area, suddenly felt sick. Because there, bold as brass, looking even more handsome than the day he had left her, was none other than Scott Scanlan, ex-fiancé and current soap love rat – holding a bunch of flowers almost as big as himself.

Cat ran into August's office and shut the door. 'Jesus! Today is turning into a real-life soap opera. Are you OK?' August was literally shaking. 'Do you want to talk to him? I can tell him to leave.'

Tyler was now fawning over Scott, who had put the flowers down on the reception desk and was doing some sort of stretching move with his arms. Max had stormed off in his Range Rover up towards the farm.

'That's what Max just told me to do.'

'What, leave?' The redhead nodded. 'Oh, August.'

'I said too much, just like you said.'

'He loves having you here, I can tell. He won't mean it. You know that.'

'He meant it. He really meant it. And while we are at it, he was also angry that I've been sleeping with someone else.'

'Oh!'

'And that someone else happens to be your son.' August's face screwed up in anguish.

'Double Oh!' Cat laughed. 'But of course, I knew that already. I wasn't born yesterday. And I can't think of a nicer woman to bear grandchildren for me, to be honest.'

'Not helpful, right at this moment, Cat!'

'Yeah, sorry.'

'I don't think I can avoid talking to him, now he's here.' She took a deep breath. 'Do I look OK?'

'You look beautiful. Now, go!'

Chapter Thirty One

'Outside,' August spat as a beaming Scott approached her with flowers in the reception area. Refusing to take them, she marched out of the door and ahead of him, only stopping when she got to the car parking area. The handsome actor duly followed. August could tell that all of the others – bar Max – were eavesdropping behind a blind.

'What's wrong, Augi? I don't get it.'

And nor did she. She felt as if the connection between her mind and her face had malfunctioned, and it was making expressions of sorrow and joy and confusion and rage all at the same time. She had loved this man with the same intensity with which he had hurt her and she was finding it almost impossible to find a way to navigate the very same mixtures of intense feelings she was experiencing right now, without bursting into tears. She noticed the actor's silver chauffeured Mercedes next to her Mini.

'She let you keep the same car then?' She shut her eyes on delivery of such a stupid comment.

'I've booked a table…for lunch…for us two,' Scott said gently, looking directly into his ex-fiancée's eyes. 'Please come. I want to talk to you.'

On recognising Scott from the television, Jaxon ushered the pair of them to the same discreet corner table that August had shared with Max. August pushed the unpleasant memories of that night from her mind – she couldn't deal with them right now, on top of Scott bulldozing his way back into her life. Jaxon replaced the reserved sign with the encyclopaedia of a wine list and a lunch menu.

Scott's fancy silver Mercedes, along with its driver, sat in one of the parking bays in the middle of the wide market-town street. Her Mini squatted next to it; she had refused to travel with him. However, on Scott's insistence, the stunning bouquet lay on the back seat.

'Clever you, reserving the trendiest bar in town.' August took in the chiselled jaw of her handsome ex, noticed how his dark-brown hair suited him shorter and that his black shirt fitted snugly to show off his muscly pecs. The pecs that she used to snuggle into, the face that she woke up to, the body that she had known every inch of for a long seven years. She suddenly felt a wave of both familiarity and sadness.

'Well, you know me: always looking for the best places for my bitches.'

'Ha bloody ha. And the arrogance of thinking I would just drop everything and come for lunch with you. You amaze me.'

'Well, you're here, aren't you?' Scott went to put his hand on hers, and she pushed it off.

'You look beautiful, August. I love your hair long like that and you seem, well, far more relaxed than I've known you to be in a long time.'

'Must be all the single-girl sex I'm getting.' August childishly pushed her tongue into the side of her cheek and smirked.

'Lucky you.'

Jaxon appeared to take their order.

'Not like you to have water?' Scott commented as the debonaire, salt-and-pepper-haired owner went back over to the bar to prepare their drinks.

'And it's not like my ex to just show up totally out of the blue and uninvited at my new workplace. What do you want, Scott?'

'Have you missed me?'

'Still the same self-absorbed bastard, I see. Does your *new fiancée* know you're here, bringing me flowers and taking me out for lunch?'

'Don't be like that, Augi.'

'I'm not your Augi any more.' August felt a physical pain in her stomach just saying those words. 'You hurt me. You hurt me badly.'

Oh, how she had imagined this moment for so long: that he would appear, begging her to come back and she would fall into his arms and forgive him, and they would live happily ever after. But they weren't on the set of a soap opera or movie now; they were in a bar in Futtingbrook. A famous actor and a successful author on paper, but ultimately just the same as anyone else. A man and a woman trying to find their way in the world the best way they could, with the tools of life and experience that they had gathered during nearly four decades on the planet. And now reality had hit, and the moment had come, she wasn't actually sure if this is what she wanted after all.

Scott Scanlan was a cheater, a liar, and by surrounding herself with new, good people who genuinely cared about her and her wellbeing, she realised that somebody who had the capacity to be so toxic really shouldn't be welcome in her world any more.

Scott's voice lowered. 'I know I hurt you, and for that I am truly sorry. I always told you I was a work in progress.'

Jaxon discreetly put a large glass of Malbec and a fizzy water on the table.

'No food, thanks, we aren't stopping long.' August handed the menus back to the bar owner apologetically.

'Oh.' Scott looked put out. 'I thought we could at least eat together.'

August was annoyed at her tear ducts betraying her. She looked up at the ceiling in an effort to compose herself. 'In answer to your question, of course I've missed you, but I've moved on now. I'm just getting my life back together and if it wasn't for your face being all over the bloody internet and in newspaper soap columns, I'd be completely over you by now. But I'm well on my way, and I'd like to keep it that way.'

'You don't have to look.' Scott took a large sup of his drink, eyeing her shrewdly.

August sighed deeply and, wishing she'd kept her mouth shut and had ordered a vat of wine herself, took an unladylike slug of her water.

'Your mum said you are volunteering too. I'm so proud of you. And that you've signed another three-book deal with Big Red. I told you they loved you. And how cool that you work out of that country Hub place now. A really great idea to get your social life moving, too. Had such a good vibe about it. I could see me living in a converted barn, actually.'

'Poor little August, needing to get out and about.' August felt her anger rising. 'For the record, I'm fine. In fact, I'm more than fine. And there's far more to do than you realise around here, when you look.' She felt even more cross now that she was justifying her very existence to a man who had quite clearly forgotten about hers for the past few months.

'There's the fire I so miss!' Scott stared right into her eyes.

'And are you really having loads of sex?'

'None of your bloody business.'

'You brought it up.'

August huffed. 'Why are you here, Scott?'

'I miss you and I miss your mum too. And Ellie and the kids. How's Grant? And...the dogs and...'

August stared at him in disbelief. 'Scott, you can't have your cake and eat it.'

'Seven years is a long time, Augi, and I realise now that I left more behind than just you. Your family are so great.'

'And I've realised that I'm great too. And if you think you can just walk back into my life with a huge bunch of flowers, say sorry and pick up where you left off, then you've got another think coming.'

He looked stricken. 'Oh God, is that what you think I'm here for? Shit! The last thing I wanted to do was give you the wrong impression.'

'What? I don't get it?' August screwed her face up. 'Why are you here, then?'

'I kind of was hoping that now the dust has settled, and you don't seem quite so angry, that maybe, well, maybe, we could still be friends. That I could still be a part of your life in some way at least.'

Her insides deflated like a balloon. 'And now I know you never loved me.'

'Augi? What do you mean?'

'Really!' August's eyes were wide. Her anger ignited, and came out in a tirade of disbelief. 'Really! If you love someone with the intensity I loved you, you could never be friends with them. You left me weeks before we were due to be married – one of the biggest days of a woman's life – and then promptly got engaged to somebody else. And as for friends, where are our so-called joint friends now? Probably still licking your boots and upping your credit cards with all the meals you treat them to, but when the chips were down for me, where were they, eh? Shallow bastards, the lot of them. As sad as it is, I don't want to be your friend, Scott. And in fact, I can't believe you've come all the way here to ask me that, anyway.'

Scott took a huge glug of his wine. 'That was only one of the reasons for my visit.' From the look on the face she had grown to know every inch and expression of, August knew that something dreadful was about to leave Scott Scanlan's lips. She dropped her shoulders ready for his destructive delivery.

'The wedding is off.'

With such a plethora of emotions flooding her, August wasn't sure if the predominant feeling running through her now was glee or nausea. 'Oh. Forgive me for finding it hard to say I'm sorry.'

'God, no need to be sorry, it's off because…well, because she's pregnant. Delila, I mean.' Sick, August was now definitely feeling sick. 'She's beginning to show and, well, we've managed to keep it under wraps for this long, but you know what the press are like. So, when I say "off", it's been postponed. Delila couldn't possibly walk down the aisle "looking like a fat swan". Her words, not mine.'

'Of course, she couldn't.' August gulped back the lump that was creeping its way up her throat.

'And, well, I felt I owed it to you to tell you face-to-face, after being so weak and not telling you about the engagement and all that.'

Standing up, August took a slow, deliberate breath. 'You don't owe me anything – nothing, nada – ever again. Goodbye, Scott. I wish you and your fat swan a very happy life swimming around in your shallow celebrity circles.'

And as she got up and hurried to the toilet, only Jaxon was privy to both the pain on the crime author's face, and the soap actor's slow, sad walk up to the bar to pay the bill.

August ran her finger over her dad's gravestone. *Ron Saunders, loving husband, father, policeman, dog lover. Always laughing. Forever missed.* When her first nephew, Wilf, had arrived, the fact that grandfather had not been written on there had caused great sadness to the whole Saunders family. Twenty years of missing someone was a lot of pain, a lot of memories and a lot of 'I wonder what Dad would have said if he'd been here's.

She began unravelling the ribbon that bound together the stems of the exquisite bouquet that Scott had bought for her. Blooms to soften the blow that her ex really was her ex. A fiancé and wife were moveable feasts, but once kids were involved, then that really was the nail in the 'there still may be a minute chance to get back together again' coffin. She hadn't realised the ember of hope had still burned within her until it had been extinguished entirely.

She was just on her knees, head in her bag, hunting for some scissors to aid her stem-cutting mission, when she heard her name being called softly above her. She looked up to see an emotional-looking Darcy Webb.

'What stunning flowers,' Darcy said softly. 'Is it an anniversary?'

August went back to her search for her scissors. 'No. More like another death.'

Darcy gasped. 'Oh my god, August, I'm so sorry.'

August suddenly felt bad for worrying the kind woman. 'Sorry, I'm being dramatic. I mean the death of a long-standing relationship.' Tears started to roll down August's cheeks.

Darcy knelt down next to August at the graveside, her legs trim and brown in her cycling shorts. She took the younger woman's hand and squeezed it in hers.

'What would your dad have made of all this, then?'

'Probably would have said, "I never liked the pretty-faced bastard anyway".'

They both laughed. August noticed the woman's red-rimmed eyes. 'There's me so full of woe and I haven't even asked how you are?'

'It would have been Sebastian's twenty-first today. I go and sit quietly in the church this time every year to try and find some kind of solace. It never works.' August bit her lip. 'I still haven't found him a suitable resting place, either. He didn't think to tell me where he'd like to be. So, selfishly, I keep him in my kitchen so I can still talk to him. Silly, isn't it?'

August shook her head. 'I'd have had my dad stuffed and propped up in a chair in Mum and Dad's place if it was legal.'

They both managed a little laugh. August squeezed Darcy's hand, which was still resting lightly in hers. 'I laugh about it to stop me howling like a wolf. I'm so sorry for your loss, Darcy. I truly am.'

'God, I remember that day so clearly. The day my Sebby was born, I mean. Three-fifteen in the afternoon, he popped out.' She checked her watch. 'About now. We lived in Suffolk, then. A little bundle with the biggest mop of dark hair and the bluest of eyes. Noisy little bugger he was, too.' Darcy's face suddenly lit up. 'Screamed the place down for at least fifteen minutes. We all knew he'd arrived in the world – that's for sure.'

'What a wonderful memory, Darcy. And it's those that we must cling on to now. Grief is…it's odd, I think. It's either all-consuming or it suddenly hides away, and you carry on as normal. And unless you're going through it or have gone through it, it's hard to describe. I read somewhere that it envelops you to honour the depth of your love. Thanks for that, grief, but nobody tells you how much it will hurt or how empty you will feel inside. And that's me talking about my dad, who lived for a lot longer than your boy. And there was me harping on about my relationship ending when you arrived… So bloody meaningless in comparison.'

'August, it's fine. You will learn this from the crisis line. Everybody's pain is relative. Yes, Sebastian should have had so many more birthdays, but he didn't, and I can't change that.'

'You're so brave.'

Darcy shook her head. 'No, I'm not. My faith has got me through, plus two years of therapy have given me the tools to try and make sense of my own thoughts. I do believe that our lives are written, and I was given this hand so that I would set up the Sebastian Line. So, for the one young life that died in vain I can hopefully save countless other kids and their parents from ever having to feel like their hearts have been ripped out and kicked over the crossbar.'

'I can't even imagine.' August's voice broke.

'You will one day, if you have kids. But that shouldn't minimise your pain at losing your dad at such a young age, or the fact your relationship is over.'

August sat back on her heels and sighed. 'I thought Scott was *the one*.'

'Unless you're lucky enough to marry your childhood sweetheart, like I did, I think there are a few *the ones*, you know?'

'Well, that gives me hope, then.' August smiled. 'He gave me these flowers for no other reason than to soften the blow that his partner is pregnant, and then had the gall to say that he'd like to stay friends with both me and my family.'

Darcy winced. 'Ouch. But sweet in a way, too.'

'I'll stick with the ouch, thanks. He was my best friend and lover for so long. How does that work? You share everything with someone and then they become a stranger.'

'Do you not think you could become friends again, in time?'

They looked at each other then both said, 'No,' in unison, and laughed again.

Darcy, her head now facing the sunshine, her legs still out straight in front of her, pulled at a loose thread on the bottom of her t-shirt. 'I read a Maya Angelou quote the other day – so simple but so poignant.'

'Go on. That woman was a marvel.' August stood up to fill the two metal vases that were behind the wire mesh, fixed lovingly by her mother to keep the greedy rabbits and deer from having a midnight floral feast.

'"Every storm runs out of rain,"' Darcy delivered slowly.

August put her hand to her chest. 'Oh my God, that's brilliant.'

'And talking from experience, it really does.' Darcy smiled and eased her way up off the grass. 'You have a big heart, August. Listen to it.'

Chapter Thirty Two

A week later, August typed in the security code and made her way into the Sebastian Line centre. She had passed a stressed-looking Melanie in the car parking area – dashing home as her partner had gone to put something in the dustbin and had locked himself out.

'Buckle up, girl. It's been an interesting evening to say the least,' were her words from the open car window as she zoomed off.

August headed to her workstation and threw her keys and handbag on the table. It had felt like a long week, writing at home. She had found herself missing the Hub and all its goings on, and was still reeling from Scott's audacity. And if she was honest, she missed Max, too.

Being away from him had given her a chance to assess the man and her growing feelings for him. She had started to make a mental list. He was so full of character and substance and, for all that he annoyed her, he made her think outside of the box about many things. He interested her. He stimulated her. And as much as he infuriated her too, he had also been kind when he thought he had upset her about Scott when she first joined. Plus, he quite often said all the right things around the loss of her father. She had always looked forward to talking to him and felt disappointed whenever she arrived at the Hub and he wasn't there. He had also stirred up feelings within her that she had not felt since meeting Scott.

But she was stubborn, and he had told her to leave. Plus, he had been ridiculously rude and angry. She had to admit that, yes, she had been prying into his business, but that was the crime author in her and if he didn't want anyone to know what was going on – if there was anything going on, for that matter – then why on earth have people working in such close proximity? And why invite her out for a drink?

Her thoughts began to swirl. The day that she and Cat had walked past the barn and heard noises inside. Mrs G's car had been there, along with a lorry similar to that which she had thought Tyler was driving all those weeks ago. Maybe even Jonah, with his naïve and honest front, was also in on it, and he pretended to be deaf so he could be the mole in the camp? She dearly hoped that Cat wasn't keeping anything from her, but maybe she was and the whole darn Hub were up to something that she wasn't privy to.

August physically shook her head to clear it of all her crime writing tendencies. Her vivid imagination had got her into trouble many times. She was probably being paranoid. Maybe Max just liked honey! Maybe he was as addicted to it as those blasted cigarettes he refused to give up. And like his reputation that proceeded him, maybe he was just a womaniser, with a particular fetish for those who drove high-performance cars. After all, he did have all those glorious Formula One original photos up on his walls. Maybe there was nothing more sinister than him liking to bathe in honey with them all in the back barn.

August laughed to herself at the ridiculousness of her own

thoughts. Probably because her week had been so dull. Aside from going round to her mum's for dinner one night, the rest of it had been write, eat, walk, sleep, repeat. Even Sean had backed off, which had been a surprise. And not a welcome one at that, as she had actually found herself missing his quirky messages, banter and wanting of her.

So, with no plans that Monday night, and with no intention of going into the Hub again in the foreseeable future, August had put her hand up for the night shift at the Sebastian Line. She had bought her laptop in that night, figuring that, as she was alone and there might be downtime, it would be great not only to help keep her awake but to up her word count too.

Checking in her paper diary, which Tyler mocked her for using, she checked her progress from last week. Fifteen thousand words, she noted, so a grand total of forty-five thousand words now, and just thirty thousand until she would be done with the first draft. Her editor couldn't believe how fast she wrote, but she had to be in the mood and solitude was perfect for this. So now, even with editing time, her Christmas book would be ready well in time for an early December release. That was good going for her. But that was what writing alone did for you. Lots of words, but little interaction. Good and bad for her mental health all at the same time.

She really could do with a break, and had been envious on finding out that Cat had booked a last-minute holiday to Sorrento so wouldn't be around until the week after. The bawdy Scot has insisted, though, that as soon as she was back, she wanted them both to go to Jaxon's so that she could show off her tan, plus look out for some new talent and maybe net some new matchmaker clients. Being wise and intuitive to the way August was feeling, she had informed her that she had not seen Max since he had sped off in his car on Scott's arrival.

Seeing a note from Melanie stating that she had left new biscuits in the tin, August went to the kitchen, grabbed herself two custard creams and made herself a strong coffee. As soon as she sat down at her workstation, ready for the six long hours ahead, the phone rang.

'The Sebastian Line, Geri speaking. Is there a name I can call you by?'

'Do I have to tell you my name?'

'No, of course you don't.' Knowing that this call could well be an inappropriate one, August raised her eyes in resignation, then assumed her calm and reassuring tone. 'So, what's going on for you tonight then?'

'It's my wife. She's pregnant.'

August paused. 'And is that a good thing?'

'Well, it would be if I hadn't had the snip.'

'Ah, OK.'

'Well, it's not OK, is it?'

'I er…didn't mean it like that.'

'Well, think before you speak. I thought you lot were supposed to be trained up for any situation.'

'I'm so sorry if I upset you,' August said, feeling her hackles rising. She downed her coffee in one as the angry man continued. 'We brought another man into the relationship, see.'

'Well, this is clearly an exceedingly difficult time for you,' August soothed through gritted teeth.

'She's forty-nine. Who'd have thought she'd get up the duff at that age?'

August suddenly found the whole concept quite amusing, and had to fight to keep her voice serious. 'Are you communicating with your wife?' Knowing full well he was probably communicating with his right hand at the other end of the line, she waited with interest for the reply.

'Oh yeah, I love her. She wants to keep it, and me.' He let out an ugly snort. 'I don't think a randy nineteen-year-old plumber would really want to be on the birth certificate, or on her arm, now – do you?'

Realising he clearly wasn't in any danger of hurting himself or in any real distress, August asked, 'I'm interested to know, what actually led you to call us today?' Her thoughts of, 'because we are a bloody crisis line', luckily remained as just that – thoughts.

'I'm worried about telling my mother. Can't lie to her, see.'

'Ah, I understand.'

'You clearly don't, you smug bitch, cos you're not in this situation. She's ninety-six. The shock will probably kill her.' The caller hung up. August laughed then put her hand to her head. What was it with these people? And what if somebody like Sebastian was trying to get through, when her time was being wasted with tales of a disastrous threesome?

Then she remembered what Darcy had said about everyone's pain being relative, and her smile faded. If she was going to be useful here, she clearly needed to bring that into this space as Geri from now on. Lesson learned, August reached for the centre notepad to register the call.

She grappled in her messy bag for the special pen that her dad had given her, but couldn't find it. She sighed. 'Bugger.' She must have left it at the Hub. The thought of going back there brought with it mixed feelings, but it meant so much to her that whatever had happened, she must find it and get it back.

Just as she was looking at emails on her mobile, a Whatsapp message from Sean flashed up. *In bed and horny. Fancy a video call? x* The message was followed by an aubergine and a winky face.

August sat back in her chair and sighed. She was actually quite pleased to hear from him, but it was as if every time she

233

came online, he seemed to be there. Suddenly this casual sex lark didn't seem so appealing. Seeing Scott again had made her realise that. The 'relationship sex' with the actor had been amazing, but although extremely important it had been such a small part of their relationship, if she broke it down.

No, it was the intimacy she was craving now. The long Sunday mornings snuggling in bed. Watching a box set together eating bags of crisps and fighting for the best chocolates in the box. Him rubbing her feet to make her sleepy. A quick bum-tweak as he followed her up the stairs. She missed that. Scott was funny. He had been caring. And what they'd had was real, warts and all. Not just suspenders, smiles and a quick jump. But for whatever reason, life in all its wisdom had decided that their path was not to be. And now that she was thirty-seven, with most of her spring-chicken days behind her, maybe it was time she started to get real. If she wanted to find a true companion, she should focus on a wholesome, sustainable roast dinner of a relationship rather than a quick-fix, although undeniably delicious, McDonalds of a muck around.

Well? Sean continued with his sexual ferocity.

'For God's sake!' August harrumphed. She really didn't want to alert him to the fact she was up or at the centre, in case he decided to come and surprise her, but her annoyance got the better of her.

Hey, it's so late and I'm dog tired

You're only allowed to say that if you have a proper job like mine. Winky face emoji. Dog emoji.

'Woah!' August slammed her hand down on the table. She hadn't heard that insult for quite some time. She deleted her angry *You try writing a bestseller then, matey,* and instead sent a *Let's chat tomorrow.*

That sounds ominous

I've got a lot going on at the moment
What do you mean by that?
Sean. I will call you tomorrow. I promise.

The centre phone rang, causing her to jump and throw her mobile back in her bag. Heart pounding, she picked up the phone.

'The Sebastian Line, Geri speaking. Is there a name I can call you by?'

The caller, a young girl, was sobbing. 'Jenny, I'm Jenny. I'm sorry to call you.' August felt relieved. She was beginning to realise that if any of her callers said they were sorry, it meant they were genuine.

'You don't have to say sorry. I'm here to listen, Jenny. In your own time, you tell me what's made you so upset.'

'I've had a huge row with my mum, and I'm scared because I feel I want to harm myself.'

August's breath caught in her throat. 'I'm here to listen for as long as you need me. OK?'

'OK.'

August took a deep breath and sat back in her chair. And in the middle of a mild June night in the Sebastian Line centre in Futtingbrook, she put her own thoughts, worries and problems to the side to allow herself to fully concentrate on a young girl's anguish. And at that moment in time, nothing else in the world mattered more.

Chapter Thirty Three

'Jesus, you didn't tell me how hot Jaxon was,' Cat announced over the Friday night music and revellers as she shimmied back from the bar with a bottle of Prosecco nestled in a wine cooler and two fancy flutes.

August gave her a stern look. 'He is also very married. Not that that's stopped you before. You weren't in Italy with the bank manager then?'

'God, no! I actually went with one of my Edinburgh mates. It was a right laugh. I needed it, to be honest. And to be among all those Italian men! Simply gorgeous! I was saying *sì, sì, sì* to them all.' Cat guffawed. 'I love a last-minute trip away.'

'I hear you. I'd love a break, but I need to keep writing, and this will sound sad, but being honest, I don't have anyone I can just shout up to go with me at the moment.'

Cat shook her head. 'Not sad at all. Happened to me. Came out of my marriage and a lot of my friends weren't in a position to just up and come away without their partners. But fear not, my friend, I'll be up for another adventure later in the year. Or could you not go somewhere alone and write?' Cat refilled their glasses.

'Cheers!' They clinked their bubble-filled flutes.

'Seven years bad sex if you don't look me in my eyes,' August laughed. 'Max says that.'

'I bet he does. Have you been back into the Hub yet?'

August screwed up her nose. 'No. I can't face another bloody confrontation; it was bad enough after the last one.'

'He will be quiet as a lamb. You wait.'

'Have you seen him, then?'

'No, I only got back last night and just popped in earlier as Tyler is helping me set up some equipment for a live podcast I'm doing. Back to it on Monday. Hoping, now summer is approaching, I will get some more horny country folk needing a matchmaker.' She peered around the room. 'To be honest, I can't see many singletons in here at the moment, but it's early. Have you noticed that men most definitely want to shag more when the sun comes out?'

'Seeing that the only person I've been seeing lately is your son, I don't really want to talk about that.'

Cat laughed. 'I'm not saying a word.'

'It's fine. It is what it is. I won't be giving you grandchildren, though, I'm afraid.'

'He did mention you may be meeting tomorrow night.'

'Umm. Yes. Maybe, but—'

Cat put her hand in the air to stop her. 'You are both adults and it's your business. Right, so…back to my question. *Would* you go away to write on your own?'

'I hadn't really thought about it, but I might have a look now and see if anywhere would be suitable.' August took a large sip of her Prosecco, and the bubbles fizzed up her nose, making her flinch. 'So, was Max in when you went in earlier?'

'No and his car wasn't there. Jonah said he'd been out for most of the week and when he did come in, and when he wasn't being short with everyone, spent most of his time upstairs.'

'Can't a man have a cave?' August laughed at her own comment.

'He is certainly an enigma, that man.' Cat looked around the room again. 'God, this place is great. The décor is spot on.' She lifted a white candle in a jar and put it to August's nose. 'Smell these; they're gorgeous.' August took an appreciative sniff and hummed in agreement. Cat's shoulders started moving to the music. 'Shall we get another bottle?'

'It's only seven o'clock.'

'Whoever put a time on fun, pal?'

August stood up to go the bar, then let out a pronounced gasp and sat back down again. 'What's the matter?'

'It's CORA13.'

Cat stared at her, mystified. 'Who? What?'

'The woman who Max went away with. I saw her car drop him off the morning he came back.'

'And?'

'Well, she also gave me a filthy glare when I parked in her store manager space at ASDIS.'

Cat's brow crinkled. 'Oh, he's seeing a shop worker.'

'Cat! I really didn't put you down as a snob.'

Cat glanced over at her. 'She is extremely attractive, though. But Cora13 – what kind of name is that?'

'It's her number plate.'

Cat giggled. 'Oh, you are funny. So, are you going to get us another bottle or do you want me to go?'

At that moment one of the handsome, black-clad bar staff appeared to collect glasses. 'Are you offering table service tonight?'

'No; too busy; we've got a private party starting at eight-thirty. Did you not see the sign at the door? Sorry, but you'll need to leave when the musicians start setting up. Come back tomorrow though, eh? We've got another singer in.'

They stared at each other in consternation. 'Oh, how disappointing. Let's just crash it.'

'Cat Bachelor! What are you like? I'll get us another drink in before we get kicked out.' Her courage fuelled by the alcohol, August made her way to the bar. She could see that Cora13 was chatting animatedly to a very tall blonde man. As the petite blonde lifted her left hand to chink glasses with him, August noticed a huge diamond ring on her finger.

'A very Happy Engagement to Cora and Dom,' Jaxon announced, placing a bottle of champagne in an ice bucket in front of the engrossed couple. 'And this one's on the house.'

August was just nuzzling up alongside them to see if she could listen in when Cora13 turned and stared right at her. She cocked her head to the side, clearly a little tipsy. 'Don't I know you from somewhere?'

Rather than August admitting to her car parking crime in the ASDIS car park, she took it as her chance. 'Umm, I work out of the Futtingbrook Farm Hub. Maybe I've seen you there?'

Thinking she would get a face of horror at having been outed for having a salacious affair with Max, she was taken aback to be met with a beaming smile.

'Ah, yes, darling Max. Dom, this lady works with Maxy.'

The tall blonde man, now deep in conversation with Jaxon over the bar, raised his glass and carried on talking.

August cringed inside, and not just at the word Maxy. 'Oh, god, maybe they were all bloody swingers, and Cora13's fiancée was very much involved in their holiday debacle.

'Such a lovely man. He doesn't like anyone to know this, but as you work there, I guess you know it already. I mean, how could he possibly hide all those jars he's ordered this year? He buys honey from my place, see. He told me he's going to deliver palettes of it to food banks all over the UK. Such a health benefit to all receiving it, and what a kind thing to do.'

'Yes, amazing,' August stuttered. 'And the fact he keeps it quiet – it makes it all the more special, doesn't it?'

Cora13 laughed. 'Very! He buzzes around like a secret little bee himself, doesn't he?'

Dom gave her a look as if to say, 'enough now, dear', but loose with champagne, the woman now, thankfully, carried on.

'My store bonus this year is going to be super-sweet on the strength of it, so it was the least I could do to invite him down to do a bit of surfing with us and stay in our holiday home in Rock as a thank you. But I guess you know that already too, if you work with him.' She smiled sweetly.

August skirted around the question. 'Is he coming tonight, then?'

'No, he's in London this weekend, I think he said.'

'Well, you have a lovely party, and congratulations on your engagement.'

Cora13 turned back to her man, and August stood deep in thought at the bar as she waited to order. Why had Max been so secretive about the honey? It was a lovely thing to do; surely it wouldn't matter if those closest to him knew about it? And where did he get the money to buy it? And what was his motivation? And why honey?

The rents from the Hub wouldn't even cover the shipping, surely? Max was the ultimate dark horse! Honey for food banks? *And* his weekends away in London. They certainly weren't to see Porsche woman, if the body language between them on the fun run day was anything to go by. So why did he keep going back to the very place he'd been so keen to leave?

To be fair to him, he had made an effort with the fun run, so maybe he was just one of these undercover secret millionaires who spread his wealth and joy to the masses. But August's crime-obsessed mind wouldn't allow her to believe that, somehow. Still, she had possibly been wrong on both counts about him shagging Cora13 and Porsche woman, so what did she know?

There were only two things she was certain of now. One: she knew even less about Max Ronson and what went through that deep mind of his than she'd thought when she had walked into this wine bar an hour ago. And two: tonight's revelations had only made her all the more intrigued to find out more.

Chapter Thirty Four

'Oh, Cat, I really don't want to come to the Hub today. I'm midway through a sex scene and the faces I pull when writing them would frighten even the alpacas.' Deleting a sentence, August gripped her handset between her ear and her shoulder.

Cat snorted. 'Lucky you. Look, Max isn't even here yet, and you'll be doing me the most massive of favours. I can't not go ahead with this podcast; T has been promoting the arse out of it for me. It would look bad if I don't go out live with it at ten as planned. I'll be all set up in one of the private offices and you'll be done by eleven. I just didn't factor in bloody illness.'

'But you've promoted it on the basis of an appearance by a professor of behavioural studies from Swinford University. What will people think when they get a jilted crime author from Upper Gamble? I'm not sure my bitter and twisted views on love will be quite so valuable to your listeners.'

'It's fine – we've kept the guest list fluid. I was rather hoping you'd do one anyway. Because, as it happens, you're starting to become quite the local celebrity, even if you don't realise it.'

August waved to a discombobulated Ellie, who was on her drive wrestling two screaming children into their car seats ready to whisk them off to nursery. To complete this picture of serenity, a barking Colin was running around her in circles as she did so.

Not liking to see her sister struggling, August jumped out of the car. 'Let me help you.'

'I'm fine,' Ellie protested. 'You get off to the Hub. I assume that's where you're going?'

'Yes, but I don't want to. Have promised Cat I'll speak on that bloody podcast I told you about.'

'You'll be brilliant, and maybe you'll have the chance to catch up with lover boy.'

'Don't!' August shook her head. 'OK. Wilfy, stop this noise.' At her command, her screaming nephew stopped his protest and started repeating the word 'Goose' over and over. She retrieved him from his pushchair and he wiped his snotty face in his auntie's hair, who without comment strapped him into his car seat securely, kissed his forehead, then put the pushchair into the boot.

'Thank you.' Ellie smiled. 'Think twice before doing this, won't you?' She handed August a wet wipe. 'And you might wanna clean your hair off before facing the general public.'

They both laughed.

As she drove along the country road to Futtingbrook, August noticed a missed call from Sean. She thought back to the way she had been treating him lately and felt suddenly guilty. It wasn't his fault that she was going through a relationship crisis of sorts. It was she who needed to sort out what she was really looking for. She called him from her hands-free and could tell from his voice how pleased he was to hear from her.

'Ah, there she is. The elusive Ms A. R. Saunders. To what do I owe this honour at such an early hour?'

'Just wanted to see how you are and to say sorry for being so shit at replying. I've been so bloody busy.'

'I've been missing those muffins. That's how I am.'

August laughed. 'What you up to today?'

'Just making my way to the Ronson turkey farm, actually. The poults are out and a couple of them have injured themselves on some wire.'

'Oh no, bless them.'

'They'll be fine. Ade has segregated them already. Turkeys love the colour red, so if they see blood on each other, it causes a bit of a bundle.'

'He told me that. I'm sure you're all winding me up with these bizarre little nuggets of turkey information. Ha! See what I did there?'

'I have better things to do with my time.' He paused. 'Seeing you, for example. It's been too long. I'll be at the farm until after lunch. If you're there, why don't you pop up and say hi? It's funny seeing the birds running around free, too.'

'I'll see. I'm on my way to meet your mum. She's talked me in to doing this *Love is…* podcast of hers. It's going out live to the nation via her website, evidently.'

'Oh god, yeah. She told me about that. What exactly is love? It does my head in just thinking about it.'

'Sean, don't scramble *my* head before I even get there. I haven't prepared anything and it's far too early for talk of such things.'

The vet laughed. 'Well, good luck with it, and if I don't see you lunchtime, drop me some nights when you're free. Sod all this love lark, give me lust any day. I just want Wiltshire's best bestseller's muffins in my face.'

August pretended to be offended. 'What are you like?'

'Horny for you, that's what I'm like. That night at the Sebastian Line will be saved in my wank bank forever more.' He laughed and hung up.

August cringed. A few weeks ago, him saying that would have made her happy and horny too. He was a decent bloke and they had had fun. But he had overstepped the friends with benefits line. And, as much as she liked his company and his cock, she would have to be fair to him and tell him that whatever they'd had, was over.

August's, 'Fuck!' at seeing Max's black Range Rover was drowned out by Ivor on his quadbike zooming past her out of the gate with what looked like Max clinging on behind him, holding on to his peaky blinder's hat. He looked back, then on noticing her staring his way, quickly away again.

'Here she is!' Tyler grinned widely and handed her a black coffee. 'You have this one; I'll make another. Good to see you, August. We thought you might not be coming back.'

'For goodness' sake,' Jonah huffed, staring intently at his phone. 'I mean, how was I supposed to know that's a joint used in carpentry? Some of the words they put in here. I've lost my twenty-day streak now.' Tutting, he stood up and kissed August on each cheek. 'Where you been? We all miss you when you're not here, you know? We thought you might have run off into the sunset with that ex of yours.'

August sighed. 'No, quite the opposite. He's going to be a father and the new sprog-to-be is clearly not mine.'

'Oh, I'm sorry.' Jonah stood up and gave her an awkward hug.

245

'Aw, thanks Jonah. Not going to lie, it was a tough day. I've also had a bit of a row with Max. He told me to leave, so I did. Which is ridiculous really, considering I pay his bloody bills with my rent.'

'It must have been more than a bit of a row – you haven't been here for ages. I guess everything is all right now?' Jonah's voice was full of concern.

'I don't know. I haven't spoken to him, but I need to tie up repayment etcetera if he does want me to leave. Where is he, anyway?'

'Hot, not or cold?' Beryl appeared in the kitchen with her notepad. 'Oh, hello August, you all right? Whatever he said to you, I'm sure he didn't mean it. And he's out. Will be back lunchtime, I think he said.'

'How did you—?'

'I know nothing, but we've had people disappear before 'cos he upset 'em. What I will say is just stick to your writing though, love. Nobody likes a sneak.'

August, despite finding the word sneak so old-school and rather amusing, felt suddenly upset that she was being thought of in this way. If Max would just explain what was going on, or even tell her to her face to mind her own business, then at least she would know where she stood. It was the lack of communication in any shape or form that was really bothering her.

She took a breath and, managing to keep her emotions in check, replied sweetly, 'Not for me today thanks, Mrs G. I'll be gone as soon as I can get away.'

Cat ran in to the kitchen and got herself a cereal bar from the snack machine. 'August, you are a complete angel, doing this. Tyler, can you quickly come and just check I haven't mucked anything up? We're going to be able to put it up on my website

246

afterwards, aren't we? August, sorry, we need to get a move on. I need to do a sound check, and I want to run some of the questions by you first.'

'Chill out, tiger, it's all good.' Tyler followed both ladies out of the kitchen.

'I hate bloody marketing, but I've always fancied myself as a bit of a podcaster.'

With briefing complete, a much calmer Cat now sat opposite August, the pair of them wearing Madonna-style microphones. 'Ready?' She put her thumb up to August, who nodded, then counted down three, two, one, with her fingers.

'Hi there and welcome to my first *Love is…* podcast. I'm Cat Bachelor, managing director of Wiltshire's one and only country matchmaking service, The Country Matchmaker, where I personally match couples using my expertise and experience, along with a hint of my very own *je ne sais quoi*, to find that elusive chemistry which, whatever age we may be, we all seek.' August was surprised at Cat's decent French accent. 'I will be doing a monthly podcast for the rest of the year, bringing in a plethora of guests to try and work out what exactly this thing called love really is. Do look out for exclusive offers on my matchmaking services after this interview in the news section of my website. We will also put a competition up to win a personally signed copy of Wiltshire's finest crime author's most recent novel – because here she is, ladies and gentlemen, the very lady herself! Welcome to my first Love is… podcast, A. R Saunders. Or can I call you August?'

August made a face at her and smiled. 'August is fine, and thanks for having me.'

Unbeknownst to the women, Tyler had rigged the sound so they could be heard over the speakers in the barn.

'I wonder if she'll mention the actor,' Tyler said in a hushed voice as he started to devour a huge steaming bowl of porridge and fruit.

'Or the vet?' Max added, creeping in behind Jonah and Tyler.

'Or you?' Jonah said quietly into the Hub owner's ear as he sat down at the desk next door.

A stony-faced Max sat with one butt cheek propped on Tyler's desk as Cat continued to interview.

'So, August, it's well documented that you write about romance as well as crime in your books. Do you base your ideas on real-life experience?'

'Yes, a good dose of reality is what draws the reader in and what makes my books so successful, I guess. Saying that, I've never witnessed a murder.'

'Well, that's a relief.' Cat laughed. 'So, Lila Lovelace – that's one of your feisty crime duo, for those who don't know – well, she seems to equate love more with just sex than the steadier Marie McGee, who is all out to find a long-standing and fulfilling relationship. Which one of your heroines would you say you are more like?'

Not expecting quite this level of interrogation, August looked open-mouthed at Cat. After a pause, she said: 'I think there's a bit of both of them in all of us, don't you?'

Cat grinned. 'I think we all want the good sex part, but does that lead to a longstanding relationship? My short-term lovers have always been better in bed than my husbands. But I guess that's the pay-off for love, attachment, affection and intimacy.

Quite frankly, I think we should just have a vast group of friends and a brothel around the corner, and we'd all be happy.' Both women laughed, as did the three men outside. Cat was on a roll. 'The bigger the dick, the bigger the ego, in my opinion. Which, again, is quite a disheartening revelation.'

'Lila Lovelace would tend to agree on that. However, I have to say that loving sex in a mutually respectful committed relationship can be equally as good as a fiery one-night stand, if you work at it. It's just different experiences, I guess.'

'So, you're saying that love is what you make it?'

'Yes, I guess so. Something I did read this week, though' – August took a sip from her glass of water – 'is that love has an important impact on wellbeing and quality of life, and that loving relationships have been linked to lower risk of heart disease, better health habits, lower stress levels, less depression, lower risk of diabetes and generally a longer lifespan.'

'Makes sense, I guess,' Cat nodded.

'So, I've ordered myself a defibrillator, booked a therapist and bought some glucose bars.'

Cat laughed out loud. 'So, nobody special in your life at the moment, then, I take it?'

August sighed. 'I think my love life has been well documented enough recently that your listeners will be well aware that there isn't. If anyone is wondering if the papers have got it right, then it is true. My ex-fiancé is marrying somebody else. I'm over that now, but can I tell you what annoys me the most?'

'Go on,' Cat encouraged.

'Men, who are not clear in their intentions. I'd much rather someone tell me they just want sex, for example. Or say, "I don't fancy you, I don't want to date you, but let's be friends." Get it all out there on the table from the start. All I ask from a man is two things. Honesty, and comm-u-ni-cation!' She slowly broke the word down.

'But surely, isn't the good part of meeting someone new the flirtation and the chase? The butterflies of uncertainty, I call it. Gives it the element of surprise and excitement.'

'I'd still rather know.'

'But maybe the man doesn't know for sure at the start what he's after.'

August paused. 'That's a fair point.'

'So, being a writer, what words would you put down on paper to describe what love is?'

'This is hard, as there are so many different aspects of love. But OK, in my humble opinion, love is – and I am talking true romantic love here – it is in equal parts electrifying, witty, exhilarating, heart-lifting, erotic, terrifying and bloody amazing. Also, somebody actually said to me just the other day that there are a series of "the ones", and not just *the one*, throughout our romantic lives, and I'm beginning to think she's right.'

'Yes, August, I wholeheartedly agree on that. Every lesson we learn in love and life is just a stepping stone, a signpost to what's to come next, and if we choose to learn that lesson first time around, then great. And if we don't, we just have to pick ourselves up and do it all again. Eventually we realise what we want.'

'You make it sound easy.' August let out a little laugh. 'But fundamentally, after saying all that, I think what we are all looking for is someone to do nothing *well* with. Well, I am, anyway.'

'I hear you. Nothing better than squashing up on the couch to watch something good on the TV with some tasty snacks and a tasty fella.'

'Exactly!' August took another sip of her water.

'You're even convincing me to want to fall in love again, after digesting all that.' Cat was clearly enjoying herself now. 'OK, time has flown but before we wrap up, please do tell us when the next A.R. Saunders bestseller is going to be on the shelves.'

'I'm just waiting to find out the final publication date, but it should be early December. And you will be able to pre-order it very soon and receive it in time for Christmas presents. The title has just been confirmed as *A Christmas Mystery in Futtingbrook Fallow*.'

'How exciting! You're actually putting Futtingbrook on the literary map?'

'Yes, and if you follow me on my social-media channels, you'll get all the latest news hot off the press. And also, don't forget to sign up to my newsletter for early special offers.'

'Ever the marketeer there, I see.'

'Well, if you can't blow your own trumpet…'

The ladies laughed in unison. 'Sounds intriguing, and I shall certainly be pre-ordering my copy as soon as I can, and will of course make sure to put all details on my website so that everyone else can, too.' Cat cleared her throat. 'Well, it's been a complete joy talking to you, August, and thanks again for being my very first guest on my *Love is…* podcast.'

'It's been an absolute pleasure.'

'Before I let you go, to close I'm going to ask all guests this question, whether they be single or married. August Saunders, what would you class as a perfect date?'

'That's an easy one for me. I would like to go for coffee at The Pilchard Inn on Burgh Island.'

Cat laughed. 'No hesitation there. That name doesn't conjure up visions of romance. In fact, I could go as far as to say Marie McGee would say it's fishy.'

'Ha! Very good! Look at you, doing your homework. But it's

a magical place for me. My parents took me and my sister there once when we were on a family holiday in Devon. It's next to the exquisite Burgh Island Hotel. It's actually where I learnt about Agatha Christie and became a superfan of her work.' August sighed. 'The views across the sea are stunning. And, well, if the date went very well and, without sounding too much like Lila Lovelace – my other naughty protagonist – maybe then we could book Agatha's Beach House in the hotel and commit a few crimes of passion ourselves.'

'Ha, now this is beginning to sound far more interesting.'

'Oh, it is. It's the perfect beach retreat, built for Agatha herself in the 1930s. She wrote some of her novels there. I keep meaning to take myself there, but never have.'

'I'm going to check my Country Matchmaker database right now and see if I can find somebody wonderful who just might be up for it.' Cat pressed a button to play some soft background music. 'And I'll be here same time, same date next month, when I will be talking to the renowned Edward Marchant, Professor of Behavioural Studies from Swinford University to get his take on what this thing called love really is…'

'Agatha,' Max called to August from his office as she headed towards reception on her way out. She sighed, then hesitantly went to him and stood in the doorway.

'While I remember, you didn't find a pen here, did you? Blue, battered, engraved with my initials.' She rested her head on the door frame casually.

'A successful author like you can surely afford a shiny new one.'

August's face fell. 'My dad gave it to me the year before he died.' Before Max had time to answer, her mouth ran away with her. 'I can't be long. Got things to do. I take it I still get a rent rebate, even if you have in effect fired me?'

'Don't be like that.'

'You told me to leave, Max.'

'I was angry.'

'Drunk last time, angry this. You need to sort yourself out.' August's expression was pained.

'I realise that. But you told me you love working here.' With his face falling, Max suddenly sounded panicky.

'I do, but how many times can you treat me like this? It's ridiculous. I'm the one bloody paying you, as well. You were the one who told me you didn't want to shoot yourself in the foot. Ironic, really.'

'Writer girl, you're so smart.'

'I know I am.'

'Modest, too.' Max managed a slight smile.

But the time for joviality was over as August suddenly remembered what she had been wanting to ask him, if she dared. 'I saw Cora on Friday. Good holiday in Cornwall, I take it?'

'Er, you did?'

'Yes. I can't believe it about the honey. Why didn't you just tell me?' August held her palms out flat in question.

Max's face dropped further. 'Tell you what?'

'That you were giving it to food banks across the UK. That is just so kind. Why would you want to hide it?'

'I don't want to talk about it.' Max turned to his coffee machine. 'Have you told anyone else about this?'

'No. I assumed you didn't want the world to know, or you would have mentioned it.'

'Good girl, and please don't.' He seemed jittery.

'It all makes sense now. The lorries and the barn, I mean. Because I guess you store it in there, as well as upstairs? Must cost you a bloody fortune, the amount of it you have.'

'Enough, OK?' Max slammed his hand down on the desk. 'I'm going to check out the poults.'

August scowled at him. 'There's no need to get aggressive.'

The Jason Statham lookalike pulled a packet of cigarettes from his drawer. He then stood up, opened the window, lit a fag and took a huge drag.

'I'm going now.' August turned to leave.

'I'm sorry, Agatha. For being such a bullish bastard.' He took another lug, then threw the half-smoked butt into the sand bucket outside.

She turned back. 'You can't keep doing this and saying sorry, Max. One day you won't get away with it. You will lose everyone who cares about you.' August stood defiant.

'And do you care about me, Agatha? Clearly not, as within seconds of meeting me you were already shagging the vet.'

'For some strange reason – and even despite comments like that – yes, I do, Max. I must be mad but I like you, yes. And if you were ever honest about your own feelings, then you'd bloody admit you like me too.'

'Oh, just go back to lover boy and talk to him. I need to go up to the farm.'

'See, again, you can't just be honest. You have to deviate. And, for the record, even though it's none of your bloody business, it's over between me and Sean. It was never more than a fling, anyway.'

Max put his hand up to stop her. 'Like I've said before, I don't want or need to know.'

'Well, it clearly wound you up.'

'It was the lie about you not seeing him that hurt, not the

deed.' His voice softened. 'Please stay. I promise to stop being such a terrible cunt if you do.' August took in his brooding brown eyes, which held so much mysterious sadness, and the full lips she had so enjoyed kissing in the lift on that balmy April Saturday after the fun run. 'I mean, three grand is three grand, right?'

She couldn't help but smile. She was just going to reply when Mrs G bonged her gong to the shout of 'Food in kitchen. Oh, and guess what? Another unannounced visitor for August.'

August screwed her face up, wondering who on earth it could be this time, and made her way to reception, closely followed by Max.

'I guessed you were busy, so I thought I'd come to you for an early lunch.' Sean was holding up two familiar brown bags of sandwiches from Mrs G and a large bottle of fizzy water. 'I got enough for two. Let's eat on the bench outside, it's a cracking day out there.'

August noticed a look of complete disappointment as Max slowly shook his head at her. Blowing out a noisy breath, she said to Sean, 'Give me a sec. I'll meet you out there.'

Max's face was like thunder as she turned to him and said, 'It's not what it looks like.'

'It never is!' Turning his back on her, Max strode to the kitchen to retrieve his lunch from the fridge. She followed him and shut the door behind her. 'You're the one who just said on the podcast to say it how it bloody is, and you're the biggest hypocrite going!'

'Oh, you listened.' Despite the heat of their exchange, August felt pleased that he'd bothered. 'So you're not a complete shell when it comes to love, then. I really don't understand you, Max.'

'Well, you'll never need to now, will you? I don't need anyone to understand me or like me.'

'Come on. We all need someone, Max.'

'Just go to your vet, will you? I'm done.'

'What do you mean, you're done?'

'I've had enough. Lie after lie. Your sweet little author image doesn't wash on me, writer girl. 'You're just like the rest of them.'

'Max? The rest of who? Just talk to me, will you?'

'No. Just leave me alone, August.'

With a heavy heart, August went outside, got into Sean's Range Rover and insisted he drive up to the top meadow so as not to aggravate Max any further.

Despite his wild contradictions, she had hated seeing him like that. It made her so angry that he felt it his right to know what she was up to and then not give anything back himself, though. It was preposterous, in fact.

He had no right to know anything about her relationship with Sean, so what had compelled her to tell him? Because she was open and honest, that's why. Something she feared that Max would never be, and if that was the case, then could she ever be with a man like that? Lie or no lie, it was over with the vet now – she just hadn't got round to telling him yet.

'What's the matter, my little bestseller? You don't seem pleased to see me.' August winced at the use of the pet name he had adopted for her. Sean carried on munching his cheese and pickle sandwich. 'And I don't know why anyone would want to sit in the car facing a field full of alpacas rather than outside in the beautiful sunshine where—'

'Look, Sean,' August interrupted, not quite knowing how to say what she needed to say without hurt.

'I've got a rug in the boot we can sit on, if you want to?' Then, as though sensing the sudden change of atmosphere shrouding them, Sean's voice began to sound decidedly desperate. 'Or it's fine to stay in here. Whatever you want to do.' He threw his door open to let some breeze through.

'Sean, listen, please.' August sighed. 'It's been so much fun.'

Sean put his unfinished sandwich back in the brown paper bag and put it in the side pocket of the car. 'Oh, shit. This is the bit when you're going to say, but I don't want to do it any more, aren't you?'

August nodded. 'I'm sorry.'

He fixed his gaze on the alpacas. 'No, I'm sorry. I broke the number one, friends-with-benefits rule of falling for you.' His face fell and August was worried that he might cry.

'You did.' She kept her voice soft and low. 'It was all a bit too much, you showing up at the crisis centre and my home.'

'I know, I know. It's like you've put a spell on me, though. I think you're amazing, August, I really do.'

'We've only known each five minutes; you don't really know me. And you don't have to apologise. It's flattering. You're a gorgeous bloke, Sean, but for someone else, not me.'

Turning to face her, Sean took both her hands in his. 'Look, I hear you. But what I do know after such a brief time is that you are beautiful and clever and sexy and fun and such great company. What if I speak like this' – he assumed an American accent – 'and get the same tattoos as Justin Timberlake.'

August laughed. 'You're way sexier than him.'

'So why don't we just carry on as we are? I promise I'll behave – or misbehave, if that's what you want me to do.' He smiled lovingly at her.

'Because it's not fair on you. You have the feels; I clearly don't. I will hurt you and the last thing I would want to do is that. You said yourself, you're not ready to settle down.'

'Meeting you has changed that.'

'Oh, Sean.' August looked into his young, honest, baby-blue eyes and suddenly realised, despite everything that had just happened, she would much rather be looking into the soulful but sad brown ones of Max Ronson. 'I don't think that changes anything, to be honest. Let's be friends without the benefits. Do you think you can do that?'

There were tears in the handsome vet's eyes. 'Give me a bit of time, and let's see.'

August nodded with complete understanding and realisation at how easy this was when the shoe was on the other foot. 'I'm going to walk back; I need the fresh air.' She got out of the car and walked round to the driver's side window.

'I listened to Mum's podcast earlier. You were great, but if you want my opinion, love is a bastard.' He bit his lip.

August brushed it with hers. 'You're great too and don't ever let anyone let you forget that.'

Sean sighed. 'I'd better get back to the clinic.' He smiled a watery smile. 'It's been a blast, my little bestseller.'

'Yes, it has. And a classic case of right place, wrong time, like so much of life.'

'Wrong time for you maybe.' Sean winked. 'But I'll be your stepping stone anytime.'

And as August and her confused heart started to walk slowly back to the Hub, the whirlwind that was Max Ronson and his muddy Range Rover sped past her without so much as a toot.'

Chapter Thirty Five

Knowing that Max was now off the premises, August went straight to his office, which she found surprisingly and thankfully unlocked, and retrieved her phone, which had slipped out of her bag and onto the chair she'd been sitting on. She could hear the camera box, as he called it, whirring in the corner, capturing every inch of every square foot of land and building.

With the whiff of cigarette smoke as her only company, she lingered to look more closely at the black and white prints on the wall. A lot of the Formula One greats she assumed, in racing action, and also the drivers in relaxed states after the event. They were stunning shots. The casual ones, in particular, which always showed personalities far better than any stiff formal ones. It was a photo of the legendary Stirling Moss in full racing gear, with his arm draped across the shoulders of a handsome man dressed in trendy sixties attire, who was holding a camera in his hand, that caught her eye. It was signed in squiggly black pen: *To Gene, pole position photographer extraordinaire, Love Stirling.* The man with the camera had hair, but on close inspection looked the spitting image of Max. The same brooding dark eyes and full mouth. The same upturned amused smile. They were in fact so similar it made her heart skip a little beat. They must be related, surely?

With her heart beating a little faster for fear of Max picking up on the cameras that she was snooping, August hurriedly closed the office door behind her and made her way to the kitchen. Not feeling hungry after all the emotional goings-on, she put her uneaten sandwich in the fridge and was just waiting for an espresso from the machine when the tall figure of Ade Ronson appeared in the kitchen.

'Oh, hi August. Is Jonah around?'

'He was earlier. You OK?'

'Yes, fine, apart from Mrs G reliably informing me that my wayward brother has cleared off for the day and night, and, even worse, that there's a huge summer storm coming later. Heavy rain – a month's worth in a day – and high winds are predicted.'

August peered out of the window. 'That doesn't seem possible. It's so lovely out there at the moment.'

'I know. Crazy, isn't it? The weather the past couple of years has no rhyme or reason about it. Cementing yet again the idea that we all need to do our bit for the environment.'

'Yes, our beautiful planet didn't get the memo that the human race thinks it gets the luxury of a dress rehearsal.' August took a sip of her coffee.

'OK. I must get everything sorted.' Ade checked his watch, a look of concern on his face.

Jonah strolled in and Ade turned to him.

'Just the man. Jonah, mate, I need your help.'

'Hey, Ade. What's up?'

'Would you mind locking up tonight, please? Mrs G is leaving shortly, and Max isn't around. Same drill as before.'

'Sure, sure, I'm doing a four-pm school run today. Was going to head off before this weather comes in. Last thing I want is to get caught by a fallen tree. Plus, Sukie is making her speciality red-bean vegan burgers tonight, and I'm not missing out on those.'

'Fine by me,' Tyler said as he strolled in. 'Sorry, couldn't help but overhear. Reece actually just told me to come home and work as he's worried I'll get blown off my scooter.'

'I'm happy with that. I'll go and tell Cat,' August offered.

'If you can close all the shutters too, please. Can't be doing with all the glass getting damaged in this place. A metal bucket flew and smashed the front door last time. The wind whips around these open meadows like a bloody tornado.'

'I can't see it being that bad,' Tyler said, pouring hot water on to his instant hot chocolate.

'I'd rather be safe than sorry. OK, I need to make sure all the turkeys are in and safe and sound – and not forgetting the seven dwarves.'

'Where has the guvnor gone, anyway?' Tyler stirred his drink furiously.

'Who knows?' August noticed the agitation in his brother's voice. 'But his timing, as usual, is impeccable.'

'OK, I'm off before the monsoon hits,' Cat announced, grabbing her mac from the freestanding hat and coat stand in the reception area. Sitting at one of the open-plan desks, August noticed her bright red lipstick and smart attire. 'Look at you, all dressed up. Going somewhere nice?'

'Meeting with the bank manager.'

'Ooh, a meeting or a *meeting*?' August cocked her head to the side.

Cat made a face. 'He's growing on me.'

'Must be the small ego.'

Cat laughed her deep, throaty laugh. 'And before you tell me off, his wife has left him.'

'No way!'

'Yes way. She sat down with him at the breakfast table on Sunday and admitted she didn't love him any more. Has been planning her escape since September, when their last kid left for university, evidently. Packed a case and just left.'

'I'm surprised you're still seeing him, now there's no escape route for you.'

Cat faked putting her fingers in her ears. 'Lalalala, I can't hear you.'

'On a more serious note, I told your Sean that I wouldn't be seeing him any more. He didn't take it too well, I'm afraid.'

'How dare you upset my son?' August was worried for a second that the brusque Scottish woman meant it, but then Cat laughed. 'Don't worry, I'll talk to him. He's a sensitive soul, my boy. Must have got that from his father. And you have to do what's right for you.' She checked her watch. 'I must fly.'

'Have fun and don't do anything I wouldn't do.' A relieved August laughed and gave her friend a parting hug.

'And T,' Cat directed at the lad, 'I'll see you tomorrow – if this place hasn't blown away like the house in *The Wizard of Oz*.'

'If it does, let's hope it ends up somewhere hot, like Barbados,' Tyler drawled, following her with crash helmet in hand. 'I'm off too. Laters.'

'Looks like it's just you and me then, kid. Fancy a cuppa?' Jonah was making his way to the kitchen.

'Yes, I'll come with you. I need to raid the machine for chocolate.'

'So, how's the new book coming along?' Jonah put his hand to his head. 'Shit, that's one thing we're not supposed to ask you, isn't it?'

August laughed. 'It's OK if it's going well – which, thankfully, it is. Living around here certainly makes it much easier to write about the sights and sounds of the countryside. Futtingbrook Fallow is a fictitious livery yard, but it's great to be able to reference a lot of local stuff.'

'I guess your readers love it too.' Jonah flicked the kettle on.

'Yes, it's amazing how having such a local following soon snowballs to a wider audience.'

'It must be so amazing having that creative skill.'

'You used to be a tailor, so you have it too, Jonah – just a different craft.'

'You are far too modest, August, but yes, I guess so. I'm super-pleased for your success.'

'Thanks, Jonah. How's business for you?'

'Fantastic, thanks. I caught the market at the right time and personally – well, the fact that I can just go and pick up the kids, like today, and have much more family time – it's changed all our lives for the better.'

'Yes, it's all about the work-life balance. I used to think that whenever I worked late at Placatac. Nobody would ever remember me for all the arduous extra work I put in – probably more for singing a duet of "Somethin' Stupid" with the finance director at the Christmas party, then whipping my sparkly top off in his face to reveal the greyest bra you've ever seen.'

Jonah smiled. 'I listened to your podcast. Glad to hear you're finding your feet again. I also overheard Max raising his voice. August...talking as a friend here. Whatever has gone on between you – and I don't wish to know – it's obvious that he likes you, a lot. He was gutted when you didn't come in. I could tell. He's a man of few words when it comes to sharing personal stuff, but Mr Empathy here can read him like a book.'

'He infuriates and amuses me in equal measure.'

'So does my wife,' Jonah smiled. 'But I wouldn't change her for the world.

'Love is…and all that.' August went across to the snack machine. 'I really like him too, if I'm honest. I find him really attractive, but most of all he stimulates me. We banter well, if that's a thing.'

'So, what's the "but"?' Jonah poured boiling water on top of their tea bags.

'He's a study in contradiction. He lashes out at the smallest thing, and demands openness and honesty in others while expecting them to put up with his extreme secrecy. In his own words, he has dark horses in his stable. In fact, he is a bloody dark horse personified.'

'We all are to a degree, and spin that on its head: the whole point of the dark horse is that they usually win in the end.'

'Please remind me to always have you in my corner, Jonah Lin.'

'I like to see the good in people.'

'You really do. And I know now, I'm ready to settle down – dare I say it, have kids – and Max doesn't seem that kind of guy. He seems troubled, he seems preoccupied. Even reckless. Prime example: the responsibility to close up the barn and make it safe should lie with him, but his brother doesn't know where he is and has had to step in. I've always been drawn to the bad boy, but ultimately that isn't what is going to make me happy. I know that, now.'

'Bad blood makes the heart beat faster and all that, August, but it is rarely sustainable.'

'Ooh, I'm going to use that – if you don't mind?'

'It's been used a millions times before, I'm sure, but use away.' Jonah went to the fridge to get the milk. 'August, I am going to tell you something now, but it is something you must never profess to knowing until you hear it from the dark horse's mouth himself.' Jonah put two cups of steaming tea down on the table and sat down. August sat opposite, her ears wide open. 'Max has a child. A boy. He must be ten years old, now, I reckon.'

'Oh my God! I can't believe it. Max, a father?' August felt sick at the revelation of yet another huge secret that this man held. 'Who's the mother? Is it Porsche woman, a.k.a. the architect, do you know?'

'I'm not speculating about anything, because I don't know. I only know this because I was here on my own one night when he came down from upstairs blind drunk and told me. It was never mentioned again. I don't think he even remembers that he told me, and if he does, it's something for sure that he doesn't want us all knowing about.'

'You can trust me, Jonah,' August said sincerely.

'I know I can. I guess in a clumsy, roundabout way, I was trying to say that he does have the capacity to be a father. Who knows if he will want to be a dad again? I'm not a mind reader, but what I do know is that I want the best for Max. Underneath that big brash bravado is a lovely and, I fear, lonely man. I wish I could peel the layers of trouble from him.'

'But Jonah, it's hard enough managing a relationship with two stable parties, let alone having to fix someone first.' August ran her fingers through her hair. 'I can't believe it. Max, a father,' she repeated.

'I appreciate that, but it would be such a waste if the pair of you didn't find love. I do believe that if people work on themselves and have a true champion, they can change. I also think that a good woman – like you – could be the making of him.' Jonah checked outside nervously. 'OK, let's drink this, then do you mind helping me get the shutters down? I need to head off soon after.'

'Sure. Bloody hell, talking of dark things, look at that sky. It's all of a sudden gone black.' August checked her weather app. 'Shit, yes, here it comes, much earlier than we thought!' Suddenly there was a huge clap of thunder and the heavens opened. 'Jonah, you go and pick up the kids. They can't be hanging around in this, and the roads may get dangerous.'

'Don't be daft. I will help you.'

'It's a few shutters on the huge downstairs windows and bifold doors. The front ones are all done already. Go on. Worst case I stay here writing all night – I've been known to do that at home.'

Despite August's pleas, Jonah ran around with her, securing what they could of the barn together.

'Get your coat, lady. Come on, let's get out of here.'

With a sudden ulterior motive in mind, August replied calmly, 'Actually, I am going to stay. I don't mind being captive. There's food in the snack machine and I'll have no distractions here, no excuses not to be writing.'

August watched Jonah head off and called Ellie. 'Hey, sis, has the storm hit yet?'

'Oh my god, yes. Grant is just moving the outdoor furniture into the shed. It's mental. Where are you? Are you OK?'

'Fine, fine. Rather than brave the road with all those trees, I'm going to stay at the Hub. Would you mind popping next door and checking on his royal highness, and giving him a sachet and some crunchies? You have a key, haven't you?'

'Sure, but be careful, Goose, OK? Is anyone there with you?'

'No, but Max's brother is only minutes away at the farmhouse.'

'OK. Love you. I'll call Mum too and warn her off any heroics. That greenhouse of hers is near to falling down, anyway.'

'Fab. Love you too.'

August went to the kitchen to get herself a drink. Wind

was now howling around the outside of the barn. A flash of lightening lit up the whole sky, followed by another huge rumble of thunder. She felt the hairs on her arms rise: she had always felt exhilarated by extreme weather. It made her feel alive.

But it wasn't just the weather that was exciting her – oh no. With Max out of the equation all night, and everybody else busy sheltering from the storm, now was the perfect chance for her to have a good old Lila Lovelace super-sleuth snoop and see exactly what the Hub owner was up to behind his closed doors. Her character's motto was 'knowledge is power', and if she were even to consider a relationship with this man, she wanted to know exactly what he was about before she considered unravelling that red flag from its pole. This now included finding out who exactly was the mother of his son and why the little lad was being kept such a secret.

Checking the front door was locked, she made her way into Max's office to turn off all power in the building via the fuse board that she had spotted in there just the other day. With all lights and security cameras off, and with her phone torch in hand, she headed to the one drawer in his desk. With trembling hand, she turned the key and opened it. Inside were a couple of packets of the familiar brand of cigarettes he smoked and a lighter. Nothing new there. Another flash of lightning lit up the room and she nearly jumped out of her skin as a stray branch hit the window with some force. Pushing her hand to the back of the drawer, she felt something else. Pulling out two photographs, she gasped. In one photo, there smiling back at her was a younger-looking Max, maybe in his mid-thirties, with a head full of hair and a smile that lit up his whole face. It was true that beauty had its foundation in happiness, because she had never seen him look so handsome or content. Grasping his hand was a black-haired mini him, around five years old, she guessed, sitting on the steps at Trafalgar Square. And in the other photo, mirroring the exact same stance and location was the same man she had seen in the signed photo with Stirling Moss, holding the hand of a little boy, a little boy who was clearly Maximillian Ronson.

Agog at the sight in front of her, she was suddenly startled by a message on her phone.

August, Ivor says your car is still at the Hub. Are you OK? Max tells him that the cameras have gone off too. Ade.

I'm fine. It must be a power cut.

August felt a swoop of guilt as she messaged back with this lie, but was still not deterred in her mission to uncover what she could before the return of Max Ronson and all of his secrets.

Ah, OK. Come up the farm if you don't want to drive home.

I have battery power in my laptop and the ambience is brilliant for the scene I am writing, but thank you. The worst of it will pass soon, I'm sure.

She would have to be quick. If Max knew the cameras were out it might spin him into a panic to come back from wherever he was. Putting the photos back exactly as she had found them, she made her way to the lift. Checking notes on her phone, she bought up the password she had since saved and keyed it in. 'Shit!' she said under her breath, realising the lift needed electricity to work. Relieved that Jonah had shared with her the existence of the hidden fire-escape stairs, she ran around the back of the kitchen and climbed them two by two. Reaching the top, she was both thankful and surprised to find the door to the flat was open. Once there, she actually wasn't sure, one, where she should look, and two, what she was really looking for. Because aside from a small kitchen, a bathroom and the bedroom, at the top of the stairs were just stacks and stacks of boxes.

Tentatively walking with her torch as low to the ground as possible for fear of Ivor or Ade driving by and seeing the light, she suddenly came across another room – an office, it looked like. Inside was a table, a printer and further boxes. Placing her hand into one of the boxes and pulling out a strip of labels, she gasped again. It seemed her gut had been right about Max Ronson not being a pillar of the community and handing out honey to food banks. Oh, no! He had obviously been buying cheap honey, relabelling the jars and reselling them as expensive Ralukar honey!

With the storm still crashing and banging around the barn, August walked slowly down the back stairs. She hadn't put Max down as a criminal, and rather than worry her, it had saddened her. He obviously needed money, but for what? There had to be an explanation as, if he really was in trouble, surely he could turn to his brother for help? Yes, he was selling hooky honey, not drugs or arms, but even so, the mystery really was thickening and August was worried that she may already be in too deep.

Turning the power back on, she unlocked the front door and stuck her head out to gauge the strength of the wind. She was startled to see, amid the commotion of the storm, Ivor tearing past on a quad bike, closely followed by Ade screeching down the lane in one of the farm vans.

On seeing her, he opened his window and bawled in fear, 'August, the alpacas have escaped. Can you come and help?'

Grabbing her keys, she ran to her car. With windscreen wipers doing nothing against the sheeting rain, she screeched to a halt at the sight of Ade's brake lights in front of her on the farm drive. As she quickly climbed out of her car, Ade screamed for her to call an ambulance. Dialling 999, she suddenly realised why. For there, in front of the open meadow gate, toppled out of her wheelchair, was Judith Ronson with blood pouring from her head, which her son, in floods of tears, was cradling.

'Is the patient breathing?' the operator asked.

'No.' August stuttered. 'No, I don't think she is.'

It was only eight pm, still light in fact, when August returned home, but it felt like midnight. The storm had left as quickly as it arrived, with nothing more now than a strong breeze and spits of rain. If it wasn't for the deep puddles and stray branches everywhere, you wouldn't even have known it had happened. August knew she looked a sorry and bedraggled sight as she got out of her mud-splattered Mini. After receiving such a shocking message from her sister, Ellie was already at the door to greet her.

Without words she went to her older sister and kissed her forehead. 'Come on, let's get you warm and dry, shall we?' August silently followed her sister inside. 'Prince Harry is fed. I grabbed your dressing gown and put it on the radiator. The shower is already running warm. The boys are asleep and Grant's helping Mrs Trinder look for her shed roof. Last seen flying towards the cricket pitch.'

Twenty minutes later, August appeared in the lounge. Her hair was wrapped in a fluffy white towel and she was wearing the cosy dressing gown she had bought with her sister at the outlet centre months previously.

'I made you a strong cuppa, but I do have some gin if you'd rather?' Ellie put a steaming mug of tea down on the side table next to the sofa.

'This is perfect.' August picked up and cradled the drink in both hands. 'I've written about countless dead bodies before, but seeing one in real life is a totally different story. And for the

Ronson boys, losing their mum in such a devastating and tragic way… I can't even imagine their horror.'

'Were they both there?'

'Ade was, but Max was meeting him directly at the hospital.'

'So do they know what happened?'

'Not exactly, but you know how quickly the storm hit.' Ellie nodded. 'Mrs Ronson had been painting in the cherry orchard meadow. When the sky went dark, Ade reckons she probably took it upon herself to go and check the alpacas were inside their sleeping barn and not roaming around. There's a stone path from the wooden gate where she could go inside and check, even in her wheelchair, you see.'

'Right.' Ellie nodded again.

'Anyway, the theory is that a huge gust of wind took the gate and it slammed back so hard that it knocked her flying out of her wheelchair headfirst on to the concrete. The paramedic said that she would have died instantly.' August started to cry. 'Poor Mrs Ronson and those poor boys.'

'Oh my god! That is so sad and I'm sorry you had to see that too, Goose.'

'Yes, tragic. I remember Ade telling me that she loved those alpacas. But to die for them…well, that is quite something.' August sniffed.

'So did they find her straight away?'

'Yes, luckily. When the storm hit early, Ade realised the alpacas would be terrified so sent Ivor – that's the chief farm hand – straight up to their meadow. It was Ivor who raised the alarm that they had escaped and then they saw poor Judith.'

'How is Max?'

'No idea. He had gone off in a tantrum after rowing with me and was having to drive back from London in all that weather. I can't even imagine the pain he's in. Because despite everything he does to piss me off, I still really like him.' August blew her nose loudly with the tissue her sister had just handed her from her pocket.

'Oh, Goose. Ade and his family will comfort him. And if that's how you feel, you must tell him exactly that, when the dust has settled from all this. How are you feeling now, that's the important thing?'

'Sad, shocked. Poor Max. If we hadn't rowed, he would have been with his mother.'

'Maybe it's better he wasn't. If she had been alive and died at the scene it would have been a different matter, but there wouldn't have been anything to be gained from him just seeing her lying there, and carrying that mental picture with him for the rest of his life.'

'I guess so. And poor Ade. How on earth will he and Beth tell their kids what has happened to their grandmother?'

'I can't even imagine.' Ellie sat down next to her sister on the sofa and put her arm around her.

'Is Mum OK?' August put her drink down and curled up so that her legs were just touching her sister's.

'Yes, aside a couple of greenhouse panels blowing inwards and a few pots misplaced around the garden, she's fine.'

'Good.'

August shut her eyes for a second and took a deep breath. Driving home, she had felt sick at the thought of what would have happened if Ade hadn't taking the initiative to rush up to the alpacas and found his mother there. What if, because she had turned the security cameras off, she hadn't been found until the next day? It was too awful even to contemplate. She had made a point of making sure all that needed to be turned on or off in the Hub was, and of locking up, just as Max would have wanted, before she left, but that didn't stop her feeling terrible about it now.

August could feel Ellie peering at her worriedly, and made an effort to smile. 'Anyway,' she said, trying to sound upbeat, 'what other news do you have for me?'

'I had my twenty-week scan this morning,' Ellie delivered matter-of-factly.

August gasped. 'I didn't realise you were going! Wow! Exciting! Time seems to have flown with this one.'

'I know. I can't believe it is July already either. And guess what?'

'Oh my god, a girl!'

'Yes.' Ellie put her hand to her tummy. 'Little Bluebell Rose is cooking away nicely in here.'

'Aww, have you told Mum?'

'Yes. She's over the moon.'

'I bet she is. And Grant?'

'He's beside himself. He said he can deal with a mixed five-a-side team, so that means we only have two more strikers to create.'

August shook her head. 'Remind me of your due date again.'

'November fifth.'

'Yeah! That means we'll be able to celebrate with birthday fireworks every year.'

'If she arrives as scheduled, that is. She already feels massive, unless that's all the chicken pie I'm eating. I mean, what's that all about? I've never craved chicken before. And tinned peaches – I can't get enough of them this time around, either. With the boys it was peanut butter and pineapple.'

'Weird, isn't it? This house of a body we live in is so clever, knowing what we need and when.'

'It really is. And talking of houses, how's your search going?'

'It's not, to be honest. Sorry. The book has taken over, but I promise I will get on to it again soon.'

'Honestly, it's fine. If we have to have three of them in one room for a while, we'll manage.'

The joyous ten minutes of 'normal' chat was over and the vision of Judith Ronson lying in the mud with blood streaming from her head took over August's thoughts once more. She sighed deeply. 'You've been amazing, Ells, but I'm going to head home now. I'm so knackered.'

'I bet you are. Just quickly, did you speak to Sean?'

'Yes, he was upset but not really surprised, I don't think.'

'And you're feeling OK about Scott's baby news?'

'Yes. If I'm being truly honest with myself, even though the obstacles are so great, it's Max who has been on my mind. I really do like him.'

'Then you must weigh up everything – the pros, the cons.' At the word cons, August suddenly remembered the dodgy honey labels, which she had decided she would not mention to a soul until she'd found out the truth. 'Set some boundaries, Goose, and follow your heart.'

'He might not be feeling the same way, anyway.' What had happened to her? He could be a potential criminal, and apparently she didn't even care!

'Well, you were the one on that podcast saying comm-u-ni-cation is key, so comm-u-ni-cate.' August gave a small laugh. 'And Goose?'

'Yes, little sister?'

'You may well lose him to grief for a while now – you realise that?'

'As long as that is the only reason I lose him, then that's fine.'

'Will you go to the funeral?'

'I'll speak to my friends at the Hub and see. Personally, I think we should support him.'

'Your friends, you say?' Ellie stood up at the same time as August, and gently put her arm on her sister's shoulder. 'Look how far you've come. New workspace, new friends, a volunteering role and a potential new man. Once you've both sorted out your differences, that is, of course, big sister.' Ellie patted her arm lovingly.

'I know. And it has kind of all just happened without me looking. It all seemed to find me, just like mama bear said it would.'

'Bless Mum. She's been through so much herself and remained so stoic.'

'Yes, we're lucky to have her.' Ellie went through to the kitchen and opened the washer dryer.

'When something like today happens, it really does make you want to hold on tight to your loved ones.'

'Absolutely. Sorry, Goose, your clothes are washed but not dry yet.'

'It's fine, I'll walk back around in my dressing gown.'

They got to the door. August kissed her sister on the cheek and gently put her hand on her rounded belly. 'Imagine if she's a mini me.'

'God help us if she is,' Ellie smiled. 'Love you, Goose.'

'Love you, too. And thanks for being there tonight.'

'Always and forever. You know that.'

Chapter Thirty Six

The day of Judith Ronson's funeral thankfully brought with it a cloudless July sky.

August stood up to lead the row of Hub mourners out of the church. The very same church where they had buried her father twenty years previously.

As she approached the doorway, all she could hear were the words, 'It was a lovely service'. It didn't sit right with her. She could never quite get her head around people saying that, especially after her dad's funeral. How could anything be described as lovely if you were burying or cremating somebody you loved. Today, she had cried, like she always cried at funerals, whether she was close to the person or not. The outpouring of grief around her reminded her of her own losses. Of her father and grandparents and her Great Auntie Betty before them. Dear old Betty, the most eccentric of the Saunders family, who not only hoarded everything and nurtured seven cats, but had swum every day religiously in the freezing waters of the little cove near her bungalow in North Devon. Maybe this cold-water-swimming lark wasn't just a modern-day fad, as Auntie Betty had lived to the grand old age of ninety-three. August and Ellie were sure now that she had been a lesbian and had sadly never felt comfortable enough to strike up a relationship with a woman. And this wasn't just because she put her old age down to the fact that she had remained husbandless and childless. 'Bloody men,' she used to say. 'No more useful than a blunt knife at an abattoir.'

August hadn't spoken to Max since the upset about Sean. She had wanted to resolve their leaving row about whether or not she had to leave, but the death of Max's mother had obviously overtaken everything. So, in order not to tamper with his emotions further, she had decided to stay away completely and write at home. She had learnt from Cat that for the past two weeks he had mainly hidden himself away at his brother's farmhouse preparing the funeral, or when not there, she had seen him heading out of the gate, off to wherever he went. She said that Ade had more often than not closed up the Hub each evening with just a silent wave and an attempt at a smile. Not wanting them to think that she didn't care, though, she had written condolence cards to both brothers and posted them to the farmhouse.

On reaching the doorway of the church, she saw both brothers thanking people for coming, in parrot fashion. Mrs Dye was of course in attendance, like the grim reaper herself, ready to spread gossip around the village like muck around a field.

August had never seen Max looking more handsome, or more sad. His tailored black suit, shirt and tie were sharp and immaculate, his shoes highly polished. There was no hint of stubble. He was wearing his black-framed going-out glasses. But despite this outward perfection, he looked haunted. Vacant, somehow.

'Hey.' She kissed him on both cheeks, causing tears to run down hers as if the meeting of their skin had somehow passed over his intense feelings of grief to her. 'Every storm runs out of rain,' she had managed to whisper to him, then on reaching her car realised what a ridiculous thing to have said, seeing as his mother had died during a bloody storm. She cursed her lack of sensitivity, but there was nothing she could do about it now but hope that he was so dazed it wouldn't have registered. Being there also made her realise just how much she missed seeing him.

Cat approached her. 'Aw, August. Bless you, getting so upset.' The Scotswoman put her arm gently around her Hub mate.

'I'm good, it's just – you know. Death.' August made a strange noise, a laugh mixed with a cry.

'Yes. Funerals make me want to embrace life more, though. Not waste a second of it. Are you going to the burial or back to the farmhouse for the wake?'

'Neither. I just wanted to show my respects here. And there's no way I can face the actual committal, especially as this is the very same churchyard where my dad is buried.' August reached for a tissue in her bag and blew her nose.

'Oh, bless you, pal. OK. I drove Jonah and Tyler, so we are all heading back to the Hub now too. Well, I'll hope to see you soon then. We must go to Jaxon's again, and why don't you do the December *Love is…* podcast? That will be near your publication day, won't it?'

August turned the key in her car ignition and was just pulling slowly out of the church car park when she noticed *the* silver Porsche pulling into a space two along from her. Pretending to fiddle around in her handbag, she watched intently as the stunning, raven-haired beauty got out, dressed from head to toe in Prada – black hat and huge sunglasses included. But her biggest accessory of all was the same little boy she had seen in the photograph, now not so little, but also dressed head to toe in black. And as she watched the pair join the tail end of the small group of mourners following the coffin down to the graveyard, August wondered how anyone could be so late for a funeral. And who exactly was this mystery woman with Max's ten-year-old son?

Ellie was just taking a parcel in from the front door when August arrived back home. 'Hey you. How did it go?' Her voice was soft and caring.

'Horrible, really horrible. So sad.' August sighed deeply.

'Did you get to talk to Max?'

'I just kissed him and said sorry and then I said the most ridiculous thing, which on a normal day would be so sweet because it's a beautiful Maya Angelou quote. But in the context of what happened, it was the worst thing I could possibly have said.' August gave a loud sob. 'Oh, Ells.'

'It can't be that bad, surely. What did you say?'

'"Every storm runs out of rain."'

'Oh, Goose. Don't worry, he won't think anything of it. He's too busy just getting through today.'

'You think so?'

'I know so. Hang on a sec, let me get you your clothes. I keep forgetting to give them to you, and I ironed them too.'

August tutted as Ellie handed them to her. 'What would I do without you, eh?' She turned her face to the sun. Thank goodness it's summer and warm. So much easier than a winter funeral, when it's cold or raining.

'Yes, totally agree. So, what are you up to for the rest of the day?'

'I'm going to have some early dinner then go to bed for a few

279

hours, as I'm on a night shift at the Sebastian Line.'

'What's that then, a midnight start?'

'Yep, until six am. I've only done one before. It's a killer but if I get some shut-eye first, I should be OK. I'm on with someone else tonight, so the chat will keep us going if it's not busy.'

'OK, well, take care of you. I'll try and keep the little monsters quiet.'

'I'll put my earbuds in. Don't worry.'

August headed inside and shut the door. She hadn't been in the mood to share further details with her sister – of Max and his son and the mystery woman – but when the time was right and she had all the information, she would.

Chapter Thirty Seven

'Hello,' August called as she walked into the Sebastian Line centre and threw her handbag down in the left-hand call room. She checked her watch: five minutes past midnight. The person who was joining her was obviously a bit late. She was just about to go and put the kettle on when she heard very loud snoring coming from upstairs. 'Hello.' She called again, loudly up the staircase this time. There was then a cry of, 'Oh, fuck!' and a dishevelled David appeared, shirt hanging out of his trousers. August could smell whisky on his breath. 'Darcy's not feeling too good with her hormones again,' he said blearily. 'You'd have thought her UHT would have kicked in by now. Anyway, I said I'd do a double shift. Young Melanie left, I went to rest my eyes and must have fallen asleep. What's the time?'

'You're fine, it's only ten past midnight. Why don't you go back up and if the second phone rings, I'll just call your mobile?'

'That would be amazing, thank you,' he said, his voice weak with gratitude. 'You won't tell Darcy?'

'I promise. Now get some rest. It's fine. No point two of us sitting here waiting.'

Ring, ring, ring, ring... 'Here we go!' August said to herself as David disappeared upstairs and back to the little single bed, and began to snore immediately.

'The Sebastian Line, Geri speaking. Is there a name I can call you by?'

'You sound really pretty, I bet you are really pretty. What's your name, then?' The gruff man continued in a lecherous manner.

August hid her sigh. 'We're not here to talk about me. So, what led you to call us tonight, then?'

'I'm depressed.'

'I'm really sorry to hear that.'

'Yeah, and when I'm depressed it makes me want to touch myself to make me feel better.'

August kept her tone level and kind. 'Well, touch away, but I'm afraid I'm not going to listen while you do it.' She hung up, exclaiming aloud, 'This is a crisis line, not bloody Babe Station.' The phone rang again immediately.

'Surely, not,' she said under her breath. She took a huge glug of coffee and reached for the biro and notepad in front of her.

'The Sebastian Line, Geri speaking. Is there a name I can call you by?'

'Look, I'm really sorry for bothering you and I've never done this before and…I don't know what to do, and do I have to tell you my name?' the man blurted.

August's heart began racing at one hundred miles an hour. She knew that voice, and tried to deepen hers to disguise it. 'Take your time, you're in a safe space and it's OK, you don't have to tell me your name if you don't want to.'

'Just call me…call me Gene.' Remembering that that was the name on the photo she had seen in Max's office, August put her hand to her heart. A racking sob came down the phone. August opened her eyes wide in horror. 'I just need to talk to somebody.' August blew out a deep slow breath from pursed lips.

'Just take your time.'

'I buried my mum today. Well, me and my brother did, and I'm at a real low point in my life.'

'That's tough stuff.' August did her best to keep the shake out of her voice. 'Do you mind me asking how she died?' August just needed to be one hundred per cent sure it was him.

'If it hadn't happened to someone I loved dearly it would be true black comedy. A gate flew open and hit her in that storm we had a couple of weeks back. Knocked her clean out of her wheelchair and she hit her head on the concrete and died.'

'I'm so sorry. What a terrible shock for you.'

'I'd ruined her life already, though.' From the way his voice was slurring, she could tell that Max had had a drink.

'Why do you say that?'

'I've always been a cunt of a son. Played up. Sorry, sorry my language.'

'It's fine, swear away.'

'I was the bad boy at school compared to my brother, who was always golden bollocks. But when I was thirty, I started to sort myself out. Got clean, got a job in London. I had picked myself up, started working as a broker in the city and I think I had actually started to make her proud. A massive bonus bought me a Ferrari and I wanted to show her how well I was doing, you know?'

August was umming in all the right places. She knew she should fess up that it was her, but he need never know he had spoken to her.

'So I drove up the driveway to the farm where she and Dad lived. It's a turkey farm and, well, one of the little blighters had randomly escaped. Must have been near Christmas and he was making a run for freedom. I've blocked it out, I can't even remember. How bad is that!' Max made a funny noise, a cross between a laugh and a cry. August couldn't believe that he was still cracking jokes when he was so obviously in despair. 'And in swerving to miss it, I accidentally put my foot on the accelerator by mistake. She had been riding her horse down to meet me, see, and I careered straight into them both. Désirée, her beautiful big black mare, died instantly, and Mum was paralysed. Has been in a wheelchair ever since. Or had, I should now say.' Max continued to sob.

Tears streamed down August's face. How awful! There was a pause and she knew he was waiting for her to speak, so she forced herself to take a deep, calming breath and did her best to keep her new-found deep voice level. 'That must have been unimaginably difficult for you both. But it sounds like your relationship was a good one.'

'My mum is – for fuck's sake, was – my angel. Even when I was at my worst, she still loved me, was always there for me. She's one of the reasons I kept myself together.'

'And the other?' August took another sip of coffee in preparation of what was to come.

'Other what?' She could hear Max swigging back a drink.

'Reason,' August replied gently, slipping slightly out of her assumed voice.

'Matteo, my son. And this is why this is so difficult.'

'What's so difficult?'

'How can I leave him? How can I possibly leave him?'

'What do you mean when you say leave him?' August tried to keep the panic out of her voice.

'Without my mum by my side, I don't know if I can do this any more.'

August dug deep, remembering how Darcy had dealt with suicide calls in the past. But this was not any old suicide call, this was Max. The man who, on hearing this outpouring of grief, she now knew she cared for more even than she had realised. She turned to the notes in the back of her book, then promptly shut it. Instinct would get her through. Nothing was going to happen to Max Ronson. She would never let it.

'And where would Matteo be without you by his side?'

Max sniffed. She could hear him taking yet another drink. 'You are grieving now. Your world seems dark now, but maybe you're just stuck in a moment.'

'I love Matteo so much.'

'There you go. And I'm sure he loves you too.'

'He does, when I'm allowed to see him. And that's brings me down too.' Max's voice was full of despair. 'His mother. Nobody can hear me, can they? Calls aren't recorded, you promise?'

'I promise. It's just you and me.'

'Giulia. She's Italian; stunningly beautiful. I fell for her charms. Her sexiness. How shallow was I? Because she is a complete and utter sociopath. She just wanted a baby; she never wanted me. And from the minute my gorgeous son was born, she made that very clear. She insisted I gave her a ridiculously high monthly allowance and when I said that it was totally unfair and that I was going to go through the authorities to sort joint custody, her argument was that if I didn't give her the money that she wanted, then I would never be able to see him.'

'That's blackmail,' August piped up without thought.

'I know. It gets worse as, when I said that I would go through the courts, she threatened to leave the country with him. And it's stressing me out so much, trying to find this money every single month. When I worked in the city, I could manage it, but everything got on top of me and I just had to get out.'

Finally, some answers! Finally the truth! Forgetting everything about her role as a listening volunteer, August shifted into full on Lovelace & McGee mode.

'Why don't you turn it on its head and tell her she won't get the money if you can't see him?'

'Geri, you said, didn't you? You're amazing saying that,' Max slurred. 'But the bitch has thought of everything. She told me the law will be so much in her favour that if she insists I was violent towards her, she will get a court order against me.'

Thinking she was just in a room with Max and not at the end of a confidential suicide crisis line, August suddenly blurted, 'What a fucking awful bitch.'

'Oh wow – a sweary woman. I love that!' August had to smile at such a Maxism. And all the time he was thinking these things he wasn't thinking of harming himself. Maybe his moment had passed; maybe she had switched the tracks of his tragic thought train. He was talking, she was listening; there was hope. 'So, my brother bailed me out, but I lied about how much money she wanted, so he lent me thirty grand, thinking that would cover a couple of years' allowance for Matteo plus get my business up and running. And that has almost gone, and I'm shit at marketing the business I've started. So, I've had to turn to fucking crime myself.' August gulped and took a drink of her now-cold coffee. 'This is definitely confidential, isn't it?' Max repeated. 'I feel I just need to get it out.'

'Yes, yes…it's just you and me. I don't know who you are, a number doesn't flash up and I never will know who you are.'

'Are you a man or a woman?' Max questioned. 'Must be the booze, I'm sure your voice was deeper earlier.'

'I've got a bit of a cold,' August lied.

'Don't worry, I haven't killed anyone or anything.' She could hear Max light a cigarette and take a long drag. 'My plan is to sell cheap honey as a posh honey – that's all. Seems like everyone is falling for it, too. Just shows you what people will believe if you stick a fancy label on a bottle.'

'So how are you selling it?'

'I haven't actually sent any out yet, just been going around various markets in London chatting to people to gain some interest. But marketing really isn't my forte.'

'It sounds ingenious to me. Maybe you're not as bad at marketing as you think.' August hoped this would humour him.

'You're funny.' Max then suddenly sobbed again. 'But this isn't funny. I can't cope. I have to keep this façade up to keep paying Giulia and it's getting too much. If only my real dad was alive. If only he hadn't left me too.'

'Your real dad?'

'Everyone fucking dies who I love. I'm so fucking over it.'

'Oh, Gene. I'm so sorry you are feeling like this.'

'He took his own life after my real mum died of cancer. Selfish prick.'

'How old were you?' Silent tears ran down August's cheeks.

'Seven. I was seven. An orphan at seven. Thank God for Judith and Tony. They saved me when they adopted me. I couldn't have asked for better parents and now they're both gone, too.' Another sob.

'That's so tough, and I'm so sorry you've suffered such loss.'

'And I try not to blame him for leaving, but it hurts still. I loved him so much. He was a photographer. A really good photographer. Such a waste of a life. And I am angry that he did it!' Max shouted suddenly.

'Have you thought of getting professional help?' August offered calmly, taking a sip of her now-cold coffee.

'I've had buckets of therapy, but it doesn't remove the pain, it just dulls it. It has given me tools to try and move forward but I'm not sure I want to move forward any more.'

'Where are you, Gene?'

'I'm in my poxy excuse for a flat above the poxy business I

run, because I can't afford a place to call home. And to make it worse, I think I've fucked it up with the first woman I actually could have feelings for.'

'Oh.' Feeling the flutter of butterflies within her heart, August tried to keep her voice on a level. 'What's happened there then?'

'She's a stunning redhead – feisty, clever, kind. She would take no shit from me and that's what I need. She's been hurt, too, so she would get my pain. I really like her. Really fancy her, as well. She seems real, if you know what I mean? But I just seem to keep fucking it up.'

August put her hand to her chest. 'So why don't you tell her how you feel?'

'Because I think she thinks I'm a selfish prat. I've screwed her around already and I can't tell her about Giulia or Matteo or my dodgy dealings because she would probably run for the hills.'

'She might surprise you?'

'I haven't been truthful with her, though. I feel like all this would be too much for anyone to bear.'

'Well. You haven't got her now anyway, so what's to lose by trying to talk to her?'

Max let out a huge sigh. 'I don't know. I need some peace, Geri. I'm so sick of running and trying to stop my house of cards from falling down. I'm just an added pain in the arse to my brother, who is such a good man. We grew up so close in age and he put up with all my tantrums without any jealousy. He didn't even blame me for Mum's accident. I love him so much, and his wife and my precious nieces.'

'It sounds like so many people would miss you, Gene.' August now had a constant hot flow of tears running down her cheeks. Not wanting to blow her nose or show any sign of emotion to throw Max off his path or reveal who she was, she reached for the box of tissues in front of her and dabbed lightly at her face.

'You sound like an amazing man, Gene.'

Max was now crying softly down the phone. 'I do?'

'You do.' August put her hand over her mouth for a second to try and stop a huge outpouring of emotion from her side.

'I have tablets here.' Max said matter-of-factly. 'Enough to kill me, I reckon.'

The word NO formed like a huge brick in August's mouth. She dug deep into her memory bank from what she had learnt on previous suicide calls.

'You called your dad a selfish prick for doing what he did,' she said evenly.

'I understand how he felt now, though. I'm going now, Geri.'

'You don't have to.' August failed to keep the panic out of her voice as a feeling of white fear spread through her body. 'I can talk to you all night. And if you don't want to talk to me, then you can get help. Talk to a counsellor, maybe go to rehab, even.'

'Thank you so much, but I think I want to be alone now.'

'What about Matteo?' she said softly. 'You know yourself how hard it is losing your dad at such a young age.'

There was silence, but he was still there. August held every breath within her, every muscle rigid, waiting for Max's response. Surely if anything was going to persuade him to stop, it was his son?

She could hear his deep breathing, and as he went to speak she felt herself exhale deeply, with hope and relief.

'You've been amazing, thank you. But I'm in so much pain.' The phone clicked off.

Now in complete panic, August stared at the handset for a second and then knew exactly what she had to do. Running upstairs, she shook David, who was deep asleep, violently by the arm. 'David, David, you have to come down. I have a family emergency I need to deal with. NOW!'

Chapter Thirty Eight

August drove as fast as her Mini would allow out of the high street and down the quiet lane to Futtingbrook Farm. She froze for a moment when she reached the gate, thinking that she had forgotten the code, but she pulled the digits from the back of her brain then tore down the drive towards the Hub. So thankful it wasn't a traditional key-lock front door, she screeched up right outside it, pressed in the code and let herself in. Darkness and silence greeted her as she entered. Turning on the main light, she ran across to the lift and pressed the button. It seemed to take an age to make the short journey to the top, and when the doors began to slide open, she experienced a moment of sheer terror and dread at what she might find.

Scrabbling to find a light switch, she found Max fully dressed, lying on his side, absolutely still. Another white panic of fear shot right through her body. She shook him. 'Max, Max. It's me, August. Wake up, it's OK. It's going to be OK.' She was just about to dial 999, when all of a sudden his eyes opened and he spoke. 'Agatha. What are you doing here? Am I dreaming?' His voice was slow, his breathing laboured.

It was as if nothing had ever mattered more to her in the whole world than just hearing his voice.

'Oh, Max. What have you taken? Show me the bottle.'

Max pointed to the floor on the other side of the bed. 'A bottle of Mr Jack Daniels, that's what I've just taken. Half in one go.' He laughed, manically.

'Nothing else?'

'I thought I had painkillers.' He slurred. She noticed a bottle of herbal joint remedy tablets on the bedside table. 'I can't even bloody kill myself properly.'

'Max, I'm so sorry you're feeling like this.' She climbed onto the bed next to him and held his drunk, floppy body close to her.

'I'm so tired of everything, Agatha.' He snuggled into her as if he were a child.

She stroked his cheek. 'I know you are. But I'm here now and we are going to get you sorted, do you hear me?' She burst into tears at the stress of it all.

Too drunk now to realise how upset she was, he flopped back onto the bed.

'You need to drink some water.'

'You need to drink some water,' he mimicked, as August reached for a bottle of it on the floor and tried to sit him up to take some. He took a few sips, then plonked himself back down again.

'Do you want to get some of these clothes off?'

'You just want to see me naked, don't you?' he slurred, smiling the amused smile she had grown to adore. Without thought, she pulled off his trousers and t-shirt. His chest was smooth and toned, his arms firm with muscle. He dragged his white duvet up to his chin, turned to his side and sighed heavily. 'Don't leave me, Agatha.'

'I'm not going anywhere.' Kicking off her shoes, a fully clothed August climbed in beside him, gently placing her arms around his waist, then pulling herself tightly into his naked and shapely back. She was suddenly exhausted, but fought to keep her eyes open. It wasn't until she could hear his breathing shallow and be sure that he was sleeping that she allowed herself to fall into a restful slumber.

Chapter Thirty Nine

Max awoke to the late-July sun streaming in through his window, his mouth as dry as the Sahara desert. His head was pounding and he was sticky with sweat. His breath smelt like a camel had shat in it. But he was alive.

Groaning as memory snippets of the night before began to come to him, he slowly put his arm out to his side, expecting August to be there. On realising she wasn't, he couldn't work out if he was sad or glad, given the state he was in now. He reached for the bottle of water on the bedside table next to him and drank it all down in one go, then ran to the toilet to promptly throw it all up again .

'Hot, not or cold—'

'Or Pizza!' Max intercepted Mrs G's lunch cry as he appeared from the lift, huge dark glasses covering his drink-swollen and tear-stained face. 'I know it's not Friday, but I need pizza, so we'll all have pizza.'

There was a sudden squawking commotion outside. 'Aw.' Tyler stared out towards the back meadows. 'The turkeys are out in the front meadow. Look how many of them there are.' He started to laugh, as did Jonah, as the prehistoric-looking birds stepped on to the fresh green meadow grass and started running around like crazy things.

Cat looked on. 'Like the charge of the light brigade, poor buggers. Thank God we don't know out futures, eh? Saying that, if I knew I was going to be culled in December I'd be making far more use of my Country Matchmaker database than I am now.'

'How're you feeling today, Max?' Jonah followed him into the kitchen.

'Like shit, to be honest. I drank a whole bottle of JD last night. These glasses will be staying on for the duration of the day, maybe even the rest of the week.'

'Don't beat yourself up about it. Losing a parent at any age isn't easy, and that was a terrible shock what happened. She was a good woman, your mum.'

'She really was,' Max sighed. 'Is August around?'

Jonah carried on filling his water bottle. 'No, you know she hasn't been in for ages. She was at the funeral yesterday, though. You saw her. That speaks volumes in my book. And it's not too late to tell her how you feel, Max. She's a great girl.'

The hulking frame of Ade then appeared in the doorway. 'You got a moment bro?'

'Sure.' The brothers made their way to Max's office.

Ade shut the door behind him. 'Sit down and take your glasses off. I want to talk to you properly.' Max did as he was told as Ade balanced on his desk.

'How're you doing?'

Max's eyes welled up. 'Not great.'

'Nor me.' Ade took a deep breath.

'I need some help, Ade.' Max started to cry.

'I know you do, and that's OK. And I'm so glad you've said that, as it makes what I'm going to say to you next so much easier.'

'Shit, that sounds ominous.'

'It is, I'm afraid.' Ade bit his lip. 'I don't say it often, but I love you very much, Max. We may not be brothers by blood, but I feel like we are.'

Max let out a sob. 'What's all this about? You're not ill, are you? Please don't tell me you are ill. I couldn't bear to lose you too.' He put his hand to his face.

'No, no, of course I'm not ill. What I am is worried about you. I don't want you to be mad, but I've arranged some help for you. A couple of weeks somewhere for you to talk to some professional counsellors about how you're feeling and maybe discuss your drinking too.'

'Rehab, you mean? If so, just say it.' Max was resigned. 'OK. I get it and I think that's it's time I got my head straight.'

'You do?'

'Yeah. I'm a mess. It's built up, my real mum going, Dad's suicide, Matteo, the accident and now losing Mum, so soon after Dad. It's been a lot. I'm in such pain.'

'I don't know how you've held it together for so long, to be honest. Just Mum and Dad going has thrown *me*.' Ade sniffed back his own tears.

Max sighed and reached for a cigarette from his drawer. 'What about this place?'

'It's fine. It will run as usual.'

'Have you seen August, this morning?'

'No. No, I haven't.' Lies didn't sit well on Ade's tongue and he squirmed in his seat.

'I don't know what I'd do if she went back to London, either.'

'Jonah's a safe pair of hands to open up when Mrs G's not about and hopefully you won't be gone long,' Ade diverted.

'When does my holiday start then?' Max managed a smile.

'Today. Pack a bag and I'll drive you there. It's only in

Ottersbury, so not far away.'

'I can't afford it.'

'I can.'

'But bro, I owe you so much already.'

'In time. It's important we get you better first.'

Despite her having her mobile literally tied to her side since she had got back home from the farm that morning, August's heart leapt at its ring.

'August, it's Ade.'

'Hi, Ade,' she effused. 'How did it go?' A huge sense of relief washed over her, just to know what was going on.

'Surprisingly, he agreed immediately. He was ready. Thank you so much. It can't have been easy coming to me this morning.'

'I knew I had to do something. He's lucky to have such an amazing brother as you.' August stifled a yawn – she was exhausted, but so happy to hear that Max would soon be getting the help he needed.

'Just so you know, he didn't mention anything about calling last night. Maybe he doesn't remember.'

'OK, good. And like I said earlier, I would really appreciate it if people didn't find out I work at the Sebastian Line. It was breaking our moral code really, me even talking to Max last night.'

'Of course, I totally get it, but thank God you were there. Anything could have happened. It's not worth thinking about.'

August shuddered. 'No, It's not. I think it was just a cry for help, though, so don't worry. I'm sure, with professional people on his side, he will get through this. Did he realise I stayed with him, do you think?'

'He didn't mention that either.'

'I always have that devasting effect on men.' August let out a little laugh.

Ade smiled. 'Joking aside, more reason to get his drinking under control. I'll call the family lawyer guy you mentioned, too. Poor Max. But we'll get this ridiculous Matteo situation sorted as well. My brother is so hard in some ways, but so soft when it comes to his boy. I had no idea it had got as bad as it has.'

'Ade, you're the best, and I'm so sorry for your loss too. As if you haven't got enough on your plate already, without this. If ever you want to chat about anything, you know where I am.'

Ade sighed. 'August, you're clearly one of life's angels, but please look after yourself too. Everyone needs someone to hug them in the night, and that includes you.'

August felt her eyes welling up. 'Let me know when he's settled in, won't you?'

Chapter Forty

Pamela Saunders was sitting at her garden table doing a crossword when August arrived, wearing a floaty flowery sundress and a huge sunhat to keep off the warm evening sunshine.

'You look as pretty as my wildflower beds. Hello, darling.' She kissed August's cheek. 'There's some elderflower cordial and fizzy water in the jug. Help yourself. Good day at the Hub?'

'Yes, it was OK, thank you. The turkeys are all running around now. It's hilarious – they are so inquisitive, they come up to the fence when we park our cars and I swear they talk to us. When Ade appears and says anything to them, they all go wild.'

'I doubt if they'd be having such a good time if they all knew they'll be on someone's Christmas table in a few months' time.'

'Mum, don't break the magic,' August grinned. 'But I know, bless them. But business is business, I guess. And the main thing is that they're happy now. You got your greenhouse fixed then?' She joined her mum at the table.

'Yes, I got some putty from that little DIY place in Lower Gamble and me and Margaret from the W.I. fixed it ourselves. The panels didn't smash, amazingly – flew straight out and landed on a bed of petunias.' They laughed. 'Good old Margaret.

Mrs Dye tells me that Max Ronson has been in rehab for nigh on two weeks, now.'

'Mrs Dye is a nosey old cow.' August took a sip from the gorgeous, sweet summer drink her mother had prepared and licked her lips.

'Is he OK?'

'His brother tells me he's doing really well. He's home on Saturday, I believe.'

'Well, that's good, then. Maybe he can sort his troubles out once and for all. I told you he'd never been right, that one.'

August sighed. 'I wish you wouldn't be taken in by the village gossip sometimes, Mum.'

Pam Saunders tutted. 'You know I like to know to what's going on. Anyway, have you heard from Scott since you last saw him?'

August noticed the mention of his name didn't make her recoil in dreaded anticipation any longer. 'No, why?'

'Just wondered. I see that he and his new fancy piece have got a deal in *Celeb* magazine for the pregnancy.'

'I don't care any more.' August silently rejoiced that she could honestly say this now.

'Good girl.'

'We can't ever go back, Mum, and I feel more sorted than I've felt in a long time.'

'Well, that's smashing. Eleanor tells me you're moving out.'

'Of course she has. Good old Ells. Yes, well, I haven't found anywhere yet. I've just started looking again. Thankfully, she decided not to rush to do the work on my place, but I'm ready for a new adventure now. A place of my own will be amazing.'

'Around here?'

'Yes, around here. I'm surprised she didn't tell you that, too. I can't even think of living in London again now. Not for the foreseeable future, anyhow.'

'How jolly exciting. And I can't tell you how happy I am that you're staying local.' Pamela Saunders took a sip of her drink. 'Ooh, yes, something else I meant to tell you. I went for coffee and cake with Hattie Somersby – do you remember her?'

'Remind me, she's one of Dad's mate's wives, isn't she?'

'Yes, that's her. I haven't seen her for years, but her husband died just last year, and I happened to bump into her at the farm shop. She lives a mile outside Swinford, so I will definitely be seeing her again.'

'Even better.'

'Her son is a policeman. She mentioned something about surveillance over this way – some sort of trading standards issue involving honey.'

August's ears pricked up high, but she managed to keep her voice level. 'A crime in our neighbourhood? Maybe it would make a good story for Lovelace & McGee.' All of a sudden thankful for her mother's place on the village gossip grapevine, August leaned in. 'What else do you know?'

'Evidently there is going to be a big swoop at the weekend. Sounds all rather exciting.'

August finished her drink and stood up. 'I need to go.'

'But you've only just got here, love.'

August checked her watch. 'I'm so sorry Mum, but I forgot, er…I forgot I had to get something over to my agent before eight pm.'

'Oh, that's a shame, but of course, you must fly. Come and see me for tea in the week.'

'I will do for sure, and so sorry to rush off.'

Chapter Forty One

Seven am, Thursday morning found Mrs G, Tyler, Ivor, Cat and Jonah all stood in front of August in the reception area of the Hub. The crime writer's face was solemn.

Tyler yawned. 'This had better be as serious as your face looks. I don't usually get out of bed for anyone before eight am.'

'Is Max OK?' Cat asked nervously.

'He will be, once Operation Honey is completed.' August said.

'Operation Honey?' Is this another book you're writing, or am I still tripping from last night?' Tyler took a glug of his water bottle, then, waking up to what was going on, murmured, 'Operation fucking Honey. I get you, girl.'

'I will explain all as we go along but we haven't got much time.' August's determined look stayed constant. 'Ivor, Ade has no clue about the back barn, does he?'

Ivor grimaced. 'I feel very bad about this, but no, he knows nothing.'

'And the turkeys are all in and out of the way? We don't want them scared by anything.'

'Yes. Done.'

'Oh shit.' Tyler ran his hands through his long hair. 'Don't tell me we've been busted.'

'Not yet.'

'Jonah and Cat, sorry to involve you, but Max is in trouble.' The two looked totally perplexed.

'Well, *I'm* not getting involved if it means me getting in trouble, too.' Jonah announced. 'I've got a family of six to feed.'

'OK, you don't have to do anything, if you don't want to,' August sighed. 'Why don't you stay here with Cat and Mrs G? All you need to do is go upstairs and find all labels with *Ralukar Honey* printed on them.' Jonah's eyes opened wide in disbelief. 'Ivor has moved the alpacas in with the turkeys, and has started a bonfire in the back meadow. Every single sign of them must be gone. They must all be burnt. Tyler, you need to delete any sign of labels off your computer, too. There cannot be a trace of even one anywhere, or on any jars, so Ivor, me, you and Tyler need to start soaking off the already labelled-up jars that are stored in the back barn. There aren't any anywhere else, are there?'

Ivor shook his head.

'Good!'

'Will somebody please tell me what's going on?' Cat whined.

'I will,' Mrs G inputted. 'And if you don't want to help, then that's up to you, too.'

'No. If Max is in trouble, then count me in.' Cat was defiant in her solidarity.

'OK, OK, I'm not being the odd one out,' Jonah added. 'But if I get arrested, I'm going to turn my hearing aids off and just keep signing "no comment".'

'And Ivor, make sure the fire looks like a normal bonfire, so as not to create suspicion. And all of us need to be as discreet as we can, as we are probably being watched.' She peered around at them all. 'Right. Is everything clear?' she said loudly.

'As a winter's day in the Highlands,' Cat muttered, earning a hearty scowl from Mrs G.

Chapter Forty Two

It was a hot Saturday morning in August when everyone stood silently assembled in the Cross Barn, watching the main gate camera that Tyler had set up on his iPad for all to view.

The young lad yawned. 'When is Max back from Ottersbury?'

'Hopefully, not until lunchtime. Ade was going to let me know.'

'Cat, you're doing the first bit of talking as agreed, OK?' The sexy Scotswoman, dressed in little denim shorts and a revealing top, put her thumb up.

'How many do you think will come?' Jonah was at his dedicated work station, wearing his Team Vegan branded t-shirt.

'They're here!' Tyler suddenly shouted. 'Jesus, there's two bloody cop cars, with sirens and lights blazing, and a Mercedes van with blacked-out windows.'

'What do I do?' Mrs G said, her voice loud with panic.

'Just open the gate,' August said casually. 'We have nothing to hide.' She brushed down her handkerchief dress and took a deep breath. 'Are you all ready?' The Hubbers and Ivor replied 'yes' in unison. 'Then, action stations!'

With Ivor having already opened the Cross Barn gate in

anticipation of their arrival, the cars screeched to a halt right outside the barn's entrance. Doors slammed and there was a loud knock on the main door.

On opening it, Cat was pleased to encounter a short, suited man nose-height to her over-spilling breasts. 'And you are?' she asked with a huge smile and a jiggle.

The man stuttered at the sight of the tall, seductively clad woman before him. 'Jeffff…Jeffrey Barnard from Swinford Trading Standards.'

'How lovely to meet you, Jeffrey.'

She looked across at the four policemen standing behind him. One of them stepped forward. 'We have a warrant to search this property. Step aside please, madam.'

'What exactly are you looking for?' Cat asked innocently, batting her eyelids. The policeman did his best not to stare at her voluptuous bosom.

'We have been given reason to believe that you are selling a fraudulent product,' Jeffrey Barnard said officiously.

Cat assumed an expression of innocent confusion. 'Oh, how very odd. Do come in.' She stepped aside. 'And do what you *think* it is you need to do.'

The barn was a hive of activity, with the boys packing and taping up the boxes of honey that were on their workstations. Loose jars with the ASDIS label were very obviously dotted about everywhere.

August stepped forward, smiling sweetly. 'Let me show you exactly what's happening here. My name is August – you may know me as A.R. Saunders, the famous local crime writer.' She beamed at the now completely flustered middle-aged balding man, as the police began searching around the main barn and office area.

August led him to Tyler. 'Tyler here is in charge of packing.

Not sure how much you know, but we have one hundred pallets that are nearly ready to go out to food banks around the UK. It's taken time for us to get a courier on board to help us distribute – there's only so much we can do with just the one spare lorry.' The man fingered the ASDIS jars and checked inside the box that Tyler was packing.

'Oh, great, great. And you have all the paperwork from ASDIS?'

At that moment Max walked in the side door followed by Ade. There was a distinct hush across the barn. August noticed how calm Max seemed, his eyes brighter. He was somehow holding himself taller. She rushed over to the pair and said in ventriloquist style. 'He's asking about the supermarket paperwork.'

Ade, now fully apprised of Max's money making scheme, and relieved that ASDIS had agreed to take half the boxes of honey back, let his brother do the talking.

'Mr Barnard, Max Ronson, manager of this scheme. Apologies for not being here when you arrived, but I take it you did arrive unannounced. Is there a problem here?'

'I have been given reason to believe that you are selling a fraudulent product.' Jeffrey Barnard's left eye started to twitch.

Max laughed. 'The only crime being committed here is you having to give up your Saturday morning. Did my lovely friends here explain about the foodbanks?'

'Er, yes.'

'Good, good, and I deal with Cora Brown, the general store manager at ASDIS. She can provide you with all the paperwork required to show what I've bought and when.'

'Nothing here,' one of the policemen directed at Jeffrey Barnard, who nodded. 'We'll head back to the station, OK?'

'Yes, thanks lads.'

August stepped forward. She smiled at Max. His melting brown eyes drilled into hers, and she gulped.

She held out her hand to Jeffrey Barnard, who eagerly grabbed it and started to shake it furiously. Managing to prise her hand away, she kept her smile. 'I have the pleasure of working at the Hub, a fine collaborative working space just down the lane from here. The Hub, which Max Ronson here manages superbly, as well as finding time to give to charity. He is an upstanding member of the community and I find it unbelievable that such a slur on his character is even being insinuated. He was heavily involved in the fun run for the local suicide crisis line charity, too.'

'So you are the *actual* A.R. Saunders? The *Love, Lies and Lupins* A.R. Saunders? I devoured that book in one sitting. We could all do with a Lila Lovelace in our lives.'

'Yes, it seems like she'd have done a much better job on this than the local police have, that's for sure.' August's smile was set in stone.

'Ha ha. Look at that, funny as well as extremely talented. I've never met a real-life author before.' He was almost childlike in his excitement.

'Then you must have a signed copy of my next book.'

'I would be honoured.' Jeffrey's other eye started to twitch, beads of sweat now dripping down his forehead.

'I do have to tell you, though, Mr Barnard, that not all the honey is being given out to food banks.'

Everyone's face slightly fell. She could see them all peering at her anxiously, wondering if she was about to betray them. Max and Ade both looked at her, worry etched painfully on their faces.

'My next book will be out in December, swiftly followed by *A Honey Trap in Futtingbrook Fallow* in the spring.'

Seemingly oblivious to the honey reference, Jeffrey nodded. 'Well that's one for my reading list, for sure. Is it going to be raunchier than the other one?' August, feeling slightly nauseous at the thought of him leering over the pages of her work, nevertheless carried on the façade. 'Oh, yes, it's going to be filthy, Jeffrey.' She looked right into his eyes. 'And not only that, I've still time to name you as a character in it, if you so wish.'

Max gave her a wicked grin, and she had to work to suppress her returning smile.

'Also, as part of the marketing plan to push it, I will be setting up a raffle prize, which will have five winners. The prizes will not only be a box of honey, but also a box set of all of my back copies and of course my honey trap book, which I will be signing personally for all the lucky winners.'

'That sounds lovely, August – if you don't mind me calling you that.' She was certain Mr Barnard was flushing pink.

'Of course not…Jeffrey.' She looked right into his eyes. 'And to add to this, all raffle ticket proceeds will be going directly to the Sebastian Line charity.'

'Gosh, how generous of you.'

'It's a great charity and, well, with all the readers I have accumulated over the years, I hope it'll be a good enough prize to get them the twenty-four-hour service and free phone line they so want and deserve.'

Max sat opposite August in his office, the window wide open to let the summer breeze float in.

'Oh, Agatha, Agatha, Agatha.' Max put his feet up on the desk and stretched his arms up high. 'Has everyone left?'

'Yes, it is Saturday after all. Diamond people you have around you, Mr Hub, you know that, but they do deserve some sort of weekend.'

'Yes, yes I really do. And you, my pretty writer girl, shine the brightest of them all.'

August smiled. 'You could have been in deep shit – in prison, in fact. What were you thinking of?'

'Quite clearly not my long term future.' Max bit his lip. 'They kind of convinced me life was worth living – at Helios House, I mean.' He brought his new vape pen to his lips and took a long drag, covering the room with a huge plume of white smoke. 'Liquorice flavour with no nicotine, might I add.'

'I'm impressed.' August smiled. 'And, it's not even our birthday.'

'You know how hard it is to give up the demon nicotine, so I may be a slightly irritable cunt for a while.'

'Nothing new there, then.'

Max gave the amused smirk that August had missed so much.

'I've got a long way to go, but I already feel so much better. I'm going to be attending regular counselling and Ade has been so understanding about me getting the money back to him. I'm going have to do some marketing for this place, aren't I? It can easily hold thirty people in here and the five we currently have, though lovely, aren't quite going to cut it. Do you agree?'

'I do, and thirty times those three grands a year that you love – well, that ain't too shabby an income, is it?'

'Yes, time to get proactive, like I should have been from the start.'

'If you play your cards right, I might even be able to fit in a few marketing bitch shifts to help you out.'

August expected Max to laugh at this, but instead tears filled his eyes.

'Words aren't enough to convey how much I appreciate you digging me out of this shit, Agatha.'

'Then let's not use words.'

August made her way around to Max's side of the desk. Sitting on his lap, she put her arms loosely over his shoulders and nuzzled into his neck for a second. Max groaned. 'You are such a sexy bitch.'

Her voice was breathy. 'I've been wanting to do this for months.'

She gently pulled him towards her, and they were soon kissing with the same intense passion as when they had first kissed in the lift.

But this time, they were both sober, and this time, it really mattered.

And as she melted into him, August realised that maybe Darcy Webb was wrong: that in life, there really was just one 'the one', after all.

Chapter Forty Three

It was a sunny September morning when Max pulled his Range Rover into a layby, leant over the seats and began rifling through his overnight bag.

'Max, what are you doing?' August looked perplexed.

'I need to blindfold you for this bit of the journey. After all, this is our first proper date and I want to it to be super special.'

August laughed. 'Don't be getting all kinky on me this early in the day.'

'If only. Voilà!' He handed her a piece of navy-blue silk.

'I think you missed the memo about what a blind date actually means. You don't have to be quite so literal,' she giggled. 'I'm delighted enough just to be in Devon, let alone wherever you're taking me.'

'Very funny, writer girl, but that's why I like you so much. Now you have to trust me, OK, and put that blindfold on.'

They drove on for another ten minutes, until Max pulled over again and gently removed the silk scarf. 'Oh my God!' August's mouth was wide open. 'No! I can't believe it. Max! Burgh Island! Are we going across on the sea tractor? This is too much.' She held herself like a little girl. 'I am so excited! Oh Max. I haven't been to the Pilchard Inn for so many years.'

'I know,' Max said quietly.

'How did you…?'

'I do listen to you sometimes.'

August racked her brains. 'The podcast! Shit. I forgot you were listening and that I'd mentioned this place!' She jiggled around with excitement and joy. 'I can't tell you how exciting this is. In fact, it's possibly the most romantic thing anyone has ever done for me.'

'Good. And if this place is good enough for your namesake, Agatha, plus the Beatles and Noel Coward, then it's just about good enough for you. You deserve the best of everything after all you've done for me, you really do.'

'So you said to pack a bag. Are we actually staying here, too?'

'We might be.'

'Oh my god, don't tell me you've booked Agatha's Beach House?'

'You'll have to wait and see. But first, to the Pilchard Inn.'

They sat in silence for a moment, quietly soaking up the stunning sea view from the wooden bench outside the inn. The soothing sounds of water lapping on the shore, seagulls cawing and the gentle murmur of chatter and laughter as people enjoyed their own little moments of peace and tranquillity made August sigh deeply with contentment. She then began to rattle off her recent history lesson.

'So, the barman was telling me this place was built in 1336. Imagine what it's seen and heard. Apparently it first served the fishermen who lived on the island and mainland shores, then the smugglers and wreckers who lured ships on to the rocks. Now its punters are no one more exciting than hotel guests and local visitors.'

'I'd have made a good smuggler.' Max lifted his designer shades to catch her eyes, then dropped them down again.

August gave him a disbelieving look. 'Max, you nearly didn't get away with sticking labels on jars of honey.' They both laughed. 'I wonder who grassed you up?'

'I don't know. Maybe I was pissed somewhere and somebody overheard me telling a mate – who knows? The less I think about it, the better. Being sober isn't as bad as I thought it would be, actually.'

'Are you stopping completely, do you think?'

'I'm not putting a label on it. I'm not very good at that, clearly.' They both laughed again. 'But I do feel so much better for staying in the moment. I was a bad drunk, as you witnessed. I'm so sorry I've been so awful to you.'

'Max, no more apologies. The future is now. Cheers!'

They chinked their Diet Cokes.

'Oh yeah. Before I forget, I've got something for you.' Max leaned down and rifled through the overnight bag at his feet. He pulled out a beautifully wrapped present, tied with a silver ribbon.

'More? Bringing me here is enough. In fact, just being with you, sitting here overlooking the sea, is a dream come true.'

'Read the label.'

To Geri, for saving my life. Max x

Tears filled August's eyes. 'If you knew it was me, why didn't you just say?'

'Comm-u-ni-cate, you said on your podcast. I'm rubbish at that. I was at my lowest ebb. All I wanted to do was talk to you and tell you, but I didn't know how. I didn't know you'd be at the Sebastian Line that night and then in my drunken despair when I realised it was you, it gave me the chance I'd been waiting for.'

'I put on a voice.'

'I didn't know it was you at first, but all of a sudden I just knew it was you. I can't even remember the phrase you said that gave you away, but even in my drunken stupor, I realised. Call it intuition, I don't know. I wanted to be saved. I don't want to die; I don't want to leave you, Matteo or Ade and his beautiful family. And if it hadn't been for you and what you said, I don't think I would have so readily gone to therapy or rehab. I'm a stubborn fucker.'

'I should be angry that you pretended not to know, but then again, I should have told you it was me.' August took a sip of her drink.

'I knew you stayed over too.'

'Max!'

'I needed you more than I've ever needed anyone in my whole life at that moment. Just you being there was enough... without words.'

The summer breeze caught her hair and whipped it in front of her face. Max gently pushed it away. 'Don't be angry. It was supposed to happen like it did. Like you just said, the future is now. I'm so glad that you know all about Matteo and that situation, too. You can see now why it was difficult for me to get involved with anyone else. She's so volatile that I dared not start seeing anyone. Also, it would have been so hard to maintain a relationship with someone when I was never sure when I would be able to see my son.'

'I understand now. Ade spoke to the family lawyer, I take it?'

'Yes, and I've met him. Madame Fleurot's husband, no less. Thank you. He's as switched on and bolshy as she is, and is adamant that he will be able to sort regular custody now, with an allowance that will not break me. And now they know what she's been doing, she won't be able to get away with saying I've

313

hurt her or that she'll leave the country.'

'Such a relief.'

'Yes.' Max was thoughtful for a second. 'You were brilliant on the phone, by the way. Made me realise I'd want you as my wing woman any day, and the fact that you are donating the raffle takings to the Sebastian Line – well, that is incredible. Darcy will be made up, as am I.'

'So, did you know I'd started volunteering there? Did she tell you?'

'No. Darcy's husband was at Jaxon's one night. He was a bit pissed. Let out that he had been on a shift with some red-headed author totty, so I knew straight way. You are so amazing doing that.' He brushed her lips with his. 'Now, open this present. Then we can head to the hotel and get comfy in Agatha's boudoir.'

August opened her mouth wide in mock disbelief. 'How presumptuous, but I am so up for that!'

She ripped off the paper to be faced with a navy-blue leather box. When she saw what was in it, she put her hand to her mouth and tears started streaming down her face. 'My signing pen. The one my dad gave me.' August put her hand to her heart.

Max nodded. 'You forgot to pick it up after you threw it at me that day, remember? I got it cleaned up and the engraving made a little sharper.'

'It truly is the best present you could ever give me. I thought I had lost it forever, like I thought I nearly lost you, too.'

'I'm not one for big expressions of love, but you bring out the best in me and, well…' Max cleared his throat and took both her hands in his. 'August Rose Saunders, if you will agree, I would love for us to start writing our own future together. I can't see a life without you in it. I promise to be honest, communicate and love you through thick and thin. There's a lot going on, I realise, and it's a bit naff asking you to be my girlfriend, but I think asking you to be my wing woman is OK, don't you think?'

'Hmm, now what would Lila Lovelace say about this?' August cocked her head to the side.

'Just tell me!' Max appeared suddenly nervous.

'I think she would say yes but she would want babies and a dog and maybe two more cats and a cottage that backs on to a stream. Oh, and a huge diamond eventually, to seal the deal.'

'Would she now? So, is that a yes, then?'

'It's a big fat yes from Lila and me. I will happily be a wing woman to your wing man, any day,' August grinned.

'Jesus, I was anxious that you wouldn't agree to that and now…well, you're not disappointed it's not a marriage proposal, are you?'

August kissed his lips softly. 'Max, let's just enjoy each other. We don't need a piece of paper to tell us how we feel – at least, not right away. I think it's sensible to take our time, Marie McGee style.'

'I've never been sensible in my life.'

'Exactly. This is a fresh start for us both. Let's get Matteo safe and happy and the Hub up and running as it should be. I can help make your flat a proper home, now that all the bloody boxes are out of it. And…well, I'll be homeless myself soon, so if all goes well – and I realise it's all very early days, but maybe in time, I can join you there, too.'

'I'd have you there with me tomorrow.' Max's eyes were sparkling with happiness as August continued to gabble.

'Plus, I've got three more books to get out there. Saying that, we might have to make a baby before I'm forty and past it – what do you think of that?'

'I think, Agatha, that we should stop talking, get into the hot tub at your namesake's beach house and start practising how to make one, right away.'

315

Epilogue

The Hub had never looked so homely. There was a grandly decorated Christmas tree taking up a large area of the main office, and a plethora of holly garlands and strings of sparkling fairy lights hanging from the beams. A pull-up banner with 'A Christmas Mystery in Futtingbrook Fallow by A. R. Saunders' greeted everyone in the main reception area, the desk of which had been converted into a bar.

'I've never been to a book launch at a turkey farm before,' August's editor from Big Red said, as she wafted by with a glass of Prosecco in hand. 'Anyway, happy publication day, and Happy Christmas. Some great reviews coming in already, by the way.'

Brigitte Fleurot charged over. 'Augoost, I see you delivered – on time –another bestseller, I do think.' Her voice descended to a whisper. 'I only travelled out of London to make sure they have your advance payment in my bank account before Christmas Eve.' She rushed off to do some more editor schmoozing.

'I love that woman!' Ellie stuffed a second sausage roll into her mouth as she gently rocked her new baby daughter, snuggled tightly to her chest in a blue papoose.

'How's our little Bluebell Rose doing?' August gently touched the sleeping baby's downy hair. 'Look at her – she's like the cutest doll. And those red locks – I told you she was going to be a mini me.'

'She's actually the best-behaved baby I've had to date. Sleeps through without a murmur from six to six. I'm going to have to head home soon because I daren't get her out of that routine. I would have left her with Grant and the boys if I wasn't feeding her myself, and you know how I can't abide expressing. He sends his love, by the way.'

'I'm just so happy you could come, even for a little while.'

'How's lover boy?' Ellie grinned.

'He's gorgeous.' August was surprised to feel herself welling up.

'Aw. I'm so happy for you, Goose. And I told you you'd meet the love of your life in deepest, darkest Wiltshire.'

'I'd forgotten you said that!'

'It was a sign!'

August gave an exaggerated eye-roll. 'You and your signs. But yes, I'll give you that. You did push me to come here.'

'How's it going, living in the flat upstairs? I honestly wasn't pushing you out, you know. You could have bedded down with the five of us, if it came to it.'

'I like my sleep too much.' August gently touched the baby's downy head again. 'She is SO scrumptious. And it's wonderful here. So peaceful, and such lovely views to wake up to. We live together well already.'

'That's great to hear. And how about Prince Harry?'

'Hmm. He isn't so sure about having to go up and down in a lift, but he's getting used to it.'

'Is it a bit weird living above where you work?'

'Well, that's the thing. Now we've got more people using the space, we can afford to move out. There's a little place in Salton Priors we both love, with three bedrooms and a stream running out the back. One of the new Hubbers is keen to rent the space upstairs when we move out, so it's a win-win, really.'

'Ooh, three bedrooms – is there something you're not telling me?'

'One is obviously for when Matteo stays over and the other – well, let's just say I might need some of your sisterly advice on motherhood in the near future.'

'Goose! You're not, are you?'

'Not yet, but not through want of trying. I have a feeling it'll happen soon.'

'That is the best news.'

'Isn't it?'

Pamela Saunders, giddy after a glass of Prosecco, pitched up next to the pair of them, with Margaret from the W.I.

'I am so proud of you, August Rose, I can't even tell you. Book eight, isn't it? I literally can't believe it. Your dad would be over the moon, too. I said to Margaret you'd sign her a copy. Is that OK?'

'Of course. Here.' August took the copy from her mother and signed it on Margaret's instruction.

'Thank you, August, and well done, dear.' Margaret held her glass aloft. 'I wish my Annabel had been a creative type, rather than becoming a funeral director. Can hardly cheer her on from the side-lines for what she does, now, can I?'

Mrs G was waddling around with a platter of sandwiches. 'Jonah, turkey sandwich for you?'

'Er, no thanks, Beryl. I don't eat meat, remember?'

'Of course, you don't. You're one of those aren't you? I keep forgetting.'

'Tyler? Cat?' The pair were arguing over whether *Die Hard* was a Christmas film or not as Mrs G approached. Tyler turned his nose up at the sandwiches, too. 'I know it sounds stupid, but I grew to love those turkeys so much that over the months they were here, I can't eat them. It seems so quiet now they're all gone.'

'Well, it's not stopping me.' Cat picked a couple of the neat, white-breaded triangles and started to scoff. 'I need a drink to wash them down now, though. See you in a bit, T. Ah, there's my number-one son.'

August noticed Sean entering the barn with a friendly-looking red-head of a similar age to him. She was pretty, too. He kissed his mum on the cheek, then headed straight towards her.

'Hey August, this is Kelly, my girlfriend. Kelly, meet August. It's her book launch today and she's a – well, she's a friend of mine.'

August felt herself warm inside at Sean's comment. She smiled at him widely. 'I'm glad you could make it. How're you doing?'

'Good, really good – and you?'

August could see Sean was finding this difficult.

'Yes, busy and—'

'Happy, I hope, August, that's the main thing.'

'I really am.'

'Good.' He gave her one last look of affection, then turned and smiled at Kelly. 'Right, come on my little firecracker, let's get ourselves a drink.' The pair of them headed to the bar.

August was just saying her goodbyes to Ellie when Cat came over. 'Number three – you're brave,' she said, nodding at little Bluebell.

'Mad, perhaps. Anyway, I must get back. See you ladies. Have fun!'

'So, mate, I guess this is it for us for a while.' Cat looked visibly moved as she put her hand on August's shoulder.

'I know. I'm so sad you're going. It's been a blast getting to know you Cat, it really has. And as soon as I can, I am coming to Portobello Beach to spend some time with you.'

'Portobello? Morningside, darling. I knew I'd get my way. I'm proof that it's not all about the cock, darling – personality counts too. I mean, who'd have thought I'd end up with a five-foot-seven, silver-haired bank manager with a small...'

'Ego,' they said in unison, and burst out laughing.

'And yes, his bank account obviously takes the pressure off. The Country Matchmaker is no more, thank God. I was getting sick of it. People are a hard commodity to sell and if I'm honest I was only doing it to ultimately find somebody for me.'

'Retired at fifty-five? Can't be so bad. What are you going to do now?'

'I can't just do nothing, so I'm going to keep the podcast running, but we plan to travel and just enjoy each other for a bit.'

'Sounds bloody amazing. I'm so happy for you, Cat.'

'And me, you. Max is looking hot to trot, and it seems like you've tamed him a bit, too. Underneath, he always was a good man. I could sense it. OK, I'd better spend more time with that son of mine before I go.'

'Kelly seems nice.'

'Not as nice as you, but I guess I'll have to live with that.' Cat winked and headed back over to her son and his girlfriend.

'What was that about a good man?' August looked around to find Ade approaching, glass of Prosecco in hand. 'Cheers to you, August. Well done on the new book and for making my brother – and this one's dad – so bloody happy.' Ade ruffled Matteo's black curly hair.

'August, I don't want to be rude,' the young lad said quietly. 'I know it's your launch and everything, but is it OK if I go back to the farm and play with my cousins?' the little boy asked awkwardly.

'Of course, it is, darling. I don't blame you not wanting to be down here with all these boring grown-ups.'

'I'm going back up with him.' Ade added. 'Beth sends her love. Never mind morning sickness, she's got all-day bloody sickness with this pregnancy. Didn't have it with the girls.'

'Let's hope it's a boy then.'

'Literally everything is crossed, and if it is, then snip, snip.' He made a cutting motion with his fingers.

August laughed out loud, then carried on smiling as Max approached and gave her a kiss on the cheek.

'Hey, Matty?' Max smiled broadly at his son.

'I'm going back to the farm, Dad.'

'OK, see you later then, matey. We won't be long. I thought we could go FIFA crazy on PlayStation later?'

'Sick!' the lad grinned. 'Uncle Ade, can we go on the quad bike?'

'Yes. Come on, then.'

'What was so funny?' Max looked super-smart in his black suit and matching black silk shirt. 'You know I hate missing out on a joke.'

'Oh, just Ade telling me he's having the snip if it's a boy this time.'

'Well, there's no chance of me having that done. I want a five-a-side team, like your brother-in-law.

'Oh my God, don't you start.'

Max looked her up and down. 'You look stunning in that dress by the way. Good enough to eat, in fact.'

'You can do just that later, when Matty's asleep, if you fancy.'

'I always fancy, you know that.' He kissed her lightly on the lips. 'You should be so proud of yourself, Agatha. Eight books, you've written. I mean, that's incredible. Such an achievement.

And be honest: did I ever make it as one of your characters?'

August tried not to grin. 'Well…you made for such a good villain.'

'August Saunders! I can't believe you never told me!' She went to run away, and he whisked her back into his arms. 'I think we've written our own happy ending anyway now, don't you?'

By eight pm everybody had left, apart from the hardcore Hub crew, who had stayed to help clear up. Mrs G, who had been loading the dishwasher, appeared, wiping her hands on her lap apron.

Cat popped the cork of the last bottle of real champagne in the fridge. She filled a glass for everyone and, on Max's direction, poured just a mouthful into one for him.

August cleared her throat. 'I just want to say thanks so much for coming tonight – it means a lot. And you didn't all have to buy a copy, but I'm happy that you did. Don't worry, I don't expect you all to read it.'

'He already is!' Tyler pointed to his partner Reece, already head down at one of the desks, totally engrossed. 'Yeah, thanks for that August – no sex for me tonight!'

Everyone laughed.

Cat tapped her glass. 'My turn. I just wanted to say a few words before I leave you all. Firstly, congratulations to August on her new book.'

Max, Jonah, Tyler and Mrs G raised their glasses in unison. 'Cheers to August.'

'Also, a big cheers to Max and August, who we all know will be incredibly happy together forever.' Matteo, now back from the farm, stood between the smiling couple, looking pleased as punch .

Another united, 'Cheers!'

'A special thanks to Mrs G for her continued production of some of the finest food in Futtingbrook.'

Even Beryl laughed as they raised their glasses yet again.

'Joking aside, I don't think I've worked anywhere that has had such camaraderie between such a small group of people. And all that is held together by one man: Max Ronson. Max, you've made us all feel so comfortable, provided a great working environment and possibly the best snack machine I have ever come across in my life.'

More laughter ensued.

'So, my final cheers is to the Hub. It's great to see you filling this place up and making the most of its potential.'

'Although no one will ever be as cool as the original famous five,' Jonah heckled.

'I second that, and I will miss you all, but will be back to visit. Don't you worry.' Cat's voice started to crack. 'So, let's drink to The Hub, and all who may work in her. Happy Christmas, everyone!' Cat was beaming.

'The Hub!'

"Do they know it's Christmas" started to blurt out over the barn speakers.

'The turkeys definitely do. Bzzzzzzzz.' Max pretended to Taser August's head.

'There he is, my inappropriate Mad Max!' August's shoulders rocked. You make me so happy.'

'Likewise, writer girl.'

Max was just sharing a cheeky kiss with August when the music was turned down and the penetrating din of Mrs G's gong resounded around the barn, followed by her dulcet tones as she shouted: 'Who was it?'

Thanks

With special thanks to Simon Windsor from Copas Turkey Farm, Cookham, for providing me with invaluable information on turkey farming. And yes, the birds really do have instruments to play, a sunflower field and alpacas watching over them!

If you have enjoyed your time in Futtingbrook – with both the turkeys and the Hubbers – an online review from our readers is worth its weight in gold to us author-types. Thank you.
Love Nicola xx

The Corner Shop in Cockleberry Bay

The number one bestseller

Rosa Larkin is down on her luck in London, so when she inherits a near-derelict corner shop in a quaint Devon village, her first thought is to sell it for cash. However, while the identity of her benefactor remains a mystery, he or she has left one important proviso: the shop cannot be sold, only passed on to somebody who really deserves it.

Rosa resolves to get the shop, in the small seaside community of Cockleberry Bay, up and running again. But can she do it all on her own? And if not, who will help her succeed – and who will work secretly to see her fail?

A handsome rugby player, a sexy plumber, a charlatan reporter, a selection of meddling locals, and a dachshund named Hot Dog, together with a hit-and-run incident and the disappearance of a valuable engraved necklace, all play their part in an unpredictable journey of self-discovery in this runaway bestseller from chick-lit publishing phenomenon Nicola May.

A sunny, funny, lovely story guaranteed to warm the cockles of your heart'
Milly Johnson

Meet Me in Cockleberry Bay

The second in the bestselling series

The cast of the runaway bestseller *The Corner Shop in Cockleberry Bay* are back – including Rosa, Josh, Mary, Jacob, Sheila, new mum Titch and, last but by no means least, Hot, the adorable dachshund.

Newly wed, and with her inherited corner shop successfully up and running, Rosa Smith seems to have all that anyone could wish for. But the course of true love never did run smooth and Rosa's suspicions that her husband is having an affair have dire consequences. Reaching rock bottom before she can climb back up to the top, fragile Rosa is forced to face her fears, addiction and jealousy head on.

With a selection of meddling locals still at large, a mystery fire and Titch's frantic search for the real father of her sick baby, the second book in this enchanting series takes us on a further unpredictable journey.

A brilliantly written, feel-good, fantabulous read
Kim Nash

The Gift of Cockleberry Bay

The third in the bestselling series

All our favourite characters from Cockleberry Bay are back, including Hot, Rosa Smith's adorable dachshund, and his newborn puppies.

Now successfully running the Cockleberry Café and wishing to start a family herself, Rosa feels the time is right to let her inherited corner shop go. However, her benefactor left one important legal proviso: that the shop cannot be sold, only passed on to somebody who really deserves it.

Rosa is torn. How can she make such a huge decision? And will it be the right one? Once the news gets out, untrustworthy newcomers appear in the Bay, their motives uncertain. With the revelation of more secrets from Rosa's family heritage, a new series of unpredictable and life-changing events begins to unfold.

The Gift of Cockleberry Bay continues this phenomenally successful series in typically brisk and bolshy style and will delight Rosa's many thousands of fans.

Something for everyone: romance, humour and a mystery. A fantastic end to a wonderful trilogy
Lucy Mitchell

Christmas in Cockleberry Bay

The conclusion to the bestselling series

Meet old and new characters in the Bay for Christmas fun and frolics.

With both the Corner Shop and Cockleberry Café in safe hands, Rosa turns her attention to Ned's Gift, the charity set up in memory of the great-grandfather who turned her life around.

Over at the Ship Hotel, Lucas has his work cut out with his devious new girlfriend and the mystery poisoning of an anonymous hotel inspector. Will the hotel still get its 3-star Seaside Rosette?

Will Mary find true love at last? Can Titch cope with the demands of the shop and being heavily pregnant. And can Rosa, with a baby of her own, pull off the Cockleberry Bay Charity Christmas Concert in time?

Christmas in Cockleberry Bay is a festive delight for fans of Rosa and her cheeky mini dachshund Hot, delivering a feast of unpredictable events and surprises.

This is a fabulous series and I adored this festive instalment. A wonderful heartwarming read that has some drama, lots of friendships, dogs, babies and all mixed in with a wonderful storyline
Me and My Books

Working it Out

Ruby Matthews has a plan. Twelve jobs in twelve months, until she finds the one of her dreams...

After redundancy, Ruby launches a mission to find the ideal job.

Her year of gainful (and sometimes painful) employment includes: nannying in the South of France; dealing with embarrassing ailments in a Harley Street clinic; waiting tables in a buzzy Soho café; and meeting celebs of years gone by in a home for retired actors. And, although love is no longer top of her list, relationships start happening along the way – which sees her handing out some P45s of her own.

Will any of the jobs – or men she meets – see her dreams come true? Or will Ruby end up back where she started?

Let Love Win

The sequel to *Working it Out*

Ruby Matthews never expected to be starting over. But, after a sudden tragic loss, she questions whether she will ever be happy again.

A chance encounter with handsome author Michael Bell throws her fragile heart into turmoil, while a dark family secret adds to her confusion. Only when she starts volunteering at the Bow Wow Club (Boyfriends of Widows, Wives of Widowers) does she begin to tackle her grief head on.

Will she let love win? Or allow her past to continue to haunt her? In this charming sequel to Working It Out, you'll laugh and cry as Ruby searches for inner peace.

School Gates

They all meet at the school gates, but their kids are the last thing on their minds

At 3.10pm every weekday, parents gather at Featherstone Primary in Denbury to collect their children. For a special few, the friendships forged at the school gates will see them through lives filled with drama, secrets and sorrows.

When Yummy Mummy Alana reveals the identity of her love-child's father, she doesn't expect the consequences to be quite so extreme. Earth Mummy (and former au pair) Dana finds happiness in her secret sideline, but really all she longs for is another child. Slummy Mummy Mo's wife-beating husband leads her down a path she never thought possible, and Super Mummy Joan has to cope when life deals her a devastating blow. And what of Gay Daddy Gordon? Will he be able to juggle parenthood and cope with his broken heart at the same time?

Four very different mothers. One adorable dad. And the intertwining trials and tribulations that a year at the primary school gates brings.

About the Author

Nicola May is a rom-com superstar. She is the author of sixteen romantic comedies to date, all of which have appeared in the Kindle bestseller charts. Two of them won awards at the Festival of Romance, and another was named ebook of the week in *The Sun*. *The Corner Shop in Cockleberry Bay* became the best-selling Kindle book in the UK, across all genres, in January 2019, and was Amazon's third-bestselling novel in that year. Described by Winifred Robinson of BBC Radio 4's *You and Yours* as 'the invisible bestselling author', Nicola campaigned successfully for the introduction of ebook charts in the publishing trade press.

She lives near Ascot racecourse with her black-and-white rescue cat, Stan.

Also by Nicola May